RIVALS *OF THE* REPUBLIC

RIVALS
OF THE
REPUBLIC

— A BLOOD OF ROME NOVEL —

ANNELISE
FREISENBRUCH

**DUCKWORTH
OVERLOOK**

First published in the UK in 2016 by
Duckworth Overlook

LONDON
30 Calvin Street
London E1 6NW
info@duckworth-publishers.co.uk
www.ducknet.co.uk
For bulk and special sales, please contact sales@duckworth-publishers.co.uk,
or write us at the above address

NEW YORK
141 Wooster Street
New York, NY 10012
www.overlookpress.com
For bulk and special sales, please contact sales@overlookny.com,
or write us at the above address

Cataloging-in-Publication Data is available from the Library of Congress

Book design and type formatting by Bernard Schleifer

ISBN: 9780715650998

FIRST EDITION
1 3 5 7 9 10 8 6 4 2

For Julian

ACKNOWLEDGEMENTS

I WOULD LIKE TO THANK MY BRILLIANT AGENT ARAMINTA WHITLEY AND also Peta Nightingale, Jennifer Hunt and everyone at LAW for all their hard work in helping me bring Hortensia to life. I am equally indebted to the legendary Peter Mayer, who saw Hortensia's potential and whose sage advice has made this a much better book. My friends Katie Fleming, Daniel Orrells, Aude Doody and Miriam Leonard are an unfailing source of support and I'd like to thank Aude for reading an early draft and giving helpful advice. Helen Lovatt generously read the book with a Classicist's eye when she had better things to do – any historical errors that remain are entirely my own. Bridget Cowan told me she loved the sound of the story when I first mentioned it – thank you, Bridget, that was more encouraging than you probably intended at the time. To the staff, parents and pupils of Chafyn Grove School and Port Regis School – where I have successively taught Latin as this book has taken shape – my thanks for your understanding and support. I am very lucky to have parents who positively encourage me to borrow money off them and eat all of their food – the ideal support system for a writer. Finally, I want to thank Gabriel and Fabia (the 21st century one) for letting me practice my cooking on them at weekends, and above all Julian, who proves John Irving's maxim that all you really need is a good, smart bear.

A HISTORICAL INTRODUCTION

ROME HAS RECENTLY SURVIVED A PERIOD OF BLOODY CIVIL WAR AND the embers of conflict and thwarted ambition are still smouldering. *Rivals of the Republic* is set in the year 70BC, four decades before the end of the ostensibly democratic era of the Roman Republic and the beginning of the age of one-man rule, when emperors such as Augustus, Claudius and Nero would make their colorful mark on ancient history. It is a period of high drama in Roman politics. In principle, the Senate holds the reins of power in trust for the people. Two consuls are annually elected by popular vote to share executive powers, standing down after they have served their year in office. But new rivalries and antipathies are emerging, most notably that between the year's two serving consuls, the wealthy Marcus Licinius Crassus and the military titan Gnaeus Pompeius Magnus – better known to history as Pompey the Great. Meanwhile, an ambitious young politician named Julius Caesar waits in the wings.

With its themes of betrayal, conspiracy and blood rivalry, the story told in *Rivals of the Republic* reflects the currents of conflict that would eventually culminate in the rise and assassination of Caesar, and the death of the Roman Republic.

Rivals of the Republic is the first in *The Blood of Rome* series of historical crime novels.

DRAMATIS PERSONAE

THE HOUSEHOLD AND FAMILY OF HORTENSIUS HORTALUS
Hortensius Hortalus. Flamboyant king of the Roman law court.

Hortensia. His precocious daughter.

Lutatia. His downtrodden wife.

Quintus. His disappointment of a son.

Lucrio. A gladiator with a mysterious past.

Elpidia. A slave woman.

Rixus. A gardener with a taste for the dramatic.

THE HOUSEHOLD AND FAMILY OF SERVILIUS CAEPIO
Caepio. Hortensia's delightful second cousin.

Cato. His moralizing brother.

Servilia. His seductive sister.

Brutus. His nephew. A boy with a future.

Eucherius. A loyal young slave.

THE POLITICIANS, THE LAWYERS AND THE MILITARY.
Lucilius Albinus. A member of the Roman Senate.

Caecilius Metellus. An elderly member of the powerful Metelli clan.

Claudia. His garrulous wife.

Marcus Licinius Crassus. The richest man in Rome.

Gnaeus Pompeius Magnus ('Pompey'). Rome's greatest general.

Mucia Tertia. His third wife.

Sertorius. A renegade Roman general.

Metellus Pius. Conqueror of Sertorius (with Pompey) and high priest of Rome.

Tiberius Dolabella. A sinister one-time soldier from Pompey's army.

Publius Dolabella. His arrogant young nephew.

Gaius Verres. A former governor of Sicily.

Cicero. Hortensius's legal rival.

Terentia. His sharp-eyed wife.

Gaius Julius Caesar. A rising young orator and politician.

THE TEMPLE OF VESTA

Fabia. An intrepid Vestal Virgin.

Cornelia. Chief Priestess of the Temple.

Felix. A young slave boy.

OTHER CHARACTERS

Drusilla. A wronged wife.

Marcus Rufio. Her unpleasant husband.

Petro. A wily forger.

Didius Flavius. A scribe.

Pernilla. His wife.

Laelia. His daughter.

RIVALS *OF THE* REPUBLIC

I

THERE WAS A LONG SILENCE AS THE ELDER OF THE TWO MEN READ the letter that had been handed to him. He raised pink, rheumy eyes to the face of the man sitting opposite him and spoke in a tone of bewilderment. "But why now? He said there was no rush to repay the debt."

His visitor tilted his head to one side, the glow from an oil-lamp on the table between them illuminating furrows of deep scarring on the left side of his face. A grey cloak was swathed about his shoulders and a bitter green scent tainted the air around him.

"If all men of business ran their affairs like a charity, Senator, I venture to suggest they would have no business left to speak of."

"But it's six hundred thousand sesterces . . . I don't have that kind of money – it's more than my house is worth. I promised him my support in the election, he said that was payment enough . . ."

"I am not sure your colleagues in the Senate would see it that way."

The old man slumped in his chair and re-read the letter. His visitor waited, his eyes watchful as a cobra's.

"How long do I have?" the old man finally asked, a rasp in his throat.

"I would say a few days. He has some . . . projects looming which require urgent cash flow."

"Why has he sent you?" asked the old man roughly. "Why not some debt-collector, one of his ruffians from the Subura?"

The man in grey appeared to weigh the question carefully.

"I think he thought it would be better coming from a friend." He smiled as though in rueful sympathy but there was only malice in his voice.

"A friend . . . I see."

"There is an alternative, Senator, as I believe the letter in your hand explains. I have previously tried to persuade you of the benefits . . . your loyalty does you credit, though I believe it is unwarranted."

Carefully, the old man placed the letter on the table in front of him. He hauled himself up from his chair, limped over to a cabinet in the corner of the room and fumblingly extracted a key from his tunic pocket. A moment later, he dropped a small silver-embossed box in front of his visitor.

"You may tell him that this is all there is for now. I will have the rest for him later, and . . . I ask for his patience."

Lifting the lid of the box, the man in grey inspected the pile of coins inside before closing it again with a snap and tucking it into the crook of his elbow. "I shall pass on your message," he said as he got to his feet and lunged toward the doorway, his grey cloak swinging gently about him. He paused to glance back at his host, who was now staring at some spot on the ground, and the watchfulness in his expression was replaced by satisfaction. "A very good evening to you, Senator," he said softly, before withdrawing.

The old man slowly returned to his chair and continued to gaze into the distance. Eventually he summoned a slave and gave orders for a bath to be prepared in his private quarters. Picking up a pen and drawing a piece of papyrus toward him, he began the letter, "To my dear Pompey, greetings . . ." and scratched out a few lines in small, swooping letters. Slipping a seal-ring off his finger – embossed with the head of a griffin – he fastened the seam of the roll with wax and placed it on the table alongside the ring. Next he shuffled down the passageway toward his private bathing room and dismissed the waiting slave with instructions that he would not need anything else that night and to see that the letter on his desk was dispatched first thing in the morning.

His hands shook a little as he fumbled with the buckle on his belt. Dropping it to the floor with a clatter, he peeled off his tunic and stood naked in the steam. His skin hung in wrinkled folds from his shoulders, and his belly draped like a sack over his genitals. With one hand against the wall for support, he lowered himself gingerly into the water and for several minutes he lay there, staring up at the tiled ceiling as though committing it to memory. Then he picked up the small silver knife which he had placed on the shelf next to him, pressed the sharp tip to his wrist and dragged it across the delicate purple skin. The spoiled limb fell back into the water with a splash. Blood spiraled into the bath in blossoming threads. The old man's head slipped a little to one side, and he sucked in shallow breaths of steam.

Through a crack in the doorway, the man in grey stood watching from the shadows of the corridor. He softly retraced his footsteps along the corridor to the vacant study and picked up the sealed roll left on the table. Breaking the seal, he read the contents and smiled slightly before holding up the corner of the document to the glowing wick of the terracotta oil-lamp. It curled and blackened in the flame before it was dropped, still smoking, into a deep clay pot against the wall. The same treatment was given to the letter which he himself had delivered earlier, and which had been left open on the table. Then he produced a loose coil of papyrus from inside the sleeve of his grey cloak and unfurled it. It was covered in a small, swooping script closely reminiscent of the old man's handwriting. Re-rolling it into a tight cylinder, he anointed the seam with a dab of red wax from the pot on the table and pressed the imprint of the griffin seal-ring to it. He placed it on the table and blew out the dancing flame of the oil-lamp.

Returning to the bathing room along the corridor, he frowned to see the senator sitting up with a confused look on his face and trying to clamber out of the bath. The water lapping at his wrinkled stomach was tinted a gentle vermilion.

"Amateur," the man in grey muttered to himself, and beckoned toward the shadows, from which three figures emerged. The old man's eyes flickered as he tried to focus on the four men entering his bathing room.

"Hold him."

The senator's cry drowned in his throat as his head was forced underwater. His frail right arm was extended and presented like a side of meat for inspection. The man in grey picked up the knife and ran his finger along the blade. His strange amber eyes glinted as the sound of threshing and gurgling echoed around the tiled room.

"Too blunt. That's where you went wrong," he said, addressing himself conversationally to the face staring up at him wide-eyed through the water. "Human flesh is tougher than those little slivers of fattened bird your slaves chop up into mush for your evening meal. A mistake too, the way you were cutting. You have to go down the vein, not across. Like so, you see?"

Blood spattered across the tiles. The old man stared helplessly, his mouth open in a silent scream as the man in grey continued to cut. One of the slaves holding him lost his footing on the newly slippery floor. Then the threshing stopped and the water ceased to churn. Wisps of silver hair fanned gently around the old man's head. His visitor stood up and let the knife drop in the lurid crimson water with a splash.

"Honorably done, Senator," he murmured, before pushing the griffin seal-ring back on the dead man's finger.

Capua, southern Italy.

THE APPIAN WAY WAS ALWAYS FULL OF TRAFFIC AT THIS TIME OF YEAR AS Rome's wealthy elite began their annual exodus out of the stifling heat of the city toward the cooler coastal resorts of Campania. But the promise of a spectacular day of gladiatorial games and entertainment to be hosted at Capua by Rome's richest man – and one of its two ruling consuls – had swelled the number of carriages and carts on the road. Angry voices barked out expletives as drivers traveling in opposite directions refused to yield the right of way and the debris of numerous accidents could be seen along the route. Such mishaps did not affect Hortensius Hortalus, Rome's great orator and king of the law court, whose capacious wheeled carriage swept past more cumbersome vehicles like a gilded trireme.

Of the five occupants of the carriage, none felt as satisfied with their situation as the orator's sixteen-year-old daughter Hortensia. Twisting her black locks around her fingers, she glanced surreptitiously at her cousin Caepio, sitting opposite her. At twenty-five years of age, with his glossy chestnut hair and laughing brown eyes, Hortensia could not imagine that there was a more handsome man in Rome. Though no one could rival her Papa's magnificence of course. Famed for the exquisite style of his clothes and elegant mannerisms in the law court, Hortensius had bequeathed to his daughter his striking coloring of black hair and bright blue eyes and at the age of forty still cut a sleek figure, despite his love of fine wines. Noticing Hortensia's scrutiny, he smiled indulgently.

"Not far now, *carissima*."

His peacock-blue gaze narrowed once more on Hortensia's younger brother Quintus, whose skin, delicate as papyrus, was even paler than usual. Travel sickness was making the boy shift in his seat and clutch his belly with his thin forearms.

"Again. And this time, try to sound a little less like an asthmatic pigeon."

Quintus sat up straighter and took a deep breath.

"If we look to the laws, they afford equal justice to all in their private differences. If we look to social standing, advancement in public life falls to reputation . . ."

He trailed off as a long sigh emanated from the other side of the carriage. Hortensius cooled himself languidly with his fan.

"It is quite extraordinary. No diction, no clarity of tone whatsoever. Are you sure he's really mine?"

The question was directed at Hortensia's mother Lutatia, sitting between her two children. She was a small, thin woman with watery eyes and sallow cheeks now flushed with embarrassment. But she was saved the necessity of answering by Caepio, who peered out of the open window and said, "I think we're here. Look, isn't that Caecilius's carriage?"

Hortensia smiled gratefully at him and squeezed her mother's hand.

An attendant in blue livery appeared and waited for them all to disembark, Quintus almost falling out in his eagerness to get out of the swaying vehicle. Hortensius refused to proceed until he was satisfied that his garments were nicely arranged. Then they were escorted past the queues and through a shaded side-entrance in the amphitheater wall to a staircase at the top of which Hortensia could see a perfect oval of blue sky. In the sandy eye of the arena, an extraordinary parade was underway – panthers, lions, bulls, bears and elephants and, at the very back of the line, a leathery crocodile, his muzzle bound tightly shut with rope. Hortensia followed close behind her father along the front row where an elderly bald man with a peevish expression was directing a slave to place more cushions behind his back. Hortensius ostentatiously swatted himself with his fan.

"You look positively dyspeptic, Caecilius," he observed in the richly sonorous tone of voice for which he was celebrated. "Are Crassus's entertainments not to your liking?"

"Hortensius, good to see you, good to see you." Caecilius Metellus heaved himself to his feet and extended a liver-spotted hand in greeting to his friend. "No problems on the journey I hope? Those damned Cilicians have been seen on the Appian Way again lately . . . it's coming to something when you can't travel down the greatest road in the empire without fear of a pack of bloody pirates relieving you of your purse. Not sure why Pompey and Crassus haven't tackled it properly, it'll be up to you and me when we take over the consulship next year."

"Careful my friend, careful. We still have an election to win."

"Oh, that's just a formality. Caepio, in good health I trust? Ah . . . Hortensia, Lutatia, how charming."

Caecilius sounded unenthusiastic and leaned in conspiratorially toward Hortensius. "I didn't bring Claudia with me. Not sure I approve of it you know. Women at these events."

But since Hortensius seemed more interested at that moment in the choice of wine being offered him by one of the slave attendants, Caecilius straightened up and addressed himself in bracing tones to his friend's son, who was still looking queasy.

"Quintus, good to see you my boy, how's the declamation coming along?"

"Excellent," interrupted Hortensius, having made his selection. "If anyone ever needs an advocate who sounds just like a cat being drowned in a sewer, Quintus will be their man. Now, if only your prejudice against women at the amphitheater did not also extend to women in the law court . . ."

Caecilius's brow creased and Hortensius's smile widened.

"Come now, I brought her along just so you could hear her latest lesson. Hortensia, show Caecilius how well you have learned Pericles's funeral speech."

Hortensia glanced first at Caepio, then at Quintus, torn between the desire to show off and a sense of sisterly feeling. Sisterly feeling lost. She feigned a modest smile then cleared her throat, lifting her chin and fixing her dark eyes on a point in the middle of the crowd above.

"If we look to the laws, they afford equal justice to all in their private differences." Her surprisingly rich and melodic voice rang out like a bell, each syllable precisely enunciated. "If we look to social standing, advancement in public life falls to reputation for capacity, class considerations are not allowed to interfere with merit; nor does poverty bar the way, if a man is able to serve the state, he is not hindered by the obscurity of his condition. The freedom which we enjoy in our government extends also to ordinary life . . . but all this ease in our private relations does not make us lawless as citizens. Against this, fear is our chief safeguard, teaching us to obey the magistrate and the laws, particularly such as regard the protection of the injured, whether they are actually on the statute book or belong to that code which, although unwritten, yet cannot be broken without acknowledged disgrace."

The delivery was over-dramatic but she was clearly audible even over the hum of the stadium. Caepio led the applause of the spectators around them and Hortensia acknowledged their praise with a delighted smile. Only Quintus and Caecilius did not join in.

"Superb, *carissima*. Superb. What do I always tell you? Give them a show." Hortensius affectionately reached up a hand to his daughter's rosy cheek, before patting the seat next to him and throwing a provocative sideways glance at Caecilius, whose face was etched with disapproval.

"It's a mistake, and so I have warned you before, Hortensius," Caecilius muttered, shaking his head. "Rhetoric exercises . . . declamation practice . . ." He leaned in closer toward his friend again. "I know Quintus has been a disappointment to you, but if females were meant to speak in public, their voices wouldn't grate so on the ear."

Hortensia looked around, flushed from her triumph. "Where is Quintus anyway?"

"Oh dear. He was here a moment ago," said Lutatia vaguely.

"Don't worry, my dear." Hortensius sounded bored. "I can't imagine anyone would kidnap him, he's far too unprepossessing."

Hortensia stood up. "I'll go and find him."

"I can go," offered Caepio. "You shouldn't go off by yourself."

"No, you stay here and talk to Mama." Hortensia smiled at him. "She doesn't like it when the fights begin, she'll need someone to calm her nerves. Quintus won't be far away."

She turned around, not realizing that a man had paused beside them while on his way to his own seat, and that he was now standing very close to her.

"Excuse me."

She started, and hoped her face did not betray the sudden revulsion she felt. The man had black hair and a thin, creaturely face, and though he was smiling down at her, she thought his eyes were strange, yellow and glassy like a snake's. He also wore some bitter green perfume she did not like. But it was the deep, raw scar etched across his cheek which had startled her.

"Forgive me. I did not mean to alarm you. I was just stopping to pay my respects to your father."

Hortensia glanced back at her father and saw that he was eyeing the man in shrewd recognition. Knowing him as she did, Hortensia thought there was something odd in his expression, a watchfulness, or perhaps it was simply dislike. He did not offer to introduce her to the man, who was now smiling at her in a way she found she did not enjoy.

"I'm sorry. I believe you wanted to get by me."

He only just gave her enough room to pass, and she was glad to put herself beyond the reach of his twisted gaze.

HORTENSIA DID NOT EXPECT TO HAVE TO EXERT HERSELF TO ANY GREAT degree to find her brother. She assumed Quintus would be by the sausage stalls at the top of the staircase. When he wasn't there, she walked down to see if he had returned to the carriage. But still her brother was nowhere to be seen. She was just starting to feel quite cross and that she had done all that could be expected of her, when she heard a strange distant roar somewhere beneath her feet and suddenly realized she knew where Quintus had gone.

To her right, there was a narrow staircase leading underground. A thick, sour smell of sweat, mud and urine wafted up from the dark tunnel and she could hear short barks of male laughter from somewhere in the depths. She hesitated. It was too bad of her annoying little brother to put her in this position. But she also knew that Quintus would get a hiding from their father if it was discovered where he had gone. Her white silk-shod feet gleamed brightly against the dirty steps as she tripped down them.

At the foot of the stairs was an ill-lit passageway scattered with gritty sand. Hortensia could hear the sound of a blade being sharpened and voices through the opening of a chamber further down, rough, male voices, speaking in a crude idiom that she had not heard before and which she found intimidating. The metallic clang of a door being shut drew her attention to the opposite end of the corridor where she saw a man with a patch over his eye emerging into view, a bucket in his hand. Pressing herself back into the shadows of the staircase, she held her breath as the man strode past, clenching her nose against the meaty stench of blood that lingered around him. As soon as he had disappeared, she looked around the corner again and saw her brother, creeping out from the alcove where he had been hiding, and peering through a gap in the door from which the one-eyed man had just exited.

"Quintus," Hortensia hissed furiously.

He turned his head and scowled at her. She knew exactly what had brought him down here. Among their father's many famous idiosyncrasies was the collection of wild and exotic beasts that roamed his country estate at Laurentum, just outside of Rome. They had spent their childhood playing among these specimens, and Quintus had long begged their father to add an Egyptian crocodile to the menagerie, but his requests had so far fallen on deaf ears.

Hortensia watched her brother slide back the bolt on the cell door, shooting a defiant look at her as he did so. She shook her head furiously at him but he disappeared from view. Holding her veil under her chin, Hortensia hurried along the dark passageway, trying to tread lightly. She peered around the door and saw her brother standing with his back to her, curiously observing as the wizened crocodile crunched its way through a slithering pile of raw poultry carcasses. Like a vast piece of discarded armor, the beast's shiny grey torso was stretched almost across the entire width of the narrow cell.

"Quintus, you come with me right now," she warned.

Ignoring her, Quintus reached down and picked up a stray scrap of chicken from the floor with the apparent intention of throwing it to the animal. As he did so, Hortensia took a step forward, meaning to grab her brother by the tunic and haul him back. But the sight of Quintus taking a piece of its food had made the crocodile suddenly clamp its jaw shut and open wide its bulbous yellow eyes. Very slowly, like some monstrous puppet being operated by unseen hands, the beast turned to look at them and a rumble echoed from its belly. It shifted its weight onto its right foot, the scaly black claws gripping the sand tightly. Hortensia held the fold of her brother's tunic clenched tight in her hand.

"Don't move," she whispered. "Don't move."

She didn't have to tell him. Quintus was frozen to the spot just as she was. Hortensia had suddenly become very aware of her breathing and she imagined that she could hear the blood rushing around her body. How far behind them was the door? Would she have time to push Quintus behind her and give him a chance to get out? All the while, the rumbling noise was growing louder and the animal's eyes were fixed on the piece of chicken flesh still clutched in Quintus's fingers. Hortensia tried desperately not to blink, almost mesmerized by the animal's jagged yellow teeth. All she could think about was what the pain would be like.

The next thing she knew, she could feel someone's arm around her waist and suddenly her feet had disappeared from beneath her. Both she and Quintus were dragged violently and unceremoniously backwards and out of the cell before she could see if the beast had reacted too. Loud voices were raised around them and she heard the sound of the door slamming shut again. For a few moments Hortensia kept her eyes clenched tightly shut. Then the arm around her waist relaxed its hold and she opened her eyes to see the one-eyed man standing in front of them, gabbling angrily in a foreign tongue and conducting his argument with someone behind her, who also spoke in a language she couldn't understand. Finally, the one-eyed man looked down at Hortensia and Quintus and spat something at them, waving a finger in front of their faces before stalking off down the corridor.

Turning around slowly, Hortensia found herself looking into the face of a tall, powerfully built young man with thick dark hair and a broken nose. His torso was bare, revealing a number of other healed wounds, some of which looked fresher than others, but he wore the wide leather belt, armband and thickly padded leg-greaves that denoted the heavyweight category of gladiator known as the Thracian. On his walnut-brown left forearm, Hortensia noticed a strange smeared mark burnt into his skin, circular in shape.

"Hello," she said, her sense of embarrassed gratitude making the greeting sound more offhand than she had intended.

The gladiator nodded and replied with an ironic twist of politeness to his voice, "Hello to you, *domina*."

Hortensia did not recognize his accent, which was not Roman.

"Are you Helix the Thracian?" demanded Quintus. Hortensia glanced down at him in exasperation.

"Is that all you can think of to say? You idiot, I was almost killed because of you."

The gladiator smiled slightly. "No. I am not Helix the Thracian. I am sorry to disappoint you."

"Who are you, then?" asked Quintus.

"I am Hannibal the Conqueror."

Quintus rolled his eyes scornfully. "I'm not a little kid, you know."

"You do not believe me? Look outside. That's my elephant tied up there."

Hortensia was surprised to hear her brother laugh. She felt there was something improper in this gladiator's manner of addressing them and out of nerves and embarrassment, she adopted a haughty tone of voice.

"You should tell us your name. Our father is a very important man, you know. You might be doing yourself out of a reward."

"That is most intimidating, *domina*. But I am Hannibal after all. Is your father good with a sword?" The Thracian mimed a pass with an imaginary blade, much to Quintus's delight.

"Our father doesn't need a sword," said Hortensia slightly contemptuously. "He fights people with words, not weapons. He has won more than thirty cases in the law courts of Rome. How many fights have *you* won?"

The Thracian gave a low laugh.

"Not as many as your father. I see I will be no match for him after all."

"How many fights *have* you won?" asked Hortensia, her curiosity getting the better of her hostility.

"None at all, *domina*," he replied.

"None?" she exclaimed.

He shook his head slowly. "None in the arena."

Hortensia stared at him, taking in the scar lines on his face, forearms and shoulders. She knew from her father that some of those who fought on games-day were convicts, serving out their punishment in the arena as fodder for more experienced gladiators. But this strong man, with his cool green eyes and droll way of parrying her questions, did not fit with her notion of a criminal.

"You are quite an unusual gladiator," she said.

"And you, *domina*, are quite an unusual girl."

Hortensia couldn't decide whether or not to be offended by this statement.

"Who's your opponent?" asked Quintus.

He pointed to the end of the corridor where a sinewy gladiator she recognized from his high leg-greaves and long spear as a hoplomachus was now talking to a heavy-set Samnite. They were glancing curiously at Hortensia, looking her up and down, and when they saw her looking at them, the hoplomachus whispered something that made his companion chuckle unpleasantly. Hortensia suddenly felt uncomfortable and the Thracian seemed to read her thoughts, moving to block her view of his fellow gladiators.

"You should go back to your seat, *domina*. Your family will wonder where you both are."

Hortensia allowed herself to be shepherded along the dirty corridor once more and up the stairs into the light. Quintus was chattering away, asking questions about the different types of gladiators. At the exit, the Thracian beckoned a passing attendant and gave instructions for their escort. Quintus was still interrogating him and Hortensia waited until his attention was back on her, feeling rather reluctant all of a sudden to end the acquaintance. As he turned to take his leave of her, she favored him with a smile.

"Good luck with your fight, Hannibal, if you truly won't tell us your real name?"

He bowed. "My name is Lucrio, *domina*."

"I am Hortensia and this is my brother Quintus. Our father is

Hortensius Hortalus," she added with a grand flourish. "I'm sure he would wish to thank you."

The gladiator inclined his head and his lips creased slightly.

"No thanks necessary, *domina*. Goodbye Quintus. Goodbye Hortensia, daughter of Hortensius Hortalus."

"Goodbye," she said and watched him disappear back down into the dark tunnel.

IV

HORTENSIUS OBSERVED HIS SON AND DAUGHTER'S RETURN.
"Where was he? Carousing with prostitutes?"
Lutatia gasped.

"Don't be silly Papa," said Hortensia reprovingly. "He was just buying something to eat."

Hortensius shrugged. As Hortensia sat down next to Caepio, he gave her an approving smile and she felt everything she had just been through had been worth it. She was relieved to see the scarred man had gone.

A great cheer went up from the crowd around them. The gladiatorial entertainments had begun and a decision was awaited by the referee, now standing between a triumphant Samnite and his badly wounded opponent. All faces were turned in the direction of a group of men sitting just along the row from Hortensius and his family, and for the first time, Hortensia noticed the presence of their neighbor from the Palatine Hill, Marcus Licinius Crassus, consul of Rome and the sponsor of the games. A tall, broad-shouldered figure, Hortensia didn't think she had ever seen Crassus without his all-embracing smile. Now he rose to his feet as the crowd appealed to him for a verdict, and theatrically cupped his ear as though he couldn't hear the crowd urgently begging for the order of death.

"Doesn't he make you want to open your own veins?" sighed Hortensius.

"Speaking of which . . ." Caecilius leaned conspiratorially toward

Hortensius. "Did you hear the news about Albinus? Found dead in his bath, poor fellow. Looks like he made a bloody botch of it, terrible mess all over the place. Left a letter saying he'd run up too many debts. I thought you would have heard, didn't he help you with a trial a few years ago?"

Hortensius's reply was drowned out by the crowd. Urged on by the others in his party, Crassus had finally pointed his thumb in the gesture sanctioning a kill and the people cheered as the loser was dispatched with a clean thrust to the neck. Lutatia's whimper of disgust was drowned out by her son's howl of ecstasy, but Hortensia did not see the moment of slaughter as Caepio had put his hand over her eyes at the last moment.

Then a Thracian gladiator emerged from the competitors' entrance just below them. Even though their rescuer's face was now hidden by a griffin-crested helmet, Hortensia recognized him by the strange mark on his arm. She watched intently as he and his opponent raised their arms in salute to Crassus, who gave a lazy acknowledgement in return. The Thracian was armed with a short curved sword and oblong shield, while the hoplomachus wielded a long razor-tipped spear in his right hand and a circular shield in his left. The fight referee brought his cudgel down and immediately the hoplomachus lunged with his spear in a bid to catch his opponent off guard. But the thrust – aimed squarely at the heart – was deflected by the Thracian's shield, and he countered with a swinging blow from his own sword, which left a brilliant red gash of blood on the hoplomachus's right shoulder. There was a great roar from the crowd, its temperature quickly rising at the prospect of a hard-fought contest.

"That's got their blood up," remarked Caecilius.

Now the combatants began to circle each other, each looking for an opening. The hoplomachus kept darting forward in a bid to sneak the point of his spear past his opponent's guard but the Thracian was lightning-quick in his response, often turning defense into attack. Allegiances were already being declared among the audience, and although there were some who admired the hoplomachus's quick footwork and cunning, the loudest, most partisan cheering was for the Thracian, who was acknowledged by seasoned games-watchers to be a prodigious new talent.

Hortensius, who in-between glances at the action had been trading idle gossip with Caecilius, suddenly leant forward and peered closer at the combatants, now exchanging blows by the fence just in front of them.

"So that's why he's so good," he remarked to no one in particular.

"What's that?" asked Caecilius curiously, squinting as he followed Hortensius's gaze.

"That Thracian. Look at his arm. The left one."

Caecilius whistled. "The Grass Crown . . . what in the name of Jupiter . . .?"

Hortensia's attention was momentarily dragged away from the fight. "What's a Grass Crown?"

It was Caepio who answered for her.

"It's one of Rome's highest military honors, awarded to those who have saved an army in war."

"You mean, that Thracian won it?" demanded Quintus excitedly. "He saved an army in war?"

"Hardly," drawled Hortensius. "He's obviously a relic of Sertorius's rabble."

Quintus looked puzzled and it was left to Caepio to explain once more.

"Sertorius was one of the Roman army's most celebrated commanders – and one of the few ever to have been awarded a Grass Crown. But he took the populist side during the recent civil war, fled to Hispania and became quite a hero both there and with the Lusitanians, who've resisted Roman rule for decades. Even embarrassed Pompey's army a few times until he and Metellus Pius managed to stop the rot."

"And gave Tiberius Dolabella his good looks at the same time," interjected Caecilius with a grim chuckle.

"Who?" asked Hortensia.

"Fellow who stopped by earlier. Got those scars at Sucro when Pompey left his entire wing exposed, trying to claim the victory before Metellus got there. Can't say I blame the barbarian who did it. Unsavory fellow if ever there was one, Tiberius. Still surprised to find out you're on terms with him, Hortensius."

"I told you," said Hortensius tetchily. "I defended a kinsman of his some years ago. You saw, it was all I could do to remember the man's name."

Hortensia looked curiously at her father, who rarely suffered either a failure of temper or memory, but she was distracted by another roar from the crowd around them. With the hoplomachus off balance, the Thracian had leapt forward and seized his shield, tearing it from his startled opponent's hand. Flourishing his prize in the air, he flung it like a discus into the crowd where it was caught by a group of drunken spectators who bellowed their appreciation. Now the hoplomachus was armed only with his long spear, which he clung to with both hands, holding it out in front of him like a farm laborer keeping an angry bull at bay. Almost all the chants were for the Thracian now, who was advancing steadily while the hoplomachus receded, prodding and jabbing as he went. At last, backed into a corner of the arena, the hoplomachus made one last desperate charge. For a miraculous moment it looked as though his weapon would find its target, but at the last second the Thracian turned his body to one side, leaving space for the spear to pass into harmlessly. In the same movement, he brought up his right, heavily-muscled forearm, and smashed it into the advancing hoplomachus's exposed windpipe.

The hoplomachus fell backwards and lay gasping on the ground. The referee stepped between them, his wooden baton held aloft to keep the pair apart, and turned his head toward Crassus's box. Gradually, the wall of sound echoing around the arena organized itself into choruses of chanting. But it soon became apparent that there was a difference of opinion among the spectators, some of whom were greedily calling for the hoplomachus's execution, while others evidently felt that neither contestant in so exciting a fight deserved to die. This presented Crassus with a dilemma, and it was apparent from the way he was affecting to encourage the crowd's partisan chanting while simultaneously craning his head back to listen to the advice being hissed into his ear by other men in his party that he was unsure which faction he should satisfy.

Meanwhile, the Thracian continued to stand by, neither raising his sword in readiness for the order to kill, nor walking away from his stricken opponent. Hortensia stared at him intently, wondering what he was thinking. Suddenly there was a cry from a woman in the crowd behind her. The hoplomachus, who had been curled up in a fetal position on the ground, had uncoiled himself with the speed of a cobra and a flash of silver glinted in his hand – a dagger, surreptitiously drawn from inside one of his leg-greaves. He dived beneath the referee's baton and with a sickening crunch drove the blade of the knife into a gap in the leather strapping on the Thracian's right knee. The Thracian crumpled like a jointed doll, his right leg collapsing underneath him.

There was a thunderous holler of outraged disapproval from the entire crowd. Crassus leapt to his feet, shaking his head ostentatiously and motioning to the fight referee, who with the help of two assistants restrained the hoplomachus. At a further signal from Crassus, the hoplomachus was dispatched with a knife to his neck to the cheering accompaniment of the whole crowd. Meanwhile two other attendants came on and lifted the prone Thracian onto a stretcher. Blood ran from his knee as he was carried off, leaving a red stain across the white sand.

With the Thracian's exit, the hollering of the crowd was quickly replaced by a low undulating wave of chatter that pulsed around the arena. Hortensius looked around for one of the blue-liveried attendants to bring him some more wine but instead found his daughter's anxious face in front of his.

"What will happen to him now?"

Hortensius blinked. "I beg your pardon?"

"That Thracian, what will happen to him now?"

"In the name of the gods, my dear, why should you or I or anyone care? They'll send him to the mines to finish out what's left of his miserable existence, I expect. If they don't give him to the lions as a chew toy. Where has that wretched boy gone with my wine?"

"Papa, we have to help him."

"Help? Help who?"

"That Thracian. Please." Hortensia hesitated and glanced back at

Quintus, who was looking shifty, then squared her jaw resolutely. "He saved our lives."

Hortensius's expression was now one of exasperation. "What *are* you talking about?"

"He saved our lives. I didn't tell you before but . . . I went down to the holding area under the arena because . . . I wanted to get a better look at the crocodile."

Hortensius's eyes narrowed.

"Because *you* wanted to get a better look at the crocodile?"

Hortensia continued hurriedly.

"Yes, and Quintus agreed to come with me, only we got a bit too close and that Thracian pulled us away just in time. Please, Papa."

Hortensius eyed his cowering son.

"I see. Quintus, you can be sure I will deal with you later so stop hiding behind your mother. Hortensia, what you are asking me is quite ridiculous and I don't know what you expect me to be able to do anyway."

"Go and offer to buy him," she said immediately, blocking his re-newed attempts to catch the attendant's eye. "His name's Lucrio, he can come to work for you at Laurentum. You've hundreds of slaves working for you there anyway, one more can't possibly make a difference. It's a debt of honor, Papa."

"Debt of honor?" Hortensius looked incredulous. "I, Hortensius Hortalus, do not owe debts of honor to barbarian gladiators, particularly not one who would probably kill us all in our beds given half a chance. You haven't a hope of persuading me, Hortensia, and I absolutely forbid you to plague me any more about this wretched Thracian."

Hortensia fixed her eyes on him in a mulish stare. Caepio laughed.

"Care to place a bet on how this one will turn out?" he murmured to Caecilius, whose face was a picture of disapprobation.

"If I've told him once, I've told him a hundred times. He should never have taught that girl how to speak."

V

*Hortensius's summer villa at Laurentum,
sixteen miles from Rome. One month later.*

ORTENSIUS PUT DOWN HIS BRONZE PEN AND FLEXED HIS ELEGANT fingers with a grimace, holding them up and examining them dispassionately for ink stains. The late afternoon sun was streaming in through the windows of the villa, casting a translucent veil over the mythological portraits daubed in cinnamon and cerulean paint on the walls of the simply-furnished room. Through the open doorway, which led on to a marble colonnade, Hortensius had a clear view of the sea, a sparkling sheet of cobalt blue flecked with white crests. He always worked in this room during the summer, finding the pulsing sound of the waves sweeping in great arcs over the sand an ambient accompaniment to his musings. Sometimes he wandered down to the beach and walked barefoot along the shore performing his daily breath and voice exercises, the music of his recitations interweaving with the cries of the gulls.

Today though, his gaze rested meditatively on the two figures who had the beach to themselves. With the damp hem of her linen dress clinging to her slender white limbs and her long dark hair freed from the severe coiffure in which her maid Elpidia usually insisted on arranging it, Hortensia looked like a naiad washed up on the shore. She was carrying her skirt bunched up in her left hand and a fishing net heavy with seashells in the other, and as she spotted another specimen in the sand, she called out excitedly to Caepio, who was fishing in the shallows. He extracted his own net from the water, and a squirming lobster was revealed inside, with which he advanced on her laughingly. She dodged away from him with a squeal, head thrown back in delight, black curls tumbling down her back.

Returning to the documents on his lap, Hortensius continued to study them with his head propped up on one hand and his lips pursed, an expression of discontent in his eyes. It was in this pose that Caepio found him some time later as he came up from the beach. Pausing to sluice the sand from his feet in the bucket kept permanently for that purpose on the terrace, he noted with curiosity Hortensius's frowning expression, the loose strands of his usually sleek hair escaping from between the fingers of his splayed palm. But he said nothing as he helped himself to a jug of water and then came to sprawl on a couch directly opposite Hortensius. Nodding to the documents surrounding Hortensius, he enquired casually, "How is your case going?"

"Quite splendidly. I know almost everything I need to know. My client Verres is venal, corrupt, mendacious and immoral. He is undoubtedly guilty of bribery, extortion, theft, false imprisonment and, in all likelihood, murder."

"No wonder you look ill," said Caepio humorously. "Are you worried about the outcome?"

Hortensius raised a haughty eyebrow.

"My dear Caepio. Where would I be if I perpetually allowed such small inconveniences as a client's guilt to stand in the way of victory? No, to answer your question, I am not worried. My most pressing problem at the moment is that upstanding citizen Marcus Acilius Glabrio."

"The praetor?"

"Were a less stiff-necked individual to be presiding over the trial, then I would have every confidence in my ability to persuade him to see things from my point of view, shall we say. But Glabrio is not half as cretinous as some of his peers and even I will have my work cut out trying to spin this one in Verres's favor. So my best hope remains to stall the trial long enough for Glabrio's term to run out and some more compliant individual to take his place in the upcoming elections – Caecilius's brother Marcus, for example, who is conveniently in the frame and will no doubt smile more favorably on Verres's fortunes."

"Isn't that a little . . . underhand?"

"Underhand?" Hortensius laughed. "My dear boy. Just doing the best for my client. Every advocate's prerogative. Cicero would do just the same, for all that he protests that he is so morally superior to me."

"Nevertheless, you seem to be taking the case very seriously. I'm not sure I've ever seen you so preoccupied with a trial."

Hortensius shrugged. "Caecilius asked for my help. We all have embarrassing family members do we not? Look at your dear brother Cato. How can I not devote myself to the task when a friend is in need?"

Caepio inspected the contents of his cup. He had a fair notion what was really troubling his friend but nothing could be gained by digging further for it. The moment Hortensius had discovered the identity of Verres's prosecutor, he had seemed to Caepio to be in the grip of an obsession which kept him closeted away in his study for far longer periods than was usual. Now the favorite topic of Rome's gossiping elite was whether rising star Cicero would finally take Hortensius's crown as the king of the Roman law court.

His brother Cato had written a typically pithy letter informing Caepio that bets on the outcome were being traded in the forum: " . . .*if you want to give Hortensius some good advice, brother, I would suggest to him that he let the Metelli fight their own battles and do not indulge the tattling classes in their appetite for this duel. He has defended too many of these corrupt governors and a victory on behalf of Verres cannot add to his credit, not when Verres has made an enemy of so many, including, I might add, Pompey himself, not that I wish to indulge that self-satisfied braggart in his inflated delusions of grandeur. Hortensius needs to be careful though, particularly if he is serious about securing a consulship. You and I both know that a man's good name is the one thing you cannot put a price on.*"

Hortensius had begun writing again. "Will any of my daughter's entertaining suitors be at your sister's Bacchanalian gathering this evening?"

"Like my besotted nephew Brutus you mean? Certainly, though I don't think there is much in that. He follows her round like a puppy, but it is exactly that, a puppyish sort of affection. Young Publius Dolabella is another matter." A frown descended upon Caepio's brow. "He is like his uncle Tiberius and all the rest of that family. Only eighteen, but convinced that life is a gaming-board, and everything and everyone on it are playing pieces for him to capture."

"Does that bother you?"

"Me?" Caepio was startled but Hortensius did not look up and Caepio, on his guard, decided to pretend he hadn't heard, and changed the subject.

"By the by, has the news reached you about Lucilius Albinus? Cato writes that he was found dead in his bath just after we left for the summer."

"Yes, I had heard." Hortensius finished his letter, picked up his own silver cup and swirled the liquid around in it, looking thoughtfully at Caepio. "You did not answer my previous question."

"I wasn't absolutely sure you had asked me one," replied Caepio cautiously.

"Then let me substitute it for another. What if I said that I wanted you to marry Hortensia?"

Caepio looked stunned. "Me?" he repeated.

"Yes, you," replied Hortensius calmly. He watched him over the top of his glass, and when Caepio automatically opened his mouth to issue a disclaimer, looked at him a little mockingly. "Do not try and tell me you haven't thought about it."

Caepio remained silent. Then he said slowly, "Of course I've thought about it. How could I help it? But to tell the truth, I am still amazed. You have never wanted to discuss the idea of Hortensia's marriage. I was beginning to wonder if you ever meant her to marry anyone."

"Of course she must marry someone," said Hortensius impatiently. "Did you think I meant her for one of the Vestals?"

"No, naturally I did not. She is just turned seventeen, she would be too old now in any case. It's just that, well for a start, most of the girls of her age are married already."

"My daughter is not 'most girls'."

"I am well aware of that. Also, that you are not 'most fathers'."

Hortensius was silent for a moment. "You think I am sentimental? Well, perhaps you are right. But tell me this." He made an expansive, sweeping gesture, silver drinking-cup still in hand. "Who *should* a daughter like mine marry? Hmm? Would you like to see her wedded to young Publius Dolabella, who looks at her like a dog would look at a wounded bird? Or are you imagining I seriously had your precocious nephew Brutus in mind?"

"Given the competition, I suppose I should be flattered," said Caepio a little drily.

Hortensius waved an impatient hand.

"She loves you. Or she thinks she does – whatever the difference is."

"I think you must indeed be a sentimental parent," said Caepio with a smile. "Not many fathers would let their daughter marry for love."

Hortensius shrugged. "I do not need money. As you see."

Caepio got up and began to pace slowly around the room, a distracted expression on his face.

"I confess I am still surprised. I have a real fondness for Hortensia, more than that . . ."

"Good," interrupted Hortensius, slipping the seal-ring off his finger and dipping it into the wax pot by his right hand. "Then you can go and tell her now."

"Now?" Caepio looked a little alarmed. Hortensius raised a sardonic eyebrow.

"Or I will do it for you if you are so chicken-hearted, but I think she would prefer it coming from you."

Caepio muttered that he was quite capable of making his proposals himself. Pausing on the threshold of the terrace, he turned back and looked hard at Hortensius.

"I do have one thing to ask and don't try and put me off. Why now?"

"I have never yet lost a case in the law courts of Rome and I have no intention of starting now, dear Caepio. In a short time, I may also be elected consul, in which case the list of my achievements might be said to be complete. But one thing I have learned during the course of my illustrious career is that it does not do to put all your faith into one strategy. If for some unforeseen reason things should not go my way in the next month or so . . . Hortensia must not be touched by my failure. I will not have her talked about as some bargaining tool with which I may top up my credit with society."

Caepio raised an eyebrow. "So you want me to marry her because no one would think me capable of improving a girl's social prospects?" he asked wryly.

"I want you to marry her so that she will be happy." Hortensius sounded tired. "Is it so much to ask, given how things already are between you?"

Caepio looked hard at Hortensius for a moment and then slowly shook his head. As he went to the door, his eye was caught by a small ivory sphinx with arching wings and an enigmatic expression, sitting bolt upright on the side table.

"That's new," he remarked, expecting Hortensius to immediately expound on the qualities of the piece and the special lengths he had gone to obtain it. He was known as a prolific collector of beautiful objects and had a library that was the envy of every man of letters in Rome. But when Caepio looked back, Hortensius was concentrating on carefully pressing his seal-ring on to the seam of his letter, and didn't seem to have heard.

As soon as Caepio was gone however, Hortensius turned and stared at the sphinx for a long time, as though wondering what question to ask it.

HORTENSIA WALKED SLOWLY up from the beach, her head full of happy daydreams. Ruefully, she ran her fingers through her damp hair, knowing that Elpidia would scold her for spoiling her coiffure. But what did any of that matter? Caepio loved her. The feeling it had given her when he put his arms around her and kissed her . . . she wanted to relive it over and over again.

As she wandered through the olive grove planted by her father at the back of the villa, she found Lucrio and Quintus standing in the shade of a tree, each holding a wooden sword. She stopped to watch them, smiling at the difference in height and build.

"Head, groin, neck and eyes", Lucrio was saying. "Always drive with the full force of your arm, and never hesitate." He illustrated the point with a thrust of the makeshift blade, which Quintus eagerly copied.

"Head, groin, neck and eyes," Hortensia repeated. "I shall have to remember that next time I find myself on the battlefield."

Lucrio smiled and held out the hilt of the sword.

"Would you care to try, *domina*?"

Hortensia saw a scowl darken Quintus's face. "No, thank you, I am not sure Papa would approve. I'm going to be late for dinner in any case. Quintus, you should go inside too."

"You can't order me around," snapped Quintus. "I want to train some more."

"No, young master, I must return to my post in the atrium. We will resume again tomorrow. Keep practicing your footwork."

Quintus stomped off, slashing at several tree branches with his sword as he went. Hortensia shrugged half in exasperation, half in apology.

"I'm sorry. I didn't mean to interrupt. It's good for him spending time with you. I think it makes the rhetoric lessons with Papa a little easier to bear."

She expected him to laugh. When he didn't, she felt suddenly annoyed with him as well as Quintus. Lucrio was like this sometimes, Hortensia had discovered in the month that he had been at Laurentum. His mood could change from relaxed and smiling to distant and formal in a heartbeat. She began to walk toward the house.

"*Domina*? May I ask you something?"

"Of course."

She waited for him to catch up. He walked with a limp now and a thick leather guard concealed the incriminating mark on his left forearm but otherwise he presented the same respectable appearance as the rest of Hortensius's household in his smart red livery.

"Will you go to Rome soon? You and your family?"

"Yes, I think so, in a few days perhaps. Papa is standing for election to the consulship next month and he has an important case coming up in the law court. Why do you ask?"

"I just wondered if I would be coming with you or staying here."

Hortensia was surprised.

"I don't know. I hadn't thought about it. Aren't you happy here?"

He bowed.

"Of course, *domina*. It's just . . ." He squeezed the blade of the clumsy wooden sword in the palm of his hand, in the awkward gesture of one trying to find the right way to put his thoughts into words. "I have always wanted to know what became of my family back home in Lusitania. My parents and my brother are dead . . . but I had other relatives alive when I was captured. I thought if I could find some migrants from my home town in Rome, I may be able to discover what became of them."

Hortensia looked at him sympathetically. It had sometimes occurred to her that some ghost haunted Lucrio, perhaps of the wars he had fought. She had seen the shadow of it pass behind those cool green eyes.

"I see. Of course I understand. I will speak to Papa for you."

"You are very good, *domina*."

"In fact . . . perhaps there is someone else I might ask." Hortensia was unable to stop herself smiling. "I am soon to be married you see."

Lucrio bowed.

"I trust you and master Caepio will be very happy."

"You could tell?" asked Hortensia in delight. "I didn't realize it was so obvious to other people. Well, Papa may not like you to leave Laurentum for long. He appreciates how good you are with the animals, even if he doesn't always show it. But perhaps he would let you come with us and be part of our household for a little while. Just while we settle in."

"Thank you, *domina*. My debt to you grows all the greater."

He bowed again, and she went past him toward the villa. Lucrio watched her go. Then he released his grip on the blade of the sword and looked down at his palm, where the skin was raw and bleeding from the splintering wood.

"Now, I will find you, tribune," he whispered, "and you will wish with the last breath you take that our paths had never crossed."

VI

The Temple of Vesta, Rome. July 70BC.

A
S LONG AS A FLAME BURNED IN THE HEARTH OF THE TEMPLE OF Vesta, Rome would come to no harm, so ancient memory would have it. The weight of that sacred responsibility lay heavy on the heads of the six priestesses who tenderly guarded both the flame and their own chastity under pain of death. Tonight, so it seemed, the city could sleep easy. A plume of smoke billowed as usual from the vented roof of the old sanctuary, slanting silver through the gaze of the moon overhead.

In the shadows of the elegant residence behind the Temple where the Vestals lived together in secluded luxury, two figures huddled close together, the pure white worn by the smaller of the pair a less effective camouflage than the grey cloak draped around the shoulders of the other.

"So you are clear? You will admit me to the Temple at the appointed hour and then you will keep watch. It shouldn't take long but I will rely on you if it looks as though I might be disturbed."

"I still do not see why you do not let me retrieve what it is you are looking for." There was a slight petulance in the whispered reply. "The Chief Vestal is an innocent fool, I can do no wrong in her eyes."

"Because you would not know what to look for, and because I prefer to conduct so delicate a stage of the operation myself."

"Very well . . . If you will have it so, I will be waiting. She insists that we are all praying in our rooms by sundown – all except the Vestal guarding the hearth of course. But they will not know I am out, they never know. I wish it were tonight!"

Tiberius smiled in amusement, running one finger down the soft, pale cheek of the passionate face before him. "Patience, little one. We both know you were not made for this life of confinement and chastity. Soon, you will be free and then all the pleasures of the world will be yours to enjoy."

The figure in white vanished through a side door of the Vestals' residence, and Tiberius emerged from the shadows and crossed from the eastern end of the forum to the west, heading down Tuscan Street toward the Forum Boarium by the river and then through a series of residential streets winding their way up the Aventine Hill. Turning right down an avenue marked "Goat Street", he stopped outside a door with a sign above it, depicting a reed pen and a pot of ink. A shaven-headed slave with misshapen features was waiting for him.

"All taken care of?" asked Tiberius.

The slave nodded, showing a mouthful of chipped teeth. "Yes, *domine*. He put up a fight. But not for long."

Tiberius stepped inside and followed the slave down a narrow, dark hallway. He paused at the sound of crying and looked questioningly at the slave.

"Wife and a little girl. We decided to lock them in their room. Unless you would rather we . . .?"

"A little girl, you say?"

"Five or six."

Tiberius tilted his head to one side, considering. Then he shook his head.

"Too many complications. I think we'll stick to the job we're being paid for tonight."

At the far end of the hallway, two more slaves stepped back to let him pass into the room at the end. A man's body lay in the middle of the floor, his face beaten to an unrecognizable pulp. Tiberius stepped over the corpse and walked toward a metal strong-box chained to a ring in the wall. The lock had already been broken for him. He lifted the lid and began to search through the rolls of papyrus stacked inside. After some time, he extracted one and held it up to the light being held for him by one of the slaves.

"This is what we're looking for. Did you ask him whether he kept more copies of his work anywhere?"

"Yes, *domine*. We asked him very thoroughly. There is nothing besides what's in there."

Tiberius tucked the roll into a small leather bag. He then extracted a folded piece of saffron-colored papyrus from the pouch at his waist. It was covered in red ink lettering, and he tucked it inside the bag as well before handing it to the shaven-headed slave.

"You know where to take these. Remind Petro it's the fee we agreed – no negotiating. When the job's done, he needs to burn both of those. We don't want any evidence. Make sure you stand over him while he does it. Bring the new document back to the villa when he's finished. I'll still be up."

The slave nodded. Tiberius followed him down the hallway, pausing for a lingering moment beside the door – behind which piteous weeping could still be heard – before continuing out into the street. He turned to one of his other slaves, extracting a folded note and handing it over. It was anointed with the seal of a dog's head.

"Take this to the villa of Hortensius Hortalus, on the Palatine Hill. No need to wait for an answer. He'll know what it means."

The slave bowed and retreated into the night. Tiberius turned and looked back at the tendril of smoke still climbing across the face of the moon, his disfigured features illuminated by the silver glow.

"If a man's hour is come," he murmured aloud, "be he brave or be he coward, there is no escape for him when once he has been born."

VII

The house of Servilius Caepio on the Palatine Hill.

THE WEDDING CEREMONY WAS OVER. PINE TORCHES LIT UP THE VIOLET night sky above the Palatine, lacing the air with their acrid smell. As the singing procession threaded its way past the homes of Hortensius's wealthy neighbors, they called out the traditional salute of *"Talasio!"* and threw handfuls of nuts, which were quickly scavenged from the ground by watchful beggar children from the nearby suburbs. The wedding guests, having been treated by their host to a lavish feast washed down with wines from Hortensius's country estates, were in a rambunctious mood as they tramped along, serenading passers-by with their wedding songs. In the middle of the crush, a saffron-colored head could just be seen bobbing along, the yellow veil blowing back in the breeze to reveal a laughing face. At last they arrived at the garlanded door of the groom's house where there was a delay while the bride received the greetings of well-wishers in the crowd and was handed a tub of animal fat with which to ceremonially anoint the lintel of her new home in premonition of wealth and plenty for her married life.

Hortensius stood off to one side with Caecilius. He had been a convivial host throughout the day, slapping backs and ordering cups to be constantly refilled and now wore a broad smile watching the final stages of his daughter's journey from maid to matron. Caecilius glanced curiously at him.

"You're in a remarkably good mood, even for a father on his daughter's wedding day. Not sure I've seen you this relaxed of late, what with all the work you've been doing on Verres's case. Very grateful to you for that of course."

"As you say, I'm a proud father today, Caecilius."

Hortensia had now finished smearing the doorway with fat. Several of the female wedding guests came forward – Caepio's sister Servilia and Caecilius's wife Claudia among them – and lined up behind the bride as a beaming Caepio emerged from the house. To the accompaniment of cheering, and a few ribald comments from individuals in the crowd, he picked Hortensia up in his arms and carried her over the threshold, followed by her matronly attendants.

Hortensius took another sip from his cup, then said calmly, "By the way, Verres's trial is to begin in five days."

Caecilius looked aghast.

"What? But I thought you were going to get it delayed until next year when Glabrio's praetorship is over? We had it all settled. My brother Marcus will almost certainly be in charge of the extortion court by then, you and I will be elected to the consulship, it will be a done deal for us!"

"That was obviously my intention but the other extortion case I contrived to get scheduled ahead of Verres's has been settled, the jury for our case has been chosen and Glabrio is insistent that we proceed."

Caecilius groaned.

"But what are you doing to do now? Tell me you have another plan?"

Hortensius swirled the remaining wine in his cup.

"Calm yourself, Caecilius. Cicero will only have ten days or so to present his case before Pompey's games begin and the court goes into recess. Let us see what he's really made of. My skill against his. May the best man win."

He put his hand on his friend's shoulder. Looking into his bright blue eyes, Caecilius thought he saw some reckless spark there, which may or may not have been down to the amount of wine Hortensius had drunk.

"I am done with stratagems, my old friend. Now I'm ready for the fight."

He nodded good night and began to walk unsteadily back up the hill toward his own villa, humming a little tune to himself.

THE VESTAL RAISED her veiled head and stared at the sanctuary door. The heat from the flames had made her sleepy and the short, high-pitched noise had caused her to start suddenly. But she was confused as to what she had heard. She was sure it had come from the sanctuary, where there was a secret entrance leading to the Vestals' private quarters, but none of the other priestesses was due to take over her duties until sunrise. She glanced in the opposite direction, toward the open doorway of the temple, and saw that the horizon was the same dark violet as it had been when she had first sat down. Should she fetch the two slaves on guard outside? But surely she would only make herself look foolish. Perhaps it was the Chief Vestal, fetching one of the bags of sacred grain that were kept there for use in special rites. But why would she do so at this time of night?

Hesitantly, the priestess rose from her ornate chair and walked slowly toward the latticed door of the sanctuary, at the back of the domed temple chamber. She bent her head and listened intently but all that she could hear was the roaring of the flames from the hearth behind her. She pushed at the door and it swung open easily. The room was in darkness, but the light from the great hearth flame behind her illuminated the sanctuary's most precious cult object – a little sacred statue of the goddess Minerva, said to have been rescued for Rome from the ruins of Troy. Around Minerva's head, the curved walls were lined with archive niches, each one brimming with precious documents belonging to Rome's wealthiest and most powerful citizens.

Then she saw him. A man, halfway up the wall of the sanctuary, balanced on a wooden ladder. He was just withdrawing his hand from one of the private archives, a roll of papyrus between his fingers. As the light from the chamber flooded the room, he turned his head and she saw his monstrous face. She opened her mouth but no sound came out. She felt dizzy, as though the walls of the room were spinning round her. He had already descended the ladder. She took a step back as he moved quickly toward her and she stumbled on the hem of her gown. Her cry was stifled by his hand over her mouth. She felt his thumbs on her throat and as the breath was mercilessly squeezed from her body, her eyes appealed pitifully to the statue of Minerva. But the goddess did not come to her aid.

SERVILIA, CLAUDIA AND the other married women had done their work and filed out of the room after bestowing smiles and embraces on their youthful charge, and in Servilia's case, a sly, whispered piece of advice that brought a flush to Hortensia's cheeks. Barefoot and dressed now only in her white bridal tunic, her black hair freed from its tight braids and her flame-colored veil removed, she sat alone on a scrolled couch in the middle of the bedroom, waiting for her husband. He came in a few moments later and sat down next to her.

"Well, here we are," said Hortensia softly.

"Here we are indeed," replied Caepio, nodding in emphatic agreement. He wrinkled his brow suddenly. "What on earth do you suppose we do next?" he asked in a tone of puzzlement.

She smiled and he sat back from her a little, looked down at the woollen orange belt at her waist, carefully tied into a complicated-looking knot.

"Your handiwork, my dear?" he enquired. "I'm very impressed. There seems to be no end to your accomplishments."

Hortensia raised an eyebrow quizzically at him and the smile between them deepened.

Reaching out to her waist, Caepio tugged gently on the orange cord, which slipped apart easily, allowing the fine white fabric to billow out around her. Leaning over, he buried his face in the curve of her neck and breathed in the warmth of her for a moment, feeling the quiver that ran through her. Then he stood, picked her up and carried her over to the bed in the middle of the room, placing her gently on the damask coverlet. He turned away to blow out one of the candles by the pillows, assuming that his bride would be shy. But when he turned back, he saw that Hortensia had already slipped the white gown over her head and tossed it to the floor. Her skin glowed the color of warm honey in the last of the candlelight, and the crimson bed linen made the perfect foil for her dark, luxuriant hair.

"Are you going to make a joke *now*?" she asked teasingly as she watched Caepio's eyes on her.

He shook his head slowly. "No," he said simply. "I'm lost for words as usual." He lay down beside her and for a time there were no more words between them.

SHE OPENED HER eyes. A glimmer of light from the hearth glowed through the slats of the half-open sanctuary door. She could just feel a breeze on her cheek from the temple entrance beyond. Was he still here? Her lips parted and she tried to breathe but it was as though her throat was caught in a metal vice, sealing in her voice and permitting only the finest filament of air to pass through. The guards outside would never be able to hear her now. Her eyelids drooped. She could still feel the man's fingers around her neck, the terrible, agonizing pain, then the feeling of light-headedness before darkness had overwhelmed her.

The man. He had taken something from the sanctuary.

Her eyes flickered open once more. She tried to concentrate on conserving the small amount of air still in her lungs as her gaze wandered around the room. She imagined where he had been standing when she opened the door. Straight ahead, directly opposite in fact. He had been balanced on the portable ladder they used to reach the higher shelves. It must have been a noise from the movement of the ladder that she had heard. He had just withdrawn something – a document – from an archive halfway up the wall. But whose was the archive? The ladder was still where he had left it. Her lips moved slightly as she counted down the number of niches from the top row of shelves, her gaze coming to rest on one next to the seventh rung of the ladder, where she thought she had seen the movement of his hand. She stared. That particular archive was fuller than the others around it. Few citizens were important enough to store that many documents here. She was almost certain . . .

The tiny pocket of air caught in her throat. Lifting her head and hauling herself on to her hands and knees, she began to crawl slowly through the half-open door of the sanctuary and into the main chamber of the temple. Her breathing was tight and desperately shallow. As she came closer to the hearth at the center of the temple, her white dress was soiled by the thin film of soot covering the tiled floor. The flames burned bright like a beacon. She knew she was not going to reach the temple door. Collapsing next to the great hearth chair where she had been sitting so dutifully until just a few minutes before, she pressed her cheek gratefully to the cool marble. Then she stretched out her hand into the shadow under the hearth chair, and with one pale, slender finger, she dreamily began to swirl letters into the dark powdery canvas.

The sound of approaching footsteps stayed her arm. She lay still now, not flinching at the man's curse of annoyance nor resisting when she felt his hands around her neck again. But the look on her face as she died was still one of shock. For as he dragged her up from the floor, she could see the person now accompanying him, a figure dressed – just like her – all in white.

OUTSIDE CAEPIO'S VILLA, the remaining guests had finally dispersed, the last few drunken revelers loudly singing as they slowly wended their way down the hill, their voices growing fainter and gradually being swallowed up by the rattle of evening traffic from the city below. The urchin children had returned to their own dark, grime-fettered neighborhood, leaving a trail of broken nut-shells scattered between the paving stones in their wake. Only Hortensius's inebriated client Bibulus – an aspiring poet – had failed to make his departure, intending apparently to spend the night sprawled over the threshold composing wedding hymnals in honor of his patron's daughter. But his happy, hazy contemplation of the stars was suddenly blocked by a dark figure standing overhead and to his alarm, he felt a strong pair of hands picking him up by the front of his robes and dragging him to his feet. A razored slant of firelight from one of the dying braziers cut menacingly across his assailant's face, and he recoiled in horror.

"Do you have a home?" came the rasping enquiry.

Bibulus nodded hastily.

"Then get back to it."

The terrified poet made no attempt to resist the shove that propelled him down the hill.

Lucrio limped a few paces down the slope after him, making sure that he had really disappeared and that no other drunken malingerers were still lurking. But then he caught sight of the view and paused where he stood, looking out at the city spread in all its dark, pulsing, undulating glory below him. Down to his right were the crowded alleyways and filthy tenements of the Subura, where the poorest residents of the city scraped out a half-existence; to his left the great arena of the Circus Maximus, where the howling mob gathered on festival days to watch chariot-racing and gladiatorial games; and in front of him, the Capitoline, the smallest and most sacred of Rome's hills, at whose foot lay the Roman forum with its patchwork of temples, shops, law courts and municipal buildings including the senate house. The city was alive with the clatter of hooves and wagon-wheels on the stone paving and the shouts of the vehicles' drivers, as they loaded and unloaded their wares or squabbled with fellow road-users over who had the right of way. From the Palatine, the noise was a distant hum. For those living in the Subura, it must have been deafening. It was only Lucrio's second night in the city but already he understood the complaint intoned by Caepio's slaves that only the rich could afford a decent night's sleep in Rome. But gazing out at this seething metropolis, one thought dominated his mind. He was out there somewhere. Lucrio knew he would recognize him the moment he set eyes on him, with or without his tribune's uniform. Every line of those angular features, every nuance of that lazy, savage Roman voice was burned into his memory. He could still see Taio falling in the dirt with bewilderment in his brown eyes and a newly drawn seam around his neck, still hear his mother's screams above the noise of the tribune's ferocious pleasure.

He glanced back into the cool, shadowy atrium of the villa. All the household slaves had been sent to their own quarters, which lay in the eastern wing of the house, just between the kitchen and the stables. The only light came from a candle on the corridor leading to the west wing where the master's private room was situated. A cool breeze rushed through the atrium and for a moment, Lucrio thought he heard a faint peal of laughter. Turning quickly away, he resumed his contemplation of the city landscape, a fire of emotions raging in his cool, green eyes.

SEVERAL HOURS LATER, as the lavender light of dawn began to dapple the murky waters of the Tiber, Bibulus woke up with a terrible headache. Squinting and moaning in protest as the early morning sun tried to prise open his eyelids, he gradually became aware that he was lying across a rubbish pile which smelt very strongly of cattle excrement. Levering himself upright and waving an arm irritably at a pair of hovering pigeons which retreated and began pecking at a pile of cabbage leaves near his feet, Bibulus tried to piece together the sequence of events that had led him to make his bed here. He had a dim recollection of that Spanish thug of a steward manhandling him down the Palatine. After that his memory became very fuzzy but one thing was clear: he would certainly alert Hortensius to the fact that his new son-in-law had some very unsavory individuals in his employment.

As the sights and sounds of his dingy surroundings came more sharply into focus, Bibulus realized that he was in the Forum Boarium where the cattle merchants habitually plied their trade. Just off to his left he could see the yellow curve of the Tiber, where some men gathered on the riverbank seemed to be shouting at someone or something in the water below his line of vision. Presumably it was this noise which had woken him from his uncomfortable slumber. Several of the onlookers were crouched on their haunches, reaching down into the river, and Bibulus caught a glimpse of something large and white being dragged up onto the bank. He wondered if it was a dead swan – they did often cluster around this section of the river in the hope of surplus food from the market being thrown into the water. Despite his throbbing headache, Bibulus was suddenly struck with inspiration. His portfolio did not yet contain an opus on Leda and the Swan. Perhaps this could be the poetic opportunity that would finally win him the notice he deserved. Dragging himself to his feet, he limped groggily toward the gaggle of workers who were now standing in a circle, looking down at their quarry. Bibulus mused excitedly over what meter to choose – elegiacs? Or should he be more ambitious and attempt an epic in hexameters?

Then a gap opened in the circle of onlookers, and with a great shudder of horror, Bibulus saw what they were all staring at. Not a swan, but the body of a woman dressed all in white, her ashen, bloated face turned sightlessly up toward the sky. Straggly brown hair clung like seaweed to her wet, pallid skin, which was mottled with purple bruising around her neck. Her eyes were glassy and bloodshot and her mouth sagged open as though her last breath had just escaped her body.

Staggering away with his hand over his mouth, Bibulus managed to make it back to his rubbish pile before adding his own contribution to it.

VIII

HORTENSIA LAY ON A COUCH IN HER PRIVATE ROOM JUST OFF THE atrium, a roll of literature unraveled on her lap. She had assured her father that she would keep up both her Greek and her rhetoric exercises, and though she knew he would have reproached her for doing so from a recumbent position, she had just been reading aloud some passages from Demosthenes. Her performance was causing much confusion among Caepio's staff, who kept peering into the room expecting to find that their new mistress was entertaining guests whose arrival they had not noticed. But after almost an hour's practice, Hortensia was now thoroughly bored and longing for some kind of distraction.

As was customary for a new bride, she had received a number of courtesy calls over the past few days from other Roman matrons, some of them friends of her mother, others noted hostesses such as Marcus Fulvius Bambalio's wife, Sempronia, who had come to inspect Servilius Caepio's young bride and pass condescending judgment on her afterwards. She had been proud to receive their congratulations on the election of her father and Caecilius to the consulship two days before, but had not been able to contribute anything to their shocked, gossipy discussion about the dead Vestal Virgin found in the Tiber on the morning after her wedding. A suicide, apparently – the silly girl had evidently broken her vow of chastity and embroiled herself in a love affair – probably she feared discovery and threw herself into the river rather than face the terrifying punishment of being buried alive. This led to some tart commentary on the Vestal's aptitude for the role in the first place, to the effect that this was what came of allowing girls from plebeian as well as patrician families to be considered for the sacred role.

These distinguishing visits aside, there was little else to fill Hortensia's day apart from accompanying her mother on social calls of their own, or submitting to the lengthy ministrations of Elpidia who, like Lucrio, had accompanied Hortensia to her marital home and insisted that she should not leave her private quarters before being properly clothed and coiffed as befitted her new position. Caepio had laughingly pleaded with his bride not to occupy herself with wool-work and she had little interest in the running of the kitchen, preferring to leave this under the stewardship of Aulus the cook. Her father's gardener Rixus had been coming over most days to replant the villa's garden. But Rixus did not rate Hortensia's horticultural knowledge and since she refused to procure for him one of the preciously rare and expensive cherry tree saplings which general Licinius Lucullus had been shipping back from his eastern campaigns, he had turned a deaf ear to all her other ideas, insisting the plants she wanted would not grow on Palatine soil. This, and his habit of taking a nap in the shade of a cypress tree during the hottest part of the afternoon, lying sprawled in such a way that his tunic often rode up to reveal glimpses of a grubby, ill-fitting loincloth straining over fleshy buttocks, soon persuaded Hortensia to abandon her daily stroll around the peristyle.

She picked up the Demosthenes again with a sigh and was just preparing to resume her reading when she heard voices in the hall outside, one of which seemed to be female. She suspected it must be another friend of her mother come to lend her patronage, and tip-toed cautiously to the doorway of her salon. A woman dressed in a chestnut brown tunic with a matching mantle drawn up over her head was standing at the threshold to the front door, palms outspread in pleading entreaty to Eucherius, the young door-keeper. He had been proud to assume temporary duty for Lucrio – to whom Hortensia had given permission to go and search the Subura for people who might give him news of his family – and was now shaking his head very firmly at the woman.

"Good morning," said Hortensia curiously. "Are you looking for someone?"

The woman had started at the sound of another voice and stared at the young mistress of the house in embarrassed dismay. "It is nothing. I was hoping I might find my husband here, that is all. Marcus Rufio? He is one of your husband's clients and I thought he might be here for morning *salutatio*. But I am sorry to have disturbed you, I will go."

She gathered up her skirts and turned back toward the street but Hortensia interrupted. "I could ask my husband if he has been here if you'd like."

"No," the woman interjected hastily. "Please, I have no wish to involve your husband."

Hortensia stared at her curiously. Her visitor was perhaps ten years older than herself, clearly no longer young but with an open, attractive face. Her dress was not expensive but it was elegant, her hair drawn up in a simple but modish style, and she spoke in a well-bred voice.

"Is it something *I* can help you with?" Hortensia pressed.

The woman paused on the threshold, looking harassed and uncertain. "I do not think so. Thank you. It is kind of you to ask but . . . I do not think anyone can help me."

She looked for a moment as though she was going to lose control of her tightly-controlled emotions and Hortensia's interest was now thoroughly whetted. She dismissed the abashed Eucherius with a wave and held out her other hand to her guest.

"Won't you please come into the garden and tell me about it? My name is Hortensia. You have created quite a mystery and I'm afraid I won't be happy until I know what it is. Is your husband in some kind of trouble?"

She indicated toward the hallway leading to the back of the house and after some hesitation, the woman followed her. Half the garden was still in shade, and they sat down on a bench in a cool corner under some olives. A large pile of smooth, flat pebbles had been heaped up next to a low stone wall where Rixus was planning to create a small fountain.

"So," began Hortensia companionably. "Do tell me your name and a little more about your husband and why you are so anxious to speak with him."

The woman began to pleat the folds of her dress between thin, nervous fingers.

"My name is Drusilla. As for my husband, I am afraid I misled you slightly when I called him that. He is not, or at least he has all but ceased to be. He . . . we are just divorced." She looked rueful but her jaw was set defiantly. "It was not my decision though I cannot say the fact grieves me."

Hortensia felt the slight smugness of the newly and happily wedded woman but schooled her face into an expression of sympathetic interest.

"Is your husband so very disagreeable?"

"I did not used to think so," Drusilla said quietly. "But I should have listened to my mother when she tried to dissuade me from marrying him."

"Presumably your father had some say in the matter?"

Drusilla shook her head. "No. My father is dead, he fought for Marius during the civil war. I have a guardian, naturally – my uncle – but he has interested himself very little in my upbringing or that of my brothers and sisters. When my mother told him I wished to marry Marcus Rufio, he dismissed her concerns and said it would be a great alliance for us. Well, now after six years I know what my mother knew all along. I married a man I thought was charming and respected. I soon discovered that he was reckless and a spendthrift who had only married me because my father's will left a handsome dowry for myself and my sisters on the occasion of our marriages. Now Marcus Rufio has stolen that dowry from me. But much more than that, he has stolen the children I bore him and does not intend to let me see them ever again."

Her head dropped into her palm and she burst into tears, the tears seeping out between her splayed fingers.

Hortensia stared at her, feeling a sense of shocked pity yet also consternation at having a strange, hysterical woman in her house. Fortunately, Drusilla regained control of her emotions quite quickly and having repressed her sobbing breaths, sat upright again and apologized for her loss of bearing.

"I am sorry if I have embarrassed you. You have been very kind to listen to me, but there is really nothing you can do. I only came to find

Marcus Rufio to see if he might reconsider allowing me to see my children at least."

"How old are they? What are their names?" asked Hortensia tentatively.

"My son Marcus is five. Cassia, my daughter, is just three. If I could just have them with me for some of the time, I would not ask Marcus Rufio for anything else. I am living with my mother again now and we can survive without the return of the dowry."

"But, forgive me, I am sure that the dowry is yours to keep," interjected Hortensia. "Presumably you were married without *manus* – in other words, your uncle is still your legal guardian, not your husband?" She received a silent nod in reply. "Well then the money is yours," asserted Hortensia triumphantly. "Your husband has no right to it and it must be returned on your divorce. I have some knowledge of these matters, you see. My father is a famous advocate," she said with a proud smile.

Drusilla shook her head despairingly. "I wish it were that simple. You see, Marcus Rufio has accused me of immoral behavior. He claims that I am an adulteress, and as such, he is under no obligation to return my dowry to me. As for my children, he claims that my influence would corrupt their character."

Hortensia wrinkled her brow. "But . . . forgive me . . ." She stopped, feeling extremely embarrassed about the level of intimacy her conversation with a virtual stranger had already reached.

Drusilla turned and looked Hortensia in the eye. "I have been a chaste wife, I can assure you," she said quietly. "But if Marcus Rufio says that I have not, then who will argue with him?"

Hortensia did not find it difficult to believe her declaration of innocence. Everything about her manner and appearance was an advertisement for the upstanding Roman matron. The embarrassment she had felt before now gave way to indignation.

"I can assure you there are people who will argue with him," she said warmly. "I am very glad you have brought this matter to my attention. My husband shall certainly hear of it."

Drusilla stood up with an expression of panic on her face. "Oh no, please! Your husband cannot be involved. If Marcus Rufio thinks that I have harmed his relationship with his patron, he will make things even worse for me."

Hortensia put out a hand to soothe her.

"I promise not to do anything that would upset you, but you must allow me to help in some way. Will you at least permit me to consult with my husband – perhaps even seek my father's advice? I assure you that I will do nothing to make things more uncomfortable for you."

After much wringing of hands, Drusilla finally agreed that Hortensia might make further enquiries on her behalf.

IX

AT THE TOP OF A TALL APARTMENT BLOCK IN THE SUBURA, A MAN WAS bent over a rickety table. He had smooth, very dark skin and the pale crescents of his fingernails were rimed with ink. A roll of papyrus lay on the table in front of him and he was holding a fine reed pen between his elegant fingers, its tip suspended like a spider quivering on the end of a carefully spun thread. Working very slowly and with meticulous precision, the man was swirling the pen up and down, glancing up every now and then to look at the other document he was copying. A shadow fell across the table and he looked up, the silver hoop in his ears glinting in the moonlight. There was a woman standing in the doorway, her skin dark like his but thickly painted and with bright eyes rimmed with kohl. She spoke in a sleepy tone of voice.

"Petro. You better run. Men outside asking where you live."

Delicately, the forger slotted his pen into place alongside a row of others on the cloth beside him, rolled it up quickly, and then went to a box in the corner of the room from which he extracted several items – pots of wax, an inkwell and several rolls of parchment. He then removed a tile from the floor and took out from underneath it what looked like a handful of clay coins and a square of saffron-colored papyrus with red ink lettering. He placed all of these items in a cloth bag, which he slung over his shoulder.

"Insurance." He grinned as he passed the painted woman in the doorway, pausing to kiss her cheek. Then he ran lightly down the stairs and disappeared into the darkness of night.

"BUT THAT IS preposterous!"

Hortensia glared across the small dining table at her husband, who shrugged apologetically.

"I am sorry, my dear, but that is the law. It is unusual for the husband to retain the whole dowry, I grant you, but there is precedent for this kind of case, and children always live with their fathers after a divorce in any case, unless they are minded to leave them with the mother. I am sorry for your friend but she is right, there is really nothing she can do."

They were lying on two couches in the summer dining room where the remains of a modest evening meal were spread on a low table. Hortensia had considered seeking out her father for advice but something told her he would consider the case beneath his attention and try to dissuade his daughter in turn from involving herself. Caepio's assistance would answer to the matter far better if he could be persuaded to confront Marcus Rufio, but Hortensia was deeply disappointed by his reaction.

"But you are his patron! Surely you can make him see reason?"

"I cannot interfere in my clients' family lives. As soon as I do that, where is the line drawn? I can advise them on their business dealings, I can withhold loans of money if I judge that they will not use them wisely, but it is not for me to tell them how to conduct their personal affairs. I agree that if your reading of this woman's character is correct then Marcus Rufio would appear to have behaved disgracefully, but he has the law on his side." He peered over at Hortensia, whose brow was furrowed in irritation, and added in a mild, placatory tone, "In my defense I did not choose him as my client. His claim on my family's protection goes back several generations."

"All the more reason for you to exert your influence," muttered Hortensia, chewing angrily on a piece of dried fig.

There was silence between them for a while, disturbed only by the call of two songbirds in a yew tree whose branches dipped over the garden. Hortensia appeared lost in thought.

"The hearing comes before a praetor tomorrow. In one of the civil courts in the forum," she said meditatively. "If she had an advocate to speak on her behalf, she might stand a better chance." She shot him a speculative glance.

"No, Hortensia," said Caepio firmly.

"You have spoken in court before," she pointed out.

"True, but I do not have anything like your father's skill. Besides, it would be wrong to speak against my own client and I cannot feel – given the accusation against this Drusilla – that it would benefit her cause to have a man wholly unconnected to her or her family arguing on her behalf."

Hortensia's eyes narrowed but she said nothing, apparently acknowledging the force of this argument. A few more wordless moments passed. Caepio had a premonition of her next question even before she asked it.

"Are women allowed to address the law court?"

Caepio sighed. "I know what you are thinking, Hortensia . . ."

"Are they?" she repeated firmly.

"There is no law to prohibit the practice yet but there is talk of one, thanks to a rather eccentric woman called Afrania, the wife of Senator Licinius Buccio, who often appears before the praetor on disputes relating to her property. But she argues on her own behalf, she is not an advocate, and I need hardly tell you her actions have made her very unpopular with the likes of Caecilius and my brother Cato."

The songbirds continued to echo each other's call. Caepio got to his feet and came to sit down on the couch next to Hortensia. She did not look at him but neither did she resist the embrace of his arm around her shoulders.

"My dearest, I admire the fact that you want to help this woman. No one knows better than I how much courage you have. But those men in that court will not know that, nor will they appreciate it. You have no evidence, no character witnesses to help Drusilla prove her claim against her husband, let alone the slightest experience of the law court. Given that, what do you truly imagine you will be able to do for her without harming yourself in the process?"

"Perhaps nothing," Hortensia admitted, raising her eyes to his. "But I cannot leave it alone, Caepio. I keep thinking of that speech Papa used to make Quintus and me recite. '*If we look to the laws, they afford equal justice to all in their private differences.*'" She shrugged and gave a little smile. "I am my father's daughter, you know."

Caepio kissed the top of her head. "That you are, though I cannot believe your father would encourage you in this instance." He remained silent for a moment. "If you are determined to go to the court tomorrow, I will not try and stop you but on condition that you promise me two things. First, you must take Lucrio to escort you through the forum. It will be very crowded tomorrow. Cicero is due to make the opening speech against Verres in the afternoon and your father needs as strong a show of support as possible, I must be there. Second, if the praetor sitting in judgment on Drusilla's case refuses you permission to speak from the outset, you must abide by his decision and not create scandal for yourself."

Hortensia nodded and raised an eyebrow at him. "Not many husbands would be so understanding," she said with a teasing smile.

"Ah but then I am a remarkable husband," said Caepio sagely.

"I promise not to create a scandal."

"Oh go ahead, why not," said Caepio, leaning back on the couch and waving a hand flippantly. "We can always move to Crete, they're very understanding about that kind of thing over there."

Hortensia laughed and raised a hand to her husband's cheek. "You are indeed a remarkable husband. You're sure you don't mind?"

Caepio smiled and gave a little shrug. "It's who you are, my darling. It's why I love you."

She kissed him lingeringly and stood up, hand outstretched. "Come to bed."

They retired to their room and one by one the oil-lamps around the villa were extinguished by the household slaves until all was quiet and dark.

DEEP IN THE heart of the city, the Subura pulsed to its own wild, erratic rhythm. There was no street lighting in the damp alleyways and few of the residents could afford the cost of a lantern-bearer to illuminate their way, but the beat of footsteps, the rattle of vehicles and the screech of voices had barely abated since the sun went down. The waft of hot chickpea soup and thick sausage stew from the cook shops competed with the stench from the underground sewer, tempting the custom of those who did not dare risk a cooking fire in the precipitous, decaying tenements that teetered like crumbling cliff-faces above the narrow streets. Stagnant pools leaked from the public fountains, soaking the feet of those who came down from the topmost apartments to replenish their supplies of washing water. A noisy stream of trade flowed in and out of the tabernas watched from nearby stairwells by groups of hard-nosed men who exchanged silent signals whenever unusually drunk or well-heeled patrons entered or left.

Most shops were still open for business, from cobblers and iron-mongers to barbers and teeth-pullers, where trays of bone and ivory re-placements were prominently displayed. A wizened man sat smoking a pipe outside an apothecary crammed with jars labeled "spikenard", "gal-banum", "mandrake" and "opium" while a roughly chalked sign pre-scribed various abortifacients, from rue and sea urchin juice to a pessary of cantharone beetles, celery seed and cuttlefish eggs. Crude price-lists etched onto the grime-covered walls advertised the services of countless brothels. As Lucrio walked along, painted girls in threadbare clothing leant out of the windows above and called out to him. "Look at this one, ladies . . . here's a prize if you can get it. How about it darling, why not die happy – it's only the price of a loaf." But he did not check his limping stride, pausing only to talk to a pair of men lounging outside a taberna, who shook their heads foggily in response to his enquiry.

A wagon carrying a shaggy-headed fir tree more than twice its length was causing havoc as it attempted to navigate a path through the twisting alleyways, its flailing branches scraping clumps of cement from the brickwork of the buckling tower blocks, much to the wrath of their tenants. Following in the tree's wake, Lucrio crossed the street to avoid the fishy stench from a stall selling garum in large vats before eventually coming to a halt beside a bread maker's where coils of dough were being briskly shoveled into a roaring oven. Next door to the bread maker was a curtained alcove with an eye painted on a flimsy sign dangling above it. Lucrio pushed back the curtain to reveal a tiny room occupied by a man swathed in filthy black robes. He was seated on the ground, an earthenware jar beside him and a strong fug of drink lingering about him. A beam of moonlight lanced across his face as the curtain was withdrawn and he squinted up at Lucrio through blueish, sightless eyes.

"Welcome, young traveler," he wheezed. "You seek your fortune?"

Lucrio squatted down in front of him.

"Not a fortune. Information."

"Information . . . that's more expensive."

Lucrio tossed a coin onto the man's lap. A scrabbling of a gnarled hand, quick appraisal of the coin's size, and it vanished into the folds of the man's clothing.

"I'm looking for someone and I don't know how to find him."

"Mmm, that *is* a challenge. My eyes are tired today . . ." Lucrio flicked another coin at him. It disappeared as quickly as the first.

"One of the rich bloods up in the hills. A tribune. From the Spanish campaigns. Who would know names?"

"A tribune you say? Perhaps one of Pompey's veterans could help you. There's a group of them who spend most of their time in the Taberna Aquila."

"I've already tried them. They wouldn't help me."

"I didn't think they would," answered the old man, unperturbed, and took a swig from the jar at his side. "Didn't like your voice I expect."

"No. They didn't. So where now?"

The man squinted and another coin appeared on his lap. As he turned his milky gaze on Lucrio, a pinprick of orange light seemed to flare in the centre of his pupil.

"One of the money-lenders on Silver Street maybe. They cater to the rich bloods sometimes, those who don't want their debts to be known. Or the forgers, there's always work for them to do. The best ones live on Mercury Street."

"And where do I find that?"

The orange glow in the old man's eyes suddenly blossomed and there was a roar behind them like a wall of water crashing against a cliff.

Lucrio turned and his gaze was dragged toward the skyline above the row of shops and apartments on the other side of the street. A crest of fire was dancing over the rooftops, sending plumes of smoke snaking into the night air.

Abandoning the old man, Lucrio darted down a tiny alleyway and emerged on the adjoining street where an entire apartment block was engulfed in flames. Pieces of burning timber were crashing down onto the street, sending up clouds of blazing embers. A few people were staggering out of the stairwell, their hands to their mouths, but screams could be heard from the smaller tenements on the higher floors where the fire seemed to be at its worst. Groups of bystanders pointed excitedly and shook their heads. Opposite the building, an argument was going on between a hysterical-looking man in a green tunic and the foreman of a squadron of fire-fighters, who instead of busying themselves filling their buckets from the nearby fountain, were leaning idly against their hooked grappling poles.

Through one of the second-floor windows, Lucrio suddenly spied the face of a terrified woman through the smoke. She had a baby in her arms and was begging one of the onlookers below to help, but they were too wary of approaching the disintegrating building. Lucrio crossed the street, dodging a falling shard of wood, and stood beneath the window with his arms outstretched.

"Drop him," he shouted. "I promise to catch him."

She hesitated. Her face was red and covered in sweat and tears. Then she leant out and let the bundle fall from her arms. Lucrio caught it, ran to place the squalling baby in the arms of a woman standing nearby, then raced back to the window. Flames were beginning to consume the woman's apartment.

"Now you."

She shook her head in a panic. "I can't," she wept.

"Yes you can. Just jump."

She clambered awkwardly on to the ledge. Roof tiles were tumbling and smashing on the ground, and she gave a little scream as one hit her on the shoulder. Then she launched herself forwards and landed in Lucrio's outstretched arms. He staggered a little but recovered himself and carried her over to a group of onlookers who applauded him as he set her down. Next he ran over to where the foreman of the fire-fighters was now waving a crumpled document in front of the anguished man in green.

"This is the deal," the foreman was saying. "We put the fire out for you but you sell the whole building plus the land it's standing on to my master, Marcus Crassus, for twenty thousand sesterces, no negotiating. All I need is that little seal from your finger right there . . ."

"Why don't you put the fire out?" demanded Lucrio. "There are people in there, why don't you save them?"

The foreman looked at him reproachfully.

"Do you mind? We're just doing a bit of business here."

He turned away and began to wave the document in front of the landlord's face again but Lucrio grabbed his arm.

"You tell your men to put that fire out now, you Roman scum!"

The foreman's mouth dropped open. "Who do you think you're calling scum, Spaniard?" he said aggressively. "Do you have any idea who I work for?"

Lucrio took a step toward the foreman and was just clenching his hand into a fist when he felt a warm hand being laid on his arm. He spun round and found himself face to face with the woman to whom he had earlier handed the baby. She was dark-skinned and bright-eyed, with a heavily painted face.

"Cool yourself, Spaniard," she said in a sleepily caressing voice, tucking her hand into the crook of his arm and forcing him to walk away with her in the opposite direction. "He's right. You don't want to cross the guy he works for."

She smiled, revealing a mouthful of brown teeth, and she let her gaze wander over him. "You're new in town, aren't you? I could show you around if you like."

Lucrio stared up at the burning building, a muscle pulsing in his jaw, the glow from the flames casting shadows across his face.

"No thanks. I'm learning my way."

He turned on his heel and walked away.

IN THE EARLY hours of the morning, Hortensia woke. For a few contented minutes, she watched the rise and fall of her sleeping husband's chest, then wandered over to the door in the corner of their room, which led out into the garden. The sky was the color of an angry sea, but a stripe of peach-colored light was beginning to warm the eastern horizon. There was a faint tang of smoke on the breeze. Wrapping a thick cloak around her white night dress, she drifted outside. The grass between her bare toes was cold and damp but there was a thickness in the air that warned of yet another oppressively hot day ahead. Placing her hand below her ribcage and filling her lungs with air, just as her father had taught her, Hortensia began to pace back and forth across the grass, steadily inhaling and exhaling as she created a trail of footprints in the dew.

X

THE JOURNEY FROM THE PALATINE DOWN TO THE RUMBLING BELLY OF the forum took no more than ten minutes, but to Hortensia, it was like passing from one world into another. As the broad, cypress-shaded avenues colonized by Rome's wealthiest citizens segued into the narrow, noisy streets snaking around the base of the hill, the temperature between the high buildings on either side rose and the atmosphere became thicker and more febrile. Lying on the cushioned pallet of her litter, screened from sight by green-and-gold linen drapes, Hortensia fanned herself nervously and held a little pot of lavender balm to her nose. It was the first journey she had made into the city unaccompanied, the protection afforded by her married status allowing her to forgo the company of her mother or another family member, yet she felt stupidly vulnerable despite the presence of Lucrio walking alongside the litter, repelling the advances of beggars who would have thrust their hands inside the drapes in search of a few coins.

As they turned on to the Sacred Way, the main street leading to the forum, the smell of bread from the many bakeries that lined the route mingled with the scent of leather from the tanneries and crushed rose petals from the perfumeries. Peering out through the gap in the curtains, Hortensia caught glimpses of greengrocers' stalls piled high with artichokes and cabbages, and snack stands dispensing hot sausages and oysters to passers-by. She spied her gardener Rixus at one such stall, opening his mouth very wide and tipping the contents of an oyster shell into his mouth, spilling the juices down his rounded, crimson-upholstered stomach.

Further along, there were drapers' merchants displaying linens, damasks and silks in a palette ranging from ivory and ochre to murex purple and sky blue. A gaggle of brightly-dressed women were crowded around another cart loaded with cosmetics, laughing and haggling with the stallholder as they experimented with smears of poppy paste on their cheeks. Just alongside, a row of children were sitting on a bench under a canopy, chanting in obedient response to the paedagogus who presided over their makeshift school. Hortensia thought back to her own childhood lessons in rhetoric with her father, smiling in guilty self-reproach as she remembered her precocious displays, often exhibited at Quintus's expense.

At last the green-and-gold entourage reached the mouth of the forum and Hortensia felt the motion of the litter slow even more. The noise from outside was almost deafening and she could see the outlines of people pushed up against the fabric of the drapes as they attempted to squeeze past. Soon they came to a complete halt and Lucrio's dark face appeared in the narrow gap between the curtains.

"It is too crowded to take the litter any further, *domina*. The whole world has decided to visit the forum today. If you wish to go on, we will have to walk from here."

Hortensia assented and Lucrio assisted as she alighted before dismissing the litter-bearers. Drawing her veil up higher over her black hair, Hortensia gazed in wonder at the scene around her. She had never seen the center of Rome so packed with people and the reason soon became apparent. There were posters everywhere, some advertising the recent elections, for which many people had traveled to Rome from all over Italy. Others loudly proclaimed the upcoming games in honor of Pompey's triumphs in Hispania and Lusitania, due to be held in the middle of the month. It was also evident that the law-courts were in full session and crowds of people were milling around the entrances to numerous wooden enclosures that had been set up in the Forum itself. It was these makeshift outdoor courts that were creating most of the pedestrian traffic problems. Only Lucrio's forbidding presence alongside her eased Hortensia's path through the crowds. Hortensia was dimly aware that her father's trial must be about to begin somewhere in the forum but she had no idea where it was being held or how she would find it in this crush.

Drusilla was waiting by the steps to the Temple of Vesta as arranged but still seemed surprised to see Hortensia approaching with Lucrio in tow.

"I didn't hear from Rufio so I realized you must have been unable to persuade your husband to speak with him," she began. "I really didn't expect you to come here today. You have been very good to me but there is no need for you to stay."

Hortensia smiled at Drusilla with a reassurance she did not feel. "Believe me, I very much wanted to be here. I'm not so easily beaten."

With Lucrio walking in front to clear a path for them, the two women made their way toward the Basilica Aemilia on the far side of the forum, where several temporary courts had been set up due to lack of space in the forum itself. As they passed under the colonnaded frontage of the basilica, which was crowded with busy pedestrians exploring the shops adjoining the building, Drusilla gasped at her first sight of the courtroom interior. Colored tiles lined the length of a long aisle, flanked by two rows of tall marble columns supporting the roof. At the far end a square dais was raised before two rows of benches set on either side of the aisle, which were intended for the competing litigants and their supporters. Further seating was provided for interested members of the general public behind and in the upper story of the portico above. In the middle of the dais was the praetor's chair. The court was apparently not in session yet but the benches were already full of people, and more spectators were milling around in the open space at the back of the court, much to Hortensia's surprise and dismay; she had assumed that domestic disputes such as Drusilla's would not attract large crowds.

A portly court clerk in a black tunic was sitting at a table by the courtroom entrance, sorting through documents. Hortensia approached, trying to adopt the kind of confident air she imagined her father would have assumed.

"Excuse me. Can you tell me if we've come to the right court? It's a dispute over a dowry – the name on the petition is Drusilla and the defendant is a Marcus Rufio."

The clerk looked Hortensia up and down and winked knowingly at her. "My my, we are in a hurry, aren't we. Got other marital plans lined up already my lady?"

Glaring at the clerk with all the disdain she could muster, Hortensia was about to reprimand him for his impudence when she caught sight of the man who had just entered the courtroom through a door at the far end and seated himself in the praetor's chair to a great deal of acclaim from the public galleries.

"What is *he* doing here?" she asked incredulously.

The clerk squinted in the direction of her gaze. "Yes indeed, my lady, we do find ourselves in hallowed company today. Consul Pompey is sitting in the praetor's chair. Didn't think you'd ever find yourself discussing your private affairs in front of him, I expect."

"But he's not a praetor, he's the consul," said Hortensia uncomprehendingly.

"Well done my lady, nothing gets past your notice." The clerk's tone was sarcastic but he suddenly perceived an unsmiling Lucrio looming over Hortensia's shoulder and reluctantly adopted a more respectful tone of voice. "The praetors are rather overstretched at the moment, my lady, and consul Pompey agreed to take up some of the slack. Looks good, don't it – makes him seem like he's in touch with us commoners, you see?"

But Hortensia was no longer paying him any attention and did not notice Lucrio bend over the clerk's desk and whisper something in his ear that made the man blench and nod hastily. Instead, her eyes were fixed on Rome's greatest general. A huge, sleepy-looking man with bags under his eyes, red cheeks and a leonine mane of dark hair which he reputedly kept long in order to emulate his hero Alexander the Great, he was receiving the banter and jokes from the crowd with much good humor. Of the two serving consuls, it was plain to see he was much the more beloved. If the wealthy Marcus Crassus was the favorite of the patricians, then Pompey Magnus was the people's champion, a man whose extraordinary military prowess had forced the Senate to bestow the consulship on him at the premature age of thirty-six. Hortensia had heard her father refer to Pompey in disdainful terms as "a fat man with an even fatter head", but she also knew that Hortensius had successfully defended Pompey against a charge of corruption early in both their careers. She was wondering whether this might in some way be turned to her advantage in her current situation when the sound of the clerk clearing his throat forced her to interrupt her musings.

"I, er . . ." The clerk's eyes darted toward Lucrio, who stood by impassively, arms folded. "I would like to offer you my apologies for my inappropriate manner before, my lady. I mistook your identity. The case to which you were referring just now will begin shortly in the court behind me. Perhaps you would like to wait on that bench just there and I will see to it that some refreshment is brought over to you."

Hortensia nodded coldly and beckoned Drusilla to come and sit with her in the alcove pointed out by the clerk. But the arrival of a group of men from the other end of the colonnade had suddenly caused the blood to drain from Drusilla's face. Hortensia had no difficulty in interpreting the identity of the weak-chinned but smoothly handsome man at the center of the group as Marcus Rufio. But she was unpleasantly surprised to realize that she was acquainted with one of his entourage, who looked equally shocked to see her, though his expression quickly changed to one of supercilious pleasure.

"Hortensia," he purred, bowing low in front of her. Publius Dolabella was a good-looking young man, though not physically imposing and with delicate, aristocratic features. Even so, at just nineteen years old, he carried himself with all the swagger and assurance that characterized all the men in his family. "What an extraordinary and unexpected privilege to find you here. It feels like an age since our last meeting. You can imagine my devastation on learning that you have since become a married lady. I must offer my felicitations to Caepio though I confess I feel some resentment toward him for stealing your hand."

Hortensia inclined her head slightly.

"I am sure such a possibility never crossed his mind," she said coolly.

Publius's eyes narrowed for a brief moment but his self-satisfied expression did not waver. "Of course not, dear fellow that he is, he has such a trusting nature," he laughed, not appearing to notice the flash of annoyance in Hortensia's eyes. "Are you searching for your father's hearing? You are in the wrong place here, he is in the extortion court on the other side of the forum, but I can show you exactly where to find him. It would be my pleasure to help you follow the proceedings and enlighten you on some of the finer legal points. I am here now merely to lend support to a family connection." He waved casually behind him to Marcus Rufio and his companions. "But I shan't be detained very long."

"You are under a misapprehension I am afraid, Publius," replied Hortensia, trying not to let the anger she felt enter her voice. "I am here to speak on behalf of a friend of mine." She indicated to Drusilla and stared defiantly at Publius, who was still smiling broadly but looked uncomprehending.

"To speak? I'm afraid I don't follow."

"I am here to address the court on behalf of Drusilla. Your kinsman's wife."

The men with whom Publius had entered had been standing in a group chatting idly until that point, completely ignoring Drusilla. But Hortensia's words, uttered in her rich, clear voice, stopped them abruptly in mid-conversation. The man whom Hortensia had identified as Marcus Rufio stared incredulously at his patron's wife for a moment before turning and bearing down on Drusilla with such a wrathful expression that she flinched and stepped back from him.

"You little whore," he hissed at her. "How dare you go to my patron's house and try to spread your filthy lies about me. You'll pay for it, you hear me?"

He brought his hand back and there was a shriek of frightened protest from Hortensia as a ringing slap echoed through the colonnade. Rufio raised his hand again but before he could strike a second time, his wrist had been grabbed by Lucrio, who spun him round and pinned him against a wall, his muscular forearm pressed to Rufio's throat.

"Lucrio, no!" shouted Hortensia as Rufio's companions advanced to help their friend. But Hortensia's cries had attracted the attention of the clerk and four burly court custodians quickly emerged from inside the court just as Publius and the others were dragging Lucrio away from a spitting Rufio. Wading into the fracas, the custodians separated the parties, though it took three of them to restrain Lucrio, whose usually cool green eyes were blazing with a fury that Hortensia had never seen before. A crowd of curious shoppers had stopped to watch and the clerk immediately began to give orders for Lucrio to be taken away. He was interrupted by Hortensia planting herself in his way.

"You will release my attendant at once," she commanded imperiously. "He was doing his duty and protecting my friend and me from the violent behavior of these men. If you dare contradict my authority in this matter, I will have you removed from your post. I am the wife of Servilius Caepio and my father is Hortensius Hortalus. I expect that name means something to you."

The clerk paused. Hortensius's name did indeed mean something to him and he had no wish to incur the wrath of one of the court's most celebrated practitioners. Seeing the clerk's hesitation, Rufio shook off the restraining arm of the custodian next to him and strode forward, jabbing his finger in the clerk's face.

"This barbarian attacked me and I want him whipped like a dog for it. I too have powerful friends and if you value your job you will do well to consider whether it is worth offending them."

Hortensia rounded on him fiercely. "Perhaps *you* would do well to consider whether you will still have a patron if my husband discovers that you violated a companion of mine in my presence," she hissed.

Marcus Rufio's face turned a deep shade of puce. He opened his mouth to speak but no words came out and he appeared to be struggling with his emotions. Finally, he turned abruptly on his heel and stalked into the courtroom, signaling curtly to his companions to follow him.

Seeing his control of the situation slipping away, the clerk's shoulders sagged and he made no attempt to stop Rufio's supporters from shrugging off their guards and leaving the scene too. But he made one last attempt to exert his authority, addressing himself sternly to Hortensia.

"Very well my lady. As long as we don't have any more of this kind of thing, I'll let the matter drop. But I am going to insist that this one" – he pointed accusingly at Lucrio – "doesn't set foot in that courtroom."

Hortensia tossed her head and ignored him. The clerk chose to take this as an indication of assent and returned thankfully to his desk. The curious crowd reluctantly dispersed.

Publius Dolabella had paused before following the others into the courtroom and was now eying Hortensia with a mixture of anger and reluctant curiosity. "They'll never let you speak, you know," he said scornfully.

"We'll see," she said shortly and turned her back on him. Incensed by this curt dismissal, Publius leant over her shoulder to issue a parting shot in her ear:

"Take my advice, Hortensia. That one's a born whore." His eyes glinted mockingly at Drusilla, who was nursing her inflamed cheek and taking in deep, shuddering breaths. "You'd do well to realize it before it's too late. People might start to speak of you in the same breath." He straightened up and glared venomously at Lucrio, whose face was a mask once more. "And I'd keep that guard-dog of yours on a leash or he'll get himself muzzled."

He strode away and did not notice the effect his parting speech had had on Hortensia. Her body had stiffened, not in anger but as though she had suddenly seen something of interest in the distance, and her head was tilted slightly like a wolfhound with a cocked ear.

Drusilla began to speak in an unsteady voice, "This is all my fault. I am so sorry. I should never have dragged you into this . . ." but Hortensia shushed her impatiently with one hand raised. Her eyes were bright and she appeared to be thinking very hard. Suddenly, she turned to Drusilla and gripped her by the shoulders.

"I have an idea. I can't promise you it will work, in fact it may make everything worse." She took a quick turn and paced about, her eyes fixed on the ground, before nodding. "But I think it may answer the purpose, if you have the courage to follow my advice. Do you think you can trust me?"

"You are the only person I know that I can trust," said Drusilla in a low voice shaky with emotion. "I don't care about the risk. All that matters to me now is seeing my children."

"Then listen to me and do exactly what I tell you." She quickly outlined her scheme and waited anxiously as Drusilla hesitated before nodding resolutely and disappearing back out into the crowds in the forum. Next, Hortensia turned to Lucrio, who was standing by, his emotions once more hidden behind his impassive features.

"Lucrio, I need you to find Rixus for me," she said urgently. "He's in the forum somewhere, I saw him on the way down. Tell him there's a whole orchard of cherry trees in it for him if he hurries."

XI

THE COURTROOM WAS PACKED BY THE TIME THE CLERK CALLED FOR PRO-
ceedings to begin in the case of Drusilla and her husband Marcus Rufio.
News that the people's favorite consul was making a rare appearance in the law court had spread around the forum and dozens more had
crowded inside the basilica to catch a glimpse of him. Hortensia had stationed herself on one of the public benches at the front, just alongside a
group of chattering women who were passing ostentatiously loud comment on Pompey's handsome person. She glanced anxiously up into the
gallery above, checking that Rixus was sitting where she had told him.
The thought of what she had persuaded Drusilla to do was making her
feel both guilty and terrified. What if she only succeeded in ruining
Drusilla's reputation? She had already wrecked any chance the poor
woman might have of seeing her children again, if the decision was left
to Marcus Rufio. It had been foolish of her to stake so much on the court
allowing her to speak in the first place. Caepio had been right to warn
her and she had not listened to him. She was on the point of turning on
her heel and going back to tell Drusilla that the whole idea had been a
terrible mistake when there was a loud, echoing gong.

Pompey was already addressing the clerk, his barking voice automatically achieving command as it resonated through the packed space.
"So, what's next?"

The clerk cleared his throat. "A quarrel over a dowry, consul. The
plaintiff is one Drusilla, daughter of the late Drusus Florentius; the defendant is Marcus Rufio. They are recently divorced."

"Divorce, eh? What a shame, what a shame. Marriage is what holds our society together." Pompey shook his shaggy head disapprovingly and sorrowfully before winking at his audience. "I should know. I've been married three times already."

Shouts of hilarity greeted this pronouncement and Pompey slapped his knee, looking very pleased with himself. "Well, well, let's hear it then. Where is this warring duo and what's their grievance?"

The clerk cleared his throat. "The husband wishes to exert the right not to return the lady's dowry."

Publius Dolabella rose to his feet, smoothing out the front of his robes. "Consul Pompey. I am Publius Dolabella, I believe you are acquainted with my father Publius Cornelius Dolabella and with my uncle Tiberius who served on your staff in Hispania." He smiled complaisantly. "My friend and client Marcus Rufio wishes to ask the court's forgiveness for taking up time in its schedule with this embarrassing domestic matter. It was not his wish but that of his former wife and I am confident that once you know her character, you will have no difficulty in dismissing her petition." He had a confident speaking manner, Hortensia admitted grudgingly, though she found his voice too unctuous for her taste.

Pompey squinted at him.

"Tiberius's nephew, yes I remember you. A bit green for this sort of adventure, aren't you?"

There were a few laughs around the courtroom and Publius Dolabella had to hide his irritation. "I believe your own illustrious career has proved that youth need not prove a bar to success," he said flatteringly.

Pompey raised an eyebrow at him. "My boy, when you've conquered half of Africa, and the whole of Sicily and Hispania, then you can start comparing yourself with me."

A rousing cheer greeted his riposte and a cry of "Pompey! Pompey!" was taken up around the room. Hortensia observed Pompey closely, noting that although he and Crassus were very different men, they shared a keen interest in their own public approval ratings, their eyes and ears always swiveling to gauge the mood of their audience. Finally, Pompey silenced the crowd with a wave of his arm and addressed the discomfited Dolabella in hearty tones.

"Come then, young Dolabella, every great man must indeed make his debut sometime or other."

Publius forced himself to adopt an apologetically amenable expression once more.

"The case is quite simple, Consul Pompey, I shall not take up the court's time with any formal speeches. My friend Marcus Rufio's wife is of bad character. To spare this court embarrassment, I will not list her misadventures and shall instead reduce the matter to its essentials, namely that Drusilla is an adulteress –" a few gleefully disapproving "oohs" greeted this pronouncement "– and as such, I would suggest that she has forfeited her right to have her dowry returned to her on the dissolution of this marriage."

Pompey blew out his lips and tilted his head from side to side in appreciation of Publius's point of view. Hortensia knew as well as everyone else in the room that no Roman court would question the word of a husband against his wife.

"A strong accusation indeed. Does the lady herself have someone to speak for her?"

The blood rushed to Hortensia's face. It was all on her now and Caepio's words of warning rang in her head. Publius glanced at Hortensia and, seeing her hesitate, made a smooth interjection.

"She does not appear to be in the court, consul. No doubt the gravity of her crimes finally weighed with her and she has elected not to bring further embarrassment on her head or that of her children."

"Well, if she has nothing to say for herself then . . ."

"Excuse me, Consul Pompey."

The sound of a female voice ringing out across the courtroom surprised its occupants into silence. People craned their necks to see where the voice had come from and a low hum slowly spread as Hortensia stood up and walked forwards out of the throng. She took up a position in front of the empty bench on the opposite side of the aisle to Publius Dolabella and Marcus Rufio's camp. Her head was held high and her blue eyes were bright and determined.

"I am here to speak for Marcus Rufio's wife Drusilla. My name is Hortensia and I am the daughter of Hortensius Hortalus. I have a notion you may be acquainted with *my* father also."

Another stir in the crowd. Hortensius's name was well-known to seasoned courtroom-watchers. Pompey leant forward and peered at Hortensia in some curiosity.

"Hortensius's daughter? He has a big case of his own today, I believe. How is my old friend?"

"He is in excellent health, sir, I thank you, and I am sure he would make the same enquiry of you."

Pompey chose not to answer this, instead tilting his head to one side and making a considered and unashamedly admiring appraisal of Hortensia.

"I must say, it has been some time since I set foot in a Roman courtroom, but I did not know that young ladies – such attractive young ladies at that – had taken to playing the role of advocate." He winked at his supporters. "If I had, I might have asked my friends in the Senate to make me praetor rather than consul."

Publius Dolabella, who had been whispering to his companions, now stood up. "I can assure you it is not common practice. Consul Pompey, you may not be aware of it but our legal system has been plagued recently by the displays of a small handful of women who have offended public decency by insisting on representing themselves and others in the courts. It is of course not for me to advise you but I have to ask, is it wise to allow this kind of unnatural public posturing to continue?"

Hortensia looked at him mockingly. "What's the matter Publius? Surely you are not afraid to argue opposite a woman?"

Publius looked scornfully at her. "Not afraid, no, my dear Hortensia. Just concerned for your reputation."

"If a woman addressing the court is so offensive to public decency, then I put it to you that it is your job to put me and my fellow offenders in our place once and for all."

The chattering group of women who had been passing dates amongst themselves gave this an ironic cheer which was taken up by others who either thought that Hortensia did indeed need to be put in her place, or who simply relished the prospect of such unusual gladiatorial combat. Pompey's eyes darted among the sea of faces in front of him. Then a broad grin crept across his pugnacious features.

"By Jupiter, I like this sport! Centaurs versus Amazons! What do you say? Shall we give old Hortensius's daughter a hearing?" The crowd obediently cheered their approval. Hortensia tried hard and only just failed to avoid smirking at Publius.

"So Hortensia, daughter of Hortensius Hortalus." Pompey waved for silence once more. "We have heard from young Publius here. The floor is now yours. What have you got to say on this lady's behalf?"

Hortensia took a deep breath. *Give them a show.*

"Thank you, Consul Pompey." The years of voice training under her father's tutelage had given strength and clarity to the husky richness of her tone. "The truth of the matter is that my friend Drusilla does not dispute Marcus Rufio's claim – quite the contrary. She has in fact never been a chaste woman and only a fool would think otherwise."

There was a ripple of surprise around the room. Pompey himself looked puzzled. "So, you're saying she is an adulteress? She admits it freely?"

"Oh yes. But I would suggest to you, consul, and to the court, that any Roman man who knowingly marries a harlot and then attempts to make a profit out of his supposed 'discovery' is worthy of censure not reward. He certainly cannot use her behavior as the basis for a claim of deception, as he is trying to do here."

Pompey looked intrigued. The crowd began debating the issue amongst themselves until they were interrupted by the sound of Pompey clapping his hands together.

"Why are we all talking about this woman and we haven't even seen her? Where is this Drusilla? Can you produce her for us?"

"I can, Consul Pompey. I will introduce her to you and then allow you to judge her character for yourself." Hortensia turned around and with as much sangfroid as she could muster, signaled to the back of the court where Lucrio was lurking in the shadows of the colonnade.

She saw him nod to someone and a moment later, Drusilla made her entrance.

Even though Hortensia had been involved in putting the finishing touches to Drusilla's toilette, she still could not quite believe the transformation that she had helped effect. Gone were the demure chestnut-colored gown and modest veil, and in their place was a robe of the most alarmingly vivid shade of green, which clashed loudly with a mantle dyed bright scarlet and a gauzy veil of the same hue, all obtained from one of the seedier drapers' stalls in the forum. White chalk make-up had turned Drusilla's face into a powdery mask and her eyelids had been very inexpertly daubed by Hortensia with saffron yellow eye paint. Her eyelashes looked like spiders' legs, so thickly coated as they were with sooty Egyptian kohl, and her cheeks were stained red with poppy paste. Cheap bead strings and a gold necklace of swimming dolphins linked nose to tail glittered against her breast, and as she tripped her way down the central aisle, the smell of orange perfume wafted from her decorated person. Her progress created a sensation among the audience and several members of the public gallery whistled appreciatively and shouted out suggestive comments. Rather than averting her eyes as any delicately nurtured Roman matron would, Drusilla shot coy glances at her admirers from underneath her fat eyelashes and ostentatiously rearranged her scarlet mantle.

As Drusilla drew alongside, Hortensia turned to Pompey, a small smile hovering around her lips, and the crowd shushed each other. She was already acquiring the trick of winning their attention in anticipation of what she might say.

"Consul – I ask you. In your *wide* experience . . ." She flashed him a naughty, conspiring look and jerked her head toward Drusilla. "Does this woman look chaste to you?"

A roar of laughter rang out around the courtroom, in which Pompey, having recovered from his surprise, joined in loudly, guffawing as Drusilla acknowledged the cheers of the crowd with a knowing smile. She then daringly blew a kiss to Pompey himself, which he affected to catch and slap on his round belly, much to the delight of his acolytes in the front rows. Publius Dolabella and his companions looked stunned while Marcus Rufio was gaping at his wife in horror.

"I have to say," said Pompey, shaking his head and wiping his eyes with enjoyment. "I had no idea the law court could be such an entertaining place."

Publius Dolabella rose quickly to his feet. "Where's your proof?" he demanded.

Hortensia looked coolly at him. "I beg your pardon?"

"Your proof! This is a courtroom, my dear," explained Publius silkily. "Didn't you know you were required to present it with proof? You say this woman was the whore we see before us when my kinsman Marcus Rufio married her." He gestured contemptuously toward Drusilla. "How do we know that these gaudy clothes were not acquired after their marriage? If they were, then you have no case."

All eyes swiveled to Hortensia, who shifted her stance. She had anticipated such a line of attack but was apprehensive about deploying the weapon she had prepared to counter it.

"Because I have a witness to the contrary."

"Oh really? And where is this witness?"

Hortensia took a deep breath and tried to sound as nonchalant as she imagined her father might have.

"See for yourself!"

Publius started and his eyes followed everyone else's in the direction of Hortensia's pointing finger. Rixus, who was sitting in the front row of the public gallery and had been helping himself to a plate of meatballs proffered to him by his neighbor, suddenly realized that this was his cue and hastily got to his feet, wiping the sauce from his fingers on the front of his tunic.

"And who might you be?" asked Pompey from the dais.

Rixus bowed and beamed at him. "My name is Rixus, *domine*." The thick regional accent of his Punic homeland, which made him pronounce his adopted Roman name as "Rickshus" caused a few giggles in the galleries. "Sincerely an honor to meet you."

"And how are you involved in this affair?" enquired Pompey curiously. "Are you a go-between perhaps?"

Rixus blinked and looked confused, his eyes darting toward Hortensia. "Go-between? No, no *domine*. I am . . . the gardener."

"The gardener?" Pompey looked puzzled.

"Yes, *domine*, the gardener." He leant forward and gave a wink. "I plant the seeds, you know?"

There were more stifled giggles around the gallery as people exchanged gleeful glances. Pompey glanced suspiciously at Hortensia, who preserved an innocent expression.

"I'm afraid you will have to be a little clearer than that, my friend."

Rixus glanced once more toward Hortensia, who inclined her head very slightly.

"Of course, *domine*." Rixus cleared his throat importantly. "This lady and I . . ." he gestured gallantly with one of his short, stubby arms toward Drusilla, "we are lovers."

His dramatic pronouncement caused all the consternation Hortensia had hoped for. Marcus Rufio jumped to his feet and mouthed inarticulately. Rixus' neighbors slapped him on the back, offering him their congratulations and more of their meatballs. Drusilla remained perfectly impassive and only by the rigidity of her jaw did she betray what it cost her to do so.

Pompey gesticulated for calm once more. "I see," he said unsteadily. "And when did this . . . ah . . . love affair begin?"

"Oh, some years ago, *domine*," said Rixus vaguely. Then, as if remembering his script and realizing he had to correct a mistaken impression, he added, "But long before she met this one, you understand." He gestured dismissively at Marcus Rufio. "I used to garden for one of her neighbors. There was an attraction between us like a bolt from Cupid, *domine*." Pleased with the reaction this produced, he warmed to his theme. "Watching me plant the *ambulatio*, she conceived for my person a red-hot passion. I knew I was not the only man in her life, of course, but . . ." he spread his palms self-deprecatingly. "I knew I give satisfaction."

"So the affair continued throughout the marriage?" demanded Pompey, holding up a hand to silence the deeply appreciative crowd.

"Oh yes, *domine*." Rixus nodded vigorously. "We could not stay apart." He leaned forward and whispered loudly to Pompey. "She said her husband was very bad . . . *in cubiculo*, you know? In the bed."

This time it took two of his companions to restrain Marcus Rufio. Publius cast a disbelieving look around the courtroom, sensing the febrile mood of the spectators swinging wildly away from his kinsman. He stepped forward, gripping the bar at the front of the court, and spoke in an urgent tone.

"Consul Pompey. This is an entertaining charade, I grant you. But I am absolutely convinced that you will not take seriously the word of a whore and a slave against that of a respected Roman citizen. Every feeling must be offended by it."

Pompey looked a little disheartened. He turned to Hortensia. "Can you in truth offer any firm proof of the plaintiff's relationship with this man?"

Hortensia hesitated, but only for a moment. She leant across and whispered to Drusilla, as though consulting with her, and then turned to Pompey once more, wearing a meek expression.

"I can, Consul Pompey. It is delicate . . . and like Publius here I am anxious to spare the court embarrassment. But the plaintiff has just informed me that the gentleman does have a rather distinctive . . . feature."

Pompey stared hard at Hortensia. "Feature?"

"Yes. A distinguishing . . . blemish, shall we say, on a certain part of his anatomy."

A delighted murmur rippled through the court. Publius threw up his hands.

"Oh spare us, madam! You cannot expect this court to be so taken in. Your client and this man could quite easily have conspired over such evidence before this hearing."

"And what outwardly respectable lady – as you claim she is – would willingly put her name to such testimony, Publius?" she shot back at him.

Pompey leant forward, staring very hard at Hortensia.

"You will have to be more precise, I think, my dear. To which part of this gentleman's . . . anatomy do you refer?"

Hortensia cast her eyes down to the floor.

"I am a respectable Roman matron, sir, and I do not think my husband or my father would wish me to say such a word in public."

"Bum. She means bum," supplied Rixus obligingly from the gallery.

Under the howl of ecstasy greeting this pronouncement, no one noticed the tiny muffled gasp of horror that escaped Drusilla. Pompey's jaw dropped open but he soon recovered enough to enquire of the stunned clerk whether this evidence might be verified. But Rixus, who was by now thoroughly enjoying his newfound celebrity, needed no further encouragement to capitalize on it.

"No, no, it's true," he called out. "I sat in a bramble once when I was doing the pruning. I can show you from here." And lifting up his tunic, he peeled back one side of his loincloth to reveal to the court a large blood blister on the fleshy underside of his left buttock.

This time it was fully a minute before Pompey was able to make himself heard, during which time Marcus Rufio could be seen engaged in a ferocious argument with Publius Dolabella and his companions.

"Enough! Silence in the court!"

A hush eventually fell and every face in the room turned expectantly to Pompey, who mopped his brow in an attitude half of amusement, half of exhaustion.

"I have heard – and indeed seen – more than enough. It seems to me quite clear that any man who would marry this woman cannot have done so in the expectation that she would remain faithful to him. Therefore, I am happy to recommend that this lady's dowry should be returned to her in full."

As a roar of approval echoed around the court, Marcus Rufio at last found his voice. Getting to his feet, his face red with anger, he shouted over the applause.

"It's a lie, it's all bloody lies I tell you!"

"What's that?" Pompey craned his neck.

Publius Dolabella was hissing, "No, you fool," and trying to drag his kinsman back down to his seat, but Rufio shook off the hand on his arm.

"It's a lie, I tell you! It's all lies! That bitch has never looked at another man, let alone persuaded one to look at her!" He jabbed his finger angrily at Drusilla. "You think I'll let you make a fool of me in this ridiculous get-up?"

A look of triumph came into Hortensia's eyes as Pompey tilted his head and observed Marcus Rufio quizzically.

"Never looked at another man, you say?"

"I swear to you, consul. I have never seen these clothes on her before." Marcus Rufio stepped forward eagerly, keen to keep Pompey's attention. "She's a drab, plain creature, usually, and rarely leaves the house. The idea of her trysting with this mud-stained fool is preposterous. She's so frigid no one could get near her without a mounting block."

He looked around expectantly as though inviting people to laugh at this remark but a ripple of whispering had broken out instead. Rufio's companions were boot-faced and a muscle twitched in Publius Dolabella's cold, set jaw. But still Marcus Rufio did not understand the mood of the room and tried again to appeal to Pompey, pointing an accusatory finger at Hortensia and Drusilla.

"I promise you, consul! These women are lying to the court!"

Everyone, including Pompey, seemed to anticipate Hortensia's answer but waited for her to deliver it. She did not disappoint, raising an eyebrow expressively and turning slightly as if to invite the whole room to share in the joke.

"What a coincidence. Because if we're lying, then so are you!"

The courtroom erupted. Publius Dolabella rose and stalked out of the room without a backward glance. Drusilla sank to her knees with her hands over her face and was immediately helped onto a bench by the chattering women from the front row, who smoothed the mantle around her shoulders and offered their box of dates to her. Hortensia, struggling to keep a broad grin from cracking her face, held up her arms for silence.

"My fellow citizens," she announced grandly. "What you have just witnessed is an attempt to defraud the people of Rome. Not of money, but of justice. This man –" she pointed at a dumbfounded Marcus Rufio "– has tried to blacken the name of a respectable Roman matron – for that is indeed Drusilla's true character. You could not find a more honorable woman in the whole of the city. These clothes and the story of an affair were indeed simply a ploy to force Marcus Rufio to reveal his true colors. You all know the story of how, centuries ago, Sextus Tarquinius raped the maiden Lucretia and then falsely accused her of unchastity. You know too how the citizens of Rome were not deceived by his calumny, and overthrew the tyrannical rule of Sextus and his fellow kings. I think we all owe a debt of gratitude to Consul Pompey for upholding the values on which our Republic was founded."

A thundering roar of approval greeted her speech, in which Marcus Rufio was the only non-participant. He stood quite still, staring at Hortensia with a mixture of disbelief and darkening rage.

"You bloody bitch," he snarled softly and for a moment he looked as though he would have lunged at her. But Lucrio, who had quietly slipped through the crowd as Pompey delivered his verdict, had now materialized at Hortensia's side. Checked by the glare in the dark Lusitanian's eye, Marcus Rufio shot Hortensia one last look of malevolent hatred before storming out of the court, roughly pushing aside a few wags who tried to prolong his humiliation with their remarks.

Hortensia meanwhile was being hailed on all sides by admiring spectators wanting to congratulate her. She received their plaudits willingly and for a time was caught up in the crowd but then noticed Drusilla trying to catch her eye. Reading the expression in her anxious face, she quickly turned to Pompey, who was heaving himself up from the judge's chair. "There is still the issue of the children in this case, consul," she said urgently. "There are two, a boy aged five and a girl aged three. Marcus Rufio is trying to prevent my friend from being mother to them."

Pompey stepped down from the dais, one calloused hand raised in a placatory gesture. "Your friend may rest easy. I think it preferable that her children should reside with her. Any mother who would go to such lengths for her children is a credit to her sex . . . as indeed are you, my dear. My felicitations on your first triumph. I should be surprised if it were the last." He smiled but cocked an eyebrow rather sternly. "I am not sure I approve, mind. A woman speaking in a man's place."

Hortensia twinkled at him. "A great general like yourself knows that sometimes one must learn to think like the enemy."

Pompey beamed and waggled a finger at her. "I shall expect you to come to supper at my villa you know."

"Only if my husband is included in the invitation," replied Hortensia demurely.

Pleased with this response, the consul exited the court on a roar of laughter, surrounded by a swarm of his adoring public.

XII

"CAN YOU FORGIVE ME?"

They were outside the court once more in the sunshine of the forum. Drusilla had swapped her colorful clothing for sober hues once more and the only traces of her recent transformation were a few faint smears of yellow on her eyelids, which had proved impossible to wash off in the public fountain. It had taken them some time to exit the court, so many people wanted to congratulate Hortensia and bestow messages of support upon Drusilla. Once outside, Lucrio had gone to arrange for Hortensia's litter to be brought as close to the basilica as possible. Rixus had not been seen since he was borne off to the local taberna by his new circle of friends from the gallery.

Hortensia waited apprehensively for an answer to her question.

"I did think I might lose control of my emotions at any second," confessed Drusilla. "It was so hard to seem indifferent to the things that Publius Dolabella was saying about me. But forgive you?" She shook her head incredulously. "You have given me back my children. For that, I can never thank you enough."

Hortensia took the hand that was held out to her. "You will let me know if you have any further difficulties? Just send me word if Marcus Rufio should still try to keep you from seeing Marcus and Cassia. Pompey has given his word that they should live with you."

"I don't think even Marcus Rufio would attempt to make an enemy of Pompey. But he will try and find some way to revenge himself on me, I know it. I have publicly humiliated him. Will your husband still act as his patron, do you think?"

"Not if I have anything to do with it," replied Hortensia drily.

Drusilla smiled but looked worried. "I fear that Rufio will wish revenge on you too. How can I ever repay you for what you have done for me?"

Hortensia shook her head vigorously. "Oh no, Papa says that advocates are not allowed to take payment for pleading a case. Just promise me that when you do marry again, you will choose a better husband than Marcus Rufio."

Drusilla slipped her hand into her pouch purse and extracted the gold dolphin necklace that she had worn in court. "Will you at least keep this? Not to wear of course, but as a reminder of me and a token of my gratitude? Although I beg that you will banish the memory of me wearing it."

Hortensia laughed and accepted the necklace. "I don't think I shall ever be able to get the image out of my mind as long as I live. But I accept the gift gladly."

Lucrio reappeared with the four litter-bearers at his heels, carrying their green-and-gold burden. Drusilla and Hortensia said their farewells and Hortensia promised to visit her. She then turned back to Lucrio, expecting his assistance in helping her climb into the litter, but realized that his gaze was instead intently fixed on something over her shoulder. Curious, Hortensia turned around to see a large, noisy crowd spilling out from one of the two permanent tribunal courts on the other side of the forum. A small contingent was detaching itself to form a small group off to one side and Hortensia quickly realized that at the center of this group was her father, his proud figure and sleek black head easily recognizable even from a distance. He was flanked by Caecilius, Caepio and her cousin Brutus – looking youthfully bullish – along with a group of older men in senatorial robes who had their heads together as if conferring intently. But the noise was all coming from the rest of the crowd, who were so large in number that some of them had to climb up the steps of the temple of Castor in order to get a clear view of the recipient of their adulation – a very tall, hawkish figure standing at their center with one arm raised aloft. Gradually it dawned on Hortensia what they were all chanting.

Cicero. Cicero.

Hortensia's eyes flickered disbelievingly back to her father. He was standing with his back to her and not by the slightest slump of his shoulders did his posture betray a hint of defeat. But she could see Caecilius shaking his bald head and there was no mistaking the somber mood of the circle around Hortensius in stark contrast to the euphoria of the opposition. Cicero's diminutive wife Terentia was standing alongside her husband with an expression of proud triumph etched across her aquiline features.

Blindly Hortensia turned back to Lucrio.

"Help me up please. I want to go straight to my father's house and wait for him . . ."

"Who is that man?"

Hortensia blinked in surprise. Lucrio had never interrupted her before.

"The man standing alongside your father."

She turned her head in bewilderment and squinted at the group standing on the steps alongside Hortensius. She could just make out the squat, flush-faced figure of her father's client Gaius Verres, who was shaking his head and grinning, as though to suggest some embarrassing mistake had been made by someone. Talking to him was a rakish individual with black hair, his arms folded over the grey cloak casually draped over one shoulder, who Hortensia recognized immediately as the scarred man from Crassus's games. Otherwise there were several men whose faces she either couldn't see or didn't know.

Hortensia turned back to Lucrio and made a gesture of impatience. "I don't know which man you mean."

"The man in grey." There was a strange quiver in his voice.

"I can't . . . Dolabella, I think, Tiberius Dolabella, but what does it matter? Don't you realize what must have happened? My father has . . ."

She broke off with a gasp as Lucrio seized her upper arms, gripping them tightly.

"Where does he live? How do I find him again?" His normally cool green eyes were ablaze with a ferocious intensity Hortensia had never seen before. His dark face was so close to hers that she could feel his breath on her cheek and smell the sweat on his skin. His gaze bored into her, as though he were trying to read the answer he needed from her face. But the look of shock in her eyes eventually brought him back to his senses and his fingers slackened their grip. For a moment he stared at the white marks on her arms.

"Forgive me, *domina*," he said in a low voice. Then he disappeared into the throng, his dark head receding toward the crowd chanting Cicero's name.

XIII

THE NEXT MORNING, HORTENSIA WALKED THE SHORT DISTANCE UP THE Palatine to her father's house, followed closely by one of her slaves holding a canopy over her head to protect her from the hot morning sun. She found her mother dead-heading roses in the garden, listlessly plucking at the brown, shriveled petals with her thin fingers.

"Where is Papa? Some of his clients are waiting to see him in the atrium."

"Oh, are they?" Lutatia sounded flustered. "I don't think your father intends to see anyone today. He is in the garden somewhere with Quintus and then he is going to court. But I know he will be so glad of a visit from you."

Hortensia flung herself down on a bench. "It all sounds quite ridiculous," she said sulkily. "I still don't understand what happened. The trial is only a day old yet Caepio tells me that it's as good as over already. Papa hasn't even had an opportunity to address the court!"

"No," admitted Lutatia. "I believe Cicero has been very clever, calling his first witnesses instead of using up his allocated speaking time. But his opening address was still very powerful, I understand."

Hortensia flared up. "It could not have been that good. I don't see why everyone is talking as though Papa's defeat is inevitable. He just needs to wait until it is his turn to address the jury. Then we shall see how smug that awful wife of Cicero's looks," she added darkly.

Lutatia looked bewildered at this but then shook her head sorrowfully.

"I heard your Papa tell Caecilius that there was no chance of an acquittal for Verres now. He said the evidence Cicero has gathered is overwhelming, that even he was taken aback by the extent of it. It will be several days before they've heard all of the witnesses against Verres."

"I have no difficulty believing in Verres's guilt," retorted Hortensia stubbornly. "But Papa would still win if he was given the chance to speak."

"I am sure you are right dear," agreed Lutatia vaguely. "But if Verres is guilty then perhaps . . ." She stopped when she realized Hortensia was paying her no heed but was now irritably plucking at the blooms nearest her, carelessly pulling away several healthy pink petals as well as the faded brown ones. "You know, darling, the odd thing is your father doesn't seem as upset as you'd think. His pride is wounded, you can tell that of course, but he actually went so far as to say that Cicero had done an excellent job and deserved credit for it."

"Well of course he said that, he's just putting a brave face on things, don't you know him at all?"

Realizing that her daughter was angrily preoccupied, Lutatia offered to go and tell Hortensius of her arrival. She found her husband on the lower terrace, wearing a look of repulsion as he watched a hunched-over Quintus spitting out a mouthful of flat, grey objects, long strands of saliva coating their progress toward the parched grass.

"What on earth is the matter with him?" asked Lutatia in horror.

Hortensius flicked her a bored glance. "Your guess is as good as mine, my dear."

"But what has he been eating? Surely those are not *stones*?"

"Pebbles. Designed to encourage him to open his mouth more and aid his lamentable diction. But I admit I had not bargained for the size of the boy's tongue. It's as though a giant sea-slug resides in his gullet, rendering all coherent communication hopeless."

Quintus dashed the back of his hand over his mouth and straightened up, cheeks flushed and eyes watering. Without looking at his father, he marched off toward the house, his usual ungainly stride exaggerated by his angrily pumping shoulders. Hortensius brushed a few specks of dirt from the hem of his tunic.

"Well, now that your son has called things to a halt in his usual el-egant fashion, perhaps you will see to it that I am not further disturbed this morning. I am due in court later. See that Rixus clears this away." He stepped ostentatiously around the regurgitated pebbles.

"I came to tell you Hortensia has called. She is waiting for you in-side." Lutatia was still watching her retreating son.

"Splendid. At least I do not have to be embarrassed for the manners of one of my children." He began to stroll toward the villa.

"You push Quintus too hard."

Hortensius stopped in his tracks, his frame suddenly rigid. Lutatia looked terrified by her own daring. "He is only fifteen years old. You said yourself that your talents only truly developed when you were six-teen, and he does not have your gifts."

"For once, my dear, we agree on something," snarled Hortensius. "He has obviously inherited his powers of speech from you."

Lutatia quailed under her husband's baleful eye. "He . . . he is in-terested in history and politics. He has made a great study of the battle at the Colline Gate, he would love to talk more about it with you and your part in Sulla's campaign . . ."

"Spare me," sneered Hortensius. "The boy does not have the slight-est aptitude for anything."

He suddenly saw Hortensia standing in her mother's shadow. Quin-tus's violent progress through the house had stirred her to retrace his footsteps and she was now watching her father, a look of questioning re-proach in her eyes.

"Hortensia! Are you here alone?" He switched tone easily. "What a delight to see you, my child. Where is Caepio?"

"He is coming up soon, Papa, he was busy with a client."

She walked into her father's embrace and pressed her face into his chest, inhaling the rich cedar and lemon scent he always wore. Lutatia drifted away, plucking at dead leaves as she went. Hortensia watched her mother's departure then lifted her head and fixed her eyes on her father.

"Papa, I know you must be angry. I heard about what happened in court yesterday. But you must not take it out on Mama. It isn't her fault that the trial isn't going well."

Hortensius's bright blue eyes narrowed but all he said was, "What nonsense you do talk sometimes my dear. Why should I be angry? Besides, the trial isn't over yet. Plenty of time for the luck to turn."

Hortensia looked doubtful but further conversation was stalled by the arrival of Caepio, striding across the grass toward them.

"Lutatia told me I would find you both here. I am sorry I could not accompany you before, my dearest, and sorrier still that I must interrupt your meeting." He addressed himself to Hortensius. "I have just seen Caecilius and he says that some of the witnesses you had lined up to speak for Verres are threatening to back out."

Hortensius seemed to accept this without demur. "I thought they might."

"Do you want me to try and bring them round?"

"No," replied Hortensius casually. "It won't make any difference. They would look like the charlatans they are, just as I will look like a monster if I even attempt to cross-examine any of Cicero's upstanding parade of paragons." He smiled, rather ruefully, Hortensia thought. "You have to hand it to old Chickpea really. He has managed to hit on the only way to best me in rhetorical combat – namely, to stop me from talking at all."

Hortensia was suddenly reminded that to her slight chagrin, no one had mentioned her own triumph in the courts yesterday. She had given Caepio an account of it on their return to the villa the previous day though at the last minute she had decided to edit out the part played by Rixus. Though the involvement of Pompey initially worried him, Caepio had been surprised and impressed when he learnt of the trial's outcome, telling Hortensia how proud he was of her; but she wondered if her father would have the same reaction. Once upon a time she would not have hesitated to boast of her triumph, expectant of her father's praise and confident of his trumpeting it to all his friends. But a small seed of doubt had planted itself and on balance, given his own recent courtroom fortunes, she decided to keep the story to herself for a little longer.

They stayed for lunch, a simple meal of cold meat, bread and fruit served in the cool of the summer dining room. Hortensius seemed his usual urbane self, devoting his entire attention to his daughter and son-in-law. Caepio made a few valiant attempts to include Quintus, who had been reluctant to come out of his room until a barked command was issued by Hortensius. Now he sat taciturn and pale-faced next to his mother who, like him, ate very little. The party broke up when Hortensius and Caepio were due to leave for court and Hortensia also decided to return home, feeling oppressed by the morose detachment of her mother and brother.

"By the way, my dear, do you know where Lucrio might be?" asked Caepio as they were standing just inside the front door preparing to depart. "Eucherius said no one had seen him since he accompanied you into town yesterday. It is really too bad that he should be so much absent like this when he's only been with us such a short time."

Hortensia was thrown off balance by the question but improvised as composed a response as she could.

"He may have gone to the Subura. I have been letting him go to search for news of his family. Perhaps he received word of something."

Hortensius tutted mockingly. "I warned you against giving that Lusitanian too much freedom. You do realize he probably only wanted an invitation to Rome because he knew he could lose himself more easily in the city than at Laurentum. I shall have to take the price I paid that trainer at Capua for him out of your dowry."

Hortensia said nothing and her father pinched her cheek. They parted in the street, Hortensius and Caepio heading off to the forum while Hortensia walked back down the hill to her own villa, shielded from the sun once more by the faithful canopy-bearer hovering at her heels. When she arrived home, she went to her room and lay down on her bed to rest, brooding deeply over her father's embarrassment and on Lucrio's strange behavior. An hour or so later she awoke from a restless sleep to find Elpidia patting her hand and whispering eagerly that she had a visitor. Out in the atrium, Hortensia found a slave-boy dressed in a plain white tunic sitting on a chair in the corner, being eyed curiously by Eucherius. The boy rose and bowed deeply to her. He could have been no more than fourteen, with long, soft black hair and a meek expression.

"*Domina*. I am Felix, from the Temple of Vesta. I bring you a message from Cornelia, the Chief Vestal. She wishes for you to wait on her at your earliest opportunity."

Hortensia stared at him in bewilderment. "The Chief Vestal? What on earth could she want with me?"

The slave bowed respectfully again. "If you will accompany me, *domina*, the Chief Vestal will be able to answer your question."

Hortensia was impressed and not a little intimidated. Ever since she was old enough to remember, the Vestal Virgins had seemed to her almost mythical creatures with their plain white robes and their aura of sacred inviolability. She had glimpsed them on a number of occasions, traveling around the city in their specially built two-wheeled carriage, or seated all six of them together in their exclusive row at the front of the theater. When she was little, she used to watch in awe as her mother arrayed herself in special clothing and wrapped up offerings in preparation for the festival of the Bona Dea. She had begged her mother to tell her the secret of what actually went on during the sacred rites, which even her father wasn't allowed to know about, but Lutatia had only put her finger to her lips and shaken her head mysteriously. Irrationally, Hortensia wondered if somehow word of her exploits in the family court had been brought to the Vestals' attention and she was going to be reprimanded for her behavior. But she knew that to refuse a request from the Chief Vestal was unthinkable and, having indicated her willingness to accompany the boy, instructed Eucherius to inform Caepio of her whereabouts should he return home before her, and warn him that she might be late for dinner.

XIV

THE FORUM WAS LESS CROWDED THAN IT HAD BEEN THE PREVIOUS afternoon and Hortensia's litter-bearers were able to find a way through to the Temple of Vesta, drawing up alongside the white marble steps which ascended toward the wide-open doors of the main chamber above. Though small compared to other temples, it was a strikingly beautiful edifice, circular in shape, symmetrical in its proportions and ringed with twenty fluted columns of marble. The doors were flanked with two slaves dressed in the white livery worn by all the Temple servants, standing guard impassively. Nervously, Hortensia put her hands up to her rose-colored mantle and made sure it was draped neatly over her dark hair before following the slave-boy Felix up another staircase leading to the upper story of the grand residence just behind the temple where the six Vestals lived. As she ascended, Hortensia glanced to her left and could just make out the plume of smoke rising from the skylight at the temple peak.

At the top of the stairs, Felix led Hortensia through an archway and along a long colonnaded corridor. Through the travertine pillars, she could look down on to the courtyard at the lower level of the house, whose inner walls were decorated with a garden landscape of trees and flowers. Statues of former Vestals lined the square, their tranquil gazes trained on the rectangular pools at its center. Hortensia glimpsed the veiled heads of two priestesses, carrying baskets of grain across the courtyard toward one of the storerooms leading off it. It seemed extraordinary that such an oasis of peace could exist so close to the seething heart of the forum and Hortensia mused that perhaps the life of a Vestal would not be such a bad one.

They reached the end of the upper corridor where Felix enthusiastically beckoned to Hortensia to follow him into a large, simply-furnished room. Standing by a latticed window was a tall woman clothed in the white veil and robes worn by all the Vestals.

"Hortensia? Daughter of Hortensius Hortalus?" Hortensia nodded. The priestess came forward and nodded dismissal to Felix. She had a high, unlined forehead and clear, wide-set grey eyes which reminded Hortensia of the sphinx in her father's study at Laurentum. "I am Cornelia, the Chief Vestal. Thank you for coming to see me. I hope I have not inconvenienced you?" What a wonderful, solemn voice, thought Hortensia.

"Of . . . course not," she stammered. "It is a great honor to visit you."

"Even so, I am sure you are wondering why I have asked you here." The priestess indicated a small, carved chair onto which Hortensia sank, fiddling nervously with the folds of her gown. Cornelia poured out two cups of scented water from an earthenware pitcher and handed one to her young guest.

"I was told of your triumph in the law court yesterday." Cornelia sat down on a chair opposite Hortensia and smiled primly. "We priestesses may devote ourselves to sacred matters but we do hear much of what goes on in the world outside. What I heard made me want to meet you very much."

Hortensia assumed her fears of censure were well-founded.

"You must think I acted inappropriately."

"Not at all," came the surprising answer. "I think you showed great bravery and moral courage. Even if your methods were perhaps a little shocking," she added with a note of severity.

"Which makes me all the more surprised that you wanted to meet me."

Cornelia did not answer immediately, subjecting Hortensia to long, searching scrutiny before speaking again in a slow, thoughtful tone. "The truth is, I am in some difficulty. And I think . . . I am almost certain that you may be the only person able to help me."

"Me?" gasped Hortensia.

Cornelia bent forward to set her cup down gently on a low table before leaning back into her chair, her posture perfectly upright as she refocused her gaze on Hortensia.

"You will have heard no doubt that the body of a member of our order was pulled from the river Tiber some ten days ago."

In the upheaval caused by Drusilla's visit and her subsequent obsession with her own court debut, Hortensia had to admit that the story of the errant Vestal had completely slipped her mind.

"Yes. I did hear of that." She did not know how to continue. The circumstances of the Vestal's drowning could not but be embarrassing to the woman in front of her who must regard such a transgression by one of her priestesses as deeply shaming. After another long pause, Cornelia stood up once more.

"If you have had enough time to refresh yourself, perhaps you will accompany me?"

She led Hortensia out into the corridor once more and down a narrow set of stairs. They emerged into the courtyard, which was now partially in shadow as the afternoon sun waned, and proceeded around its colonnaded perimeter until they came to a small door, partially concealed behind the statue of a Vestal. Glancing around with what appeared to Hortensia to be a look of fear, Cornelia ushered her through the door and closed it quickly behind them. They were now in a narrow candlelit corridor. The priestess picked up one of the candles on its holder and held it up, illuminating her face like a death mask.

"You must promise me now that you will never reveal what I am about to show you. If the Pontifex discovered I had taken a woman who was not a member of the order along this way, he would have me whipped. If not worse . . ."

Hortensia nodded in alarm and bewilderment. She followed Cornelia along the corridor and down another set of steep stairs, feeling carefully with her feet as she went. The passage was narrow, just wide enough for one person to walk along, and the light from the candle barely enough to see by. Hortensia tried to focus on its reassuring glow but the closeness of their environment and the thick must in the air was making her feel panicky and faint. Finally, just as she was about to ask in desperation how much further they had to go, they arrived at another set of stairs, at the top of which Hortensia was thankful to see a door. Climbing up, they emerged into a small circular room, its green marble floor faintly illuminated by a strange light flickering through the slats of a wooden door on the opposite wall. There was a large ornate chest in the middle of the room, flanked by a statue of Minerva and several giant vessels that appeared to be storage containers for grain. But what caught Hortensia's eye at once were the wooden shelves set all around the curved walls, reaching from the floor almost to the ceiling. Each shelf was segmented into niches with a plaque fixed beneath each opening. Some appeared to contain bundles of wax tablets, their hard frames bound together by leather thongs. But most were full of papyrus rolls, their slim coils packed together like the cells of a honeycomb.

"Do you know where we are?" the Chief Vestal asked Hortensia, who shook her head wonderingly. "We are inside the Temple, in the sanctuary at its heart. A number of sacred treasures are kept here, but they do not concern us for the moment. As you may know, one of a Vestal's responsibilities is to guard the personal papers of our more prominent citizens. Wills, treaties, papers of state – all are kept here in this room and it is a treasonable offense for anyone other than a Vestal to attempt to remove them."

Hortensia continued to gaze around her in wonder. What her father wouldn't give to see this room! Several of the rolls had obviously been there for decades, their edges gently darkening like autumn leaves. Flaring her nostrils, she detected the faint scent of cedar oil, which her father had once told her was used to protect the papyrus from moths and worms. Her attention was recalled by Cornelia's next words.

"I mentioned the death of one of our sisters to you a moment ago. You have perhaps also heard the reason for her death?"

Hortensia nodded awkwardly.

"What you will not have heard is that the day before her body was recovered, an intruder somehow gained access to this room."

Hortensia looked around her in surprise, as if half expecting someone to be lurking still in a dark corner. "Was something stolen?" she asked tentatively.

"We do not know," replied the priestess bluntly.

"Haven't you checked?" asked Hortensia incredulously.

Cornelia made a sweeping gesture with her arm. "Nothing has been taken from this room as far as we can tell. A full inventory was conducted, secretly, and at my request. Every document that should be here is here. There is no sign that anything has been disturbed."

Hortensia wrinkled her brow. "Then . . . forgive me, but how do you know that someone has been in here?"

Cornelia did not answer her immediately. The light from the slatted door cast her face into stony relief, like one of the statues of the goddess she served.

"I was called to the college of Vestals on my ninth birthday," she finally said, meditatively. "We are a closed order, and no male except for the slaves who serve us and the Pontifex himself is permitted to set foot within this sacred space. In the twenty-seven years that I have served the goddess since leaving my parents and my family home, I have come to know every stone and every tile of this temple, every sound that echoes through its corridors, every shade of light that falls through its windows." Her gaze wandered around the room with no apparent fixed object. "The day after Helena's disappearance I walked into this room and I *knew* that a man had been in here."

"How?"

Cornelia brought her limpid grey eyes to rest on Hortensia, peering at her with strangely fervent intensity.

"Because I could *smell* him."

She let the impact of her announcement settle, before beginning to stroll slowly around the room. "A bitter, green scent – galbanum, I think." Cornelia gazed up at the shelves as though still trying to discover the source of any theft. "Very distinctive. I remember my father used to wear it." She paused in a corner near the doorway. "It was strongest just here. Its wearer obviously stood here for a time, perhaps waiting his chance to escape without being noticed."

She turned to observe Hortensia's reaction.

"But, surely if the accusation against the girl was true, it is not surprising that a man should have been here? Forgive me but perhaps the person whose scent you detected was . . . her seducer?"

Cornelia was silent for a moment.

"That is what the Pontifex – Metellus Pius – concluded when I conveyed my concerns to him, and consuls Crassus and Pompey supported his decision. But I do not believe it." The priestess set her jaw and shook her head stubbornly. "Helena was a shy, pious girl. She took her duties very seriously. She was not the sort to forget herself in that way." She saw that Hortensia was still looking doubtful and nodded. "I can see you need further proof. It is understandable. There was – *is* – something else."

She peered out through the gaps in the slatted door before opening it and at once Hortensia understood the source of the strange light. They were looking into the heart of the temple itself, at the center of which was a hearth in which a bronze basin of fire was blazing. A Vestal was seated impassively beside it, her white mantle drawn up over her head so that her profile could not be seen. But then she turned at the sound of the door and Hortensia could see that she was young, only a few years older than herself, with pale, pointed features and a heart-shaped face. As they drew near to her, something about her expression made Hortensia think for a moment she had met her before but it was an elusive feeling. The younger priestess glanced around and whispered excitedly to Cornelia. "It is still there, *domina*. None of the others have noticed it."

"Thank you, Fabia. Please stand up. I would like to show our discovery to our young guest here."

The Vestal got to her feet eagerly and without being asked, began tugging at the arms of the heavy wooden chair on which she had been seated, dragging it over the mosaic tiles.

"Careful," admonished the Chief Vestal. "Do not disturb it."

Hortensia suddenly realized that the marble floor all around the blazing hearth was coated in a thin film of soot and ash. It became obvious as soon as the chair was moved because thick white lines appeared on its mottled surface as the legs were dragged across it. The young Vestal beckoned conspiratorially to Hortensia, and pointed to a patch of the floor previously covered by the chair. Squinting in the direction of her finger, Hortensia could not at first make out what was being pointed out to her. But then she saw it, one word followed by the beginning of another, faintly and crookedly daubed on the blackened floor by an anonymous, solitary finger.

P O M P E Y   M

Cornelia began to speak quickly, in a low voice as though she was fearful of being overheard.

"Helena was guarding the hearth on the night of her disappearance. I think she may have disturbed the intruder and was attacked. There were marks around her neck when she was found. But somehow she had enough life in her to scrawl that on the floor underneath the chair before her body was moved from the temple . . ."

Cornelia's voice became constricted. Hortensia could not quite believe what she was hearing. The import behind Cornelia's revelation was sensational. What did the Vestals think the message meant? Surely they couldn't be suggesting that Pompey himself . . .

"Have you shown this to anyone?" she asked.

Cornelia shook her head and nodded to Fabia to replace the chair. She seemed agitated for the first time.

"No. Fabia came to take over Helena's duties the following morning. She summoned me as soon as she discovered the hearth unguarded."

"I knew something must be terribly wrong when Helena wasn't here," explained Fabia. "It's forbidden for us to abandon the fire. Something else was odd – there were no footprints."

"What do you mean?" asked Hortensia.

"There are always footprints on the floor. Because of the fire you see. We always joke about how you can tell when someone has been falling asleep on night duty and walked up and down, trying to wake themselves up. But there weren't any prints that morning. It was as if someone had sprinkled fresh soot all over the floor, maybe to cover up the signs of a struggle, we think. Then when we moved the chair, we found that writing . . ."

". . . but by this time, Helena's body had been pulled from the river," finished Cornelia. "The Pontifex conferred with the consuls but together they concluded that her death must have been self-inflicted – the shame of an impious love affair. The Temple has been tarnished by scandals of that nature in the past, and the Pontifex declared that the marks on her neck were probably the result of an attempt to hang herself first. If I showed him this inscription . . . I did not know what the consequences might have been, for our order, for Rome. I told Fabia to place the hearth chair over it. We have managed to keep it hidden ever since."

Hortensia peered searchingly at the priestess. "What do *you* think it means?" she pressed.

Cornelia met Hortensia's gaze unflinchingly.

"That, Hortensia, daughter of Hortensius Hortalus, is what I am asking you to discover."

XV

BY THE TIME HORTENSIA EMERGED FROM THE HOUSE OF THE VESTALS, the sky was beginning to grow dark. She spent much of the journey home struggling to regulate the thoughts jostling with one another in her mind. She felt as though she had been plunged into a situation that was far beyond her powers of comprehension or deduction. A part of her reasoned that the Vestals were understandably upset and shocked by the gruesome death of their sister. The young priestess Fabia may have encouraged her superior to entertain this hypothesis of murder and conspiracy as an acceptable alternative to the tawdry reality of a girl who had simply been tempted. Cornelia had insisted that Helena was a shy, pious girl but – crediting herself with far more worldliness than might be expected in a young matron of seventeen – Hortensia could have told her that did not make her immune to the advances of a skilled seducer.

The inscription on the floor was deeply puzzling though. Was it really Helena's final communication? It was obvious what Fabia and Cornelia suspected, but Hortensia was unimpressed by such fanciful imaginings. Could Pompey in fact be the seducer? She sat upright as the thought occurred to her. That wouldn't be so difficult to believe, and would explain why the Pontifex Metellus Pius, who had shared Pompey's triumph in Hispania, had received such swift consular approval in declaring the case closed. But did that mean that Pompey himself had . . . Hortensia again had the uncomfortable feeling of being a long way out of her depth.

The sun was setting by the time she reached home. As soon as she entered the cool of the atrium, she quickly peeled the rose-colored veil from her head, anxious to feel some air on her neck after the stifling heat of the litter. Realizing that it must be past the dinner hour, she headed toward the corridor leading to her private rooms. But her attention was distracted by raised voices coming from the direction of Caepio's study. The door opened and Eucherius sidled out of the room, closing the door carefully behind him. Hortensia realized that Lucrio had still not returned.

"*Domina*, your father is here," Eucherius informed her in an excited whisper. "He is with master Caepio right now. I am not sure you should enter," he added hastily but Hortensia had already ignored the warning, walked straight past him and entered the room. She was met by the sight of her father and her husband clearly in the middle of a heated argument. Caepio was leaning back against the edge of a couch, his arms folded and wearing a closed, angry look instead of his usual sleepy smile. Hortensius meanwhile was pacing from side to side, gesticulating wildly as he talked, his usually sleek hair disordered and his face red with exertion.

"You were supposed to protect her from scandal! That was the one thing I asked of you!" They both heard Hortensia's footstep on the tiled threshold. As soon as he saw his daughter, Hortensius flung out an arm in her direction and carried on his tirade.

"Here she is now! Have you any idea where she has been, may I ask? For all you know she has been selling vegetables from a market stall in the forum. Or perhaps she has been down to the theater and enlisted to appear alongside Roscius in his next comedy!"

"Your father is here to see you, Hortensia," was all that Caepio would say.

Hortensia regarded her father with a mixture of puzzlement and concern. "What is it, Papa? Why are you angry with Caepio?"

"With him? It is you I am furious with, Hortensia! What in Jupiter's name were you doing speaking on behalf of some strange female in the public courts?"

"She wasn't a strange female, Papa," Hortensia explained patiently. "She was the wife of one of Caepio's clients. And she needed my help. I did what I knew you would have wanted me to do."

"Oh really?" Hortensius's voice became silkier and his gestures more deliberate, as if he were assuming his law court persona. "And if you were indeed so convinced of that, why did you keep the whole escapade a secret from me?"

"I was going to tell you, Papa," she said, half-defensive, half-coaxing. "But you were so busy with your trial and I didn't want to bother you. I knew that you would be proud when you heard the whole story though," she added encouragingly.

"Proud?" Hortensius gave a short bark of mirthless laughter. "How proud do you imagine I felt when that corpulent braggart Pompey sidled up to me just before the court session today and told me that I have a very gifted daughter, with all the salacious relish that I'd expect of someone telling me he had recently discovered a talented prostitute?"

A flush erupted across Hortensia's face, as though she had been slapped across the cheek.

"You weren't there, Papa," she said through clenched teeth. "They were trying to cheat the poor woman of her dowry and her children. They would have done it too if I hadn't been there to help her."

"And make an exhibition of yourself in a public courtroom?" Hortensius demanded. "Invite the jests and sallies of the common rabble? Not only that, but you enlist my gardener as a player in your farce! Don't think I didn't recognize that boil-buttocked buffoon from Pompey's description of his performance."

"I don't understand, Papa. I thought you didn't care what the likes of Caecilius and Cato thought. You were the one who taught me how to use my voice. You were the one who gave me all those speeches to read and made me practice them until I was word-perfect. You were the one who told me that eloquence was the noblest of all pursuits."

"I did not do any of those things so that you might make an exhibition of yourself!"

"Then why *did* you do them?" Hortensia flung back at him. "So that you would have a performing puppy to entertain your friends? So that you could make Quintus feel even more of a fool when he didn't live up to your expectations?"

She knew immediately that she had gone too far. Hortensius swept the end of his toga over his shoulder. His blue eyes were bright and stormy but his voice was clipped and controlled.

"You are hysterical, Hortensia, and I refuse to listen to you until you are yourself again. In the meantime, I forbid you to set foot in a public courtroom, do you hear me? Since your husband will not take responsibility for your reputation, I see it falls on me to exert my authority as a father."

"Don't you dare blame Caepio!"

But Hortensius had already swept out of the room.

Hortensia burst into tears and was quickly comforted by her husband, who wrapped his arms around her in a tight embrace.

"Don't cry, my darling. Your Papa is not himself today." But Hortensia's sobs continued unabated. Caepio stroked her hair and her back for several minutes.

"On the positive side, I hope courgette sales were good?" he eventually enquired solicitously and Hortensia's sobs were interrupted by reluctant giggles.

"Eucherius told me you were summoned to see the Chief Vestal. A great honor indeed – I trust she had kind words for you?"

Hortensia was filled with an impulse to unburden herself of everything she had seen and heard at the temple. Caepio would know what to do and she would not have to worry about it anymore. But just as she was about to open her mouth and blurt out the incredible tale she had heard, something made her hesitate. The rational part of her brain believed that the Vestals were placing too much faith in Helena's chastity. But if Pompey was involved somehow, what good could come from involving Caepio? At the last second, she decided to give her husband only an abridged account of what had taken place.

"She heard about my victory in the courtroom and wanted to tell me that she approved. At least someone appreciates what I did." She gave a watery sniff.

Caepio laughed and kissed the top of her head. "Poor Hortensia. I promise that your Papa will come round. It has been a difficult day for him."

"Is the trial still not going well?"

Caepio shook his head. "I'm afraid not. Cicero has enough witnesses to keep everyone's attention for at least another six or seven days. He won't hesitate to twist the knife as deep as possible, he'd be mad not to. All your Papa can do is sit there. It must be deeply frustrating for him but there's nothing he can do. Oddly enough, he seems to be quite sanguine about it all, more so than I would have thought."

"That's what Mama said." Hortensia thought for a while, her attention wandering back to the scene in the forum the previous day. She hesitated, then raised her head.

"Caepio, do you remember that man we met at Crassus's games? The man with the scar?" She saw that her husband was frowning. "I saw him standing next to Papa outside the court yesterday."

"Yes, I know who you mean. Tiberius Dolabella. Why do you ask?"

"I just . . . wondered. I didn't get the impression Papa liked him very much, so why would he be there?"

"I don't know, if I'm honest, my dear. I saw him approach your father just after proceedings adjourned for the day but Hortensius seemed to give him pretty short shrift . . ."

Caepio broke off, and after staring at the floor for a moment, he smiled and shrugged.

"Who knows? Maybe he wants your father to be his advocate, or to lend him money. Either one would be quite plausible in his case. I shouldn't worry your head about it, my dear. He's not the sort of man I would want you to have any dealings with."

A slave appeared to summon them to dinner, and Caepio did not notice the worried look on his wife's face.

XVI

THE CAELIAN HILL WAS A LESS FASHIONABLE RESIDENTIAL DISTRICT THAN the Palatine but popular nonetheless with members of the Roman elite who did not mind living in such a busy, crowded neighborhood. Its summit commanded the most spectacular views of the city and had in recent years been colonized by an increasing number of impressive villas whose open front doors invited envious inspection of their cavernous interiors by poorer citizens who lived lower down the hill. As evening set in, the contrast between the villas' vibrant inner walls and the darkness outside was so spectacular that some tourists to Rome made the journey up the hill just to see it. Thus it was that Lucrio was able to make a close observation of the house of Tiberius Dolabella without attracting too much notice.

The villa was one of the largest on the Caelian hill, situated in the middle of a wide avenue on the summit. Through the front entrance, Lucrio could see marble columns, rich red wall hangings and a painted corridor leading all the way to a colonnaded portico at the back of the house. A bored looking door-keeper in a grey tunic was slowly pacing back and forth on the threshold of the lighted doorway, exchanging a few words with another attendant just out of view. The door-keeper glanced only perfunctorily at Lucrio as he shuffled past, exaggerating his limp for the slave's benefit. As soon as he reached the end of the row he looked behind him and having made sure that there was nobody watching, he vaulted on to a wall that ran alongside the last house on the street. From there, he jumped across on to the roof of the adjacent villa, wincing as he came down on his weak leg.

Crouching low, he peered into the courtyard garden of the house. A low table was laid out for dining on the colonnaded terrace below but it was a cool night and he could hear from the sound of chatter beneath him that the family who lived there had evidently decided to take their meal indoors. Moving with great care, Lucrio picked his way nimbly across the terracotta tiles before springing lightly onto the portico roof of the next house. He then proceeded to the next roof and the next again, counting as he went. One villa. Two. Three. He had never been able to break the habit of counting out loud in the Romans' own tongue. Sertorius had taken it upon himself to teach him personally, first with a handful of used slingshot pebbles, then with a battered abacus. Every time Lucrio mouthed the numbers to himself, in his mind's eye he could see his adolescent fingers tentatively sliding the little beads along their row.

At last, he dropped down into the fifth garden and immediately sucked in his breath as he realized he had almost collided with a wind chime hanging from the underside of the roof. He exhaled slowly as he stared ruefully up at the swaying ornament from his crouched position in the shade of the portico. It was a grotesque trinket, the likes of which Lucrio knew hung in many a Roman garden, a fact that had greatly amused him when he first arrived in the city. A little bronze statue of the god Pan, his mouth open in an extravagant leer as he sat astride a giant phallus which appeared to be flying through the air. Bells hung from its undercarriage, attached by strings of varying lengths, which tinkled very gently as the object swung in the breeze. Glancing around Tiberius's garden, which was considerably larger than that of his neighbors, Lucrio realized that there were many of these rude little chimes dangling from various vantage points around the garden. A crude warning system perhaps, but they reminded Lucrio that he would have to tread very carefully.

He approached the house through the shadows of the colonnade. Several of the rooms were in darkness but it was clear from the shouts of male laughter and the clinking of silver on silver that he had arrived on a night when his host was having a dinner party. Lucrio was anxious for blood but would not risk his chances of success by shortening his own odds. He was prepared to wait all night for the right opportunity, if that was what it took. So he crouched down in a shady corner beneath the window of a room in which there were no lights lit and waited for Tiberius's guests to leave. He occupied himself in the meantime by studying the stars and running his fingers along the blade of the knife he had brought with him.

A sliver of moon glimmered in the night sky. Lucrio listened to the men carousing next door, knowing from his time in Hortensius's service that such occasions could go on for many hours. He could tell which course was being served by the smells that wafted out to him – oysters with pungent quantities of garum followed by roasted meat and onions. The scent of roses and honey heralded the arrival of dessert, which was interrupted by a sudden raucous chorus of approval. Lucrio quickly realized what had precipitated it. A girl had begun to sing, her dulcet voice just audible over the cheering of the men. From her accent, Lucrio guessed that she was from Hispania, almost certainly a war-prisoner like him. Later on, she would probably be offered to Tiberius's guests, who would take it in turns with her, assuming their inebriated bodies would cooperate.

The girl was still singing when Lucrio became aware of a pool of light on the ground around his feet. He looked up quickly, his fist closing down hard on the handle of his knife, and he realized that someone had entered the room behind him and lit a lamp. Squatting on his haunches, he peered cautiously over the window ledge. When he saw that it was Dolabella, and that he was alone, Lucrio's blood began to thump through his veins. He shifted his weight and watched for a few seconds as Tiberius lit a second lamp and placed it on top of a low cabinet. The light illuminated his sinewy, damaged face and ignited a glow in the strange amber eyes which had haunted Lucrio since he was a child. Everything about the man was just as he remembered, save the deep scarring on his left profile. Lucrio felt a pang of regret that one of Sertorius's men had obviously got to Tiberius before he could. As soon as his quarry's back was turned, he gripped the hilt of his dagger and prepared to spring through the open window. But at that moment a slave entered, followed by another man, tall and well-groomed in a plain white toga with a purple border.

"You will forgive me for receiving you in here, my dear Crassus." Tiberius's voice was just as Lucrio remembered it, dry and lazy. "I'm also quite certain that you will excuse me for not inviting you to join my party next door. I doubt they're really your sort of people. Especially not now that you hold such distinguished office."

Tiberius Dolabella flashed his small, jagged teeth in a smile as he poured a cup of wine for his guest. Lucrio withdrew further into the shadows, making sure he could not be seen by the occupants of the room. He could hear Crassus irritably refusing the offer of refreshment.

"I don't want your hospitality Tiberius. It's been ten days now and you have failed to respond to my repeated messages. I want to know – *where is the item you promised me?*"

"I have it safe, my dear Crassus, I assure you."

"Then where is it? I have brought the money with me now." Lucrio heard the crunch of a sack of money being thrown down. "You see? There can be no excuses. Now let's make the exchange and have done with it."

There was a long pause and then another sound of coins jangling as Tiberius picked up the sack and weighed it appraisingly in his hand.

"It's all there," Crassus asserted bullishly.

"Oh I have no doubt," agreed Tiberius. "The thing is, how do I put this without sounding indelicate? My price has gone up."

"What?" gasped Crassus.

"Well, there were added inconveniences as you know. The dead girl for a start. I don't know if you have ever attempted to smuggle a corpse through the forum in the dead of night, my dear Crassus, but believe me, it takes an extraordinary amount of ingenuity. One has to find a vehicle at short notice, transport the body to some secluded bend of the river, all without being seen of course."

"I never asked you to commit murder! That was never part of our arrangement."

"Well what would you have me do when the silly girl walked in at the most inopportune moment?" complained Tiberius. "Believe me, I found it as distasteful as you do. Well, distasteful may not be quite the right word . . . there was a certain frisson I admit. You look pained, Crassus. I take it your tastes don't run in that direction? My apologies. I didn't mean to offend your delicate sensibilities."

"I don't want to hear any more about it!" said Crassus shrilly. "We made a deal, Tiberius!"

"Yes we did and I have every intention of fulfilling my end of it. Another hundred thousand should do the trick."

"A hundred thousand?" Crassus shouted. Lucrio could hear Tiberius tutting.

"Ssh, Crassus. You wouldn't want my guests next door to hear. They're not moralists, but they would be shocked you know."

"I want what I paid for!"

"I know you do. After all, your needs are quite pressing, are they not?" By the silence that followed, Lucrio guessed that Crassus was struggling with his emotions.

"I'll give you another fifty thousand."

"How kind. But I believe the figure I mentioned was a hundred."

"Sixty – and that's my final offer."

There was a long silence. Lucrio heard a heavy tread as Tiberius walked over to the amphora of wine, followed by the sound of liquid glugging into a cup. Then he spoke in a tone which Lucrio remembered all too well.

"You need to ask yourself something, my dear Crassus. You need to ask yourself, can I really afford to *bargain*?"

After what seemed like several minutes, Crassus's barely audible reply came. "Have it your way. I'll get it to you tomorrow. You have my word."

"Splendid. You musn't think me greedy, my dear fellow." Tiberius's manner had reverted instantly to the urbane. "But the nature of the task merits generous compensation and I think you would agree that I have already proved my worth in handling Albinus for you. I will show you that your continuing good faith is not misplaced."

A key clicked in a lock, shortly followed by a rustling sound and a relieved sigh from Crassus.

"Thank the gods. Yes, that's the right document. You're sure no one saw you going in?" pressed Crassus.

"Thanks to a connection of mine on the inside, perfectly sure. Aside from the girl of course." There was a pause and the sound of papyrus rustling against fabric. "Aren't you going to destroy that?" asked Tiberius. "It's rather incriminating if it's found in your possession."

"I will when we're sure of the outcome. If we run into any problems, we may need to put it back."

"So little faith. Still, it's your show, as they say. I take it you have dealt with our stubborn friend in the Subura?"

"Bloody leech. Trying to screw more money out of me. He got what was coming to him."

A chair creaked as someone settled into it.

"Have you spoken to Hortensius again?"

A raucous shout of laughter from the room next door drowned out Tiberius's answer. Lucrio instinctively flattened himself against the wall as he saw a man suddenly poking his head of the window of the dining room next door and vomiting copiously on to the plants beneath. As soon as the man had disappeared again, Lucrio put his ear closer to the window, straining for all he was worth to hear what Tiberius and Crassus were saying.

". . . what does he think he's playing at? You showed him one of the letters, we can expose him any time we choose. His reputation would be ruined!"

"I rather think he's having an attack of conscience."

Lucrio could hear someone pacing around the room.

"Hang him. We'll do it without him if we have to."

"That may not be so easy. It might mean he has to meet the same fate as Albinus."

"So be it if it comes to that," said Crassus, after a long pause. His voice had become constricted. "We need to talk about what comes next in any case."

"Yes," agreed Tiberius promptly. "About that. I'm going to need another five hundred thousand if you want me to keep helping you."

The pitch of Crassus's voice escalated sharply. "I just promised you another hundred!"

"Yes. Expenses, you know."

There was a loud thud as Crassus's hand hit a table.

"You can wipe that self-satisfied grin off your face Tiberius. You're not going to treat me as some kind of rich uncle you can fleece at will! It was thanks to me that Metellus Pius was willing to declare the girl's death a suicide! I can implicate you! – and in Albinus's death too!"

"And I *could* make the obvious reply but what would be the use? You're going to give me the money, because you don't have a choice. If I am dragged down to Hades, my dear Crassus, then we both know who's coming with me to pay the ferryman. Don't we?"

Crassus's breathing became louder, but he said nothing.

"Another five hundred. Have a little think about it if you need to," crooned Tiberius softly. "I am in no hurry, you see."

Crassus's sandal squeaked on the marble floor as he turned on his heel and marched out of the room without another word. Lucrio heard him bark something at someone as he marched through the atrium and out of Tiberius's front door into the night. A few moments later, there was the sound of a drawer opening and the money pouch being placed inside it. Then the pool of light around Lucrio's feet disappeared and he heard Tiberius returning to his party next door.

XVII

OR A LONG TIME, LUCRIO DID NOT MOVE. THEN, RISING TO HIS FEET, he padded stealthily back along the portico. He stopped several times, feeling the desire for vengeance pulling him back toward the villa, but he made himself keep going, reasoning that he had waited this long and another night was not too high a price to pay for loyalty. He would not have had this chance if it weren't for Hortensia and her father.

There was an oak tree in one corner of the garden, whose branches clambered over the roof of the colonnade. Putting his dagger between his teeth, Lucrio set one foot on the trunk and began to pull himself up. Too late, he realized his mistake. The inner boughs of the tree were full of wind-chimes, the same little phallic baubles he had almost knocked into earlier. As soon as the lowest branch sank under Lucrio's weight, the air was filled with a high-pitched cacophony of colliding bells, the likes of which could never have been caused by a sudden breeze.

Lucrio had only a few seconds to think. A warning shout had been taken up inside Tiberius's villa and he could see shadows rapidly approaching along the painted corridor. He took hold of the dagger and wondered for a wild moment if he would be able to get to Tiberius before force of numbers overwhelmed him. But at the last moment, some instinct prompted him to throw his weapon over the portico wall. He heard it land with a thud in the neighboring garden and had just enough time to regret it before three burly slaves emerged from the lighted corridor and bore down on him. The breath was knocked from his body as they charged at him and pinned him to the ground, so that his bad knee was agonizingly twisted. He felt a fist connect with the flesh covering his ribs. Another began raining blows down on his head. Lucrio curled himself into a ball and withstood their assault as best he could. The onslaught continued until the left side of his face was shiny and swollen and he could barely breath for coughing.

"All right, all right, let him up."

The shaven-headed slave who had led the attack gave Lucrio one final kick and stepped back, spitting phlegm through his chipped teeth. Tiberius Dolabella was standing overhead, holding up a lit torch. Some of his dinner guests were gathered behind him, several still holding their silver wine goblets and giving slurred encouragement to the brawling slaves. The torch was held up to Lucrio's face, the heat of it almost scorching his skin.

"Well, my friend. That was a little clumsy of you, was it not? I fear you may have chosen the wrong house – and the wrong man – to steal from."

Lucrio spat out blood from between his teeth, thinking fast while he tried to recover his breath. "I was not trying to steal from you . . .*domine*."

"Really? My apologies. Most people come in by the front door."

"I was . . .visiting a girl."

"A girl?" Tiberius repeated incredulously.

"A maidservant. She belongs to the household of your neighbors. I was making my escape over the rooftops and I lost my footing. I apologize, *domine*."

Lucrio forced himself to sound contrite though it cost him everything he had to do so. Tiberius Dolabella held the fire closer to Lucrio's face, illuminating his own in the process, the copper-colored eyes, skin ridged and puckered. A resiny perfume lingered about him, blending with the smoke from the flames and making Lucrio feel nauseous.

"You're not from around here, are you? You look as though you come from some barbarian outpost in the west. Hispania?"

Lucrio looked him in the eye. "Lusitania, *domine*," Even though he knew it was impossible that Tiberius would identify the eleven-year-old peasant boy whom he had sold into slavery fourteen years before, he searched his interrogator's scarred face almost hopefully for any hint of recognition, some flash of memory. But Tiberius simply straightened up.

"I see. So you were out on a nighttime adventure, you say? A man after my own heart. Tell me – I am fairly well-acquainted with most of the doxies on this street. What was this very forward maidservant's name?"

"I don't know," improvised Lucrio, shrugging as though it were a matter of no consequence. "I met her in the forum. She told me where she lived and how to reach the house unseen. Like you say, she was very forward."

Tiberius chuckled. "Either you are astonishingly stupid, my friend, or you think I am. Which is it? Do you believe I cannot very quickly find out if this story of yours is true?"

Suddenly one of the men in the circle behind Tiberius spoke.

"Wait a minute. I knew I had seen him somewhere before."

Squinting around the light of the torch hovering above his face, Lucrio could just make out the aquiline features of Publius Dolabella looming above him, bending down to get a closer look.

"It's you. From the law court," said Publius slowly, more surprised than suspicious.

Tiberius eyed his nephew keenly. "You always manage to surprise me, Publius, by either knowing a little less or a little more than you should. Is this barbarian a friend of yours then?"

Publius straightened up and shot his uncle a covert look of dislike. "He belongs to the household of Servilius Caepio. More specifically to his wife." His tone was offhand.

"His wife . . . aha." Comprehension spread across Tiberius's face. "Now I know why your powers of recognition were so keen on this occasion. Well, well. This does put things in a different light."

Tiberius turned to one of his slaves. "You will take a message to the Palatine in the morning. The villa of Servilius Caepio. Make sure you deliver it personally to the lady of the house. Since I have her property in my possession, she may come and fetch it at her convenience."

"That's all you're going to do?" asked Publius aggressively. "You said you didn't believe his story."

"My dear Publius. You're the one so obsessed with poor form. I cannot possibly serve punishment on another man's slave, now that I know his provenance. Besides, I should very much enjoy meeting Hortensius Hortalus's daughter again."

He issued a curt command to the shaven-headed slave, who had now hauled Lucrio up from the ground.

"Lock him in the cellar. If you choose to tenderize him a little more first, that is your affair."

The shaven-headed slave gave a toothy grin and Lucrio was dragged away to a chorus of encouraging cheers from Tiberius's guests. With arms outstretched, their host began to usher them back toward the dining room. Only Publius stayed where he was, staring sullenly down at the patch of grass recently vacated by Lucrio. As his uncle stooped to pick up a wine cup that someone had dropped in the grass, Publius suddenly fired a question at him.

"What did Crassus want?"

Tiberius paused before slowly uncoiling himself back to his full height and staring haughtily at his nephew. Publius's jaw was set at a challenging tilt. "You were gone some time. I came to see what was keeping you from your guests. The intelligence that you were closeted with the consul intrigued me, I admit."

Tiberius's response was softly-spoken and deliberate.

"I remember mentioning to your dear father once, when I caught you in your infancy, trying to steal my finest stilus, that there was a snooping streak in you which should be snuffed out at the earliest opportunity. A shame he never took my advice. Perhaps I shall have to do it for him one of these days."

He left Publius shrouded in darkness.

XVIII

HORTENSIA WAS READING A LETTER FROM DRUSILLA THE NEXT MORNING when Tiberius Dolabella's messenger arrived. Her mind was not much engaged with the words in front of her, glad though she was that Drusilla sounded happy and full of optimism for the new rural life she was planning with her mother and her children in Campania. Lucrio's continued absence, and the connection it seemed to have with Tiberius Dolabella, continued to trouble her. On top of that, she was wrestling with the problem placed before her by the Chief Vestal. Although she was still inclined to think there was an element of hysteria to the priestess's qualms about Helena's death, she could not dismiss the scrawled reference to Pompey so lightly. There was no logical explanation for it. Had it definitely appeared on the night of Helena's death? Could the younger Vestal Fabia have written it herself? But why would she do so?

Eucherius knocked on the door of her salon, disturbing her troubled thoughts. "*Domina*, there is a messenger outside. He asked me to give you this and wait for an answer." Hortensia took the note offered to her. She did not recognize the seal – an impression of a dog's head – and broke it open without much interest.

"*Madam. I have something that belongs to you. He is not very communicative so I will have to rely on you to supply a name for him. You are free to collect him – in person – at your earliest convenience. Tiberius Dolabella, Alban Street, Caelian Hill.*"

Hortensia's eyes widened, her emotions veering wildly between incredulity and fear. She read the letter again and then, making sure that she did not betray the extreme agitation she felt to Eucherius, said, "Tell the messenger who brought this that he may inform his master that I have received his letter. He may expect a visit from me shortly."

Eucherius nodded and shortly she heard him passing on her response to the waiting slave.

It took Hortensia a few minutes to decide what she should do. Caepio was hosting clients in his study as usual. Knowing he would have prevented her from going and may even have stormed up to the Caelian Hill himself to confront Tiberius, Hortensia decided with a pang that once more she would have to act without her husband's knowledge. He would probably find out later, but for now what mattered was getting Lucrio back without further muddying the murky waters in which she already stood. For both propriety's and safety's sake, however, she decided to take Elpidia with her. It would be scandalous for her to visit the house of a man unrelated to her unaccompanied, and she felt uneasy in any case at the prospect of going alone, remembering how Tiberius had looked at her at the games. Elpidia was highly suspicious at hearing the news that she was to accompany her mistress on an errand which they had to depart on immediately and which involved a visit to the Caelian Hill where, as far as she knew, her charge was unacquainted with anyone. She was even more shocked at being informed she was to wait in the litter outside. But Hortensia told her old nurse haughtily that it was not her place to question orders and Elpidia lapsed into offended silence.

The door-keeper on duty at Tiberius's villa bowed Hortensia into the study. The first thing she noticed on entering the room was a smiling Tiberius Dolabella himself, seated in a high-backed chair with a drinking cup in his hand. The second thing was how different the room was to her father and Caepio's private sanctums. Where theirs were light, comfortable and full of rolls of literature banked up on shelves and in cabinets, this one was dark, sparsely-furnished and smelled heavily of some bitter perfume that made her wrinkle up her nose. Tiberius Dolabella smiled at his visitor and rose lazily to his feet. But Hortensia had been rehearsing her lines in the litter and before her host could utter a greeting, addressed him in her clearest, most imperious speaking voice.

"Thank you for your letter. I should like to know first of all, if you please, just how a member of my household came to be detained in your house. I demand his immediate release and a full explanation. If my husband were not away on business this morning then he should have accompanied me here and I have no doubt he would express himself far more strongly than I can."

Tiberius Dolabella subjected Hortensia to a long, appraising scrutiny. He seemed to appreciate her attempt to wrong-foot him.

"That seems unlikely. I can quite understand your outrage, my dear. But I am afraid you may be laboring under a misapprehension. I did not kidnap your servant. Indeed I cannot imagine why you think I would have. He was apprehended fleeing the scene of an amatory adventure."

"A what?" exclaimed Hortensia, much taken aback.

"Yes. One can sympathize, can one not? Apparently the girl is a neighbor of mine – from the servile classes herself you understand – and in his doubtless weakened state, the lovesick fellow lost his footing and tumbled from the roof into my garden."

Hortensia felt strangely incensed for a moment but then she realized that Tiberius Dolabella did not believe this story any more than she did. Whether it was his invention or Lucrio's she did not know. But for some reason she did not understand, it suited her host to play a game with her. She decided the best course of action was to play the innocent. The sooner she and Lucrio were away from here the better. So she drew herself up to her full height and said, "I am shocked indeed and assure you I shall punish him suitably. Thank you for sheltering him and I apologize for any inconvenience he has put you to. Perhaps you would bring him to me immediately and then he will not trespass on your hospitality any longer."

"Of course. But I am not such a poor host. You will not disappoint me by refusing refreshment."

He proffered an amphora of wine and gestured toward a bowl of figs. Hortensia shook her head but instead of accommodating her obvious desire to take leave of him, Tiberius sat back down, selected one of the fruits himself and began to slice it into segments with a thin knife.

"These figs come from a tree near your house, just outside the Lu-percal, perhaps you know it?"

"Of course," answered Hortensia scornfully. "It grows at the site where the founder's cradle washed up. I was under the impression though that it was an offense to eat the fruit from that tree."

Tiberius raised an eyebrow. "When pleasure is at stake, my dear, what are a few archaic superstitions?" He sucked loudly on the fig's soft ruby flesh. "You are obviously well read. I suppose I should have expected as much from a daughter of Hortensius. Tell me, do you perhaps also know the other myth connected to the Lupercal? Not the story of Romulus and Remus – every child knows that. I refer to the legend of Hercules and Omphale."

"No, I'm afraid I do not and since my Papa made sure I was educated in all of the important myths, I cannot therefore think it worth knowing."

"Oh but it is, I assure you. Though perhaps Papa didn't think it fitting for you to know." He watched her for a moment while he continued to flourish his knife. "You must be familiar, I am sure, with the Lupercalia festival, held near the cave in February, in honor of our twin founders. Have you by any chance ever wondered why the young priests of Faunus who preside over the festival perform their peculiar rituals without clothing. No? It all goes back, so I am reliably informed, to an encounter between Hercules and the Lydian queen Omphale. Hercules had killed the brother of the woman he loved, you see, and on the orders of Apollo, was sold into slavery for a year as punishment. Omphale purchased him and while in her service, forced him to wear women's clothes and do feminine chores. Some say that he and the queen also became lovers . . . Well, one night, Hercules and Omphale were forced to take shelter in a cave and as usual she commanded him to exchange clothes with her. He put on her jewels and her girdle – far too narrow for his thick waist of course! – while she donned his lion's skin and slung his quiver of arrows over her shoulder." Tiberius took another sip of wine and studied Hortensia to gauge her reaction to his tale before continuing.

"After a wine-soaked meal, they fell asleep, he still wearing her clothes, she clothed in his. Now Faunus, the patron god of shepherds as you well know, had seen Hercules and Omphale go into the cave. Faunus was passionately in love with Omphale and now he spied his chance. He crept into the cave and in the darkness, had a good feel around the first bed he came to and jumped back pretty quickly, as you can imagine, on feeling the rough texture of lion skin. So he switched his attention to the other sleeping figure, confident that he was now on the right track. Lying down behind the person he thought was Omphale, he gripped his manhood firmly, lifted up the soft, gossamer fabric of her dress and . . . well. You can imagine the shock he got. As a consequence, Faunus ordered that all his followers should ever after conduct their worship in the nude, thus preventing the repetition of so painful a mistake in the future."

Tiberius smiled politely at Hortensia and took a sip from his goblet. She could hear him drawing the liquid through his teeth before swallowing it.

"Your stories do not interest me, sir," she said coldly. "Where is Lucrio?"

"Lucrio? So that's his name." He was completely unabashed by her froideur. "My men reported that he wasn't very chatty. Of course. I was enjoying our conversation so much that I had quite forgotten all about him."

To Hortensia's relief, he rang a bell and a slave in grey livery appeared almost instantly.

"Would you please fetch our guest? His mistress is anxious to take possession of him."

When Lucrio was brought in, Hortensia gasped in horror. His lip was cut, his face puffy and bruised, and the swelling around his right eye had forced it shut. He was able to walk unaided, but was hobbling badly on his weak knee and there were dried smears of blood all down his tunic.

Hortensia whirled on Tiberius. "How did he get like this?" she demanded angrily. "He did not receive those injuries falling off a roof."

Tiberius spread his palms apologetically. "You must forgive me. My slaves are very assiduous in their duties. They could not be expected to take the soft option with what they quite understandably thought was a common housebreaker."

The shaven-headed slave who had brought Lucrio in bowed slightly as though in mock apology.

"I shall make sure my father hears of this!"

"You know best of course, my dear, but do you really think it wise to tell him about your visit here?"

Hortensia did not trust herself to say another word. She motioned to Lucrio to follow her and marched out into the atrium. Tiberius came outside with them and observed as Hortensia climbed into her litter.

"I do hope we shall meet again soon. Perhaps at Pompey's games," he called out. "I must say, I don't often find myself sympathizing with Publius but I can fully appreciate his disappointment."

He watched as the litter moved off slowly down the street, Lucrio hobbling in its wake. Then he turned to the shaven-headed slave now standing next to him.

"If you see that Spanish cripple anywhere around here again, you will inform me immediately."

"What if he says he's just here to meet his girlfriend?" asked the slave with a gap-toothed grin.

"He was no more here to screw slave-girls than he was just taking a moonlight stroll on my roof. Someone sent him. Someone perhaps who knows I have some incriminating items in my possession that they would like back."

"You think she knows?" asked the slave, tilting his head in the direction of the receding litter.

"No. But it's an interesting idea to play with. No father wants his little girl to be disappointed in him, after all."

Tiberius continued to watch as the litter trundled slowly down the hill.

XIX

ORTENSIA STOOD IN THE MIDDLE OF HER STUDY, A STORMY EX-
pression in her eyes. She spoke in a low, fierce voice.

"You will tell me right here and right now, what you were
doing at that man's house. Why you abandoned me in the forum, why
I have not seen you for two days, why I just had to go through that
embarrassing scene. I almost started to believe my father. He said you
had probably always meant to leave us as soon as you got to Rome
and laughed at me for trusting you."

Lucrio stared back at her, not a trace of emotion in his eyes.

"But I knew you wouldn't do that to us," she continued, a plead-
ing note entering her voice. "Not after everything we've done for you.
I knew there must be another reason. So I will ask you one more time.
Who is that man to you and why did you seek him out?"

For several long moments, it seemed as though Lucrio still did
not mean to reply. He stood with his weight resting heavily on one
leg, the heavy bruising around his right eye giving him a squint which
only added to his air of bored defiance. Silence hung heavy between
them and the only sound in the room was the faint noise of children
playing outside in the street. Then, just as Hortensia was on the verge
of dismissing him angrily, Lucrio spoke.

"He is the man who took everything from me."

Hortensia's eyes widened. "What do you mean?"

Lucrio's gaze shifted to some point on the wall beyond her head.
His voice was cold and dispassionate.

"When I was a boy, a Roman tribune came to my village. We lived on a farm close to the river Tagus, on one of the main routes used by the Roman army. My parents did their best to be on good terms with the Romans and did not object to supplying the passing troops with milk and fresh bread. But when this tribune arrived, he demanded more than we could afford. My father refused the tribune's request. Then the tribune ordered his companions to force my father's head into a water trough. They held him there until he drowned. When my older brother Taio tried to stop them, the tribune cut his throat. He attacked my mother and killed her too. I could hear her screaming but I couldn't get to her." Lucrio paused and took a deep breath before resuming in the same emotionless tone.

"One of the other soldiers put me across his horse. They sold me to a slave dealer whom they met on the road, and he traded me on to a garum merchant. When I was fifteen, I escaped and offered myself in service to Sertorius as a kitchen hand. Later they made me a soldier. I did not much want to serve under a Roman but I thought it my best chance of learning how to fight and finding the man who killed my family – and Sertorius took an interest in me. Every time we met the Roman army in battle I looked for the tribune. I thought I saw him once, at Sucro, when we met Pompey's army, but I lost sight of him. For many years, I kept looking. Then, two days ago in the forum, I found him at last."

His gaze settled on her again. Hortensia's eyes were glittering with tears.

"Why did you not tell me?" she whispered. "Did you think I would not understand?"

Lucrio shrugged. "You would have felt sorry for me, *domina*. But no, you would not have understood what was inside me."

She bit her lip. "Did you go there to kill him last night?"

He nodded. "I was very close."

"So what stopped you?"

"I overheard something." For the first time, Lucrio hesitated and looked uncertain. "Something . . . I thought your father should know about."

"My father?" asked Hortensia, mystified.

Carefully omitting any reference to Hortensius himself, Lucrio recounted as much as he could remember of the conversation he had overheard between Tiberius and Crassus, the exchange of money for the unknown document, the mystery man in the Subura and the death of the unnamed woman.

"I couldn't tell you the woman's name," he concluded. "But it sounded as though she was killed because she discovered something she shouldn't have. I think her death may just be the beginning through. There is something else they are planning, something more serious, perhaps another man's death." He studied Hortensia's face closely. "You need to tell your father what you know, *domina*. So that he can stop it . . . before it goes any further."

He waited for her reaction, but it was not what he had expected. Hortensia's hand was pressed to her mouth yet the look on her face was not of bewilderment or horror, but of fearful understanding. "Helena," she whispered through her fingers. "Her name was Helena . . ."

She closed her eyes. So the Vestals had been right to be afraid. Her mind was in turmoil, darting through a gallery of different images, sifting through the pieces of information in her possession. The dead Vestal in the river, the archive room, the message beside the hearth. Suddenly she opened her eyes with a snap.

"You said it was a document that Tiberius gave to Crassus? And that he kept it, in case he needed it to be put back? You're sure that's what he said?"

Lucrio nodded. He was now watching her in some concern. Hortensia distractedly rearranged her veil about her head.

"Listen to me. Tell Elpidia to come to me in my room, I shall need her escort. If Caepio comes home and asks where you have been, tell him he can come to me for an explanation and that I shall return home shortly."

Lucrio frowned. "Where are you going?"

"I have to go and see the Chief Vestal."

She was about to head for the door but Lucrio blocked her path with his arm.

"If what I have told you has put you in danger, *domina*, you must allow me to come with you."

"If we are to speak of danger," retorted Hortensia, "*you* were going to kill that man and count your own life for nothing. Now you listen to me, Lucrio." She fixed him with her most tigerish stare. "I forbid you to return to that man's house tonight."

Lucrio's green eyes became still and cold again. "There is nothing you can say that will stop me, *domina*. I have sworn to kill him."

"It was an order, not a request. You will stay here. I know that you want that man's blood, Lucrio, and I know that in the end I may not be able to stop you. But if you kill him now . . . you do not know what you may set in motion. I do not yet know what is behind all of this, but I may know more soon. There are many people who could be in danger because of it. People I care about. That may not mean much to you, but it does to me."

Lucrio was silent for a moment.

"As long as you promise me I have not put you in danger, *domina*, I will let you go and I will give you a little more time. But I have waited fourteen years and I will not wait much longer."

"Then just obey me for now, please. And fetch Elpidia to me."

She swept out of the room.

XX

"**A**RE YOU ABSOLUTELY SURE?**"

Felix, the little Greek slave, had been surprised to see her but had greeted Hortensia with a bashfully welcoming smile and led her through the beautiful colonnade, bowing her into the Chief Vestal's private apartment just as before. But now it was Hortensia who had taken charge of the interview, pacing about restlessly while Cornelia watched from her high-backed-chair, a hint of defensiveness in her manner.

"Of course I am sure. We have accounted for every document," insisted the priestess. "We checked every individual archive, there was nothing missing from any of them."

"But have you really checked them? Have you made sure they are all what they claim to be, I mean?"

Cornelia looked offended. "It is a sacred crime for anyone, let alone a Vestal, to read the private papers of a Roman citizen," she said repressively. "We do not break the seals. We just confirm that the item is in our inventory and move on to the next."

Hortensia threw up her hands in exasperation.

"But don't you see? If all you are doing is checking that the same number of documents are there as before, anyone could have replaced one document with another and you would be none the wiser!"

Cornelia pursed her lips. "I do not understand what it is that you want."

Hortensia took a deep breath. "I need to see Pompey's archive."

Cornelia's eyes widened. "Then, the inscription on the floor, do you think . . .?" she asked in a hushed voice.

"I do not know what I think until I see the archive."

Cornelia was silent for a moment and then rose reluctantly to her feet.

"I suppose there cannot be any harm when you have already seen the room once, though I shall be in trouble if we are discovered. Fortunately, Fabia is by the hearth at the moment." She led Hortensia back into the colonnade where Felix was hovering obediently.

"This lady is here to make a special offering to the goddess, Felix. Should the Pontifex arrive early for our meeting, you will ask him to wait in my chamber and inform him that I will return shortly."

Felix bowed reverently and Hortensia followed the Vestal down the steps to the lower courtyard, through the latticed door behind the statue and along the dark, musty corridor up into the temple sanctuary once more. Hortensia waited while Cornelia disappeared into the chamber. She heard her having a brief conversation outside before returning.

"I told Fabia what we are doing. She will keep watch for us but we must hurry, another priestess will come to replace her soon."

Pompey's personal archive was on a shelf opposite the door and Cornelia had to fetch a small portable ladder-chair so that Hortensia could reach it. Balancing precariously on the narrow rungs, the soles of her slippered feet rocking back and forth, Hortensia climbed slowly until her nose was level with the niche labeled *"Gnaeus Pompeius Magnus."* It was much fuller than most of the others, stuffed almost to its roofline with wax tablets and papyrus rolls, their yellowing edges tightly wound around wooden rollers. Leaning over and trying not to overbalance, Hortensia peered inside the musty cavity, scanning the little crimson labels attached to every roll by leather thongs which dangled limply down the wall. A few bore the name of Pompey's father Strabo; some appeared to be property documents relating to Pompey's various estates, others had the look of private letters.

Without really knowing what she was looking for, Hortensia began pulling the rolls and tablets half-out of the niche one by one and inspecting them closely in the dim light filtering through the latticed door before slotting them back into place. After several minutes of futile activity, she stopped abruptly and went back to a slim roll she had just partially withdrawn and then replaced. The red label attached to the end of its wooden cylinder was inscribed in tiny black lettering, barely legible in the murky light of the sanctuary: "*The Will of Gn. Pompeius Magnus.*" Hortensia stared at the roll, and then back at the others in the archive, trying to work out what had caught her notice.

"When was this deposited here?" she called down to Cornelia. "Pompey's will?"

"Toward the end of last year, I think," replied the Vestal, who was peering nervously through the slat of the door into the temple. "When he came back from the Spanish campaign."

Very carefully, Hortensia tucked her fingers inside the perfect cylinder of pliably soft, honey-colored papyrus, bound by no fewer than seven crimson wax seals, and withdrew it. Turning it over in her hands and holding it up close to her face, Hortensia noted that the edges of the red seals were sharp and neat, neither cracked nor abraded from attrition with their neighbors. She bent her head and much to the bewilderment of the Vestal watching her from below, sniffed deeply as though she were inhaling perfume. Then she shook her head and turned to Cornelia with a triumphant beam.

"This can't be more than one or two months old," she announced, holding out the roll for Cornelia's inspection. "See how flat the edges are? My papa receives all the newest publications for his library. After a few months, the seams always start to fray and turn darker, it's something to do with the air. That's why Papa keeps all his finest pieces in closed cabinets. Also, I can smell the lamp black, can't you?" She waved it slightly in Cornelia's direction. "It's still got that fragrance, like Papa's study when he receives something new from his copyist Pollio. That must be what caught my attention in the first place." Holding the roll up to the dappled light, Hortensia squinted at the finely-etched insignia of the topmost wax seal. She was just able to make out the outline of a griffin but this revealed nothing to her. Without thinking, she started to glide one fingernail under the seal's edge.

"Do not break the seal!"

Hortensia almost fell backwards off the ladder, so startled was she by the powerful echo of the Vestal's impassioned command. Cornelia was white and shaking.

"That is a sacred document and you have looked at it long enough, you must put it back at once."

Clutching tight to both sides of the ladder and steadying her breath, Hortensia tried to adopt a manner of reassuring confidence, as though she were speaking to a frightened child.

"But it's so important we know what it says if we are to understand what has been going on. I promise we can re-seal it afterwards."

Cornelia shook her head vigorously, clearly horrified at the suggestion.

"You cannot re-seal it. Each seal is unique to the seven people who witnessed the will, it will be clear to anyone that it has been tampered with."

"But if we explain our suspicions, then I'm sure Pompey will understand. He might not even notice the difference," coaxed Hortensia, realizing even as she said it that there was no chance that the Vestal would comply.

"You must come down from there right now! Another Vestal will be coming to take over from Fabia. By the power of the goddess I command you to come down!"

Her voice had reached a pitch of terror now and very reluctantly Hortensia slid the roll back into place and climbed back down to floor-level.

"Cornelia, please," she urged as she stepped off the last rung. "Your instincts were correct. I confess I doubted you at first. But now I believe that there is something very worrying going on here."

"Do you think I don't know that?" Cornelia bit back. "One of my priestesses is dead!"

"Then surely you can see how important it is for us to know what is inside that will?" pleaded Hortensia. "You must listen to me. I am quite convinced that will is a forgery. If I'm right, it won't matter if we open it."

But Cornelia shook her head stubbornly. "I took a sacred vow. I cannot break it."

"Even if you know it may save the Republic?" asked Hortensia incredulously.

"I trust to Vesta's guidance."

The priestess's face was a mask as she propelled her protesting guest out of the room and back along the tunnel to the Vestals' palace. Try as she might, with all the persuasive rhetoric at her disposal, Hortensia was unable to sway the Vestal and eventually was left with no choice but to allow herself to be shepherded across the courtyard and out through a side gate.

She was leaving, head bowed in restless thought, when she heard her name being spoken in an urgent whisper. Fabia was hurrying down the marble steps of the temple, clutching the folds of her veil under her chin. Her pale, pointed face was anxious and she drew Hortensia into the shade of the colonnade that ran along the front of the Vestals' palace.

"Have you discovered something? About Helena?"

"I may have. But won't you be in terrible trouble if they discover the hearth unattended?"

"Another Vestal came to take over from me. Please, you must tell me what it is you suspect."

"I can't know for sure. Your priestess would not let me confirm it one way or another," answered Hortensia darkly.

Fabia nodded. "I heard you. You wish to inspect the will of Pompey. I listened outside the sanctuary door," she explained guiltily. "It means so much to me, you see. Finding out what happened to Helena."

Hortensia was touched by her earnest concern. "She was a good friend of yours?" she asked.

Fabia nodded. "She was my best friend. We came to the order at the same time. I was ten, Helena a year older. What they say she did, throwing herself in the river to escape the shame of discovery, that's a lie." She shook her head, stubborn anger written across her face. "I understand how the affairs of these men work, you see. Did you know that when Cornelia spoke of scandals attached to the Temple, she was talking about me?"

"No," said Hortensia in surprise. Fabia nodded, twisting her hands together.

"Three years ago, someone claimed that I had engaged in . . . immoral conduct with a man. I had never even met him you understand, but this man's enemies knew that such a charge would damage him, and I was as good a Vestal as any other. Fortunately, the case came to nothing and the charges against me were thrown out. But if I had been found guilty of breaking my oath of celibacy . . . they would have buried me alive."

Fabia covered her face with her hands for a moment and breathed deeply before continuing. "The Chief Vestal believed me and I will always be grateful to her. But she does not understand how the world works beyond the walls of this temple. How could she when she has known no other life since she was a child? I wish I could help you."

Hortensia empathized with the mulish determination on Fabia's face but she shook her head warningly. "Promise me you will not endanger yourself. You are right, everything is different beyond the walls of this temple, but I fear that even here you may not be safe. I am going to speak to my Papa about all of this. He will know exactly what to do."

XXI

WHEN HORTENSIA EMERGED FROM THE COLONNADE, THE FIRST
person she saw was Caepio, pacing about at the foot of the
temple steps. He took her arm and led her to the waiting litter.
His usually smiling face was pale and tense and he looked angrier than
she had ever seen him.

"Where's Elpidia?" she asked.

"I sent her home. In Jupiter's name what has been going on, Hortensia?" he demanded. "Lucrio greets me looking as though he has been
in a brawl with Diagoras of Rhodes, and informs me cool as you like
that he has waited only to pass on your message and that he is now going
to the forum to fetch you from the Vestals' house and that you – if you
please – will explain everything on your return. You can imagine what I
had to say to him. I don't know what is going on but I do know that you
have been keeping secrets from me, Hortensia, and it stops now."

Hortensia waited for him to get into the litter alongside her and
then leant her head thankfully against his shoulder.

"You are quite right, it does. I am so glad you are here."

Caepio, who had expected to encounter Hortensia in an obstinate
mood, was wrong-footed.

"I need to talk to you and to Papa, very urgently," she added.

It was a great comfort to share the burden of her knowledge with
someone else. Keeping her voice low so that the litter bearers would not
hear them over the noise from the Sacred Way, she told Caepio everything
that had happened in the last few days, from her first interview with the

Chief Vestal and being shown the inscription naming Pompey on the temple floor, to Lucrio's report of the conversation between Tiberius Dolabella and Crassus. She was deliberately vague on the details of why Lucrio had been at Dolabella's villa, but realized she had to give some explanation, and intimated that Lucrio had heard that Tiberius may have information on the deaths of his family. Caepio listened without interrupting, his brow becoming more and more heavily furrowed. When Hortensia had finished, he was silent and it was only once they were climbing the Palatine that he spoke.

"Hortensia, do you hear what you are saying? You are proposing to accuse a consul of Rome of conspiracy against his co-consul, without a shred of evidence."

"I am not proposing to do any such thing," she said impatiently. "Not yet anyway. But you heard what the Vestals found, you heard what Lucrio said."

"What you heard is more likely to get Lucrio thrown back into the arena, or worse still, the river Tiber. A slave's testimony is inadmissible in a Roman court. Unless it has been extracted from him by torture." Caepio grimaced and admitted, "Though on seeing the state of Lucrio, they might be persuaded."

"But you believe him, don't you?"

He did not answer her straight away and when he did, he chose his words carefully.

"I can readily believe that Crassus may have hired Tiberius to steal something from the Vestals' archive for him. It's well known that Tiberius would commit any kind of villainy if the price was right. If the dead girl of whom they spoke was the Vestal – and I don't deny it sounds plausible – then that is a terrible offense without question. But you will not find it easy to persuade others of it, particularly since Lucrio, by his own admission, only overheard this conversation when he was in the act of breaking into Tiberius's house and recalled it only after his subsequent capture. It is far more likely he would be the one to face punishment."

Hortensia looked taken aback but only for a moment. "So what would you do? I agree Lucrio's name must be kept out of it but are we supposed to sit back and let them conspire against a consul of Rome without so much as lifting a finger?" she demanded.

"Did Lucrio actually hear them mention Pompey's name at any point?"

"No, but I told you about the inscription on the floor and the will in the archive."

"The inscription means nothing without proof that the priestess was murdered, which you don't have. A jury would be far more likely to believe your first instinct, that the girl was naming Pompey as her lover. He pretends to be a model of fidelity but the women of the Subura would tell you different. As for this idea of a falsified will, I'm sorry my darling, but they're almost impossible to forge. They have to be witnessed and sealed by seven people for a start, and even if you could get round that fact, Crassus knows full well that no one's ever going to believe Pompey is suddenly so fond of him that he's willing to write his will in Crassus's favor. All you have otherwise is a conversation about a stolen document, the identification and provenance of which you really have no idea."

Hortensia was silenced and after a moment's reflective pause, Caepio continued.

"Lucrio said that Crassus mentioned someone from the Subura? Someone who wanted more money? That's interesting. Crassus owns a lot of the apartment blocks in that district. He buys them up cheap whenever they catch fire and the owners are so desperate they'll accept any sum, then puts out the fire with his own brigade, fixes them up and rents them out for the best profit he can get. I heard one came down just the other day. What would you care to bet that the 'leech' he talked about was the owner of that tower? That would solve one part of the mystery."

"I want to tell Papa. He'll know what to do."

Caepio was silent for a moment.

"I really don't think you should talk to him about this, Hortensia."

"Why not?" she demanded.

"You don't know what kind of a hornet's nest you will stir up if you interfere and in all likelihood it is Lucrio who will end up in trouble. Remember how your father reacted the last time you took a hand in someone else's affairs? What if you're wrong about the will? What do you think will happen then?"

Hortensia felt conflicted. Perhaps Caepio was right. Hortensius would indeed be angry if he thought she was interfering again in matters that didn't concern her. More to the point, how could she tell him what she knew without revealing how she had come by her knowledge? It dawned on her with dismal certainty that her father would be far less inclined than Caepio to believe that Lucrio had been outside Tiberius's house for good reasons. In fact, he would be determined to believe the opposite and the consequences of that didn't bear thinking about. She also hadn't forgotten Tiberius's presence next to her father at the trial. Hortensia had some ill-formed notion that perhaps, rather as Caepio had suggested, Tiberius hoped to cultivate Hortensius's acquaintance so that he might defend him in the event that the conspiracy should be discovered. Distasteful though it was to contemplate, if there were a relationship between Tiberius and her father, it didn't improve the chances of Lucrio's story being believed.

By now they had reached their villa. Hortensia jumped down from the litter, ignoring Caepio, with whom she was by now quite aggrieved. How could her husband not see what she saw? She accepted that Lucrio's evidence probably wouldn't convince a jury and not for the world would she place him in any kind of danger. But if Tiberius and Crassus really were hatching some kind of plot against Pompey and had murdered a priestess in order to accomplish it, then it was the duty of any Roman citizen to expose them. Caepio's lack of enthusiasm for the fight was bewildering to Hortensia.

Feeling upset and frustrated, Hortensia swept through the atrium to her private salon, pointedly shutting Caepio out by loudly giving instructions to Eucherius that she was not to be disturbed for the rest of the day. Then, an hour later, she confused the young door-keeper by ordering him to fetch Lucrio and send him to her. When Lucrio eventually came in, he found Hortensia pacing up and down, fiddling with the string of rose beads around her neck. She looked up, wincing at the purple bruising around his eyes which was now rippled with yellow. The cut on his lip was hardening into a rusty scab.

"You really do look awful," she observed.

Lucrio smiled wryly, as well as he was able.

"You did not know me in my soldiering days, *domina*. I have looked much worse, believe me."

"You should put some lavender ointment on those bruises."

"Elpidia has already overcome her distaste of me and attended to it. She wanted to lay cabbage leaves over my face. An infallible Roman remedy, she said. But I told her no."

Hortensia laughed but was quickly serious again.

"You have been honest with me, Lucrio. Now I'm going to trust you with something." She locked her fingers together purposefully and told him about her two interviews with Cornelia.

"The Chief Vestal is convinced that this girl Helena was murdered because she discovered an intruder stealing something from the temple sanctuary. Now that I've heard your story I think that in fact she discovered Tiberius Dolabella replacing one document with another and was then silenced. It's the only explanation for why the Vestals haven't noticed anything missing. I've seen Pompey's archive. I think that what Tiberius stole for Crassus was Pompey's will and the one that's there now is a forgery. The question is, what do they hope to accomplish by it?"

"Pompey's death, one imagines, *domina*."

Hortensia nodded. "Yes, I fear that too. But if so, why tamper with the will? It's well known that Crassus and Pompey hate each other; no one's going to believe it if Pompey suddenly writes his will in Crassus's favor," she said, repeating Caepio's reasoning as if it were her own. "Lucrio, I need your help. I have to find out what's in that will and I have to prove whatever it is that Crassus and Tiberius are planning."

He didn't answer her immediately. A slight frown creased his brow.

"Why don't you just tell your father what you suspect, *domina*? As I suggested before?" he asked eventually.

"I did think of that, but what if I'm wrong? Then Cornelia will suffer terrible punishment for showing me a private citizen's documents. The truth is, I have no witness but you."

"I understand," said Lucrio drily. "My testimony doesn't count."

"No," admitted Hortensia, "and Papa would probably have you run out of Italy."

"I can live with that if I have the chance to kill Dolabella first."

She shook her head.

"I need your help, Lucrio. I can't do this alone."

"Are you sure you want to even try, *domina*? You don't know what you may discover."

"That's what Caepio says, but I don't have a choice. The Vestals have put their trust in me, I have a duty to help them." She saw that he was still frowning. "I promise you I have not forgotten what you told me and when the time comes I will not stop you from exacting whatever revenge you have set your heart upon, though I fear . . ." Hortensia stopped and bit her lip.

"You fear what, *domina*?"

"I fear what may happen to you of course," she confessed. "It's a capital crime to kill a Roman citizen. What will you . . . I mean, what did you mean to do afterwards? Will you flee? Back to Lusitania?"

Lucrio met her anxious gaze. "Perhaps. But if I am caught, *domina*, it is a price I am prepared to pay."

Hortensia swallowed and shook her head vigorously.

"Please no. Please promise me you will escape, if they discover you."

Lucrio smiled a little. "You have great faith in my promises, *domina*. It is very humbling." He was silent again for a time. "Tell me what it is you wish me to do first. To help you."

Hortensia nodded, unlocked her fingers, and resumed her pacing. "I have been thinking of it and I have an idea where we may start. If only I'd been able to study the seven seals on the will in the archive more closely, but it was too dark and I didn't have enough time. Each one is the personal insignia of the seven men who witnessed the will – they're the only ones besides Pompey who would know if anything had been changed or tampered with. So presumably they must be in on the plan too. But there is someone else to consider, someone I thought of before you came in. If Crassus wants the new will to convince the Senate, then he will have to have enlisted Pompey's own scribe to create it."

"Why?"

"It would look too odd if the writing was different to Pompey's other papers, the Senate would surely notice it. Crassus must have bribed him. The scribe is the only other person besides the witnesses who would know if there was anything different about the will and presumably he's also the one person apart from Pompey who might have a copy of the original to create the fake from. So the first thing I need you to do is find out who does Pompey's scribing work for him, and where he lives. See if one of Pompey's slaves will tell you. Charm the maids, since you're so good at that," she added a little archly. "Then I can go and talk to him, not to ask him outright of course but to see if he gives anything away."

Lucrio regarded her inscrutably for a moment and then nodded.

"Very well, *domina*. I will find your scribe. But you in turn must promise me two things. First, you will not go and see this scribe without me there with you. Second, you will be extremely careful. These are very dangerous men. You do not want them as enemies."

"Well they are going to find that I can be dangerous too," retorted Hortensia, a martial light in her eye.

TIBERIUS REGARDED HIS informant with beady-eyed interest.

"You are sure?"

"I am sure."

"And you say it is the second time she has visited the Chief Vestal in as many days?"

The informant nodded vigorously.

"The high priestess took her into the archive room on both occasions and today I overheard them arguing over Hortensia's wish to inspect the will of general Pompey."

Tiberius whistled softly. "Well, well. It appears I have greatly underestimated my old friend Hortensius's daughter."

He tapped a finger to his lips for a few moments and then nodded a curt dismissal.

"Go back to the Temple and conduct yourself as normal. As long as the will remains where it is, unsealed, there is no real need for concern. A pity she saw the message from the dead girl – no no, no more self-recrimination from you. I blame myself for not checking she had been properly finished off. But if Hortensius's daughter could prove anything, we would know about it by now. However you will send me word immediately if she pursues her enquiry further."

XXII

WHEN HORTENSIA APPEARED IN THE DINING ROOM THAT EVENING, she was in her most dulcet mood. Embracing her husband, she apologized for her earlier petulance and reassured him that she could see the force of his arguments about Lucrio's testimony and did not mean to meddle in affairs that did not concern her, nor worry her father. She could tell that although Caepio was obviously happy that she wanted to reconcile, he was still a little suspicious. She distracted him by introducing a new topic of conversation as the slaves entered and spread a first course of bread, cucumbers and seafood with cumin sauce on the low table.

"Did you go to court this afternoon? What happened?"

Caepio grimaced and shook his head as he settled himself on the couch next to her.

"Every day is the same. Witness after witness, all of them testifying that Verres robbed, blackmailed, tortured them, countless other charges not fit for me to repeat to you. Verres didn't even show up in court today. He claims he's ill – sick to the stomach I can believe. Your father is trying to persuade him that his only hope now is to go into exile. If that happens then the outcome of the trial will be a formality. Cicero has been very clever. He's going to win by making it impossible for Hortensius to mount a defense."

"I suppose they'll call Cicero the king of the law court now," she said gloomily, taking Caepio's silence for assent. "Will it be very hard on Papa?"

"Your Papa has many friends," asserted Caepio, "and one lost case does not ruin a career."

Hortensia hesitated before asking as casually as she could. "Is Pompey a friend of Papa's?"

Caepio paused in the act of peeling a prawn. "I thought you said you were going to leave it alone," he said chidingly.

"I am, I promise I am," insisted Hortensia soothingly. "It's just, Papa doesn't seem to like Pompey but I'm sure I heard Papa say that he defended him once."

"Yes, he did, though that was some years ago. Your Papa was still a young man, and Pompey barely out of his teens. *His* father Strabo was a great general like himself, and won a famous victory at Asculum a few years before the trial. After Strabo died, Pompey was accused of not handing over some of his father's war booty to the state as he should have done. Your Papa was one of three orators who spoke for him – the other two were Papirius Carbo and Marcius Philippus if my memory serves me correctly. I was only a small boy at the time."

"I remember Philippus," recalled Hortensia. "He used to come to the house when I was little. Papa made me declaim for him."

"Yes, Philippus used to tell your father that you had more talent than he did. A wily, cantankerous old sod, but a great man in many ways, and a fine orator."

"Was Pompey acquitted?"

"Indeed he was. One of his father's friends, Lucilius Albinus, came forward to say he had seen some of the items in the possession of one of Strabo's freedmen. Not only that but the judge, Publius Antistius, was so impressed with Pompey he gave him his daughter Antistia in marriage. She was Pompey's first wife. Mucia Tertia, to whom he is currently married, is his third."

"Are Carbo and Philippus still alive?"

"No Philippus died about three years ago and Carbo picked the wrong side in the civil war. He was executed a few years after the trial, on the orders of Pompey himself would you believe. If that doesn't tell you something about why you should stay out of the affairs of these men my dear, I don't know what will." He stopped and looked suspiciously at his wife. "Why *are* you asking me all these questions?"

Hortensia hastily retrieved her position.

"I promise I'm not trying to deceive you. It's just that I'm confused. I don't understand who's on whose side. I know that Pompey and Crassus hate each other."

"That's an understatement," commented Caepio.

"But they were both supporters of Sulla during the civil war, weren't they? Like Papa. So why don't they get along?"

"Just because a man worships at the same temple as you doesn't make him your friend. Crassus hates Pompey for being a better soldier than he is and more popular with the people. Pompey envies Crassus his money and his social standing."

"But Pompey *is* the more popular of the two?" pressed Hortensia.

"It depends on who you talk to. With the people, undoubtedly yes. With the senators, it's another matter. There are plenty among them who don't like the idea of such a big fish in their pond. They call him a demagogue and a danger to the Republic, though in truth he has little more desire than they do to distribute more powers among the people."

"And Crassus has friends among the senators?"

"Crassus has money. That's more important than having friends in this city."

"So who . . .?" began Hortensia eagerly.

"That's enough now. You promised me you would leave it alone." And Hortensia was forced to abandon the subject.

Later that night, as Elpidia took down her hair, there was a knock at the door of her room and one of the maids delivered a note to Hortensia. Recognizing Lucrio's awkward, spiky scrawl, the product of his rudimentary education in Sertorius's camp, Hortensia waited impatiently for Elpidia to finish and then unfolded the note as soon as she was gone.

"*Didius Flavius. Goat Street, Aventine Hill.*"

XXIII

To REACH THE AVENTINE HILL FROM THE PALATINE INVOLVED A JOURNEY through some of the most insalubrious parts of the city, and it was one that Lucrio warned Hortensia she would be ill-advised to make in her luxurious litter. So having descended the Palatine and left the litter and its carriers in a shady corner of the forum, they made the rest of the journey on foot.

Hortensia knew that she was taking great risks with her reputation in visiting this part of the city with no other escort than a male slave. She had been on the receiving end of a number of suspicious looks from Elpidia since their excursion to the Caelian Hill and had no doubt that her faithful maidservant was dithering on the point of telling Caepio that his young wife was up to something. Only by announcing that she and her mother were going on a shopping expedition to the forum had Hortensia been able to persuade Elpidia that her chaperonage was not needed.

Once in the privacy of the litter, Hortensia removed her elegant mantle to reveal her plainest gown and veil, chosen so that she would not stand out so much in the plebeian crowd. With the exception of her wedding band, she left off all jewelry that might attract thieves and hid it under the mattress of the litter. Even so, she felt uncomfortably vulnerable as she followed Lucrio around the perimeter of the Forum Boarium, being jostled by cattle traders and having to scurry out of the way of fast-driven carts and herders steering their animals toward the market pens. At least there was little chance she would be recognized here. She had caught glimpses of such environments before from the cloistered seclusion of her litter but never had she experienced them at such close proximity, and her eyes were wide at the sight of stray pigs snuffling through the rubbish piled up at the side of the road, and filthy, hollow-cheeked children splashing about in puddles of overflowing sewage. Coarse voices assailed her ears, barking out trading prices or arguing heatedly. The air was full of dust kicked up by the animals' hooves and the earthy smell wafting from the nearby river Tiber so pungent that in the absence of her lavender smelling balm, Hortensia had to cover her mouth with a fine linen handkerchief.

The district around the foot of the Aventine had been colonized by warehouses where river barges traveling up the Tiber from the port of Ostia unloaded their cargo. There were many workshops too, which provided a living for some of the plebeians whose crowded residential ghettos, along with those of foreign immigrants, dominated the upper landscape of the hill. Goat Street, where Didius Flavius lived, was situated near the great temple of Diana, the goddess beloved of the plebeian classes. Sticking close to Lucrio, Hortensia followed him down the street, which seemed mercifully less down at heel than some of the areas they had passed through, although she squealed in horror when someone threw the contents of a chamber pot out of an upstairs window, just missing them. At last they came to a small, one-story residence, where Lucrio stopped and pointed. Hortensia followed his finger and saw a small sign just above the door with a picture of a reed pen and a pot of ink, beautifully and neatly drawn.

The door itself was closed, so she stepped forward and knocked tentatively.

There was no sound of a response inside and Hortensia was about to try again when the door opened a crack and a barefooted little girl with solemn brown eyes peered out. Slightly taken aback not to see a servant, Hortensia bent forward and spoke in a kindly tone of encouragement:

"Hello there. I think I might be looking for your papa. Is he at home?"

The girl blinked at Hortensia several times without answering and then disappeared, leaving the door ajar. Hortensia and Lucrio could hear her calling to someone within the house. A moment later, another face appeared in the doorway, this time of a middle-aged woman with a care-worn expression and deep lines in her brow. "Yes?" she said quietly.

Hortensia inclined her head. "I'm very sorry to disturb you but I'm looking for Didius Flavius and I'm told he lives here?"

The woman stared at Hortensia.

"What did you want with him?" Her voice was almost a whisper.

Hortensia had already devised a pretext for her visit.

"Your husband has been described to me as one of the finest copyists in Rome. My father is a great collector of literature and I would like to commission something special for his birthday."

Even before Hortensia had finished, the woman had already begun to shake her head and there was a quiver in her throat as she responded.

"I'm sorry. My husband won't be able to help you. He was killed this past month."

Hortensia's jaw dropped and she glanced at Lucrio, whose face as usual betrayed little emotion, though his eyes had narrowed attentively. Turning back to the woman, Hortensia bowed her head respectfully.

"I am so sorry. Truly I am. May I ask . . . how it happened?"

The woman shook her head.

"There was a robbery. They broke into his workroom and took everything from his money-chest. We were at home. We could hear them beating him . . ." She broke off on a gesture of apology and pressed a shaking hand over her eyes.

Hortensia glanced again at Lucrio and saw by his return look that they were thinking the same thing. Turning back to the woman in the doorway, she spoke gently. "I am so sorry. Do you have family? Someone to help you?"

The woman shook her head again and blotted her eyes with a corner of her veil.

"My brother owns a bread stall in the forum," she said shakily. "He is giving me what he can and I may be able to earn more by helping him with his accounts. Otherwise my daughter and I are on our own." She collected herself. "But all of this has nothing to do with you of course. I am sorry that you will have to look elsewhere for someone to do your work for you." She bowed and was about to close the door but Hortensia put out a hand and stopped her.

"I know this will seem a strange request and I do not wish to impose on you in your grief. But would you let us, myself and my attendant here, have a look around your husband's workroom?"

The woman stared at her. "Why would you want to do that?"

Hortensia hesitated.

"I won't lie to you but I'm afraid I cannot tell you the truth either. The only thing I can say is that I have a suspicion who may have been behind your husband's death. If you let me look, I may be able to prove it. My name is Hortensia. My father is the advocate Hortensius Hortalus, perhaps you have heard of him?"

The woman looked at a loss. "I don't see how you could know anything about my husband's death. Didius was a quiet, honest man, he didn't have an enemy in the world. They were just thugs, after his savings."

Hortensia waited, imploring the woman with her eyes.

"But, if you really want to look, you may come in. I am Pernilla." She gestured to them and they entered the small dark atrium.

By contrast, the workshop at the back of the house was a relatively light, airy room, flooded with sunshine from a skylight in the roof. There was a sloping bench all along one wall and a cunning rack above, into which a row of bone and bronze pens with differing sized nibs had been neatly slotted, along with a small knife to sharpen them. This was the only sign of order in the room. An alcove containing rows of wax tablets was messily stacked, some of the contents spilling out haphazardly. Both the bench and the floor were strewn with a patchwork of papyrus pieces, most of them covered with the same elegant, swooping handwriting. A pool of some black, viscous substance had half-soaked into the tiles in one corner of the room and for a horrible moment Hortensia thought it was blood. But then she realized it was just the contents of an overturned inkwell, still lying on its side.

"Did he always work in such disarray?" she asked.

Pernilla shook her head vigorously. "No, never. Didius was very meticulous, he got cross with me if I moved so much as a stilus. *They* did this. Trying to see if he had any more money hidden anywhere. Didius would be heartbroken if he could see it but I haven't wanted to come in here since . . . since I found him." She began to weep silently once more and Hortensia averted her eyes.

Lucrio, who was standing by the bench, was rubbing some pieces of papyrus between his fingers. "Why do they feel different?" he asked Hortensia.

"Different grades," she explained, walking over to him and picking up some of the scraps herself. "The best papyrus comes from the middle of the plant, neither too thick nor too thin. If it is too thin, the pen goes straight through. You can see how the fibers run horizontally here – that's the direction copyists usually prefer for writing, it makes the script flow better. See this thicker material here though? This is called parchment, they make it from animal hide, stretched over a wooden frame. It's becoming more popular because it's more flexible than papyrus and lasts longer. Papa has a little notebook made from it to record his thoughts on various cases."

Pernilla nodded wonderingly.

"You know my husband's work. I've never met a woman who could explain it so well. He would so like to have met you. I think he grew a little tired of my conversation sometimes. He hoped to teach Laelia one day, not that there are many females in his profession of course. But he thought it might make her a more useful companion to her husband."

While Lucrio continued to sift through the half-finished documents on the workbench, Hortensia began to walk slowly around the room, breathing in the smoky scent of lamp black ink which was so comfortingly familiar to her from her father's study. It was evident that the people who had ransacked Didius's workshop were looking for something, but there seemed little way of knowing whether or not they had found it. She asked Pernilla whether anything had been discovered missing from among his papers but the widow shook her head.

"Didius didn't share much of his work with me. He preferred to be alone in here."

"But presumably he kept copies of everything? The documents he produced for his customers?"

"Yes, I think he did, the important ones anyway. He was often asked to, in case the original should be damaged or go missing. Some of his customers liked to take copies of the originals on long journeys abroad. I believe he kept them all in that chest over there."

She pointed to a plain metal strongbox chained to a ring against the wall. Lucrio went over to inspect it and beckoned Hortensia.

"The lock is broken," he muttered, lifting the lid to show her. Inside was a pile of beautifully bound tablets and rolls which to judge by their jumbled arrangement and creased corners had been violently rifled through. Hortensia picked them up one by one, examining each of the labels, and then finally shook her head.

"It's not here. They must have taken it, knowing a second copy could incriminate them."

Pernilla asked exactly what it was they were looking for. Hortensia hesitated, one hand fiddling with a spare fold of her drab mantle in unconscious imitation of her father's famous habit.

"Your husband did some work for consul Pompey, didn't he?"

"Why yes. Pompey was his most important patron of course. But what has that to do with anything?"

"I think that the men who killed your husband were looking for something to do with your husband's work for the consul and I believe they found it. I am not saying Pompey himself was responsible of course," added Hortensia, seeing the shock on Pernilla's face. "But I do need to find out exactly what was in the document they took. Is there anywhere he could have kept any more copies of his work? In particular, of any wills he was asked to scribe?"

Pernilla was wide-eyed with distress. The old wooden door in the corner of the room creaked slightly and they all turned quickly. But it was only the little brown-eyed girl, Laelia, who padded over to her mother and pressed her cheek against her stomach, clinging to Pernilla's tunic and peering curiously up at Hortensia and Lucrio. Pernilla stroked her daughter's hair with one hand and made a hopeless gesture of despair with the other.

"I don't know what to tell you. As I said, Didius did not share much of his work with me. Now you tell me that he may have been killed because of it. It doesn't seem real, any of it."

Her eyes wandered around the room and came to rest sadly on the section of the workbench that was most worn and smeared with ink stains. "As for more copies, no, I don't think so. I know that he was usually asked to be present at the sealing of wills and he would often make a spare copy while he was there. Sometimes he was late returning because he was asked to stay and drink a toast with the signatories, who would then put their names to the additional copy as well. But as far as I know, he kept everything in that chest and I don't believe he would have made any other copies without the knowledge of his patron – that would be quite wrong."

"What about the people he met during his work? After all, your husband was employed by some very important men. Is there anywhere he might have kept a record of the witnesses to the wills he created?"

Pernilla shook her head doubtfully and Hortensia felt as though the gate to her last avenue of enquiry was being shut in her face when she was afforded a faint glimmer of hope. "Unless there was something in his commentaries," concluded Pernilla.

"Commentaries?" asked Hortensia in surprise.

Pernilla nodded, a reminiscent smile creeping into her eyes.

"Dear Didius, he was quite a vain man. I shouldn't say that of my husband, I know. What I mean is that he was very proud to work for men such as Pompey and he liked to keep a record of his commissions. I believe great men of state keep similar accounts of their various achievements. Sometimes I found him in here, reading through it as he sipped his evening drink, a proud little smile on his face. I think he hoped to pass it on to Laelia, as a reminder of all of the great men her father had worked for."

"Can I see it?" asked Hortensia eagerly.

"You could if I knew where it was," confessed Pernilla. "I didn't even think of it until just now. It must be in this room somewhere."

They began to search but there was little furniture and few obvious hiding places. Hortensia and Pernilla sorted through the scattered sheaves of parchment on the floor while Lucrio investigated the tall cupboard in the corner which appeared to contain little more than empty inkwells and broken stili. The little girl Laelia meanwhile had detached herself from her mother and went to sit underneath the workbench. From this vantage point she watched the adults intently as they became increasingly frustrated with their lack of success.

"Nothing. These are all drafts of letters and legal documents. Are you sure it couldn't be in the house somewhere?" asked Hortensia in desperation.

A sudden loud knocking noise made them all jump and turn around in surprise. Laelia beamed hesitantly, pleased to find herself the subject of their collective scrutiny, and rapped her knuckles again on the underside of the workbench.

"Not now, darling," admonished her mother. "Mama will play games later."

But the knocking started up as soon as the visitors began scouring the room again, becoming louder and increasingly persistent, until they were forced to pay attention. Laelia beamed conspiratorially at Lucrio, showing a mouthful of half-grown teeth, and beckoned him over.

"I think you've made a conquest there, Lucrio." Hortensia smiled in spite of her disappointment with the outcome of their failed expedition.

Crawling obligingly underneath the workbench, Lucrio sat down alongside Laelia on the floor and laid flat one of his hands which the little girl thumped her fist into with a spluttering giggle of pleasure. Then she pointed at the bottom of the workbench and knocked on it again. Lucrio put his own hand up and knocked as well. Understanding dawned on him, and he looked at Laelia, pointing upwards with one finger in wordless interrogation. Laelia nodded and reaching up, she pushed a little finger against a weakened patch of wood next to one of the bench legs. She couldn't quite press hard enough though and Lucrio added his weight too. Immediately, the panel of wood dropped down and a hollow opening was revealed in the underside of the bench.

Lucrio gave a long, low whistle. "Clever Papa," he murmured. Laelia nodded solemnly and then the gleeful grin creased her cheeks once more.

"What is it?" asked Hortensia, crouching down to have a look and squealing with excitement when she saw the hiding place. "Is there anything in there?"

Lucrio reached up and felt around before withdrawing an assortment of items – a beautiful ivory-bladed pen, a jar of wine containing a few inches of liquid which by its rich blood-red hue was clearly of an excellent vintage, and a canister of brown leather.

"That's it!" exclaimed Pernilla in some excitement. "I remember, he used to put it away in that case when he had finished adding to it."

Lucrio dipped his fingers inside and extracted a very thick document, bound with a piece of linen. He handed it to Hortensia, who unraveled it eagerly across the ink-spattered floor and began to read, tracing the writing down each column with one finger as she knelt. Laelia, who now appeared to regard Hortensia with almost as much fascination as Lucrio, sat up and peered over Hortensia's shoulder as if she too were reading along.

"This is where the entries for this year begin – see here where he's headed it, *In the consulship of Pompey Magnus and Marcus Licinius Crassus.* But Pompey's will would have been made last year so we want the previous year's consuls . . . here we are, it's this column – *In the consulship of Publius Lentulus Sura and Gaius Aufidius Orestes.* She squinted at the tiny, elegant handwriting and soon jabbed her finger excitedly at a point near the bottom of the roll.

"Here it is! *The Kalends of December. Today I attended the Villa Pompeius on the Caelian Hill and served as actuarius for Pompey Magnus in the matter of his will. Also present* – yes! The names are all here! You marvelous man, Didius Flavius, may the gods keep you in Elysium! Now we shall see who else is involved in this."

Hortensia bent her head. "*Also present were seven very distinguished witnesses who in due course signed their hand to my work. Senator Gnaeus Lucilius Albinus . . .*" Hortensia stopped and her brow furrowed.

"I've heard that name recently, but where?"

She pondered a moment longer before returning her attention to the roll in her hand and continuing to read aloud. "*Former consul Marcus Aurelius Cotta* . . .yes, I know that name, Papa introduced him to me at a party once . . . *Gaius Julius Caesar* . . . I'm not too sure about him. Look, Lucrio! *Tiberius Dolabella*! Well that explains why he knew there was another copy of the will, he was there when it was made. I wonder why he turned against Pompey? Maybe he's just in it for the money. You said Crassus was paying him a huge amount."

She looked down and continued reading. "*The Pontifex Maximus Metellus Pius* – now that's interesting! Maybe that's why he was so willing to call Helena's death a suicide? He was co-commander with Pompey against Sertorius, I remember Caecilius telling us. But there was some sort of rivalry over who would claim the victory . . . That's five anyway . . . *Marcus Licinius Crassus* – so *he*'s a witness too! Well, I suppose he *had* just been elected to serve as consul alongside Pompey when this will was drawn up."

There was one name left on the list. Lucrio and Pernilla waited.

"That's six," said Lucrio. "Whose is the last name?"

Hortensia went very still before haltingly reading it out.

"*Quintus Hortensius Hortalus.*"

She looked up to find Lucrio watching her and gave an unsteady little laugh.

XXIV

"ARE YOU ALL RIGHT, *DOMINA*?"

They were walking back down the Aventine Hill, having left Pernilla with a promise of answers about her husband's death and placated Laelia with an assurance that Lucrio would come to visit her again. Hortensia was quiet and preoccupied, a flush in her pale cheeks. But she lifted her head at Lucrio's question and directed a defiant look at him.

"Of course. So Papa witnessed the will. He's an important man, he witnesses many wills. That doesn't mean he knows what Crassus and Tiberius are planning."

There was a long pause.

"I think perhaps he does know, *domina*."

Hortensia stopped and stared at Lucrio. "What are you talking about?"

"I am sorry I did not tell you before. Perhaps I should have but I did not want you to be . . . you see, when I was at the house of Tiberius and Crassus, I heard them mention your father's name. They talked about him as if . . . as if he knew what was going to happen."

There were two bright spots of color in Hortensia's cheeks now.

"Tell me what you heard. Tell me exactly."

"Crassus asked Tiberius if he had spoken to your father. I admit I did not hear everything that was said. But Tiberius seemed to be saying that your father would not agree to something and this made Crassus angry. He said . . . if they had to do it without him, they would." Lucrio paused. "He also said they had letters which would be embarrassing to your father and which they would use to expose him if they needed to . . . I'm sorry, *domina*. I hoped perhaps that if he realized you knew something, it would be enough to persuade him to take a step back and protect himself. To protect you."

He expected her to be angry, to tell him he had misheard or even that he was making it up. But instead, after frowning at him for several long moments, a dawning smile of realization spread across Hortensia's face.

"Of course! Lucilius Albinus!"

Lucrio blinked.

"I beg your pardon, *domina*?"

"Don't you see?" Hortensia's eyes were bright with fervent zeal. "He's a witness to the will too! I *knew* I'd heard his name before. He's the one who Caepio told me was a witness for Pompey at his trial, and he's the senator who was found dead in his bath! I remember them talking about it at Servilia's dinner party when we were still at Laurentum. Everyone said it was a suicide but I'd wager you a million sesterces Crassus and Tiberius killed him because he wouldn't join them . . ."

She broke off and the smile left her eyes. "Which means Papa is in terrible danger too if they've realized he won't give them his support. Oh if only I knew what . . ."

She began to pace about, then stopped and looked distractedly at their surroundings.

"I need somewhere to think," she said abruptly. "Somewhere out of the sun."

There was a low-roofed taberna nearby, its shuttered doors open onto the street. A mange-ridden dog was sleeping by the threshold, pointedly ignoring the pedestrians passing right in front of his nose. The walls behind the dog were scrawled with crude graffiti and a dirty wooden sign depicting a bunch of vine leaves was hanging from its hinges above the entrance. Lucrio peered through the door uncertainly.

"I don't think you should go in there, *domina*. It isn't a place for the likes of you."

"I told you, I need somewhere to work all of this out and I need some kind of refreshment too," said Hortensia petulantly. "There's hardly anyone in there and it's not as though anyone is going to recognize me. I look destitute in these clothes."

Lucrio raised an eyebrow but said nothing.

One of the dozing dog's ears flickered as they went inside. It was a dark, low-ceilinged room, fetid and reeking of wine and sweat. A platter of congealed chicken wings lay untouched on the serving counter, which was presided over by a pot-bellied proprietor in a greasy apron. The hour was not advanced and only two of the tables were occupied, one by a group of elderly men playing a game of knucklebones, another by a jowly craftsman sitting on his own, carefully painting what looked like crude wooden figurines of Diana, her ill-defined fingers occupied in stringing a bow. A disproportionately large hunting dog peeped out from behind one of her legs. Hortensia recalled seeing a stall further down the hill where these and other such clumsy cultic souvenirs were being sold.

The only other person in the taberna was a woman on a stool beside the serving counter. She was considerably older than Hortensia, with sallow skin and deep lines in her cheeks, and she was wearing a man's toga, dark in color, which was slipping just enough to reveal a protruding collarbone. Hortensia was a little puzzled by the hostility in the woman's expression, but decided to ignore it and allowed Lucrio to shepherd her over to the small table in the corner of the taberna next to the man painting figurines while he went back to the serving counter. While she waited, Hortensia tried to ignore the curious glances of the men playing knucklebones in the corner. She suddenly noticed another man slumped at a table just to the right of the entrance. His eyes were cloudy with drink but it was obvious he was staring at her and as soon as he knew he had her attention, he made an obscene gesture with his fingers and nodded encouragingly to her. Hortensia gasped and averted her eyes quickly, feeling hot outrage rushing to her cheeks. She was now wishing she had never suggested coming in here. But then Lucrio returned carrying two tankards and sat down in front of her, blocking her view of the rest of the room.

"What is it?" asked Hortensia cautiously as Lucrio placed one of the tankards in front of her.

"Best you don't know. But I wouldn't drink their wine."

Hortensia sniffed and then took a sip, scrunching her face up in immediate disgust.

"Urgh, Lucrio what *is* that?"

"Fermented goat urine," he answered with the ghost of a smile. Hortensia stared at him slack-jawed as he drained his own cup. He laughed at her expression.

"It's called posca, *domina*. An old soldier's drink. A little sour wine, water and herbs."

"It's revolting."

"But refreshing," he grinned.

Hortensia took another small sip, wrinkling up her nose as she did so. The men in the corner had now resumed their game of knucklebones and the drunkard at the counter was leering at the woman sitting by the serving counter, who seemed to accept without demur the fumbling creep of his hands around her waist. Hortensia began to tap her fingernail against the rough clay of the tankard.

"Let's think about what we know so far."

"We? You forget, *domina*, I am only here to ensure you come to no harm. If it were up to me, I would already have played my part."

"That's not very helpful and I've already explained why you can't go after Tiberius Dolabella until I say so. So you might as well help me. As I was saying . . . there is one thing we know now at least. Didius Flavius obviously wouldn't do the job for Tiberius and Crassus. So they killed him and made sure they took Didius's copy of Pompey's will so that it couldn't incriminate them. But that leaves us with another question. Who made the will which is currently in the temple archive?"

Lucrio drew his finger around the rim of his own tankard, idly watching the delicate movements of the craftsman's brush.

"A forger," he supplied eventually. Hortensia looked questioningly at him. "Perhaps you are looking at this the wrong way, *domina*. Maybe they never expected Didius to help them. Maybe the copy of the will was what they wanted in the first place. So that a forger in their pay could use it to create the new one."

Hortensia nodded slowly.

"Yes. That makes sense. They couldn't rely on Didius not to betray them to Pompey. But could a forger really produce something that would fool the Senate? He would have to reproduce not just Didius Flavius's writing, remember, but the witnesses' signatures too – well enough to fool those who know them well – and then he would also have to create counterfeits of the seven different seals to bind the will, one for each witness."

"A good forger could do all of that, even the seals. They are not so hard to reproduce. I imagine your father's seal and that of the other men are fairly well known," replied Lucrio. "Sertorius had just such a man on his staff. He used to compose fake dispatches purporting to be from Roman commanders, claiming that Sertorius was putting them to rout and they needed reinforcements without delay, and then directing the soldiers to the wrong location. He found it extraordinarily funny."

Hortensia nodded slowly as she took this in, still drumming her fingertips restlessly against the tankard.

"There's something else that's bothering me," she said at last. "How did Tiberius get into the sanctuary in the first place?" She chewed her lip, while Lucrio watched her. "I suppose he could have bribed the guards and then slipped behind Helena without her noticing," she said thoughtfully. "Crassus could certainly have provided enough money for that purpose. The only other way would be through the tunnel from the House of the Vestals. But that would mean someone from inside the Temple would have to have helped him . . ." Her voice tailed off and the restless tapping resumed.

"I wonder what the letters are," she said abruptly after another long silence. "The letters you heard them talking about, the ones they want to use against Papa."

Lucrio shrugged.

"Most men have secrets, *domina*."

Hortensia's eyes narrowed.

"Just what are you implying?"

"Nothing, *domina*. Only, that I think we never know the ones we love as well as we think we do."

Hortensia digested this for a while.

"Well. Whatever they are, they won't do Tiberius and Crassus any good. Papa will never give in to blackmail."

"Are you sure, *domina*? You don't think he might in the end do what Crassus and Tiberius want just to prevent these letters, whatever they are, from becoming public? Even if his reputation – and the reputation of his family – were at stake?"

"None whatsoever," answered Hortensia in an icy tone of voice which clearly signaled that she would brook no further discussion of the matter. "You don't know my Papa. He is completely honorable."

While Hortensia and Lucrio were talking, a shaven-headed man with a broken nose and wearing a grey tunic had entered the taberna and was now leaning up against the counter, exchanging familiar banter with the proprietor. The drunkard and the woman in the toga had disappeared. Hortensia, who unlike Lucrio now had a clear view of the counter, was immediately aware that she had seen the man before but could not decide why she recognized him. Had he been in the law court at Drusilla's trial? She whispered to Lucrio, who turned around at the same moment that the shaven-headed man did. At that moment, Hortensia remembered why she knew the man's face.

"Oh no," she whispered under her breath.

The man observed them for a moment and then strolled over, a menacing leer on his face. The bones in his skull protruded unpleasantly from his scalp.

"Well, well, well. Isn't this cozy?" He picked up a chair, thrust it down with a loud bang on the dirty floor next to Hortensia and Lucrio's table, and leant heavily on it, one hand on his hip, his eyes going back and forth suggestively between the pair of them. The hands of the men playing knucklebones stilled and the craftsman silently picked up his box of half-painted figurines and removed himself to another table.

"That cut on your eye's healing up nicely." The man in grey nodded to Lucrio. "Didn't put up much of a fight, did you? All the same, you Spaniards. My master had you read from the start though, didn't he? There's no fooling him. Little stumble getting away from a girlfriend wasn't it?" He shook his head mockingly and shot a sly look at Hortensia.

"Still, nice of you to take the mistress out. Not part of most slaves' duties, is it? Not like most fine ladies to enjoy a drink of the good stuff."

He leant over the table, closer to Hortensia. She flinched away from his hot, stale breath.

"How about it my lady?" he whispered lasciviously. "If you're ready to slum it with this one, then maybe you'd fancy a go with me."

At which point, Lucrio, who had been observing the man with cold, still watchfulness, produced from under the table a small Diana figurine which he had secreted from the box next to the craftsman, and drove it like a small blunted dagger – arrow first – into the groin of his adversary.

As the man clutched his hands around the affected area, howling like a spiked bull, Lucrio and Hortensia fled into the street to the accompaniment of the dog's frenzied barking and ran down the slope of the Aventine, darting amongst the dock-workers carrying cargo to the ships. By the time they had reached the Forum Boarium once more and been swallowed up in the loud, bustling crowd, Hortensia was unable to hold back her laughter any longer, and although Lucrio did not join in, his face eventually relaxed in reluctant appreciation of her enjoyment.

Once she had recovered, Hortensia asked Lucrio where they would be likely to discover the identity of a possible forger. He had an answer ready.

"The Subura. There is a street where such individuals are known to operate. I have heard mention of it."

"Excellent. We can go there tomorrow," began Hortensia, but Lucrio shook his head.

"No, *domina*," he said firmly. "The Subura is no place for you. I go alone. You may give me any instruction you choose to pass on."

XXV

THE STREETS OF THE SUBURA WERE BATHED IN A GHOSTLY SHEEN OF silver. The cook shops heaved with customers as usual and some local residents were leaning out of their windows, chatting loudly to neighbors across the street. Two young boys hung out of their fifth-floor home ambushing passers-by on the street below with gobbets of well-aimed phlegm and provoking howls of fury from their victims. But a warning glance was all that was needed to spare Lucrio similar treatment. The boys maintained a respectful silence and allowed the tall Lusitanian to pass by unscathed.

He wandered deeper into the neighborhood, turning this way and that until he came to a sign that read Mercury Street. Carefully avoiding the piles of excrement fouling the narrow avenue at regular intervals, he passed several brothels and a fuller's through whose open door he could see barefooted young boys with their tunics tucked into their loincloths stamping around in laundry vats full of watered urine. Above his head, drying linens hung from cords strung across the street, grey liquid leeching out of them and puttering the ground. A group of men were sitting in a doorway, playing a game of dice. Lucrio paused to exchange words with them and was directed toward the end of the street. He continued on his way, now counting the numbered tiles on the apartment blocks under his breath. As he muttered, "Twenty-one, twenty-two, twenty-three . . ." a grim premonition suddenly took hold of him and he stopped before the number "twenty-four" had left his lips.

He gazed for several minutes at the skeletal remains of the apartment block, resting on a small mountain of ash and rubble. He knew it for the same tower he had rescued the woman and her child from just days previously. There was bad scorching on the two adjacent buildings and the bitter tang of smoke still lingered in the air. Moonlight beamed through the vacant space, like ghostly sunlight through dark clouds, picking out jagged pieces of blackened timber and lead water pipes half-buried in the grey dust. Lucrio looked back toward the men playing dice, who were laughing at him and raising their drinking cups in ironic salute. A child's wooden doll lay at his feet, its rough woollen hair singed on one side. He bent down and picked it up, slowly moving its jointed arms and legs back and forth in reluctant fascination until he was distracted by a burst of coughing from a nearby doorway.

Lucrio crossed the street and hunkered down next to the old blind man, dropping a coin into the tin begging plate at his side. The wooden sign with the painted eye was propped up next to him, the curtain from his old alcove draped over him like a blanket.

"Thought I knew your voice," whispered the man. "Did you find your tribune?"

"Yes. But I'm looking for someone else now. A forger called Petro, the best in his trade so they say. I was told he lived at number twenty-four. But I see my timing is unfortunate."

The beggar nodded vaguely. "Yeah, yeah . . . he lived there. But the most you can hope to find of him now is his fingernails. So if he owes you money, forget it." He wheezed with laughter and took a swig from his jar.

"Did you know him?"

"Sure, sure, everyone knew Petro," muttered the old man. "Every-one knows everyone round here. In the same game, aren't we? Or we were til . . ." the man waved his hand wildly in front of his sightless, bluish eyes. "Not much call for a blind forger is there?" An insane cackle suddenly burst out of him. "More money in the fortune-telling business."

"But you're sure he's dead?" pressed Lucrio.

"Course he's dead," mumbled the man. "They're all dead. Some had to jump from the top floors. I heard them landing. Dead, dead, dead

. . . all dead and gone." The faint grey pupils of the man's eyes darted helplessly behind their sea-green veil as he began to wheeze and weep at the same time, and Lucrio withdrew quietly.

He was passing the fuller's once more when he heard himself being addressed by a sleepily caressing female voice.

"Well hello again Spaniard."

He turned and saw that he was being regarded by an alarmingly pale-faced woman. But as he looked closer, he realized that it was an effect created by a thick layer of lead-paint and that underneath was the dark-skinned woman from the apartment block fire. This time her curly hair was elaborately twisted and coiled about her head, and by the fact that she wore a man's toga over her flimsy, low-cut tunic, Lucrio understood what Hortensia had not in the taberna on the Aventine. Her mouth curved in a slight, challenging smile as she watched him.

"What do you want with Petro?" she asked.

Lucrio nodded. "I thought I might have been able to put some work his way. But I seem to be too late." Lucrio jerked his thumb toward the rubble of the apartment block.

The woman surveyed the Lusitanian for some time, apparently subjecting him to close scrutiny. "You can give me your message," she said at last in her languid drawl. "I'll see that it finds him."

Lucrio raised an eyebrow. "You know that he's alive then?"

The woman's smile deepened and she bared her brown teeth.

"Sure he's alive," she said in her strange, knowing voice. "Don't you know Petro? Petro doesn't burn."

After a moment's pause, Lucrio produced the note written earlier that day in Hortensia's hand.

"If you find him, tell him to come to the slaves' entrance of the address in that note and ask for Lucrio. It's urgent, so if you do know where he is . . ." He handed her the note along with a silver denarius also provided by Hortensia.

The painted woman examined the elegant writing on the thin slip of parchment, then tucked both it and the denarius inside the front of her tunic. "No problem, Lucrio. I'll tell him." She resumed her scrutiny from beneath heavily kohled eyelashes. "Anything else I can help you with?" she purred.

Lucrio shook his head with a slight smile of his own. "No," he replied simply, and with a last glance at the gently smoking pile of ashes where the tower had once stood, he turned back the way he had come and was soon lost in the shadows of Mercury Street.

XXVI

"**F**OR THE LOVE OF JUPITER, STOP FIDGETING, HORTENSIA."

Hortensia grimaced apologetically at her father and stopped playing with the crimson tassels on the litter drapes, instead leaning back so that she was shoulder to shoulder with her mother. She tried to resist the temptation to fiddle instead with the string of purple amethysts around her wrist, a wedding gift from her husband. They were rounding the spur of the Velia, halfway to the Carinae district atop the Esquiline Hill where Pompey lived. Hortensius and Caepio reclined opposite Hortensia and Lutatia, with Quintus forced to prop himself awkwardly on one elbow next to his mother. With so many other luxury vehicles making their way along the street, all of them carrying guests to the party, their progress was slow and Hortensia had plenty of time to wonder whether Lucrio's latest search of the Subura was bearing any fruit.

It had been three days since his hunt for the elusive forger began but there had been no reply to the note he had handed to the prostitute in Mercury Street. Hortensia was beginning to despair that Petro – whom Lucrio assured her was acknowledged by almost everyone he spoke to as the undisputed master of his craft – must indeed have perished in the apartment block inferno. She was under no illusion, particularly after Lucrio told her the identity of the condemned building's owner, that the fire could have been the work of anyone but Crassus. He and Tiberius were eliminating anyone who could tie them to the false will in the archive. Hortensia fretted that her time was running out and more than once was on the verge of blurting out the new information she had discovered to Caepio. But she knew what the outcome of that conversation must be and something still held her back from telling her father what she knew. In part it was because she suspected that he would angrily deny any knowledge of the affair and claim that it was all a fabrication on Lucrio's part – which would then of course lead to Lucrio's banishment. She needed proof that would clearly demonstrate Tiberius and Crassus's guilt and thus exonerate her father. Then there were the letters, the letters that could cause her father embarrassment . . . what could they be and how . . .

Hortensia gave a start as she heard Hortensius addressing her, feeling guilty at the trend of her thoughts.

"The Temple of Tellus, Hortensia, come on, just outside there, look – enlighten your brother as to the story behind it."

Quintus scowled and fired up. "I know all about Tellus! She's the goddess of mother earth, the Roman sister of Gaia. I don't need *her* to tell me."

"I would expect a six-year-old to know who Tellus is," replied Hortensius witheringly. "It is the story of the temple itself that I was asking your sister to explain to you."

Hortensia glanced at Quintus, whose jaw was now set like a rebellious bull. She wouldn't have been surprised to see wisps of smoke coming out of his nostrils. Feeling a pang of sympathy, she spoke with apologetic constraint.

"I'm sure Quintus has heard it before Papa. The temple is built on the site of Spurius Cassius's house. He was executed a few years after the fall of the Tarquins for trying to restore the monarchy and make himself king. The temple is about two hundred years old. It was built after an earthquake struck the city."

"Correct, and if you took your head out of those low-brow comedies you're always devouring, you might have been able to tell us the story too, Quintus," murmured Hortensius.

There was a short, uncomfortable silence, eventually broken by Caepio.

"I don't think I've ever seen so much traffic in this part of town," he observed conversationally. "That's Cato's litter I think, just up ahead of us. If we've gone past the Temple of Tellus we must be nearly there."

But such was the crush of vehicles that it was some time before they were eventually set down by the gate leading into Pompey's private gardens. There they joined the chattering throng filing into the property, the women like butterflies in brightly-colored gowns of every hue from sky blue and violet to crocus yellow and myrtle green, the men swathed in their best togas, purple stripes advertising their rank. Tiny lantern-lights sparkled in the trees around them and two rows of pine torches lit up the path ahead, along which purple-liveried slaves were stationed like a guard of honor, some bearing baskets of exotic fruits, others proffering trays of drinks – wine for the men, orange-scented water for the women. The doors of Pompey's villa had been thrown open, revealing a startling crimson color scheme and an atrium full of enormous, swirling murals beneath the blank-eyed death masks of Pompey's ancestors. A bank of flute players welcomed the new arrivals and beyond the atrium the central corridor of the house opened up into an enormous peristyle where jugglers and conjurors were entertaining a group of revelers, their spellbound faces lit up in childish delight. Pompey was standing in the atrium, greeting his guests alongside a plump woman whom Hortensia assumed must be his wife Mucia Tertia.

Pompey was quick to notice Hortensius's party arriving and, abandoning Mucia, he immediately made a beeline for them, his broad, broken face displaying every sign of pleasure.

"Hortensius, my old friend and defender," he boomed, slapping Hortensius on both shoulders. "Wonderful that you could make it, and your charming wife too" – he bowed formally to Lutatia, who smiled timidly in return. "You must forgive me being so remiss in not hosting you here sooner, madam, I've had so little time to entertain these past few years . . ." He spread his hands in the eloquently apologetic gesture of one who had been too busy winning Rome's wars to host dinner parties. "Who's this lad then, surely it can't be your son?" Pompey indicated incredulously to Quintus, who was even more tongue-tied than usual at being in the presence of one of his heroes.

"It seems impossible, doesn't it?" replied Hortensius sweetly. "But apparently true – or so I'm told."

"Well I'll be damned." He gave Quintus a friendly punch in the ribs. "Are you going to be a lawyer like your father, young man, or a soldier like me?"

Clutching the spot where Pompey had poked him, Quintus shot a quick glance at his father.

"A s-s-soldier I hope," he stammered half-eagerly, half-defiantly.

But Pompey had already lost interest in Quintus and had turned to Hortensia.

"No need to ask this young lady if she's going to be a lawyer or a soldier. I shouldn't be surprised if Hannibal himself were not foiled by her stratagems. A delight to see you again, my dear. I told you I would have you to dinner."

His restless gaze wandered to Caepio, who was looking faintly amused. Pompey's grin deepened.

"Ha! Servilius Caepio! How's that seductive sister of yours? I hope she may come tonight if her stick of a husband will let her off the leash. Speaking of sticks, your brother Cato's here somewhere too." His gaze flickered back toward Hortensia and he shook his head wonderingly. "It seems quite wrong to me. What do you mean by snapping up this little lady for yourself, completely out of your league. Were I not a married man . . ." Pompey roared with laughter and dug Hortensius in the ribs just as he had Quintus. "I am your daughter's greatest admirer, Hortensius. I make no secret of the fact."

Hortensius raised a faintly contemptuous eyebrow but to Hortensia's relief, made no remark in reply to this sally.

"Go, go and enjoy yourselves –" Pompey waved them magnanimously toward an open door off the atrium, leading into the garden. "– we're going to eat outside – they're just laying the food out. All very casual, no standing on ceremony at my house as you know. My wife Mucia will want to greet you all. I'd better go and rescue her from Crassus, he's giving her the full charm offensive."

Hortensia started at the mention of Crassus and turned around quickly to see his tall, sleek figure arching over Mucia Tertia like an obsequious willow tree, smothering her with the full impact of his all-embracing smile. Pompey rolled his eyes, winked conspiratorially at Hortensius's party and disappeared back into the throng.

They wandered outside as instructed and were soon joined by Caecilius and Claudia. The latter wanted nothing more than to engage Lutatia and Hortensia in a gossipy appraisal of the fashions worn by all the women present.

"Will you look at that necklace Tertulla is wearing, Crassus must have paid a fortune for it, I don't think I've ever seen larger pearls . . . Oh, there's your sister-in-law Servilia, my dear, I do wish someone would tell her that shade of yellow is really not the thing, such a vulgar color. How lovely our hostess looks, though with her figure I can't help but feel a less voluminous choice of material would have been wise . . . Well, well, so *she's* here – Clodia Pulcher, look, she's pregnant you know, though the rumor is the father *isn't* her husband . . ."

Since Hortensius, Caecilius and Caepio soon began discussing political affairs, this split of the conversation left Quintus standing on his own, and after several minutes spent staring, sulkily scuffing the grass with his sandals, he soon wandered off in the direction of the peristyle, ignoring the concerned enquiry of his mother.

Hortensia soon felt equally bored, and though she maintained an expression of polite attention as Claudia continued her commentary, her ear was soon caught by snippets of what her father and his colleagues were saying. ". . . Another raid on the Appian Way yesterday . . . one of them's got to get a grip on the situation . . . coming to something when pirates think they can dictate to Rome . . ." She listened with mild interest, letting her eye wander around the gardens on the pretext of joining in with Claudia's observations.

The majority of those present were from her own family's social set and Hortensia recognized several people she knew. There was her brother-in-law Cato, looking severe as he sipped abstemiously from an elaborate goblet and who soon came over to join the circle around Hortensius. Over by a fish-pond in the middle of the *ambulatio*, a separate court had formed around Crassus. Hortensia saw him nod in the direction of her party and say something which made those around him roar with laughter. She fumed silently, guessing it was a joke at her father's expense. A few other knowing smirks as they arrived had already brought it home to her that her father's impending loss to Cicero was being much enjoyed as a topic of gossip. Her brooding thoughts were then interrupted by her mother, who took advantage of a lull in Claudia's monologue to ask Hortensia anxiously if she would go and see that her brother was all right.

"He doesn't know anyone here, I'm worried about him going off by himself."

"You shouldn't fuss so much over him, Mama, he's probably just gone to watch the acrobats. Besides, he does know people. If Servilia is here then Brutus must be too, they're not so far apart in age. Brutus will look after him."

Lutatia looked doubtful. "Quintus gets into such a rage sometimes. I do wish . . ."

But she had lost her audience. Hortensia's attention had been caught by a sudden change in atmosphere among the group of men alongside them. They were muttering and glancing surreptitiously toward the villa, while Cato had his head bent toward his brother and was issuing some apparently urgent instruction. "I think he means to approach us," she heard Caepio say in apparent surprise.

"He has a nerve if he does," Caecilius growled.

"Calm yourself, Caecilius," came Hortensius' urbane reply. "It is a party after all. Old Chickpea probably feels he has a duty to mingle."

Hortensia glanced around and to her astonishment realized that none other than Cicero and his wife Terentia were making their way through the chattering crowd in their direction, attracting a great deal of notice as they went.

Although he had been pointed out to her in the forum, this was the first time Hortensia had ever seen her father's adversary up close. He was extremely tall, with at least a head's advantage on Hortensius, and his pale, angular face was dominated by intense black eyes. Though not yet forty, his close-cropped hair was already graying at the temples, but there was a restless energy about him, quite different from her father's magnificent air of unruffled insouciance. They came to a halt in front of Hortensius's party and for a moment nobody said anything. Hortensius's blue eyes glittered and a strange little smile tugged at his lips, but he made no attempt to break the tense hush and as usual the task of peace broker fell to Caepio.

"A very good evening to you both," he nodded. "Wonderful night isn't it?"

"Good evening indeed, gentlemen. And ladies," Cicero added, nodding to Claudia, Hortensia and Lutatia, who kept glancing nervously at her husband.

"Are you enjoying the party?" persisted Caepio, realizing that no one else was going to come to his aid.

Cicero shrugged. "Terentia enjoys these affairs more than I do. Personally I would have preferred to spend the evening at home but we live close by so we can always leave early. I have another busy day in court tomorrow."

Hortensia was incensed by this provocative allusion to the ongoing trial, and glanced at her father, who was still wearing a seemingly relaxed smile. But out of the corner of her eye she could just discern the twitchy movement of his fingers by his side, twisting and tugging at a fold of his clothing in that way which advertised to all who knew him that he was not as calm as he looked. She wished he would say something, come up with one of his characteristically acerbic set-downs and put Cicero in his place.

She felt Caepio take her hand in his and was momentarily reassured.

"You must allow me to present my wife Hortensia. I don't believe you have met."

Hortensia could hear the warning note that she knew was meant only for her and she bit her lip, suppressing her first instinct to snatch her hand back from her husband. She returned Cicero's nod with an infinitesimal one of her own, aware that a great many eyes were focused on their party.

"A great pleasure," said Cicero. His voice, Hortensia reluctantly owned, was compelling – strong and smooth, but with a slight rasp which she could imagine him using to great rhetorical effect in the law court. "Allow me in turn to present my wife Terentia."

He gestured casually toward the woman next to him and there was nothing for it but to go through the formalities of greeting once more. Terentia tilted her head and peered at Hortensia with disconcerting curiosity. Despite her small stature, she had a presence about her and a strong, characterful face. Looking at her up close, Hortensia was reminded of someone, but could not think who.

"Yes, I should have called on you after your marriage," she said in a forthright, matter-of-fact voice. "You'll have to forgive me for not doing so. It all seemed rather awkward." It was difficult to tell whether Terentia meant the remark maliciously or not. But she carried on in apparent disregard of the perilous social terrain into which she was plunging. "You are not quite as I expected. I was told you take after your father in a number of ways, and you have his coloring certainly. But the cast of your features is more your mother's."

She turned to Lutatia, who looked mortified at suddenly becoming the center of attention. "I haven't seen you in some time, tell me, are you well?"

"Quite well, I thank you," stammered Lutatia.

"You must be very proud of your daughter. She is an excellent advocate, or so I am told. My husband will have to watch his back."

Cicero looked rather amused and not a little disdainful at this suggestion but Hortensia was taken aback. Terentia smiled knowingly at her.

"I have my sources, you see."

She leant on her husband's arm in a clear signal that they should take their leave, and they sauntered on to join another group of partygoers, leaving a pregnant silence in their wake. Claudia was the first to break it.

"Awful woman," she expostulated. "Terrible dress."

Caecilius looked both cross and confused. "What did she mean at the end there? Excellent advocate? What on earth was she talking about? Hortensius?"

Caepio glanced first at Hortensia, who seemed in no mood to speak, then at Hortensius, who also said nothing. He answered for both as diplomatically as he could.

"You have not then heard about Hortensia's great success? She was kind enough to speak on behalf of a lady married to one of my dependents, in the family court a few days ago. She acquitted herself quite splendidly and the judgment came down in her favor."

A cloud of disapproval descended over Cato's austere features and Caecilius looked thunderstruck.

"I warned you Hortensius, where all this would end," intoned Caecilius, shaking his head. "Declamations, rhetoric training . . . it is no education for a girl and so I told you."

Cato cleared his throat. "Far be it from me to pass judgment myself but I confess I am surprised at you, Caepio. She will be talked about in the same breath as that harpy Afrania."

"Nonsense, I'm very proud of her," replied Caepio bracingly before adding, "Besides, it's unlikely to happen again." Everyone looked at Hortensius.

"Shall we go and eat?" he suggested with a bland smile and strolled off toward the stretch of grass outside the portico where clusters of tables had now been laid out, with large cushions and low couches arranged around them. After a moment's hesitation, Claudia seconded this proposal with great alacrity, scolding Caecilius and Caepio for dawdling so long with their own companions, and propelling them toward the dining area, all the while talking at the top of her voice and managing to greet any number of people as she went.

They took up their places on a group of couches which had been thoughtfully draped with blankets for the warmth and comfort of the guests, and were brought a succession of courses including peppered mushrooms, peacocks' eggs, spit-roasted boar, thrushes with honey, ham with figs and bay leaves and finishing with a fricassée of roses and sweet-wine cakes. Children darted around from table to table, vying for the attention of the adults or retreating in groups to play catch with a harpastum ball in the surrounding gardens. Pompey occupied a huge couch of his own at the central table and his loud, booming laugh echoed over the happily buzzing throng and the gentle accompaniment of the lyre players. As the sweet course was served, he clapped his hands and a troupe of Hispanian musicians appeared, a triumphalist allusion to the conquest that his upcoming games would celebrate.

Listening to the high, echoing call of the Hispanian players' pipes, Hortensia briefly thought of Lucrio and a vision came into her mind. A long road stretching as far as the eye could see across a rust-red landscape, shimmering with the dust kicked up by passing legions of Roman soldiers. A small farm-worker's cottage, surrounded by grazing goats and roughly marked-out patches of dark brown earth. A mother and father with their two small boys, standing respectfully to attention as the invading army passed by. For a moment, Hortensia felt confused. Why should she not do as her husband advised and leave these men to their games of war? Rome was not the beacon of prosperity and peace to its empire that she had once believed it to be. Did it really matter who governed it? What – or who – was she trying to protect? She glanced at her father, who was smiling at something Caepio had said to him.

Then she saw Marcus Licinius Crassus, seated at the table next to Pompey's. He was diverting some of the younger guests by making silver denarii disappear and reappear out of his sleeve before bestowing the coins on the children, who of course begged him to perform the trick again and again and called over their parents and friends to watch. A lock of his oil-sleek hair flopped over his face but he didn't notice, so intent was the look of greedy pleasure on his wine-flushed cheeks.

Hortensia made her resolution. Petro or no Petro, she had to warn Pompey that there was a plot against him. To let a man like Crassus win was unthinkable and she had to protect her father too. She would not betray Cornelia's confidence and risk reprisals for the Vestals, nor would she mention the involvement of Crassus – that would be to throw fat on the fire when she still did not really know the nature of the plot which might not succeed in any case. But she would put Pompey on his guard, encourage him to take care with his safety, perhaps increase his personal bodyguard. He seemed to have taken a liking to her and perhaps that would help her word carry more weight.

Resolved in this decision, Hortensia waited hopefully for an opportunity and was rewarded toward the end of the evening when Pompey came over to their table and sat down on the couch next to her. She had a shrewd suspicion that he had timed his moment, since Caepio, Hortensius, Cato and Caecilius had all got up from the table and joined a group of senators in the far corner of the garden. Claudia was gossiping with friends nearby and the only people still reclining around the remnants of the feast were Hortensia and her mother, who was fretting about Quintus. He had made a brief appearance at dinner but disappeared during the main courses and Lutatia was wondering aloud to Hortensia whether she ought to go and look for him.

"Enjoying yourselves I hope?" asked Pompey enthusiastically as he sank heavily on to the blanketed couch, leaning over to scoop a handful of nuts from a bowl and popping them rapidly into his mouth one by one.

"Hugely, thank you, sir," smiled Hortensia.

"Ah well, I can't take too much of the credit," said Pompey, looking gratified all the same. "Mucia handles this sort of thing. But I'm glad if you're pleased with it. Nice to see so many families here. I'm always telling Crassus, that's what Rome's all about – family. We should get a little portrait done and put it on the coins." He laughed uproariously.

Lutatia spoke up. "Are your own children here somewhere, sir?"

"Oh yes, yes I expect so. They're still pups you know, barely out of short tunics. Ah, see, there's little Pompeia over there, clinging to her mother's skirts. My boy Gnaeus has just turned five, he'll be tearing around somewhere, takes after his Papa."

Lutatia sighed. "I wish the same were true of Quintus. Hortensia, you wouldn't ask Caepio to have a quick look for him, would you?"

Pompey's face brightened.

"Better than that, I can tell you just where to find him, madam. He's over by the balustrade, saw him there myself a moment ago. Here." He snapped his fingers and a slave came running over. "Faro here will show you. Do go, you get one of the best views over the city from that part of the garden. I insist on you seeing it and then you can bring the boy back and we can talk more about those soldiering ambitions of his."

Lutatia looked doubtful glancing at Hortensia, but Pompey winked and gave a little salute.

"You may leave her safely in my care, madam, fear not. My wife will play chaperone. She's like a dragon with a hundred eyes, believe me." He gestured with his thumb toward the neighboring couch where Mucia Tertia formed one of the group which Claudia had joined.

"Do go, Mama," encouraged Hortensia. "Quintus would be so disappointed to think he had missed an audience with the general."

After some more anxious indecision, Lutatia allowed herself to be led away by Pompey's slave. Pompey turned back to Hortensia and gave a comical roll of his eyes.

"You're not really that pasty-faced boy's sister, are you?"

Hortensia couldn't help but laugh though she tried to be reproving in her reply. "That is indeed my brother, sir, and I'll thank you not to insult him. He's a great admirer of *yours* and has studied all of your campaigns – he'd very much like to emulate you."

"Impossible. Never seen such skinny knees on a boy. Reminds me of a pet chicken I had when I was a nipper."

Hortensia looked around to make sure that no one was standing behind them and then lowered her voice.

"These pleasantries about my brother aside, I am glad to have a moment to talk with you, sir. I have heard something . . . a whisper only . . . but I feel honor bound to inform you of it."

Pompey raised his brows in surprise.

"This is a city of rumors, sir, as you well know, but one has reached me which I hope you will take seriously. You must forgive me if I do not reveal my sources, but I have received word that there may be a conspiracy against you. I wish I could give you more information and indeed I don't know exactly what is being planned, but I am anxious on your behalf sir and I can only urge that you have a care to the possible danger."

She expected Pompey to be intrigued at the very least and was prepared for him to press for more information, even to become angry and defensive. But instead he waited for her to finish, and then chuckled.

"I am indeed in danger, my dear. Great danger, from an assassin sitting right next to me on this couch."

Hortensia was bewildered. "What do you mean?"

"Don't you know you could fell a man with one dart from those eyes?" he asked solemnly.

Hortensia set her teeth. "I am quite serious, sir, and if you do not believe me –"

"Oh I believe you, my dear, I believe you," Pompey waved a hand in lazy dismissal, "and I don't doubt that you are serious. In fact your concern does you credit and I applaud the feminine sensibilities which are no doubt making you so anxious. But if I had a denarius for every time someone warned me that my number was up, I'd be richer than Crassus over there – and that's saying something."

"I don't think you should dismiss this so slightly, sir," she persisted. "My sources are very credible."

"And just who *are* these credible sources of yours, my dear?" he asked in a tone of mock seriousness.

"People I trust, sir," she said with dignity, "and I wish you would too. Promise me that you will at least pay some heed to my warning."

"How could any man refuse to promise you anything?" teased Pompey.

But Hortensia did not smile. She was annoyed, and also uncomfortably aware that a few people were now glancing in their direction.

Despite Pompey's reassurances, she knew that Mucia's presence was not enough to mask the impropriety of being seen in such intimate conversation with the consul and she made her excuses, claiming that she wished to help her mother find Quintus.

"Oh, don't coddle the boy. Tell me, shall I see you at my games? I'm going down to my villa at Albano tomorrow but I'll be back on the Ides. Promise me you'll come?"

He reached out and tried to squeeze her hand, which Hortensia disengaged as quickly as she could. Mumbling her excuses, she wrapped her rich plum-colored mantle around her shoulders and began to weave round the groups of party-goers sprawled out across the gardens, many of them now in a deeply mellow mood from the fine Pucine wine served with dinner.

She found her progress checked almost immediately by Publius Dolabella, who was passing in the other direction, accompanied by another man. He had seen her too and for a moment she thought he was going to cut her dead and carry on walking. But at the last moment he forced his patrician features into a smile.

"My dear Hortensia. A pleasure to see you. And in great beauty as always."

"You are too kind, Publius," Hortensia answered evenly.

He gestured to the older man alongside him, a tall, slim individual with a round face, thinning hair and very dark eyes. "Allow me to present to you my patron – Gaius Julius Caesar, a close friend of our host. Julius, do you know Hortensia, wife of Servilius Caepio?"

"Of course. The famous advocate," answered Publius's companion slowly, raising his glass in wry acknowledgement. "I know all about you."

There was something a little sly in his tone and Hortensia resented it. "*I know a little about you too,*" she thought grimly, thinking of his signature on Pompey's will. An awkward silence descended. Publius looked discomfited at having his humiliating courtroom defeat alluded to by his patron but still he hovered uncertainly, despite being given no encouragement to linger.

"Your family are well, I trust?" he persevered. "Your father is in good health?"

Hortensia was about to return a cool answer and move on when she was startled by an interruption from someone standing just behind her.

"You always did have such lamentable tact, Publius. What a clumsy thing to say to the girl. No wonder she wouldn't marry you."

Tiberius Dolabella loomed over Hortensia's shoulder, his eyes bright and keen like a satyr's, his lower lip slightly stained with wine. He smiled down at her. "Charming to see you again, my dear," before adding loudly for the benefit of his nephew's companion, "I recently had the good fortune of restoring an errant slave to this young lady you see, Julius. Poor fellow became a little disorientated during a nighttime adventure. Well, we've all been there, haven't we?" The wolfish smile reappeared.

Hortensia didn't bother to keep the disdain out of her voice. "Forgive me for not staying to hear more of your edifying conversation, gentlemen, but I am on an important errand for my mother."

Julius nodded and Publius bowed, a touch of embarrassment in his manner, but Tiberius suffered no such discomfort, and as Hortensia swiftly detached herself and began to stride toward the balustrade he accompanied her for a few steps, keeping up easily as she attempted to outpace him.

"That must have been quite an interesting encounter you had a little earlier," he murmured.

Hortensia could feel her pulse surge and her cheeks growing hot.

"I don't know what you're talking about and I wish you would leave me alone, sir," she snapped, hoping that the bite in her voice would disguise the consternation that she felt. "It can't have escaped your notice that I don't welcome your company."

Tiberius smiled, showing his thin, crooked teeth. "Your father and Cicero of course. I must admit, I would dearly love to have been within earshot."

Hortensia relaxed a little, reminding herself that Tiberius had no idea of her knowledge of the conspiracy, but her brow darkened all the same. "It's unlikely you would have the opportunity," she threw at him haughtily. "My father is very particular about the company he keeps."

Tiberius laughed. "Though not so particular about his clients in court. Tell me, is it true that Verres has already gone into exile? I hope your father is not feeling the disgrace too deeply."

Hortensia stopped dead and turned to confront him. Her eyes flashed and her hands clenched into balled fists. "My father will *crush* Cicero at their next meeting," she announced in a quaking voice. "Then the whole of Rome will know who is the greatest orator of them all."

Her rich voice had carried over the hum of the Hispanian musicians, silencing the conversation of several nearby groups of guests, and a number of curious stares were directed at her. People began to whisper and Hortensia felt her cheeks glow hot again.

"I would never dare contradict you, my dear," replied Tiberius softly. "Tell me, do you enjoy Pompey's company? He certainly seems to enjoy yours. It's something I've always found remarkable about him – his total lack of shame about pissing in other men's territory. By the way, my dear, a piece of fatherly advice. It might not be wise in the future to let yourself be seen in a taberna on the Aventine in the company of a male slave. Tongues will wag, you know. You wouldn't want to hurt your father's reputation even more."

Hortensia opened her mouth to utter another retort when she heard a light tread behind them and spun round to find her father standing just behind her, silver wine-cup in hand.

"Hortensius. I was just telling your daughter how much we all admire the way you are handling your current difficulties in court."

Hortensius took a sip from his cup, regarding Tiberius thoughtfully over the top of it. Hortensia took advantage of the pregnant silence.

"I'm going to find Quintus," she muttered. "Mama is worried about him."

She walked away quickly, wrapping her mantle closer about her.

"A charming young lady, your daughter," said Tiberius admiringly, watching Hortensia's retreat. "I remember thinking so when I first saw her. She's obviously very proud of her Papa too. As any daughter of the great Hortensius, king of the law court, would be."

He raised his own cup in tribute. Hortensius spoke softly

"Perhaps I should make something clear to you, Tiberius. If you ever attempt to speak to my daughter again, I will see to it that that scar is the least ugly thing about you."

Tiberius's smile faltered for a moment, but then it returned.

"I can understand your anxiety. After all, it's extraordinary what secrets one can let slip after a few cups of wine, isn't it?"

He nodded and rejoined the group surrounding Crassus.

* * *

Feeling enraged and on the verge of tears, Hortensia made her way over to the edge of the estate where a low marble balustrade formed an ornamental boundary wall. As she drew closer, she saw a crowd of children gathered around a conjuror, their eyes lit up in wonder as he made a small ball disappear from underneath one inverted cup and reappear under another in the row of three. Every time they tried to guess which one the ball was under, their guess was wrong, much to their delight. Hortensia began to walk along the balustrade a little, trying to calm her breathing and letting the evening breeze cool her face. Pompey had been right about the view at least, which afforded her a rare perspective on her home up on the Palatine, with the pulsing hub of the forum just below. On the summit of the Capitoline hill above the senate house, she could see where, under the supervision of her uncle Catulus, they were rebuilding the great temple of Jupiter – like a vast white bird looming over the heart of the city.

She was about to walk back in the direction of the main party when she caught sight of Quintus standing in a small courtyard, throwing a harpastum ball against the villa wall. As Hortensia came closer, she realized that he was trying to hit a particular spot on the brickwork, cursing loudly every time he failed.

"Mama is looking for you," she announced without preamble.

"I saw her. She can keep looking. If I needed a nursemaid, we could have brought Elpidia," replied Quintus, continuing to fling the leather ball savagely at the wall, letting it fall to the ground and then picking it up to try again.

"You shouldn't keep doing that, you're leaving a mark," Hortensia said reprovingly. "This isn't our house and if you cause any damage, Papa will have to pay for it."

"What a hardship for him. What a terrible setback. Now he'll never be as rich as Marcus Crassus."

Hortensia resented the sarcasm in her brother's response.

"I don't see why you would say something so horrid. Papa is wealthy, that's true, but he isn't interested in money. To compare him to someone like Marcus Crassus is terribly disloyal of you."

Quintus snorted, punctuating the sound with a particularly vicious throw of the harpastum ball. "You think you're so clever, especially now that you're married. But you don't know anything."

"I know a great deal more than you as it happens," Hortensia replied loftily. "All you have ever been interested in is blood and battles. It is quite childish." She saw that Quintus was about to flare up and continued in a more conciliating tone. "I know that Papa has not always been kind to you. I'm not so unfeeling a sister that I haven't noticed it. But he really has tried his hardest to help you learn. It's neither his fault nor yours that you don't have an aptitude for the things he can teach you."

This time Quintus did not pick up the ball from where it had fallen.

"So Papa isn't interested in money, is he? Then tell me, darling sister, *enlighten* me in your wisdom – why do you think he defends the likes of Gaius Verres? Why do you think he married Mama for that matter?"

"He defended Verres as a favor to Caecilius, and Mama came from an excellent family, just like Papa's," replied Hortensia, trying to remain dignified, but she was unsettled by the hatred suffusing Quintus's sallow face.

"Mama came from a *wealthy* family," he spat. "Papa married her to get his hands on her money and don't think he won't cast her aside as soon as he wants more. He makes out that he's a noble advocate and that the law is the only honorable calling. But he's a fraud. He'd sell Rome to the highest bidder if the price was right," he concluded with bitter relish.

"How dare you?" spluttered Hortensia, momentarily about to revert to her childhood self and lunge at Quintus to claw at his face.

"It's true." Quintus knew he had the upper hand now and having stooped to pick up the harpastum ball, was tossing it in the air with irritating nonchalance. "He defended Verres for the money. All that rubbish about how an advocate can't accept payment, who do you think gave him that sphinx in his study, which is probably worth about fifty thousand sesterces? Verres did. Payment for making sure Papa did whatever it took to win."

"But Papa's losing! So there goes your argument, doesn't it?"

Now Quintus came closer to Hortensia. The light from the moon cast an almost ghoulish look across his already pale face. His voice was low and taunting.

"Have you never wondered how Papa lives the way he does? How he pays for the paintings, the houses, his wine collection, his precious library? Think hard, darling sister, use that famous brain of yours. No? Well I'll tell you. By taking anything he can get from those crooks and thieves he calls his clients. Did you honestly think he wins all his cases because he's the greatest orator in Rome?" Quintus gave a hysterical squawk of laughter. "Bribery and corruption, dear sister. Our Papa's a cheat and a liar."

"I don't believe you," whispered Hortensia. "You'll never make me believe you."

"No? Then explain why I found a letter hidden under the rug in his study, from one of his clients, thanking him for getting him acquitted and promising final payment soon. It's all there, praise for Papa's brilliance, how clever he was to forge the evidence and pay off the judge. Go and look for yourself if you want. But Cicero's wise to Papa's little tricks, isn't he? He's outwitted Papa, and now *he's* the king of the law court. Everyone knows it, everyone's glad about it. And do you know what, my dear sister? *I'm glad too.*"

He leaned in to make sure his words had hit home, then stepped back, a satisfied smile on his face.

"Not so unlike Marcus Crassus after all, is he?" he crooned, before sauntering back toward the lights of the party, throwing and catching the ball as he went.

XXVII

HE COULDN'T SEE THEIR FACES, ONLY TWIN OUTLINES LOOMING OVER her, silhouetted against the evening sky. Something was falling on her face, dry and light like a shower of tiny spiders. Her feet felt strangely heavy, she couldn't lift them, and her arms were pinioned to her sides. She tried to speak but when she opened her mouth, she tasted dirt seeping into her mouth. Coughing and spitting, she choked out a cry for help but the men were so far above her and the patch of light around their heads was growing dimmer and dimmer. Now the falling soil was in her eyes. Her lashes and lids flickered desperately against the deluge and a scream built in her throat, but it was stoppered by clumps of wet mud. As the blackness enveloped her, there was a drumming in her ears, whether from the sound of her heart desperately trying to keep her alive or the noise of mud and stones raining down on her prostrate body.

Hortensia woke up and realized that the drumming in her ears was actually the sound of someone tapping very gently on the door. She blinked rapidly as she came back to consciousness, feeling waves of heat ripple across her sweat-drenched skin. The tapping continued and she managed to swing her legs round to the floor, wrapping her thick mantle around her shoulders before treading gingerly over to the door and opening it a crack. Lucrio was standing there. He spoke very quietly.

"I'm sorry to wake you, *domina*. But you have a visitor."

Hortensia stared at him uncomprehendingly for a moment. Then her eyes widened.

"It's really him?" she mouthed.

Lucrio nodded and Hortensia slipped out into the corridor, tip-toeing past Caepio's room next door. They arrived in the atrium, which was in darkness apart from a single moonbeam pouring through the skylight. A slight figure was sitting on one of the chairs and as he got up and came forward into the silver light, Hortensia saw that he was young and dark-skinned with a silver hoop in one ear.

"Petro?" she whispered. He nodded, a crooked little smile plucking at the corner of his mouth, and she beckoned for him to follow her into her private salon. Lucrio came too and shut the door behind him. A lamp burning in the corner cast flickering shadows around the room.

"You received my message then?" Hortensia asked. "I'm glad to see you escaped the fire. We didn't know what to think when Lucrio discovered the remains of your tower block."

The forger grinned at her and held up his forearms to the light from the lamp, as if inviting her to inspect them.

"Petro doesn't burn," he intoned. He spoke with a slightly slurred Punic accent, placing a strange stress on shorter syllables.

"You must know my name from the message I left. I'm very grateful to you for answering it. I've invited you here because I'd like to ask you a few questions about a man I think you may know – Marcus Licinius Crassus – and some work you may have done for him."

Petro eyed Hortensia appraisingly for a moment but did not respond. Instead he began to walk slowly around the room, looking up at the shelves of literature and lifting a hand to toy with some of the labels, turning them over to read the contents. Hortensia's eyes were drawn to his forger's fingertips, which were pinched and wrinkled as though they had been resting in water.

"Good collection," he said approvingly. "Demosthenes . . . Euripides. That's from Sabinus's workshop. Single-roll Livius Andronicus – those aren't easy to find. Must have cost you." He flicked another speculative glance at her.

"Petro, I think that the work you did for Crassus almost got you killed in that fire." Hortensia waited for a reaction and didn't get one. "Don't you think so too?"

"Maybe so, maybe not so," drawled Petro, still inspecting the rolls on the shelves.

"Then wouldn't you like to get revenge?" she pressed. "Because the best way would be to tell me what you did for him. I can make good use of the information. He's no more my friend than yours."

Still Petro contemplated the shelves, seemingly uninterested in what she was saying.

"Look at this," he said reverentially, extracting one of the larger rolls from its compartment. "Mago's *De Agri Cultura*. Twenty-eight books, single roll. Hieratic papyrus, middle of the plant. Cedar oil finish. A beautiful piece." He turned to Hortensia and grinned broadly.

Hortensia was exasperated. "I don't understand why you came here if you weren't willing to talk to me."

Petro did not seem the slightest bit abashed nor did his grin slacken.

"I can see you're a little new to the game. Everything's got a price in this city. Even revenge."

Lucrio took a step forward but Hortensia put up a hand to check him.

"I understand. You want payment. I don't have much money about me but I can get you some – though I won't be held to ransom," she added.

Petro eyed her quizzically then turned back in reverential contemplation of the roll resting in his hands. "A beautiful piece," he repeated. Hortensia glanced at it and at last she understood.

"It's yours," she said quickly.

Petro seemed delighted. He tucked the roll carefully inside his tunic before seating himself nonchalantly on a small couch.

"Petro's listening," he said grandly.

"I think that Marcus Crassus asked you to forge a will for him. Am I right?" asked Hortensia bluntly.

Petro put one finger to his lips. "A will. A will . . . let me think now . . ." He appeared to deliberate for some time, then withdrew a small, crumpled piece of saffron-colored papyrus from inside his tunic and offered it to Hortensia.

"What's this?" she asked, taking it from him.

Petro smiled and laced his fingers behind his head. "Read it," he invited.

Hortensia stared at him then unfolded the note with trembling hands. There were several lines of writing there, in a hand she vaguely recognized, inscribed in red ink.

"*To the Senate and People of Rome,*" it began. Hortensia's breath quickened and she began to read a little louder.

"*It is my wish that in the event of my death during the period of my consulship, Rome should be spared another civil war of the kind that has done such damage to our Republic in recent years. Therefore, for the sake of our people and in the exceptional circumstances I have specified, I urge the Senate to do as it has done in the past during times of crisis and confirm my co-consul, Marcus Licinius Crassus . . .*"

She stopped. Lucrio waited but it was Petro who finished the sentence for her, speaking in a slow, mockingly pompous tone.

"*. . . as sole consul and dictator of Rome for such time as is necessary to secure peace and prosperity for the Republic.*"

Hortensia stared at the sentence Petro had just spoken aloud. "*As dictator of Rome . . .*"

She read it again and again then sank down on to the couch behind her, staring with unseeing eyes at the words in front of her.

"What is this?" she asked incredulously. She looked up to find Petro watching her with an anticipatory smile.

"That's what they told me to write at the end. Keep everything else the same, they said – estates, bequests, legacies and the rest of it. Just add that on and make it look neat. Then burn the note. But that meathead they sent to watch me do the job wouldn't know one piece of papyrus from another. Petro likes a little insurance. Helps persuade people to pay on time. Marcus Crassus didn't pay on time." He laughed gleefully. "Tried to get rid of Petro instead. But Petro doesn't burn . . ."

Hortensia's eyes moved down to the next sentence and she read on in a half-whisper.

"*I urge all members of the Senate to unite behind this proposal which I know will be supported by all patriotic citizens of Rome . . .*"

Hortensia's voice tailed off, and she finally looked up at Lucrio and Petro and shook her head in bewilderment.

"I don't understand. How can Crassus expect this to convince the Senate? Everyone knows how much he and Pompey hate each other; the idea that Pompey would willingly cede power to Crassus like this is inconceivable."

Petro shook his head, evidently enjoying her reaction.

"Petro's no politician. Petro's just the messenger."

Lucrio spoke up. "What does it mean by '*as it has done in the past*'?"

Hortensia fidgeted distractedly with the document in her hands.

"There *have* been occasions when certain men have been given such powers temporarily by the Senate," she admitted. "Cincinnatus – twice of course – when Rome was under attack from the rest of Italy. Fabius Maximus, during the invasion of Hannibal. But those were exceptional circumstances, times of crisis, not the result of one consul dying."

"But if Pompey did die . . . wouldn't that be seen as a time of crisis?"

Hortensia stared at him, a deep furrow in her brow. Yes, the death of so popular a consul could trigger terrible upheavals. But wouldn't that work against Crassus? It was possible if it weren't for the fact that there were plenty of senators who might well be glad of Pompey's removal. Who was to say that Crassus hadn't already bought the support of key members, just as he obviously had some of the witnesses to the will? The general populace might rage and riot, but perhaps that would be to Crassus's advantage, enabling him to persuade his fellow aristocrats that a period of strong, decisive government was needed to soothe the troubled waters. Some liberal redistribution of Crassus's sizeable fortune would no doubt persuade dissenting members of both patrician and plebeian camps. Hortensia's grip on the document in her hand tightened in anger. She could just imagine the form that Crassus's persuasion would take – games, public handouts of grain and money, hypocritical posthumous tributes to Pompey.

There was still the matter of the will itself and Hortensia clung hard to the belief that no one could seriously be persuaded of its authenticity, no matter how good a forger Petro was. But after much thought, she was forced to acknowledge, however reluctantly, that it would be a brave senator who accused a man of Crassus's power and influence of breaching the sacrosanctity of the Temple of Vesta, particularly if the priestesses themselves had not reported a theft. Moreover, if the witnesses to the will were willing to verify that the contents reflected Pompey's true wishes, then the skeptics would be forced to keep their insinuations to themselves.

"Ugly game isn't it?" Petro interrupted Hortensia's thoughts. She stared accusingly at him.

"Why didn't you take this to someone? Didn't you realize what it meant?"

"Like I told you. Petro's no politician," he repeated. "Doesn't matter to me who sits at the top of this dungpile."

Hortensia said nothing at first.

"There's something else I have to know."

Petro tilted his head to one side.

"The other men named in the will, the seven witnesses. Did you ever have any dealings with any of them?"

A knowing smile appeared in Petro's eyes.

"You mean did they know what was going on?"

Hortensia nodded, her eyes fixed on him.

"Hmm. Well, I'd only be guessing . . . but I'd say maybe at least *one* of them didn't want to play the game."

"Which one? How do you know?" she asked eagerly.

"Got me to write a suicide note from one of them. Old man's writing, real small and shaky, took an artist like me to get it right."

"Lucilius Albinus?"

"That's the one. I guess the writing was on the wall for him." Petro laughed.

"What about the others?" Her desperation was palpable and Petro seemed to enjoy toying with her.

"Well, now I come to think of it . . . there was at least one more I reckon they weren't sure if they could count on. Which one was it now . . .?"

"Hortensius Hortalus?" came the whispered enquiry.

"That's the one. Should have thought of it, his name being so similar to yours." Petro beamed innocently.

"But how do you know? How do you know he wasn't involved?" she asked eagerly.

"Well, I don't *know* of course. But it seemed to me a possibility when they asked me to write some letters addressed to this . . . Hortensius, was it? Quite a few of them, if I recall."

Hortensia's brow was furrowed.

"I don't understand. You wrote to my father?"

Petro laughed.

"Well, in a manner of speaking. Sort of thing that would be embarrassing to a man, if you get my meaning."

Hortensia stared at him.

"The letter! The letter Quintus saw!" She almost grabbed Petro by the arm. "The one from his client, the one where he talked about how Papa fabricated evidence and bribed the judge! That was you? It was just a forgery all along?"

Petro's smile widened. Hortensia closed her eyes and slowly let out the breath she had been holding. She glanced over at Lucrio.

"Didn't I tell you?" she said triumphantly. "If only Quintus were here! Tiberius gave Papa one of the letters, to scare him into thinking there was going to be a scandal and persuade him not to say anything when they eventually killed Pompey. Papa must have known the letter was a forgery but he was worried about what it would do to his reputation, the family's reputation, you were right, Lucrio! That must have been why he was so preoccupied when we were at Laurentum . . . I knew there was something not right with him . . . oh poor Papa, what he must have been going through . . ." She broke off, now brooding deep in thought.

"What do you want to do now, *domina*?" Lucrio asked in a low voice.

Hortensia stood up and paced around the room. At last she shook her head in frustration.

"We're no better off than we were before. This," she held up the saffron-yellow scrap between finger and thumb, "counts for nothing. Petro's evidence carries about as much weight as yours does. Who's to say he wouldn't be accused of forging this?"

"There may be a solution."

"What?"

"You let me do what I came to the city to do in the first place."

She stopped pacing. "No."

"Without him in the picture, Crassus might lack courage. It would buy time at least."

"And Crassus will simply buy someone else to do his dirty work for him," she threw back at him. "One thug is much like another after all . . ."

Hortensia trailed off mid-sentence. Her eye had been caught by the gap on the shelves where Mago's *De Agri Cultura* had recently rested. She walked over and in imitation of Petro's actions a few minutes earlier, brushed her fingers over the edges of the rolls stored there, tugging meditatively on their little tags. Suddenly she swung round and advanced on the forger, who had remained on the couch in supremely relaxed pose, swinging one sandaled foot to and fro as he observed his two new acquaintances arguing. "What do you charge for your work?" she asked him peremptorily.

Petro's expression brightened. "For a lady like you, I could do a special rate." His gaze traveled greedily around the room once more.

"Good." Hortensia's eyes too held a gleam. "Because I have a very special commission for you."

XXVIII

LAUGHTER RANG OUT ACROSS THE NIGHT SKY ABOVE THE PACKED AUDI-
torium as the great Roscius switched back and forth between the
grotesque one-eyed mask of Polyphemus the Cyclops and the incon-
gruously beautiful one of Galatea, conveying the giant's declaration of
passion and the nymph's horrified reaction with comic contortions of his
body. The last tints of sunset had since faded but thanks to the largesse
of the theater's sponsor, Crassus, the temporary wooden framework of
the three-storyed stage had been heavily gilded so that it caught the light
from the flaming braziers set in the bronze statues all around its perimeter, illuminating not only Roscius's bravura performance but the rapt
faces of the spectators sitting in the front rows.

Hortensia felt her husband squeeze her hand and smiled up at him
before joining in the laughter and applause that greeted the end of the
first act. A buzz of chatter filled the theater as acquaintances hailed each
other and people wandered outside to stretch their legs.

Several stagehands hurried on to change the scenery and members
of Crassus's blue-clad household made their way along the rows spritzing
saffron wine among the spectators to freshen the air and handing out
platters of Syrian dates. Hortensia's eyes flickered over to their right
where the Vestals were just entering the theater and being led to the special row of their own which they were always allocated. Cornelia led
them in and from her ramrod posture and censorious expression, Hortensia guessed that pantomime was not to her taste. Immediately behind
Cornelia was Fabia, and as the Vestals seated themselves, the young

priestess locked eyes with Hortensia. Receiving a firm nod in response to her silent question, Hortensia leant over toward Caepio.

"My darling, I've just seen an old friend of mine going outside with her husband, excuse me for a moment while I say hello to her."

Caepio, who had been hailed by one of his clients, nodded amiably, and Hortensia extricated herself from her row and joined the flow of spectators heading toward the narrow exit. Over on the far side of the theater, she was aware that Fabia was watching her intently.

She emerged from the theater onto Tuscan Street, which linked the Forum Boarium with the main forum. To her right was the great sunken belly of the Circus Maximus, empty and silent for the evening, and just behind her, forming one corner of Crassus's temporary theater, was the little round temple of Hercules Victor, encircled with offerings laid in honor of this, his festival day. A strong waft from the river Tiber made her pinch her nostrils and hurry toward the other end of the square where beneath a ramshackle wooden canopy shaded by laurel trees, litters belonging to the theater's wealthier patrons had been laid down on the paving stones, their jewel-colored drapes fluttering in the evening breeze. Their carriers had convened around a blazing brazier a little way off and were passing around a jar of wine, laughing and joking though staying close enough to deter any loiterers from inspecting the vehicles more closely. Alongside the litters, a solitary two-wheeled vehicle was drawn up, the distinctive traveling carriage of the Vestal Virgins. Its driver had not joined the gaggle of litter-bearers but was standing by the heads of the two mules who drew it. Shifting their weight heavily from hoof to hoof, they bobbed their sleepy grey heads now and then and snuffled for wisps of grass between the paving stones. The driver picked his teeth and looked bored.

In a dank passageway opposite the canopy, Lucrio waited alongside Rixus and Eucherius for Hortensia's appearance. The young door-keeper was extremely over-excited.

"He looks puny," he remarked confidently of the carriage driver. "Why don't we just go and knock him over the head and drag him into the trees? Problem solved."

"Because they'll arrest you and pack you off back to Cilicia where you belong with your pirate cousins, hippopotamus brain," explained Rixus, administering a small smack to the back of his friend's head with one hand and taking a bite of his overripe peach with the other. "We're trying to do this on the quiet."

Lucrio, who had been peering around the corner, had already seen Hortensia emerge from the theater, her green dress bright against the dark silhouette of the theater behind. His dark head turned toward his two accomplices.

"Stick to the plan. The mistress is depending on us. Now get moving."

Rixus and Eucherius nodded. Creeping out of the passageway, they wrapped an arm around each other's shoulders and began to make circumambulatory progress down Tuscan Street in the direction of the little square where the litter-bearers were holding their convention. From his shadowy hiding place, Lucrio watched, first keenly, then appreciatively, as Rixus began to lean heavily on Eucherius, pushing him into the filthy ditch at the side of the street. In retaliation, Eucherius pushed back.

"Stop pushing me!" slurred Eucherius.

"You're the one doing all the pushing," came the belligerent reply.

"You're on my side of the road."

"You're on *my* side."

Their squabble began to turn more physical, Eucherius splaying his fingers across the side of Rixus's face, trying to force him to look straight ahead. In return, Rixus hooked his right leg behind Eucherius's and caused him to overbalance. Soon the pair of them were crawling around on the dirty paving stones, Rixus attempting to charge Eucherius like a bull while Eucherius in turn did his best to sit on Rixus's head. The litter-bearers, whose attention was caught by this comic side-show, quickly left the warmth of the brazier and gathered around the squabbling pair to shout encouragement.

Lucrio glanced at the Vestals' carriage driver under the laurel trees. He had not moved from his post by the mules' heads but his attention was also focused on the struggling pair.

"Come on," he whispered. "Come on."

As if he had heard Lucrio's plea, the driver took a few steps away from the mules, craning his head to get a better view, and then with a hesitant glance back at his sleepy charges, hurried up the street in order to join the amused spectators watching the comic combatants.

Further down the street, Lucrio could see Hortensia waiting for his signal and gave her a quick nod. She walked over to the litter station, as though she were going to retrieve something from her own vehicle, which had been set down near the back of the canopy. Then, glancing around to make sure that all eyes were still on Rixus and Eucherius, she slipped behind the row of litters toward the Vestals' carriage and, with another nervous glance around to make sure she was concealed by the shade of the laurels, she slid her arm under the canvas awning which provided cover to the priestesses on their journeys around the city. The vehicle creaked slightly and one of the mules threw its head up and gave a loud snort. But it soon resumed its whiskery exploration of the paving stones. Blindly groping around the right-hand corner of the compartment, which Fabia had said was her customary seating place, Hortensia began to feel panicky when she couldn't immediately find what she was looking for. But then her fingers brushed against something that rustled and her fist closed on the curtain which shielded the Vestals from view and whose hem had become wedged under the mattress. Rolled up snugly inside a fold of the thick drapery was a roll of papyrus, an extra piece of linen wrapped around it to protect its seven fragile seals. Quickly tucking her prize under her voluminous myrtle green mantle, Hortensia retraced her steps back to her own litter, where Lucrio was now waiting and keeping a lookout.

"Tell him he must work quickly," she whispered, handing him the roll. "We must –" A roar went up from the theater down the street, signaling that the second part of the entertainment had begun. "We must have it ready before the play ends. If for any reason I can't get out of the theater in time, you'll have to put it in the carriage, though you must make sure no one sees you anywhere near it. Men are expressly forbidden to so much as touch the vehicle: it is a sacred offense. Back right corner, rolled up inside the curtain."

Lucrio nodded. Hortensia shook out her cloak and hurried back to join the crowd of spectators re-entering the theater. Ducking his head between the green-and-gold curtains of Hortensia's vehicle, Lucrio held out the linen bundle to Petro, who was sitting cross-legged on the luxurious upholstery, calmly testing the point of a fine reed pen. A small oil lamp hung from the frame of the litter, illuminating the short roll of clean papyrus which lay partially unraveled across a plank of wood on his lap. Balanced on his knee was an inkwell, and in front of him, on a faded cloth wrapper, a row of tiny reed pens had been carefully laid out in ascending order of size, with a small pot of red wax at the end.

"You've got about an hour," Lucrio told him shortly.

"Not going to stick around? See the master at work?" enquired Petro with a grin, flexing his fingers.

"Just do your job. I'll be out here doing mine."

Lucrio straightened up and glanced over to where Rixus was now attempting to press Eucherius's face into a puddle. He would have given them a signal that they could stop now but for a time there was nothing he could do to attract their attention.

HORTENSIA'S FOOT JOGGED slightly during the second part of the performance, eliciting a glare from the elderly patrician seated alongside Cicero and Terentia. Noticing her restlessness, Caepio asked if she was feeling well and offered to take her home but she assured him she was enjoying herself and it was just the heat of the theater which was making her feel a little nauseous.

Claudia, overhearing their whispered conversation, clutched Hortensia's arm.

"My dear! Might you be expecting? Goodness me, you've been married less than a month, but for some women it is like that you know, Juno smiles upon us! I myself became pregnant with little Caecilia in a very short time, Caecilius was terribly startled. One or two of his relatives made little jokes to him about it," she trilled merrily, oblivious to the furious stare that her husband was shooting at her from her other side. "Take my advice, dear. If you want know the sex of the baby, get an egg from a setting hen and keep it warm – or have one of your maids do it. If a crested cock hatches, you know you'll be having a boy," she finished triumphantly.

Caepio raised an eyebrow at Hortensia, who flushed and whispered that she had no reason to think such an event might be in the offing. She returned the squeeze of Caepio's hand however and in order that he wouldn't suspect anything was amiss, laughed warmly at his whispered aside that Roscius's flamboyant arm gestures and mannerisms clearly owed much to the actor's careful study of his idol Hortensius. But all she could think about was how far Petro had got, whether he would finish in time so that she could substitute the new version of the will back in the Vestals' carriage and whether Fabia would be able to replace it in the archive undetected. She was well aware that of them all, Fabia was taking the greatest risk. Yet it was the young Vestal herself who had proposed the theater scheme, pointing out that even if she were able to remove the will from the archive as Hortensia had enquired, its absence would not go long unnoticed. "Cornelia has been holding daily inventories of the chamber," she confided in her note to Hortensia. "Ever since your last interview with her, she has been terrified that something else is going to go missing and the Vestals will be blamed for not doing their duties. But with all of us out at the theater, there will be a window of opportunity – you must seize it. I can provide the will if you can manage the rest."

As she watched the enraptured faces around her reacting obediently to the antics on stage, Hortensia had a brief, wild vision of herself standing in a courtroom, surrounded by a sea of hostile spectators, while her father and Cicero traded rhetorical blows over her guilt or innocence before a jury that included Caecilius and Cato. What was the penalty for her particular crime? Exile? Or would they condemn her to live burial, like an errant Vestal? Her train of thought was interrupted by a sudden burst of applause as the actors bowed themselves into the wings and the team of stagehands appeared once more to rearrange the sets. There was only one act of the play to come. She leaned over and whispered in Caepio's ear.

"If you don't mind, my darling, I think I *am* just going to go and get some fresh air, it's so terribly stuffy in here with all these people."

"Are you alright?" asked Caepio with concern. "Let me come with you."

But Hortensia put her hand on his shoulder and stopped him getting up. "No, you stay, I have seen this play several times before, there is only this last act to go and Lucrio is just outside the door, I shall be quite safe."

She saw that her husband still did not look convinced and made her departure before he could lodge another protest.

At the far end of the Forum Boarium the litter-bearers were warming their hands around their brazier once more. There was no sign of Rixus and Eucherius. Lucrio was pacing up and down in front of the litter.

"Is he almost finished?" asked Hortensia breathlessly. "There's only one act left."

"Almost, *domina*," nodded Lucrio. "He's reluctant to be rushed though."

"Where are the other two?"

"They made themselves scarce once the night patrolmen arrived. I'd be surprised if what you saw in the theater was any more entertaining."

Hortensia poked her head through the curtains of the litter. Petro was bent over almost double, his nose very close to the papyrus – now covered in writing – as the ink from his reed pen slowly leeched into its honey-colored surface in perfect swirling script. A strip of metal lay beside him, used to measure an equal distance between columns. The roll which Hortensia had taken from the Vestals' carriage lay unraveled in front of him, across the green coverlet.

"How much longer?" she demanded.

Petro didn't look up. "Only the signatures and seals to go," he replied.

Hortensia watched in some fascination as Petro perfectly reproduced the autographs of first Pompey, and then the seven witnesses, finishing with her father's flourishing signature. She noticed that Petro barely had to glance at its twin on the earlier copy laid before him for reference. At his side was a pile of what she thought were coins but then realized were crude little clay discs, baked hard in an oven and embossed with different images – a griffin, a dog's head, an armed representation of the goddess Venus. Hortensia picked up her father's own seal and marveled once more at its accuracy.

"Where did you learn to do all of this?" she couldn't help asking.

"Father taught me. His father taught him." He grinned at her as he laid his pen down on the cloth.

"Done. Now seal it, we don't have much time," urged Hortensia.

"Not yet," said Petro calmly. "One more signature to go."

"But you've done them all," protested Hortensia. "See, there's eight names – that's it, Pompey plus the seven witnesses."

Petro didn't reply. Instead, he picked up an unused reed from the end of the row in front of him and dipped it into a pot of what looked like water. Hortensia watched as he dipped the nib and then scrawled something in the bottom right hand corner of the document. But she couldn't see what he had written, the ink seemed to have left no trace.

"What was that?" she asked.

He grinned at her, enjoying her confusion, and held up the pot.

"Tithymalus milk. Some people call it goat lettuce. Grows near the seashore. Shows up brown when you sprinkle it with ashes. Stays invisible the rest of the time."

"But why?"

"Petro's an artist, isn't he? An artist always puts his name to his work."

He blew gently at the papyrus strip before rolling it up very carefully between his dexterous hands. Finally he picked up the first of the little clay discs. Using the metal strip to ensure an equal distance between them, he dipped the counterfeit seals one by one into the pot of soft red wax, holding them up to the glare of the oil lamp for a minute or two first and then carefully pressing them in descending order against the seam, mirroring the arrangement on the original will.

"That ought to do it," he murmured to himself, holding up the roll and inspecting it from all angles for what seemed like an age to Hortensia before he finally let out a satisfied sigh. "Another beautiful piece of work from the workshop of Petro."

She held out her hand. "Careful," warned Petro, laying it gently across her outstretched palm. "Seals still need a little time to dry."

Suddenly Hortensia heard Lucrio whispering urgently and she straightened up.

"What is it –"

But she never finished the sentence. The reason for Lucrio's warning was already plain to her – her husband, approaching from the direction of the theater. Caepio's eyes were fixed upon her and she daren't pass the will in her hand to Lucrio in case the movement attracted Caepio's attention. So, with the roll clutched behind her back, she waited with what she hoped was a tolerable impression of equanimity.

"Darling, I promised I was fine, I was just going to have a little lie down, like I said."

"Well I didn't like to think of you feeling unwell. To tell the truth, I'm rather tired myself. Let's both take the litter back up to the Palatine, then you can get an early night. Lucrio, go and tell the litter bearers that we're ready to go. At least we'll avoid the crush this way."

Lucrio glanced at Hortensia, who appealed desperately to her husband.

"Oh no, don't be silly, I haven't said goodbye to Caecilius and Claudia, they would think it so rude of me. Why don't we go back inside and watch the end of the last act?"

Caepio looked curiously at her. "What's the matter, my dear? You look very flushed. Are you sure Claudia wasn't right – could you be . . .?"

Behind her back, Hortensia felt the roll being twitched out of her fingers.

"It's really nothing," she said in a strangulated tone.

"Come, I honestly think you should lie down."

Before she could stop him, Caepio had grasped the edge of the green curtain and drawn it back. Her squawk of protest died abruptly. There was no sign of Petro nor his makeshift workshop. Wax, pens, knives, even the little oil lamp had all vanished.

Feeling very weak, Hortensia allowed Caepio to assist her into the litter but soon sat bolt upright again. The new copy of the will had to be hidden inside the Vestals' carriage or else the whole scheme would be exposed.

"Wait. My bracelet," she said wildly, clutching at her wrist.

"What bracelet?"

"The little amethyst one you gave me, it must have fallen off in the theater."

"But you weren't wearing it."

"Yes I was, I remember fiddling with it in the first act . . ."

"Hortensia, we're going home," he interrupted firmly. "You're not well and you're acting quite strangely. I'll buy you another bracelet."

"Please, Caepio, I couldn't bear to lose it," she wheedled. "Just have a very quick look for me. I promise I'll keep very calm and quiet."

Caepio sighed heavily.

"Tell the litter-bearers to be ready to depart when I come back," he directed Lucrio and went back down the street toward the theater once more. "And keep an eye on her."

As soon as he was out of earshot, Hortensia scrambled to her feet.

"Quick, we've got to find Petro," she hissed, but the words had only just left her mouth when a great storm of cheering suddenly erupted from the belly of the theater. Barely had it reached its peak than a side-door opened and the first members of the audience to depart emerged – the Vestal Virgins, all in white, with Cornelia at their head. They walked in stately procession behind the two lictors charged with accompanying them.

Hortensia's heart leapt as she saw Fabia walking just behind Cornelia. If they weren't able to restore the new will to the carriage in time, there was no telling how much danger the young Vestal would be in. Hortensia closed her eyes at the thought of Fabia's reaction when she felt in the pocket of the curtain and the will was not there.

"In the name of the gods what do we do?" she whispered desperately. "*Where is Petro?*"

"Did somebody call my name?" drawled a voice behind them.

She spun round. Petro had appeared out the darkness and was leaning nonchalantly against the litter frame, his arms folded. Hortensia almost grabbed him by the front of his tunic.

"Where is it?" she asked in desperation. "Quick, *what did you do with it?*"

He put his head to one side and it appeared as though he were going to take pleasure in toying with her. Then, as Hortensia beseeched him with her eyes, he seemed to relent.

"Back right corner, rolled up inside the curtain."

Hortensia's jaw dropped. Then she exhaled deeply, only just managing not to sink to the ground in relief.

"Petro keeps his ears open," he added by way of explanation.

The Vestals were now being helped one by one into their covered carriage, Fabia among them. Hortensia just managed to catch her eye and was able to reassure her with a slight nod of her head that all was well.

"Praise Jupiter," she breathed, blowing a kiss in the direction of the temple rising from its ashes on the Capitoline high above them. From inside his tunic, Petro produced the will which Hortensia had earlier removed from the Vestals' carriage, its crimson seals now splintered and broken. "Figured you still had a use for this one."

Hortensia clutched hold of it gratefully. "Yes, I certainly do. Thank you, Petro. You've certainly earned your fee."

Petro shrugged. "Shame I couldn't stick around for the rest of your conversation. I'd have given something to hear you trying to explain to your husband what I was doing there," he said with an appreciative gleam in his eye.

Lucrio went to tell the litter-bearers to prepare for departure. Hortensia reached into a side compartment of the litter and withdrew the single-roll copy of Livius Andronicus's translation of Homer. Petro took possession of it as if she had handed him his first-born child, stroking its soft leather wrapper and crooning something in his native tongue.

"Thank you again," she said. "I'll know who to summon if . . . well, if ever I have need of such services again."

Petro tucked the Homer carefully under his arm and gave an ironic little bow.

"Nice doing business with you. Don't have too many lady customers. Surprised to see a lady that day, but as it turns out, a pleasant surprise." He bowed again and began to saunter toward the forum.

Hortensia turned back to her litter and was about to settle herself, ready for Caepio's return, when a thought struck her and she swiveled around.

"Why were you surprised?" she asked.

Petro checked his departure and raised a questioning eyebrow.

"You said you were surprised to see a lady," she repeated. "But you had my name and direction from the note I left. Who were you expecting to see?"

Petro showed his teeth in a smile, this time a rueful one.

"Well, how about that? You've got sharp ears just like your father. See, when I got your note, thought I must be reading the name wrong. But I figured, maybe he wants to meet somewhere other than his own house. Then you turned up and . . . well, I didn't think he'd want me to let on to you that I knew him. He got pretty agitated that day he ran into Tiberius Dolabella at my place a few months ago. Hope it didn't cause trouble for him."

He subjected Hortensia to an assessing look.

"You're both pretty alike I reckon, so maybe you won't mind knowing. You send him my best. Good man, your father. Haven't seen him in a while but I guess he hasn't had anything for me to do. And you tell him not to worry about those letters I cooked up for Tiberius and Crassus. He can show them up for fakes any time he wants. They may not know how to find my signature but old Hortensius does."

He waved and disappeared into the throng of theater spectators and late-night shoppers now spilling across Tuscan Street, leaving Hortensia staring after him, a stricken expression on her face.

XXIX

THE DOORS TO TIBERIUS DOLABELLA'S HOUSE HAD BEEN CLOSED TO THE street almost an hour since, nightfall having set in and his servants not expecting any more visitors. When a frenzied hammering echoed through the villa's painted corridors, it took the startled doorkeeper some time to scramble to his post and he was even more surprised when he saw that the person doing such violence to the dog's head door knocker was none other than the consul, Marcus Licinius Crassus.

"Where is your master?" snarled Crassus, barging past the bemused slave.

"He has retired for the evening, *domine*. He is in his private room. But . . . *domine* . . ."

Ignoring the slave's protestations, Crassus marched down the corridor leading to the inner sanctum of the house, his sandals squeaking angrily against the paved floor. He passed several lurid wall paintings depicting highly eroticized versions of traditional myths before arriving on the threshold of Tiberius's room, only to discover that his host was not alone. A naked girl was kneeling on the floor, her fleshy brown back and buttocks facing Crassus. Tiberius, who was fully clothed, was holding the girl's mane of silken black hair in his fist and carried a chariot-racer's coiled whip in the other. He turned to survey his visitor.

"Crassus. Dear fellow. You have such timing."

Stubbornly averting his eyes, Crassus addressed the wall over the girl's head.

"Get rid of her, Tiberius. We have urgent matters to discuss."

"We do? And I always used to think myself a man of leisure. Meeting you has truly made me realize what I've been missing." He made a speculative gesture toward the kneeling girl. "Unless . . . I don't suppose you'd care to . . . After all what's mine is yours, Crassus – no? Ah, your morals. I forgot."

He let the girl's long hair fall from his fist. "We shall have to continue this another day, my dear. You know the way out I believe. Tell your father he will have to wait a little longer until his debt is paid off."

With her gaze lowered, the girl picked up her discarded clothes and vanished into the corridor. Tiberius sat on the edge of his sleeping couch and leant back against the cushions.

"So. What was so important that you had to interrupt my evening?" he asked sweetly.

"*This* was just delivered to my door."

Crassus threw the papyrus roll down onto the couch next to Tiberius. A few splinters of wax fell from the broken seals, scattering over the black coverlet. Tiberius's eyes widened but otherwise he evinced no sign of surprise.

"Well, well," he intoned. He picked up the document between thumb and forefinger and inspected it closely.

"Is that *all* you have to say?" Crassus ran his hand through his already disheveled hair. "Can't you see that's the damned will? The fake one – the one Petro made – the one we planted in the temple archive!"

"Yes, I did understand you the first time."

"So? We have been discovered!"

"*We?*" repeated Tiberius slowly, still examining the roll closely. "I *think* you said this was delivered to *you*."

A shadow passed across Crassus's contorted face. "You know damned well I'll take you down with me, Tiberius! You killed the priestess, don't think I can't pin that on you."

"I'd be fascinated to see you try, Crassus, but there is really no need for these childish threats. Tell me, out of interest, when did you say this arrived and how was it delivered?"

"About an hour ago." Crassus flung himself down on a chair and buried his face in his hands, breathing heavily through his splayed fingers. "My slaves say they heard a knock on the door and when they opened it, *that* was lying on the threshold, wrapped up in a bit of cloth. Any bloody passer-by could have picked it up."

"I take it there was no note included."

"None. But the message is damned clear. It must be from Pompey himself, but what I don't understand is, why send it to me?" He shook his head in frantic bewilderment. "Why not take it straight to the Senate as evidence? Not that it counts as evidence of course. He can't prove I had anything to do with it. Your men dealt with the scribe, the fire took care of the forger. He's obviously trying to intimidate me, make me think he's biding his time. But what does he think he can do? Kill me?" A hysterical laugh escaped him. "How does he propose to explain that away to the Senate?" Crassus continued to brood twitchily, the frown sinking deeper into his brow. "But if not Pompey, then who? What I wouldn't give to know!" he muttered.

Tiberius, who had been absorbed in his own reflections, raised his eyebrows. "How very interesting. What would you give, out of curiosity?"

"At this precise moment, my entire fortune," retorted Crassus with a hollow laugh.

"Might I have that in writing? I am still waiting for that other five hundred thousand you know."

"Why in Jupiter's name would you want it in writing?"

"Because I know exactly who sent this to you."

Crassus took his hands away from his face and stared incredulously at Tiberius. "You know?"

Tiberius's amber eyes seemed to glow as he perused the document in his hand. "Cheeky little minx," he said, an admiring caress in his voice. "I have certainly underestimated her. Not as much, I fear, as she has underestimated me, but a salutary experience, nonetheless." He smiled at Crassus, who was still gazing at him open-mouthed.

"Yes, I use the word *me* on this occasion. This was always going to be my show from here on in anyway. You can tell your balls to come out now, Crassus – the game is still very much on. It includes some new players but that is going to make everything so much more exciting. We will proceed three days hence, on the Ides, as planned, and I will arrange for this –" he held the will between thumb and forefinger "– to be put back where it belongs. I sense that Petro may have betrayed us, slippery customer that he is, but there are other forgers who can counterfeit the seals for us. You, meanwhile, will send five hundred thousand sesterces round to my house tomorrow – cash, Crassus, don't think you can fob me off with a deed of ownership on some decrepit tower block in the middle of the Subura – and I'll want another fifty thousand in interest payments. After that you can sit tight and dream of sitting on your throne all by yourself. I'll send you word when it's done."

"But damn it, Tiberius," spluttered Crassus, "what are you talking about? *Who* are you talking about?"

There was a brief silence, broken by a faint rustling in the corner of the room. Swinging round, Crassus realized that someone was standing there, partially concealed by a tall cupboard. As they emerged into the light of the room, the white of their clothing seemed to glow with an unearthly brilliance and Crassus thought for a moment that he was seeing a ghost.

"You were not my only visitor this evening, you see." Crassus's eyes darted in the direction of the door through which the naked girl had disappeared earlier. Tiberius saw it and shrugged. "They live such a sheltered life in the Temple of Vesta. I thought it might be an education of sorts," he offered by way of explanation.

He put out a hand and beckoned the slim figure further forward.

"Come, don't be shy, that isn't like you. Now why don't you tell the consul here just what you told me a little earlier?"

XXX

HORTENSIA WINCED AS ELPIDIA SCRATCHED HER SCALP WITH YET another wickedly sharp hairpin. "Ouch! I'm sure there must be enough flowers now, Elpidia, please?"

"Just a few more," said Elpidia coaxingly.

Hortensia squinted at her dim reflection in the polished metal mirror. Elpidia had washed her black hair in scented water and curled it, and was now deftly weaving a crown of violets and white oleander around her head. A garland of the same flowers lay across her breast and she wore a pale dress the color of creamy candle wax. Her rich purple mantle lay on the bed. Outside, she could hear a steady progression of vehicles making their way cautiously down the Palatine toward the start of the Appian Way, where they would join up with the procession making its way to Diana's shrine at Lake Nemi. Hortensia jigged her knees up and down, earning herself a reproof from Elpidia for making her work more difficult.

There was a knock at the door and Caepio entered. He beamed admiringly and complimented Elpidia on her handiwork. "You look like a dryad, my dear."

"She'll look like a hedgehog, if she doesn't sit still," said Elpidia admonishingly.

Caepio sat down on the bed and tweaked one of his wife's curls. "Excited about the festival?"

She nodded and bestowed a happy, self-satisfied smile on him. Caepio tilted his head, a humorous glint in his eyes.

"Anyone would think me a cruel and tyrannical husband to see you so relish the prospect of an evening without me."

"Well, why do you think men are forbidden to attend the Nemoralia?" she responded with a twinkle. "To give wives a moment's peace of course."

"Or husbands. You do seem to be in an extraordinarily good mood."

"And what if I am?" she said, tapping him nonchalantly on the nose. "Isn't that what kind and benevolent husbands want for their wives?"

Caepio caught her hand and squeezed it. "I am pleased of course. It's just that you have been rather distracted these last few days. I was worried about you at the theater the other night, you were very quiet on the way home."

"I was just tired," she said heartily, returning the pressure of his hand before disengaging her own.

Caepio nodded and picked up a pin that had fallen to the floor, restoring it to the dressing table. "I wondered if perhaps Claudia's suggestion wasn't as silly as it sounded . . ."

She stared at him uncomprehendingly for a moment, then burst out laughing. "Oh. No! No, no, no. I really don't think it's that." She saw the slightly rueful look on his face and put a hand out to squeeze his again. "Not all men can be as potent as Caecilius you know."

He grinned in response to the mischief in her eyes. "No, indeed," he replied, his eyes on Elpidia's deft fingers as they continued to build the elaborate coiffure. "And I trust that business with the Vestals is now over and done with?"

"Completely at an end." Hortensia seemed absorbed in contemplating her reflection in the mirror but she spoke calmly and reassuringly. "There's nothing to worry about now. You were quite right. Papa is more than a match for Crassus. I should have known it."

There was a blandness in her voice and her maidservant eyed her mistrustfully, but Caepio seemed reassured and stayed to watch Elpidia complete her task. "Beautiful," he said admiringly, as the last flower was gently eased into place and secured with one last long pin. "You look like Diana herself. I trust the journey won't be too uncomfortable, it's a cursed long way to Nemi. But you will have your mama for company and there should be enough traffic on the road to deter any lurking pirates."

"How very comforting," she said wonderingly.

He laughed. "Well, your papa is going to provide you with a couple of outriders, just in case, and once the festival is over it's only a short distance to Caecilius and Claudia's villa at Aricia. You should be safe in their company."

"As long as Claudia doesn't provoke the pirates too much by objecting to the cut of their tunics."

He laughed and kissed her cheek. "I shall see you tomorrow. Enjoy yourself and try to see to it that your mother does too. She hasn't had an easy time of late."

He left, and a few minutes later, Hortensia was making the short journey up the Palatine toward her father's villa, where she had arranged to meet Lutatia. The faithful Eucherius scurried along behind her, holding a canopy over her head to protect Elpidia's creation from the breeze, and as they made the climb, they passed several descending vehicles containing aristocratic ladies whose hair was garlanded just like Hortensia's and who were clutching votive offerings for the goddess, which they would eventually lay at her shrine. Under her mantle, Hortensia was herself holding a small figurine of the goddess, very much like the one Lucrio had used to disable Tiberius Dolabella's henchman.

To reach Hortensius's villa, they had to pass Crassus's house. Hortensia tried but failed to resist the temptation to steal a surreptitious glance into the villa's atrium. It was past the hour of *salutatio*, and there was no sign either of the illustrious owner or his clients. Hortensia wondered if Crassus was at home, sweating under fear of exposure as he tried to deduce who could have discovered what he was up to. What wouldn't she have given to see his face when he discovered the will on his doorstep! She had listened first with apprehension, then with a dawning smile of satisfaction as Lucrio told her how he had watched the villa from a safe distance and confirmed the discovery of the will by Crassus's doorkeeper; then how the consul himself had emerged a short time later, obviously in a state of some disarray, climbed into his private carriage and set off down the Palatine at pace. Hortensia was lured into thinking for a wild moment that the success of her scheme had terrified Crassus into fleeing the city but Lucrio dashed these hopes, saying that the consul had eventually returned, though clearly in a somber state of mind. Hortensia congratulated herself nonetheless on her masterstroke, finding a way of letting Crassus know that his scheme had been discovered without revealing the identity of the one who shared the secret. As long as Crassus labored under this confusion, she was confident that he would not dare to act. The final months of his consulship with Pompey would pass off harmlessly and the mantle would be transferred to her father and Caecilius at the end of the year. Hortensia's only disappointment was that she was not allowed to tell anyone what she had done.

A few minutes later, as she continued to brood on these gratifying thoughts, closing her mind to a few more troubling ones, they arrived at the villa of Hortensius. Hortensia expected to find the traveling carriage drawn up outside, but to her surprise there was no sign of the vehicle or the two mules that would pull it. Even more surprising was the absence of her father's door-keeper, Ancho, who usually presided over entry to the villa. Leaving Eucherius outside, Hortensia stepped into the dark cool of the atrium. The house was eerily quiet, but at the end of the long corridor which led toward her mother's rose garden, she spied Rixus struggling to maneuver a large terracotta pot through the doorway, and called out to him.

"Rixus, where is everyone? Where's Mama?"

Rixus turned with some difficulty and stared at her in surprise.

"She's gone to Antemnae, *domina*. A letter was sent up to you. Did it not arrive?"

"No. What happened?"

Rixus had put down the pot and come hurrying along the corridor into the atrium.

"Your mama's uncle Gaius is sick," he announced.

"What's the matter with him?"

"A note arrived this afternoon. He fell from his horse and has not woken up."

Hortensia screwed up her face in recollection. She had a dim memory of this gouty relative, recalling that she had met him once at a family wedding and he had let her sip from his wine cup. But other than that there were no ties of affection to make her feel any particular concern on his behalf.

"Has Quintus gone with her?"

"Yes, *domina*. Reluctantly –" Rixus chuckled conspiratorially "– but yes."

"Where's Papa?"

"In court, *domina*. For the conclusion of the trial. He was out when the letter came. Ancho must have gone to find him. Do you want me to send a message?"

Hortensia shook her head distractedly. "No, there's no sense disturbing him. But what am I to do now? We're supposed to be leaving for the Nemoralia."

Rixus nodded obligingly. "Yes, I heard about this. Your mama said to Ancho that if you still wanted to go to the festival, you could send a message to your sister-in-law and see if she would give you a seat in her carriage."

Hortensia grimaced. Even at the best of times, she was not terribly fond of Servilia, who had a way of making Hortensia feel uncertain and gauche, and smiling superciliously so that her younger sister-in-law wished she could think of a suitably devastating response, but somehow the right words never came. The thought of a whole afternoon spent in a stuffy, rolling carriage with her was not appealing.

"I don't see why I have to have company," she complained. "Has Mama taken the carriage then?"

"No, she went in the two-wheeler, she thought it would get her there quicker. But I don't think the mistress would want you to travel alone, *domina*."

"I wouldn't be alone," Hortensia pointed out. "Half the city is on its way to Nemi today."

Rixus shifted nervously from foot to foot. "Yes but, *domina*, what about the pirates?"

"Oh, if there are other vehicles around it won't signify," insisted Hortensia, who was very attached to the idea of attending her first sacred festival as a married woman but equally determined not to throw herself on Servilia's mercy. The success of her stratagem with Crassus and Tiberius had emboldened her. There was no chance they could know who had thwarted them so she had no fear of reprisals. Instead, she was enjoying the euphoric sensation of being a force to be reckoned with and even conjured up a pleasing vision of herself confronting a band of swarthy pirates, imperiously demanding what they meant by accosting her. But she realized this portrait was unlikely to placate the anxious Rixus and so added a reassuring postscript. "Besides, Papa said he was going to send two outriders with me. Mama hasn't taken them, has she? I can always send for Lucrio if she has."

"No, *domina,* Antemnae is on the Salarian Way and your mama did not think it necessary, but . . ."

"Then there is nothing for anyone to worry about," said Hortensia complacently. "Have the carriage brought round and tell Glaucus and the riders to get ready. I shall leave a note for Papa explaining everything."

Although Rixus would not have hesitated to exert his authority in the days when Hortensia was still a little girl thieving apples from his beautifully tended orchard, he found her grown-up self much harder to argue with. All his suggestions met with resistance. Hortensia had no intention of allowing her pleasure to be spoiled and knowing that Caepio would have seconded her mother's suggestion to accept Servilia's escort, she turned down Rixus's proposal that she seek her husband's permission for her journey, pointing out that any further delay would mean not reaching Nemi before nightfall. After some more futile pleading for her to at least wait until her father could be consulted, Rixus at last admitted defeat and went to convey Hortensia's orders to the stables, reasoning that no one could blame him for not being listened to by his owners. His preoccupation with this thought meant that he did not notice the grey-liveried slave taking a close interest in his movements on the opposite side of the street.

Half an hour later, Hortensia was safely ensconced in her mule-drawn traveling carriage, heading for the Porta Capena with two of her father's grooms bringing up the rear. The sun was high in the sky but she knew it would take until dusk to reach Lake Nemi. So she settled down into the cushions and hoped that the rocking, juddering motion of the wheels and the hot sun flooding the carriage with its soporific warmth might eventually lull her to sleep.

XXXI

HORTENSIA OPENED HER EYES AND SHUT THEM AGAIN QUICKLY against the strong glare from the sun, uttering a small moan of protest. She twitched the drape slightly and realized with a pang of frustration that they were no more than three or four miles outside the city limits. She knew the route well, having traveled it every summer on their way to family holidays at Laurentum, and could tell their rate of progress by the names on the tombs lining the roadside. When she was little, Hortensius had made her practice her letters by picking out the inscriptions on the mausolea of the more famous occupants.

The topmost branch of a pair of tall wooden crosses drifted past. Hortensia suppressed a little shudder of revulsion. She had a vivid memory of the previous summer when her mother had mysteriously insisted on the drapes to their carriage being drawn as they drove along the road. Impatient with the stuffy atmosphere this produced, Hortensia had stubbornly dragged them aside and been transfixed by the sight of a naked man hanging from a cross at the side of the road, his flesh raw and scorched from the sun, his broken body limp like one of the dolls she used to play with as a child. She'd had just enough time to register that the man's tongue was lolling from his mouth and that his sightless eyes were rimmed with flies before her mother grabbed her round the waist and snatched the drapes shut again. Later, Quintus had gleefully told her the truth. The man was one of the rebel slave Spartacus's army, whose survivors Crassus had ordered to be nailed up alongside the Appian Way. The crosses were empty now of course, the carcasses of those who had once hung from them rotted away to nothing, but no doubt Crassus wished to ensure that his purge of the runaway gladiators of Capua had not been forgotten. The entry of Crassus into Hortensia's thoughts reawakened her sense of triumph and she was allowing herself some satisfied contemplation of his current predicament when the carriage jolted and the landscape outside came to an abrupt halt.

Hortensia waited, unconcerned, assuming that they were pausing to allow a wider vehicle to edge past, or to make way for a cohort of soldiers returning to Rome from the port of Brundisium. But the absence of any sounds that might signal such an approach and a battery of loud cursing from Glaucus, her father's coachman, prompted her to sit up and look through the opening to the driver's seat.

"What's the matter?" she called out.

Glaucus slung himself around and waved an arm in a gesture of impatience. "Stupid mules won't go, *domina*." Over Glaucus's shoulder, Hortensia could see the rearing head of one of the two animals who pulled the carriage. Its ears were set flat either side of its poll, its eyes rimmed with white. "They just stopped, but there's nothing that should scare them. It's like they think there's a ghost in the road."

The novelty of this thought brought a look of slight nervousness into his eyes but he flapped some more with his arms and poked their soft rumps with his whip, still to no avail. Hortensia watched as one of the attendant grooms rode into view, dismounted and grabbed the harness underneath the off-side mule's chin, attempting to urge it forward. But instead the mule began to retreat skittishly. Hortensia, who was still sitting bolt upright, had to grab the side of the vehicle to steady herself. As hard as the groom pulled, the mules stubbornly resisted.

A tiny voice of worry whispered in Hortensia's ear, though she could not have said why at the time. It struck her that the traffic on the road had thinned out and that they had lost touch with the carriages that had been just ahead of them when they left Rome. The last changing post had been passed some time ago and there were no houses or buildings on this section of the road, which instead was flanked with a thick pinewood on one side and high, lonely tombs on the other. Quintus used

to try his best to scare her with the same ghost tales which were now giving Glaucus pause for thought – of discontented souls emerging from
their graves and setting upon passers-by, or the spirits of dead legionaries
being seen marching toward Rome. His efforts were always in vain. Hortensia was unmoved by such stories and not for a moment did she think
there was any truth in them. Yet there was something about the wide,
echoing silence all around them that she found eerie, and she felt uncomfortably foolish recalling her insouciance in the face of Rixus's warnings
about the threat of Cilician pirates on the road.

The cry of an eagle lanced across the pale sky overhead, making
her jump, but just as quickly quiet was restored, disturbed only by the
sound of the mules' hooves pawing and scraping at the smooth paving
stones. Then came a long whistling sound, as though another bird of prey
were soaring above them, followed by a surprised exclamation from the
groom at the head of the mules. Hortensia watched uncomprehendingly
as the man sank out of her sight and then screamed as a second arrow
buried itself with a crunch in Glaucus's neck, and the coachman too
slumped from view, his hand raised uselessly to the bubbling wound.

Panic wrapped its hot fingers around Hortensia's heart. The arching
canopy of the carriage blocked her view of what was going on but she
could hear scuffling outside, the scrape of metal on metal, and she could
feel the vehicle beginning to tilt precariously as the terrified mules, freed
from the check of Glaucus's hand, began to shy off the main road onto
the dirt track alongside. Desperately, she tried to yank up the thick
awning from the near side of the carriage in the hope of being able to
reach the shelter of the wood. But just as she felt the ties of the heavy
material begin to give way, a pair of hands grabbed her waist and tugged
her backwards. Hortensia couldn't see her assailant but even if she hadn't
been anticipating the attack, she would have known who it was by their
bitter scent. A damp hand wrapped itself around her mouth and
Tiberius's voice hissed breathlessly in her ear.

"Now. Let's not be too hasty. You don't even know what I'm going
to say."

Hortensia kicked back with her heels but felt Tiberius pinioning them together with his own. She opened her mouth and tried to bite down on the fleshy hand clamped against her mouth but a vicious tugging on her long hair forced her head upwards and a cry of pain escaped her throat.

"You need someone to break you to bridle, that's all." Tiberius was lying half on top of her now, his weight pressing her body deep into the soft mattress. Hortensia could feel his breath on her cheek and tried to turn away, closing her eyes as she did so.

"That's right. Relax. You'll only excite me if you struggle. And right now we need to be very clear-headed, both of us."

The precarious, juddering motion of the carriage had not abated but Hortensia could hear voices close by and she felt the wheels turn suddenly and purposefully to the left. Tree branches scraped against the roof and the sides, raking deep patterns into the soft canopy as the carriage was guided into the forest.

FABIA GAVE A nervous start as she heard a murmured word at her shoulder. She had been staring into the dark dancing flames of the hearth, her fingers playing abstractedly with a fold of her white priestess' gown, much preoccupied with her role in the events of the past three days. But now she realized that her period of duty had come to an end and stood up so that the next priestess could take her seat at the hearth. She made her way along the passage leading from the sanctuary, emerging into the peaceful oasis of the palace courtyard, and walked slowly up a staircase to the light, airy room she occupied on the second floor of the Vestals' living quarters. It was lit by a single, half-melted candle and simply-furnished with nothing more than a sleeping couch and white woollen blanket, a wooden clothes box for her robes and a stand supporting a large marble basin of water which she and her fellow priestesses were commanded to use for frequent ablutions. Fabia twisted her veil into a knotted skein behind her before dipping her hands into the basin and carefully flicking cold water over her face.

A small pitcher of oil stood beside the basin and she poured some out into her hands, rubbing hard between her rigidly splayed fingers. As she leaned over the basin to rinse them, she saw a white shape flicker in the water's reflection and turned round to find Felix standing immediately behind her.

"Felix!" she expostulated indignantly. "What are you doing here? You know you're not allowed along this corridor, we have told you any number of times. You have to stop peeping or we'll tell Cornelia and she'll ask the Pontifex to have you sent back to the orphan house."

She groped for a linen cloth and pressed it to her face, trying to calm her breathing as she felt the water being absorbed from her skin. When she looked up again, she expected to find Felix looking abashed and seeking forgiveness as usual with one of his beseeching smiles. But instead there was a curious blandness to his expression, belied only by a watchful keenness about his eyes.

"What is it?" she asked uncertainly. Then her eye was caught by the glint of silver in his hand. She stared at it uncomprehendingly for a moment, recognizing the special knife kept in Cornelia's chamber and used for slitting the throats of sacrificial beasts. Her gaze snapped back to his face and she saw that the smile was there now but not a trace of its usual boyish sweetness was visible.

"You shouldn't have interfered," he said in his soft voice, shaking his head slightly. "I knew it was you all the time. You thought I didn't see you. But I did."

Fabia shook her head in dawning horror as she backed slowly away, clutching the sides of the basin stand as she put it between herself and Felix. He didn't make a move to stop her but raised the knife, flexing it in his fist, a glow of childish satisfaction flaring in his eyes as he saw the effect this had on her.

"I bet you wish you hadn't told that bitch you'd help her now, don't you? I saw you sneaking through the door into the sanctuary just before you all went to the theater yesterday and I saw you sneaking back. I waited for you."

Still she didn't understand. "Felix, you don't know what's been going on. I'm sure you think you're doing the right thing but you have to let me explain, I promise I would never have deceived anyone but there was going to be such terrible trouble . . ."

"Don't know what's been going on?" His face was suffused with gleeful incredulity. "You stupid whore. I know more than you do." He took a step toward her, the knife in his hand catching the light from the candle in the corner.

"I swear if you come any closer I'll scream." Her panicked voice caught in her throat as she struggled to get the words out. "You know what they'll do to you if you so much as touch me, Felix, they'll tie you up in a sack and throw you in the Tiber."

"What, just like I helped throw that bitch friend of yours?"

Fabia's eyes dilated and she gazed at him while he beamed with delighted pleasure.

"She made a lovely big splash," he crooned. "Like a sow flopping in the mud."

She shook her head, terror and disbelief contorting her pale, heart-shaped face. "It can't have been you! You killed Helena? You stole Pompey's will? But why . . .?"

"Of course not, you dumb cow. What do I care about some politician? But I have a new master now – one who trusts me with his greatest secrets. It was me who let him into the Temple sanctuary, and now he will reward me with anything I want."

He advanced purposefully and the pitch of her voice escalated.

"I'll scream! I told you I would scream and I will."

"Scream all you want," he said mockingly. "It won't matter. In a few hours, my master's word will be the only one that counts in Rome. Your bitch friend is probably dead already – if my master's done with her. As for you, they'll say you killed yourself just like Helena, and call you a whore too. After all –" he shifted his grip on the knife in his hand "– it's not as though you haven't been called one before, is it?"

He lunged too quickly for her to react and the terrified cry that escaped her was one of anticipation. But his knife caught in the voluminous drapes of her gown and grazed her flesh instead of burying itself in her ribs. His thin white arm came back again but with her good hand she overturned the marble basin and he was forced to jump backwards to stop it toppling on his feet. Clutching her side where the blood was already beginning to seep through her dress she tried to run to the door but her legs would not carry her and she slipped and fell to her knees on the rough stone floor. Sensing Felix's shadow above her, she quickly hurled herself forward and rolled under the low sleeping couch, pulling up her knees as she felt Felix trying to stand on her ankles and pinion her down. With her back pressed against the cold wall of her cell, she curled herself up into a ball, kicking wildly at Felix's grasping hands as he reached in and tried to grab hold of any part of her flailing body. After a few frenzied seconds, Fabia felt his fingers wrap around her bare calf and his grip tighten. The stone floor began to move underneath her, scraping agonizingly against her injured side, and she grabbed the underside of the couch, clinging on so hard that it began to drag across the floor too.

Just as she realized that her grip was not strong enough to resist another violent tug from Felix, there was a loud, hollow thud. The tightness around her calf slackened and she opened her watering eyes to see the top of Felix's head now lying at an awkward angle in the space between the couch and the floor, his thin silky hair splayed over his eyes, the silver knife partially concealed beneath the lifeless fingers of his left hand. To the right of his prostrate body was the gently swaying hem of a long white robe beneath which she could just see a pair of sandaled feet. Crawling forwards and peering out from underneath the bed, Fabia looked up to see the tall figure of Cornelia looming overhead, the thick wooden fire stick normally used to kindle the hearth in her room clasped across her body at an angle like the weapon of a warring goddess.

"I *knew* I should have complained about him to the Pontifex," she cried wrathfully. "But you girls were all so soft-hearted over him, insisting that he was just an innocent boy. Well I hope you've learned your lesson."

She dropped the fire stick with a clatter as Fabia dragged herself out from under the bed, leaving a red smear on the floor. Still lying on the floor, the wounded priestess prised open Felix's loosely curled fingers and extracted the knife. Cornelia stared at it in horror.

"That's the knife from my chamber. You're bleeding! In the name of the gods my dear, what has he done to you?"

Fabia stood, wincing as she clutched her side but with a determined look on her face. "It's only a cut, *domina*, it doesn't signify. We must go to the villa of Servilius Caepio at once."

"But why?" asked Cornelia in bafflement.

"She has put herself in danger. Felix is the least of our worries. Please, *domina*, we have no time to waste."

XXXII

HORTENSIA'S SCALP BURNED WHERE HER HAIR HAD BEEN VICIOUSLY pulled and as she came to from her faint, she had to close her eyes once more against the insistent drumming of blood in her head. Waves of nausea and fear flooded over her, scrambling her brain. Her nostrils were full of the smell of pine-sap from the forest outside and another unpleasantly familiar scent, bitter and green. She felt something gently brushing against her head and cringed as she realized that it was Tiberius's hand, his fingers dislodging the flowers so meticulously woven into her hair by Elpidia. Opening her eyes just enough to see his thin, scarred face swimming into focus above her, she realized she was lying on her back, staring up at the vaulted canopy of the carriage. A tightness around her wrists and ankles was soon explained, and a length of cloth had also been wound around her head and mouth, preventing her from speaking. She stared warily at her captor, who was looking down at her with an expression of satisfied greed.

"Apologies for any discomfort, my dear, though I confess it's been very pleasant, watching you sleep a little while. I hope this isn't too tight?" He plucked at the cloth stretched across her cheek. "You know I enjoy listening to you almost as much as looking at you. But you'd be too tempted to draw attention to our presence here. We're only a few feet from the main road even if no one will see us until we want them to."

He correctly interpreted the flicker of her eyes toward the opening in the canopy.

"Yes, your coachmen and other companions are dead, I fear. You'll appreciate the necessity. A few of my men are outside, keeping an eye on the traffic. But we have an hour or two yet. So what shall we talk about in the meantime?" He wound one of her curls around his finger, smiling as she tried to tug her head away.

"You mustn't feel too foolish, my dear. You did very well for a beginner. Your only mistake – and that of your friends in the Temple of Vesta – was in assuming that I was quite so inept a player as Crassus. Clever of you to find the forger. A mistake on my part in fact, letting Crassus handle his disposal. One can only hope he'll make a better fist of governing by himself. I was rather hoping to be able to fade into the background by that point though I see that I may have to take a hand now and then. You're probably wondering why I even took on so clumsy a partner in the first place," he mused in a philosophical tone before chuckling as she mutinously shook her head from side to side.

"Money, you think? Well, maybe. Money's a nice thing to have. I enjoy it as much as the next man. Particularly if the next man's your father." He studied her face for a reaction and smirked with pleasure.

"That was a little unfair of me, I admit. Your father has proved a more stubborn foe than either Crassus or I expected. Did Petro tell you that I ran into Hortensius doing business with him in that squalid tower block of his in the Subura? It wasn't long before I first met you, at Crassus's games – do you remember that? An embarrassing moment for Hortensius. He feared then, of course, that I would expose him. It's always been an open secret that your father doesn't exactly fight fair in some of his trials, but to be able to offer evidence of it . . .well that would be a coup. I admit, I thought that all I had to do was to threaten your father to make him compliant. That's why I sent him one of those rather embarrassing letters Petro gave us. Both Crassus and I assumed your father would by then be so terrified of losing the reputation he'd built for himself that he would pledge himself to whatever scheme that was proposed. But I underestimated Hortensius. Just as I underestimated you, my dear. Your father gave me to understand by return post – in his own inimitable way! – that he considered me a cockroach scurrying through the rubbish tip of humanity and that if I chose to expose him, it was my own affair."

Tiberius smiled.

"Naturally, he didn't know then what Crassus and I were planning of course, if that's any consolation to you. Crassus was convinced Hortensius would come around once Pompey was dead and that we could buy him off if we had to. But if you ask me, I expect only death would have would have silenced your father in the end. Thanks to you, that won't now be necessary . . . but where was I? Ah, my own motivation!"

His hand was still moving in her hair, but his attention seemed to wander from her a little toward an unspecified point in the distance, his copper eyes open and unblinking. Then he fixed his sphinx-like attentions on her once more, bending his head close and speaking softly.

"Do you have any thoughts on why the people love Pompey more than our friend Crassus? Do you imagine it's because he understands them, because he has so much greater an affection for them than Crassus does?" The fingers of his other hand traced an aimless pattern on her breastbone. "Nonsense. It's not even down to all his great victories on the field of battle, remarkable though they are. It's because he has a very special talent – a talent for making sure that when he walks into a room, people's eyes are on him, and no one else. Our Pompey would sooner taste defeat than share a triumph with the soldiers who sweat in his service." Tiberius's eyes gleamed with fervor as he put his face closer to Hortensia's.

"Do you know whose idea it was to coin that name, '*Magnus*' for him? Not ours, not the men who served under him, who followed his orders unquestioningly. Oh he may have been forced to share a little of the limelight from time to time – with Metellus Pius for example, after the victory over Sertorius – but will you wonder at it if Metellus Pius turns a blind eye to Pompey's untimely death when Pompey would happily see Metellus Pius eaten by rabid wolves if it meant he could have ridden in that triumphal procession by himself?" A fleck of spittle landed on Hortensia's temple. She could feel his breath on her cheek now, his voice very low in her ear. "We're all just a pot for him to piss in, my dear. And Rome laps it up like a dog."

For a long minute, the only sound was of Hortensia's lungs expanding and contracting, and the rustle of pine branches against the canopy. Then Tiberius propped himself up on one elbow again, and his wandering finger traced a pattern over her rigid face. The viperish intensity of his expression had lessened and his voice was soft and casual once more.

"You despise Crassus for his weakness, his money, his cowardice. Don't think I blame you my dear. But you shouldn't fool yourself into thinking that in doing everything you've done to protect Pompey, you've been helping the better man. He's not worthy of your patronage." Tiberius's fingers speculatively probed the cloth covering her mouth. "Which makes it a great pity that your name will now, I suspect, forever be coupled with his."

He answered her fearful, questioning look.

"Pompey rides to Rome today. Those much-vaunted games of his begin tomorrow and even as we speak he's on his way from his house at Albano, ready to milk every last drop of adulation he can suck out of that adoring crowd. But quite soon, my friends at the Porta Capena are going to close the road out of the city and put out the report that Cilician pirates have been seen lying in wait for unwary travelers. Not long after that, my men stationed at the next milestone will light a beacon for our benefit, alerting us that General Pompey is passing, before diverting any travelers who may be in his wake. You see how the trap will be set? The news will reach Rome that their beloved consul and favorite son has been ambushed and killed by pirates. I imagine that once the Senate has agreed to put Crassus in charge, his first measure will be to announce a mission to rid Rome's highways of the Cilician menace once and for all. That should help his popularity, shouldn't it?"

He leaned close to her again, this time letting his hand wander downwards to her neck and collarbone before easing it underneath the shoulder of her white gown, grazing her pale flesh with the tips of his sinewy fingers.

"As for you, my dear . . ." he whispered, "it very much pains me to report that you also will be a victim of this terrible tragedy. An unfortunate coincidence of timing you might think, for you and Pompey to be passing just at the key moment. Although the rumor that Pompey's body was actually discovered inside your carriage and that both of you were in a state of some undress –" Hortensia shivered as he exposed her shoulder and pressed his lips to it "– will cause quite a storm, one that won't be calmed by the protestations of your husband and father, however eloquent they should both prove to be. A blemish on a beloved general's reputation, though more on account of the embarrassing manner of his demise – his sword sheathed rather than bared, as it were – but an indelible stain on yours, and one which I'm afraid those familiar with both your courtroom exploits, your habit of frequenting tabernas with your slaves and your intimate conversation with Pompey at his recent party won't find too difficult to believe."

He winced as her knees came up and connected painfully with his shin but was quick enough to snatch her bound hands and prevent her from clawing at his face. She continued to struggle, her heels scrabbling at the soft upholstery of the carriage, and at one point managed to catch his jaw with one of her flailing elbows, which seemed to amuse rather than anger him. But when the keening issuing from her gagged mouth threatened to escalate into a full-bellied scream which would have been heard by any passer-by on the nearby road, he put his hand to her throat and secured her silence with one threatening squeeze.

"Not yet, my dear. There will be time for this sort of thing later. But I like an audience and I wouldn't want you to miss the opening act. Afterwards you can scream all you like. Believe me, I'm not going to stop you."

LUCRIO POURED MORE water over the mare's withers, watching a dark satin glaze spread out over her chestnut coat. With a flat strigil, he smoothed away the excess moisture as the animal's ears twitched contentedly. It wasn't one of his duties, caring for Caepio's horses, but one that he often took on voluntarily, enjoying the opportunity to escape the cool, close confines of the villa and feel for a moment as though he were back home on his family's farm in Lusitania. It was unusual for him to allow himself to remember that far back. The memories of his childhood were tightly sealed in a compartment of his mind which he rarely opened. But today he dwelled heavily on them. He had kept his promise to Hortensia. Tonight, at last, he had determined, he would finally exact his revenge on Dolabella.

His violent imaginings were interrupted by hurried footsteps approaching along the street. Lucrio glanced up to see Eucherius's lively face appear above the stable door.

"You had better come," came the breathless announcement. "There are two women here, looking for the master."

"What sort of women?" asked Lucrio, checking that the mare had enough drinking water before letting himself out of the stall.

"Strange women. They came in a strange carriage. They say they are priestesses. From the temple of Vesta. I think they might be telling the truth though I have never seen such women before. One of them is young, the other one is older and looked very stern. She told me that it was very important they speak to the master or the mistress," added Eucherius.

Lucrio quickened his pace and swiftly made up the distance between the Palatine stables and the villa. On stepping over the threshold, he was confronted by the sight of Fabia and Cornelia, pale, ghostly figures in their spotless white robes. Recognition flickered on Fabia's face.

"It's you," she said eagerly. "I remember you, from outside the theater. You have your mistress's confidence?"

Lucrio nodded, his dark gaze fixed intently on her. But it was Cornelia who spoke next, her low voice rippling impressively around the atrium.

"Is your mistress here?" she demanded.

"No. She has gone with her mother to the festival at Lake Nemi."

"Oh no, we are too late!" The cry came from Fabia. "You must go after them, please. They know." She took a step toward Lucrio, an urgent message in her eyes. "It was Felix, the slave-boy. He saw me taking the will from the sanctuary, he was helping them all the time, the people who took the will, the people who killed Helena. Do you understand? They *know*."

Lucrio had already thrust the strigil in his hand at Eucherius. He raced through the house to the slave-quarters at the back of the kitchen. Overturning the thin straw mattress on which he slept, he prised up one of the wooden floorboards underneath and retrieved a dirty canvas bundle which he shook open to reveal an eclectic assortment of objects – a flat red pebble, a small cloth pouch that jangled when it dropped on to the hard floor, a short length of crimson thread, two swords – one straight, one short – and a close-fitting leather helmet. There was also a frayed slingshot made of thin, flexible flax and a handful of small muddied objects the size of acorns. Rapidly gathering up the weapons and the helmet and tying them in the canvas, he went back to the atrium and was on the verge of issuing curt instructions to Eucherius when he caught sight of Lutatia, just arrived and evidently stunned at the sight of the two Vestals.

"Lucrio? What's going on, I just came to . . ."

"Why are you not on the way to Nemi?" he demanded.

She blinked at his unusual lack of deference.

"I . . . I received a note summoning me to Antemnae, it said that my uncle Gaius was ill, but when I arrived he was in perfect health. So I came back, and Rixus said that Hortensia had gone to Nemi by herself. But it's too dangerous along the Appian Way. I came here to ask you if you would go after her. It's so strange that –"

"Find the master," commanded Lucrio. "Take the priestesses with you to the forum if need be, they will be able to explain. Then tell the master – tell both of them – to follow me along the Appian Way."

"Why, what is it, is Hortensia in trouble?" asked Lutatia in bewilderment. "Please, you have to tell me!" But Lucrio was already gone.

Within seconds, the chestnut mare was clattering at breakneck speed down the southeastern slope of the Palatine toward the Porta Capena. The two swords were wrapped in canvas concealed under Lucrio's arm, the helmet stowed in a saddlebag hung from the pommel. Urged on by her rider, the mare wove her way through heavy foot-traffic, her haunches cannoning off angry pedestrians, until they were suddenly caught up in a heavy swell of vehicles filling the road leading to the city exit. Wagon drivers jostled and swore at each other and up ahead Lucrio could see the source of their discontent. A line of men was advancing up the street, waving their arms and directing travelers back into the city. Behind them, the heavy wooden gates which marked the start of the Appian Way were being slowly swung shut. Digging his heels into the mare's sides, Lucrio fought his way through the crowd, ignoring the objections of those being funneled in the opposite direction. He rode up to one of the men, a portly individual whose fat fleshy palms were bared to the crowd as he fanned them back.

"I have to get through."

"Sorry, gate's closed," came the indifferent reply.

"Let me pass you Roman pig," hissed Lucrio through clenched teeth. But the man standing in his path simply grinned.

"Now now, temper temper. Pirates up ahead. Try the next gate, Latin Way's open – hey!"

He was forced to take evasive action as the mare charged straight through him and into the open space behind the line of guards. Oblivious to the shouts behind him, Lucrio bent low over the mare's flying mane, his green eyes fixed on the ever-narrowing gap between the slowly moving gates. For a moment, it looked as though there was going to be a sickening collision, but the sight of the determined little mare bearing down on them had transfixed the men pushing the cumbersome gates shut and they slackened their efforts for a moment. Lucrio's right knee missed the side of the archway by the finest of margins and with a whisk of the mare's flaxen tail, they were out in the open, the famous old road stretching long and straight into the distance.

XXXIII

HORTENSIA LAY WITH HER HEAD TURNED TOWARD THE FRONT OPENING of the carriage, through which she could just glimpse the watery light of the dipping sun through the green tops of the slender white trees all around them. Streaks of violet were beginning to stain the sky. The festivities in Nemi would already be underway. Was there a chance that Caecilius and Claudia would notice her absence and send someone back to look for her? Even if they didn't assume she and Lutatia had simply been delayed, Nemi was ten milestones distant. It would take several hours for anyone to track back this far.

She flexed her jaw. The gag around her mouth was cutting into her cheeks and her throat ached where Tiberius had wrapped his hand around it. She had drawn her bound wrists up to her chin and her knees to her waist, trying to create any kind of barrier between herself and her captor. She kept her gaze resolutely away from him, but for now, he seemed content to lean against the cushions on the other side of the carriage, his copper eyes alert to her every breath and blink. He seemed to know that he had stifled the fight in her, his manner that of a beast keeping lazy watch on his cornered prey.

A shadow fell across her face and she flinched before realizing it was Tiberius's shaven-headed henchman, addressing his master through the opening in the canopy.

"The beacon is alight, *domine*. Pompey is on his way."

"You know what to do," came Tiberius's indifferent reply.

The man nodded and disappeared.

"Not long now, my dear," crooned Tiberius. "I hope you're sharpening your claws for me."

Hortensia squeezed her eyes shut and shook her head helplessly, fighting to clear her mind, trying to find a reason why Tiberius's plan would fail, why the Senate would never agree to hand over the reins of power to Crassus, why they wouldn't be deceived by the false will which must have been re-sealed and restored to the archive by now. She couldn't bear to think what must have happened to Fabia. Precisely who had betrayed them she didn't know, but Hortensia was certain that it was her own hubris that had placed the young Vestal in such terrible danger. If she had listened to Caepio, to Lucrio even, who had told her to be wary of what she might discover, then Pompey might still be riding along this road to his death, but at least Fabia would be alive. And she herself would not be counting down what was left of her own life, though that depended on whatever depravities Tiberius was concocting. A wave of terror and despair swept over her. The thought of what Caepio would feel was too much to bear. He would see through the slanders, of that she had no fear, but to his grief would be added the burden of hearing such unjust accusations bandied about freely by others. As for her father, how would he live with the aftermath? She saw all too clearly how her recklessness had strengthened Crassus and Tiberius's hand – Petro's false proof of courtroom corruption was no longer needed to shame her father. Who would accept the word of the man whose own daughter had been discovered in so compromising a position at the scene of Pompey's death?

Hortensia's eyes flickered open. In the distance, she could hear the stuttering clatter of horse's hooves on the smooth paving stones of the famous road. By the pattern of the noise, she could tell that there were several riders – perhaps four or five – but she had no doubt that Tiberius would have brought enough men to deal with Pompey's entourage. As the hoofbeats became louder, she wondered desperately if there was anything she could do to give the approaching horsemen warning but the sharp point of a knife placed at her temple scotched any such thoughts.

"Quiet as a mouse now," whispered Tiberius in her ear.

With her breathing quick and shallow, Hortensia strained her ears.

The noise of the riders approaching grew louder and louder until they seemed so close that she wondered if in fact they had the wrong man and they were going to be allowed to pass by. Then there was a sudden shout from the direction of the road. A series of whistling noises like the ones she had heard just before Glaucus toppled from the carriage, and the sound of a horse screaming. More shouts, the clashing and scraping of blades, a man's bellowing voice and then, close by, the pounding of hooves and the cracking of branches as a loose horse charged past. She heard the scuff of sprinting footsteps – someone was running along the road – followed by a grunt and then a long period of silence. Then another whistling noise, this time clear and lower-pitched, repeated three times. The dagger was removed from Hortensia's temple.

"Looks like the show's underway. Come along my dear – you'll want a ringside seat."

The trees in Hortensia's sightline began to move. Slowly, she felt the vehicle trundling down the shallow slope once more and coming to an abrupt halt. The fastenings securing the green awning were loosened and the side panel suddenly flung up, giving her a clearly framed view of the road and its surrounding landscape. Struggling on to her left elbow, she looked around. There was a body on the verge just in front of her and two more sprawled across the highway itself, dark liquid from the deep slashes in their purple livery filling the gaps between the paving slabs. Some distance further up the Appian Way, Hortensia could just see the outline of another prostrate figure, lying face down. Pompey was sitting half-upright in the middle of the road, clutching his right thigh from which the slim shaft of an arrow was protruding, its buried head surrounded by a dark circle of blood. He was cursing and barking at the grey-liveried men standing guard over him, "Bloody mercenaries, haven't got a bloody clue who you're dealing with, I'll have the bloody lot of you torn to pieces by dogs!"

But as soon as he saw Tiberius jumping down from Hortensia's carriage, his ruddy face seemed to turn to stone. As Tiberius strolled forwards and came to stand over him, a sword in one hand and a dagger in the other, Pompey monitored his progress warily.

"What in the name of the gods do you think you're playing at, Tiberius?"

"The gods?" Tiberius shrugged. "No, I never play in their name. Sore losers, most of them. Best to play for your own stake. And there's one very big pot of gold on offer today."

A look of incredulous comprehension came into Pompey's face. "Is that what this is about? You think you can hold me for ransom?" He gave a short crack of laughter. "Who did you have in mind for my bene-factor – the Senate? Crassus? Ha, that's rich! Crassus would rather see me swinging from that tree."

Tiberius raised an eyebrow and grinned. Pompey's expression changed and Tiberius hunched his shoulders again, this time as though in apology. "I'd hate for you to think I did all this for Crassus's sake, mind," he added in a pacifying manner.

"What then?" growled Pompey. "You want to go down in history as the man who killed me? Because you know, you'll never make a name for yourself any other way."

"History?" This time Tiberius shook his head and made a tutting noise. "That's the difference between you and me, Pompey. I don't really mind if no one remembers my name. In fact, I couldn't care less."

He jerked his head back toward the carriage from where Hortensia was silently watching them and waved his sword in her direction.

"She tried to warn you, didn't she? But you could never take an-other's advice. Not even when it meant leading others into disaster." He squatted down and began to toy with the end of the arrow protruding from Pompey's thigh, causing the consul to wince in agony. "How many men was it you lost at Sucro?" probed Tiberius. "All because you wouldn't wait for Metellus Pius, no matter how many times we tried to warn you. You were so worried that he would steal your thunder. So you sent me and my officers off on that suicide mission, knowing that Serto-rius was in charge of their left wing, while you took the soft option at the other end. Then while we fought all the way to his camp, you turned tail and left us the minute Sertorius switched to the right and the going got too rough for you. Leaving us to be picked off. Like carrion at the mercy of vultures. That's when I knew I didn't owe you a damn thing."

Pompey stared doggedly up at him, a muscle going in his cheek. "You got away, didn't you?"

"At a cost." Tiberius ran the edge of his dagger blade lightly over his disfigured left cheek.

"What of it? Most soldiers of Rome wear their scars with pride. Besides, I won plenty more battles than I lost."

Tiberius straightened up, tucking his dagger into its sheath at his belt. "Yes you did – thanks to your legions. But you never mentioned us when you celebrated your triumphs, did you?"

"My men kept faith with me!"

"No, not all of them." Tiberius shifted his stance so that his feet were planted directly in front of Pompey and gripped the hilt of his sword with both hands. "Not Lucilius Albinus, even after he lied for you about what you did with your father's loot. You let him get in Crassus's clutches rather than help him out of debt yourself. Still, he cut his own veins rather than betray you when he had the chance, did you know that?"

A muscle flickered in Pompey's cheek. Tiberius smiled.

"What was it you told us once, about what you said to Sulla when you persuaded him to give you your first triumph? That people would worship the rising rather than the setting sun." He gestured to the darkening sky around them, now veined with violet and gold. "How right you were." He raised his sword like an axe above his head.

Then he tilted his jaw, turning slightly into the breeze like a wolf detecting a scent. Hortensia, who had screwed her eyes shut in anticipation of the fatal blow, dared to open them a fraction. She could hear it too. So could the men surrounding Pompey. A frenetic thudding, like a pulse rippling through the ground. Craning her head forwards, her weight balanced across her elbows, she peered down the road toward Rome. A cloud was appearing over the fire-stained horizon, a small moving silhouette at its center. As it grew larger, the sound of galloping hoofbeats became louder. Tiberius lowered his sword. His expression was calm and closed but Hortensia could see the tension in his jaw as he nodded to his two archers.

"One horseman only. Shoot them down, whoever they are. No witnesses. We'll deal with the body afterwards."

The men nodded and jogged some way down the road. One squatted down in the sunken verge, the other took up a position a few feet behind him on the bank leading up to the forest. Slowly, like ink seeping outwards from a drop spilled on papyrus, the dark speck on the horizon took on a shape, the pumping forelegs and flying mane of the little horse coming into focus. Its ears were flat to its head in the wind tunnel of its own making, its coat shiny with sweat. More puzzling to all those watching its progress – and the glare of the sinking sun admittedly obstructed their view – was the apparent absence of a rider. Hortensia strained her eyes. There was something about the animal's head that was familiar, the shape of its white blaze . . .

The archer concealed at the roadside glanced back uncertainly at Tiberius, who brought his arm down in an irritable gesture of encouragement. Turning back, the man brought his weapon up and took careful aim. The chestnut horse was almost in range but he allowed it to come as close as he dared in order to make sure of the shot. With a twang of his finger, he released the string, but at the same instant the animal swerved and the arrow passed harmlessly behind its haunches, embedding itself in the ploughed field. A second arrow was fired almost immediately, this time by the archer stationed on the bank, but the little horse was moving at such speed that he too missed his target. As the men quickly re-armed, Hortensia suddenly noticed the leg resting along the mare's spine and the strong forearm curving over its neck, pulling heavily on its right rein. Then she saw a face, half-obscured by a leather helmet that came down over the eyes, framed between the mare's thrusting head and bulging chest.

A flash of movement, a jerk of the swinging rider's free arm and something flew across the road, a small object no bigger than a fig. The head of the man standing on the bank jerked backwards before he fell slowly, a crimson hollow where his eye used to be. The remaining archer fumbled with his bow as the animal plunged toward him. When he looked up again, he saw Lucrio suddenly swinging his right leg over the animal's back, heaving himself upright, sword outstretched and ready. The archer's arm came up but with a whirling swipe of Lucrio's long straight blade, his bow hand was severed cleanly at the wrist.

"Get your bloody swords up!" Tiberius shouted to his six remaining followers, who immediately braced themselves across the road, abandoning their guard of Pompey, who began dragging himself toward the bank at the side of the road. "Leave him," he bellowed at the shaven-headed slave who was looking uncertainly at the retreating Pompey. "He's a sitting duck, we can finish him off whenever we want."

The chestnut mare was now bearing down on the group blocking the road. Lucrio sat up straight and easy in the saddle, guiding his sprinting mount with his heels while in his right hand he brandished the straight sword, and in his left he held the shorter blade. The leather helmet covering his skull and cheekbones created a menacing foil for his broken nose and rigidly set jaw. As he closed the gap between himself and Tiberius's men, the long blade in his right hand began to swing like a cart wheel.

"Don't give way," roared Tiberius. "Hold him up."

His command came too late for the man nearest him. The shorter of the two swords, pitched like a javelin with unerring speed and accuracy, buried itself in his neck. A second follower was dispatched with a clean thrust through his shoulder from the long blade. Tiberius stepped forward, timing his move to take advantage of Lucrio's sword being engaged and attack from the mare's other side. Hortensia, who was desperately trying to tug her hands free of the ties around her wrists and had managed in the meantime to peel down her gag with her fingertips, cried out in terrified warning. But a well-aimed kick from Lucrio's good leg connected with Tiberius's jaw, and he stumbled away with a mouthful of blood and loose teeth.

"Finish him off damn you," he gargled.

As Lucrio checked the little mare's forward momentum and swung her round in a tight circle, two more men attempted to close him down, one from either side. There was a violent clash of blades, and a gash of blood appeared on Lucrio's forearm, soaking into the leather guard he always wore there. Slashing viciously with the sword in his other hand, he dragged the edge of the long blade across his opponent's neck and seconds later he had driven the point through his other attacker's chest.

The last pair hung back as Lucrio turned to face them, shifting their grip on their swords, eyeing the helmeted Lusitanian warily. One of them was the slave with the shaven head. Tiberius, who had retreated to the verge in order to empty his mouth of blood, bellowed at them. "What are you waiting for you donkeys?" but still they hesitated. He picked up a rock from the ground. "Get the bastard!" Instead of hurling it at them, he spun round and flung it directly at the head of Lucrio's mount. It hit the mare squarely on her eye and she reared up in fright and pain. Lucrio tumbled onto the hard paving stones, landing awkwardly on his weak knee. An agonized oath escaped him. Tiberius's copper eyes glowed and he spat out a bloody tooth.

"Now, let's see you fight, whoever you are."

Emboldened, the two men ran forward. Hortensia, who had finally succeeded in freeing her hands, was now being helped to undo the ties around her feet by Pompey, who had managed to crawl as far as her carriage and heave himself up into it. She watched in helpless anguish as Lucrio struggled to get up, his sword scraping uselessly across the hard ground. The first man to reach him raised his own arm, blade poised.

"No!" Hortensia cried out, distracting Tiberius, who glanced in her direction and noticed Pompey's progress.

A second later there was another cry, this time from the road. Lucrio yanked his long straight sword from the first man's gut and then launched himself into combat with his shaven-headed companion. From his first step, it was clear that Lucrio was limping badly. But as they stumbled over the bodies of Tiberius's helpmates, he was able to extract his short sword from the gullet of his first victim and, having parried his hapless opponent's blade with his right hand, he delivered a fatal blow to his adversary's rib cage with his left. Blood bubbled up through the slave's chipped teeth as he slumped sideways onto the hard ground.

Panting and spitting, Lucrio turned to look for Tiberius. He found him, not on the verge where he had previously been standing, but sitting on the open ledge of Hortensia's carriage. He still held his sword in his left hand, but his right arm was hooked around Hortensia's neck, pressing the edge of his short dagger into her throat. Pompey lay semi-conscious on the ground in front of the carriage opening, a trickle of blood making its way down from his luxuriant hairline and across his ruddy cheek.

"My congratulations," Tiberius called out to Lucrio. "I must remember not to hire Cilicians next time. Eight for one is a poor return on my investment. No, no!" Hortensia gave a strangled cry as the blade pressed deeper into the underside of her jaw and Lucrio stopped dead at the top of the slope. "That's close enough, we can chat from here. I have many questions for you my friend but let's go through the formalities. Who are you, or more importantly, since you're obviously not a passing tourist, who sent you?"

Lucrio said nothing. Hortensia stared at him desperately, trying to read a signal in his eyes. She noted his eyes flicker toward her clenched fist held across her breast and she opened her fingers slightly before closing them again.

"It's a simple question, my friend. It might even make you a rich man. Who are you here for – him or her? You see, it's quite important I know where we all stand."

"They're not my concern." Lucrio's voice was emotionless.

Tiberius raised an eyebrow disbelievingly. "Is that right? So what are you? Some kind of avenging Fury? Did those harpies from the Temple of Vesta pray for divine intervention and get you instead?"

"It's you I came for."

There was a pause. Lucrio put up his hand and pulled the sweat-soaked leather helmet from his head, tossing it onto the ground. Tiberius studied him carefully, then his eyes narrowed, and he glanced at Hortensia.

"I know him, don't I?"

"Not as well as I know you," said Lucrio.

Tiberius snorted. "You must have a highly developed sense of grievance if one night in my cellar made you so hungry for revenge on me.

But you didn't learn to fight like that in the backwoods of Gaul, or wherever you said you were from."

Lucrio spoke slowly and deliberately. "Do you remember a small farm in Lusitania, where a man gave you water and offered you food?"

Tiberius stared at him, blank incomprehension on his scarred features.

"In return, you killed him and his small son. You shamed his wife and then you killed her too. Do you remember now?"

A look came into Tiberius's eyes, an intrigued flicker of memory.

"Do you remember what you said to the little boy you left alive? The boy you and your friends sold for a bag of coins and a jar of wine?" His eyes traveled briefly to meet Hortensia's, glancing deliberately at her clenched fist, still held defensively across her body. Then he refocused his gaze on Tiberius, who was still staring at him in wary fascination. "You told him that he was lucky. That the Roman Empire was a land of opportunity, if he was willing to take advantage of it." He inched his way forward all the time as he spoke. "It never occurred to you that the boy might come looking for you one day." He spread his arms and tilted his face so that the watery light of the rising moon fell across it. "You didn't recognize me that night at your house. But maybe you recognize me now . . ."

Tiberius opened his mouth to speak and in that instant Lucrio's eyes locked with Hortensia's. Her fist came up like the arm of a catapult and the long, jeweled hairpin concealed in her palm split the skin of Tiberius's cheek just below his left eye. In the same second she ducked out from underneath his arm and rolled off the ledge of the carriage. Blood seeped out between Tiberius's splayed fingers as, howling with pain, he lunged instinctively with his sword arm. But the wild thrust was parried away from Hortensia by Lucrio, who had hurled himself forward, making up the final feet between himself and the carriage. The cost of this Herculean effort to his injured knee however meant that he was off-balance as he tried to turn defense into attack, and despite his own injury, Tiberius was able to deliver a strong riposte, forcing Lucrio into hobbling retreat. Springing down from the carriage, Tiberius advanced menacingly but in the next instant was brought to the ground by a revived Pompey, who had lurched forward to grab hold of one of Tiberius's feet and was now clinging tenaciously to his prize. With a vicious kick that left Pompey cursing, Tiberius extricated himself and scrambled to his feet before stumbling down the slope toward the road and disappearing into the violet gloom.

Lucrio stood poised to go after him, but hesitated a moment, looking down at Hortensia, who was curled up by the wheel of the carriage, both hands covering her face. "Are you alright, *domina*?"

She shivered and nodded.

"Are you sure?"

"Yes. Head, groin, neck and eyes. I remembered." A shaky laugh escaped her. "You should go or you'll lose sight of him." She lowered her hands and saw him hesitating still. "It's all right. I'm all right. Just make sure you come back," she added with a touch of acerbity. "Or I'll never forgive you."

He gave her a little salute and then limped down the slope toward the road.

XXXIV

H E WAS JUST IN TIME TO SEE TIBERIUS'S OUTLINE DISAPPEARING amongst a crowded colony of tombs that lined the Appian Way up ahead. The moon was now beginning its upward climb across the vault of the sky, casting a soft metallic glow that threw every angle of the landscape into sharp relief. Lucrio drew alongside one of the larger sepulchres, pausing in the shadow of its towering peak for a moment. Then, keeping his sword vertical and close to his body, and with his back pressed to the cold bricks, he slid into the dark little labyrinth. His steps were short and careful. Around the tombs there were numerous urns and tiny amphorae filled with wine and oil, offerings to the dead made by those they had left behind. When he knocked one over with his dragging right leg, it made a dull crack like a bone snapping and he withdrew into the deep shade of a little archway. But there was no answering movement from any of the encircling shadows, just the lazy bob and sway of tree branches in the evening breeze. He crept on, stealing from tomb to tomb, ducking silently between slanting moonbeams.

As he skirted round a grandiose mausoleum designed like a small temple, a drop of blood glinted up at him from a shard of travertine which had fallen to the ground. His knuckles whitened against the hilt of his sword and he came to a halt, letting the breeze whisper into his ears. Then he moved on, weaving slowly through the colonnaded frontage, checking his step every now and then to take a reading from his silent surroundings. A cloud passed across the face of the moon and he took the opportunity to cross the narrow avenue separating the temple-tomb from its neighbors. The slight ruffle of a cloak behind him was the only warning he had, but it was enough.

His sword met Tiberius's with a hissing clash and it was Tiberius who was forced to disengage first, though not before pushing the Lusitanian off-balance with a violent thrust driven from the hilt of his blade. He attacked again, quick as a cobra, and as the moon emerged from behind its cloud, his face was illuminated, the scarred skin now rendered even more grotesque by its veneer of dried blood, his gums, bared like a tiger's, stained crimson.

No words were exchanged as they traded savage blows, Tiberius with the advantage of speed over his lame opponent, Lucrio with the upper hand in height and physical strength. Nevertheless it was Tiberius who assumed the role of aggressor at first, hacking and slashing with almost frenzied venom, keeping Lucrio on the back foot and using their constricted surroundings to force him into awkward nooks and corners where he struggled to make the most of his large frame. But the Lusitanian's blade remained steady, and as he soaked up the relentless onslaught, his narrowed green eyes glowed with unwavering intent. Slowly, as Tiberius started to tire, his opponent's strategy began to reap dividends. Every feint was anticipated, each desperate lunge parried and returned with interest. Now it was Tiberius who was being forced to retreat along the path between the tombs while Lucrio advanced, his limp barely discernible. At one point Tiberius stumbled and fell, but the fatal blow did not come. His opponent seemed content to observe him scrambling to his feet and then continue to dog his every move with an assault of increasing intensity, all the while watching and waiting as Tiberius fought to keep up his guard.

By now, sweat was pouring down Tiberius's face, streaking across the blood smears on his cheeks, and it was all he could do to keep his fighting arm raised. Every time Lucrio brought the edge of his own blade smashing down, the sword slipped a little further from Tiberius's damp grasp. Finally, one last shattering blow sent it clattering to the ground. Lucrio stepped back.

"Pick it up," he ordered harshly.

Tiberius rocked back slightly on his knees but did not attempt to retrieve his sword. Contemplating his conqueror, his eyes came to rest on the mark on Lucrio's arm, no longer concealed by the leather guard which had since fallen away.

"So," he slurred. "You really did go a long way to find me."

"Pick it up!"

Tiberius shook his head, a gummy leer splitting his face. "Who would have thought . . . from peasant brat to soldier. Slave to savior. The Roman Empire . . . truly a land of opportunity. Strange . . . how memory plays tricks on one though. *Three* deaths, was it you said?" He held up one hand and counted slowly with his fingers. "Funny. I can only remember the two . . . maybe I should hire Hortensius to defend me on the third count?"

He swayed again, as though the gentle buffeting of the breeze swirling around them might topple him over at any moment. Then, with a last burst of effort, he swooped to grab his fallen weapon, lurched to his feet and charged. The straight sword in Lucrio's hand passed cleanly through him. Tiberius paused, looking down at the point where Lucrio's balled fist almost met his ribcage, a glinting bridge of metal in between. He blinked rapidly as though reviewing the novel sensation of a mortal wound and finding it strangely unexpected. Then he slid to the ground and lay there, his copper eyes open and fixed on the starlit sky.

For a long minute, Lucrio stared at Tiberius's body. A nightingale cried out softly, waking him from his reverie, and he dashed the sweat from his brow before bending to retrieve his sword. Wiping the blade against Tiberius's cloak, he gazed down at him for a few moments more, a deep furrow in his brow. Then he began to make his way back to the road, his limp strongly in evidence once more, and retraced the few hundred paces back to where he had left Hortensia and Pompey. As he came closer he could see four horsemen thundering along the Appian Way from the direction of Rome, one of them considerably in advance of the other. Lucrio had no difficulty in recognizing this lead rider.

"Stand where you are!" came the bellowed command. "Drop your sword!"

"It's me, *domine*."

Caepio's muddied face loomed out of the darkness, his chestnut locks wildly disordered.

"Lucrio! In the name of the gods, where is she? Where's Hortensia?"

Lucrio pointed with the sword he was still holding.

"She is there, *domine*."

Caepio whipped around and saw Hortensia making her way slowly down the slope from the forest, one shoulder lent in support to a groggy-looking Pompey, whose thigh was now tightly bound with the cloth Tiberius had used to stifle her. She glanced up as they neared the road and a ripple of emotion passed across her face as she saw Lucrio standing there. Then her gaze traveled to Caepio.

"Hortensia!"

He ran toward her and she in turn abandoned her role as Pompey's helpmate, flinging her arms around her husband's neck and burying her face in his shoulder. Hortensius, Cato and Caecilius arrived just in time to witness the scene, their horses sending up a skittering cloud of pebbles as they were dragged to an abrupt halt. Hortensius was the first to dismount and he too hurried to embrace his daughter, shedding tears as he rested his chin on her dark head. Caecilius and Cato, both sweaty and exhausted from their breakneck ride, hesitated before going to Pompey's aid but he waved away their offers of assistance with impatience before eventually consenting to sit down on the bank. An intense discussion broke out between the three men, eventually joined by Hortensius. Several times during the conversation, which was enlivened by Pompey's animated gestures, Hortensius glanced back at Lucrio, a solitary figure on the road amongst the bodies of Tiberius's men.

Eventually, Hortensius detached himself from the group around Pompey and approached the Lusitanian.

"Where is Tiberius Dolabella?"

Lucrio tilted his head slightly in the direction of the road stretching out behind him.

"By the tombs, *domine*."

Hortensius looked down at the blood-streaked sword and then up at Lucrio again.

"Did you leave any of his men alive?"

Lucrio shook his head. "None that I found here. He has more though, further up the road at the next milestone, and some more by the Porta Capena."

Hortensius nodded. "They have been apprehended. The others will be caught in due course." His expression was hard to read but he said nothing more. Caecilius came over to address himself to Hortensius.

"Can you believe it?" he asked heavily.

"Yes. A terrible windbag, isn't he? One nick from an arrow and he carries on as though he has been flattened by a siege machine."

Caecilius shook his head. "This is serious, Hortensius."

"I know it is, Caecilius. That's my daughter over there with Dolabella's fingermarks around her neck, in case you'd forgotten. If I'd had any idea what he was planning . . ."

"Why would you have known?" asked Caecilius in puzzlement.

Hortensius did not answer him. Instead he scanned the landscape, his blue eyes cold and alert. Very deliberately, he began to wind one fold of his traveling cloak around his slender fingers.

"I think we need to pay someone a visit. Don't you?"

XXXV

THE WALLS OF CRASSUS'S PRIVATE QUARTERS HAD BEEN DECORATED, AT the owner's special commission, with a tapestry of ornithological paintings showing doves, nightingales, orioles and peacocks in various poses against a garden setting. It was an idea he had conceived after visiting the house of Licinius Lucullus, who was famous for entertaining guests in a dining room which also housed an aviary – thus one would dine on cooked birds whose live cousins fluttered above one's head. But as Crassus lay there in the dark, the beady-eyed birds seemed suddenly sinister to him, as though augurs might read terrible prophecies into the way they were spreading their wings. He also knew that it would not help his cause if rumors should spread, via his more indiscreet household staff, that he had been wide awake and pacing about his house on the night that word arrived of his co-consul's murder. So he pulled the crimson linens over his head and, when the sound of the heavy knocker adorning his front door echoed through the villa, forced himself to lie still for what seemed like an interminable wait. At last he heard approaching footsteps. The door opened and the troubled face of his steward intruded.

"*Domine*. I am very sorry to disturb you. But there are some people here to see you . . ."

Crassus had already started up from his bed and was hastily swathing himself in a thick cloak. "Tell them I shall be there in a moment," he said. Then his face paled to the color of marble as Hortensius entered the room, his customary air of magnificent languor belied only by the razor-sharp glare of animosity in his blue eyes. He was accompanied by Hortensia, now wrapped in a thick cloak retrieved from her villa, her long hair falling about her shoulders. She shot a defiant look at Crassus, who instinctively pulled his robe closer about him, but neither she nor her father uttered a word, instead stepping aside to make room for a procession that began with Caepio, Cato and Caecilius, and concluded with Pompey, who strode in slowly and purposefully, clearly intent on his entrance having the maximum impact.

For a long moment there was silence as the six faces contemplated the one. Cato and Caecilius's expressions were masks of austere gravity and even Caepio looked angry for once, his usually smiling face lined with aggression. Under scrutiny, Crassus tried repeatedly to arrange his features into a surprised smile but the attempt kept going awry, presenting the appearance of a palsied twitch. When he found his voice though, it was steady and charming as always.

"Gentlemen. And . . . lady," he made a gesture eloquent of gallant surprise in Hortensia's direction. "I . . . this is quite a . . . a delegation. I trust . . . I can't begin to imagine why . . . I hope you're not here to tell me that the Parthians are advancing from the east." He laughed deprecatingly, then his tone changed from friendly surprise to solicitude. "Pompey, my old friend, you don't look well. Nicodemus, fetch a chair for General Pompey."

"Spare me the concern, *old friend*."

Crassus's smile took on a rictus quality but he maintained his easy manner. "You military men, you're like dogs who won't let anyone else touch their wounds. Come now, you must sit down."

After a slight pause, Pompey lowered himself into the scrolled chair which the steward Nicodemus had placed against the opposite wall from Crassus's sleeping-couch. He rested his elbows along the arms, stretching his leg out in front of him so that the fresh bandage around his thigh was just visible. Crassus glanced fleetingly at it but made no comment. Hortensius and the others remained standing, Hortensia shaking off the slight pressure on her arm from her father, who had indicated another chair to her. They waited while Nicodemus lit the candle-lamp beside Crassus's bed before bowing himself hesitantly out of the room.

"So." It was Crassus who once more broke the silence. "Not that I wish to be an uncivil host, but what can I do for you all? I confess I am rather anxious. It must be an extraordinary situation to bring you all here at such an . . . unconventional visiting hour."

Pompey put the tips of his fingers together and peered unblinkingly over the top of them. "We're here to canvass your opinion on a judicial matter, Crassus. As my co-consul of course."

"Very well," said Crassus with the air of one amenably indulging a child. "Though I can't imagine what I could offer in the way of judicial advice that would be superior to that on offer from present company." He made a deferential little bow in the direction of Hortensius, who was now leaning back against the wall, arms folded. "Incidentally Hortensius I was sorry to hear of the outcome of the trial today, not that I suppose it came as much of a surprise to you in the end –" He was cut off by Pompey.

"Never mind that now, Crassus, Hortensius doesn't want your sympathy. What, in your view, should the punishment be for disloyalty?"

Crassus glanced speculatively at Cato and Caecilius. He coughed slightly, as though both amused and puzzled by the question. "Disloyalty . . . that sounds more like a philosophical discussion than a judicial one. I think you might have come to the wrong house."

Pompey cut in. The intonation of his voice was even and relentless.

"Then let me be more specific still, using terms that even you can understand, Crassus. What should the punishment be for treachery?"

"I suppose it depends on the kind of treachery you're talking about, old friend," replied Crassus humorously. "I mean, if this is about you and that dancing-girl I saw you with at your party then I suppose you'd have to ask Mucia."

"I'm talking about treachery to Rome!"

Crassus licked his lips. "That would be very serious indeed . . . Look Pompey, I don't know quite what you're getting at and I'm really awfully tired so if you could get to the –"

"You lying scum."

The fierce savagery with which he spoke made everyone in the room flinch. Hortensia took her eyes off Crassus for a moment to glance at Pompey, a hint of misgiving in her face. Crassus recovered quickly, allowing a small, incredulous cough to escape him before opening his mouth to speak, but Pompey interrupted, his florid cheeks inflamed with righteous passion.

"You thought you could get rid of me?" he demanded. "Send a pack of hired criminals to eliminate Rome's greatest general? Leave me for dead at the side of a road like some common sea merchant? Forge my will and try to fool the world into thinking that I would ever entrust you with power over the Republic? This is how you repay me for sharing power with you?"

"Really, Pompey . . . I don't know what madness has seized you though I'd thank you to explain it to me. And might I add that the gift of power is not *yours* to share. We were both elected on equal merit need I remind you, by the people of Rome." Crassus was so agitated in his rebuttal that he didn't notice Lucrio sidling quietly into the room.

"Ah yes, the people of Rome," retorted Pompey. "Tell me, what did you reckon a fair price for their loyalty? I can just picture the scene – you standing on the rostrum, shedding tears for me out of one eye, giving the wink with the other that it was going to be party time in Rome from now on for everyone. Just how long a period of mourning were you planning to give me before you started hosting games and handing out free bread?"

Crassus shook his head. "Madness," he repeated firmly. "You barge into my house in the middle of the night, dragging with you some of our senatorial colleagues whom you then subject to these deluded ramblings. Conspiracies, forged wills . . . By Jupiter who has poured this poison into your ear? I thought you knew better than to believe the rumors which fly round this city."

"And what of Dolabella?" pressed Pompey. "When did he agree to the scheme?"

Crassus's breath caught in his throat for a second but his reaction was carefully studied. "What on earth does Publius Dolabella –"

"You know full well I'm not talking about that little whelp," snarled Pompey. "I give you credit for alighting on the one man in Rome with the audacity to plan such a coup, though believe me Tiberius would have fleeced you for everything you had to keep the secret. But maybe that was a price you were willing to pay – anything to get one up on me."

"Caecilius, Cato, you are both reasonable men, you must realize that these are the ramblings of –"

"Don't appeal to them! They know everything. They saw the bodies of the men who tried to ambush me, not to mention the hole in my leg damn it. Your friend Tiberius is dead too by the way. But his followers – those who were charged with closing the gate out of the city, those who sent the signal that I was on my way down the road – they're still very much alive. How much would you be prepared to bet that they can't be persuaded to talk?"

"So you've got proof that Tiberius was plotting against you!" blustered Crassus. "That's all very well, Pompey, but *tell me this*. Where's your proof against *me*?"

There was a brief, expectant pause. Something rustled in the corner. Crassus suddenly noticed Lucrio standing there in the shadows.

"Who is this?" he demanded. Then he saw what Lucrio was proffering to Pompey and it was as if all the air were suddenly sucked out of his lungs. Pompey took the crimson-sealed scroll, and ran the pad of his thumb delicately and deliberately over the topmost disc of wax, which was embossed with a griffin.

"Why don't you tell me something instead. What's my will doing in your house, Crassus?" he asked softly.

He received no reply. Crassus stared at the will and shook his head. His mouth opened and closed but no sound came out. Pompey's smile was pure malice now.

"No? Then I'll ask you one more time. What should the punishment be for treachery? Shall we ask our friends here?" Pompey turned to face Caecilius, Cato, Hortensius and Caepio, gently slapping the will against the palm of his other hand, like an axeman preparing to strike his first blow. "Gentlemen. Let's imagine that this is a court of law and you are sitting as jury. You've seen the evidence. You've heard the witness's testimony. What's your verdict?"

Cato answered almost immediately. "I think I can speak for my colleagues," he declared in tones of stern authority. "There can be only one punishment for such treachery."

"I agree with my esteemed friend Cato." The announcement came from Hortensius, still propped casually against the wall. "There can be only one punishment."

Hortensia glanced up at her father. A worried frown creased her brow and deepened when her husband became the third to speak. "I agree," said Caepio resolutely.

"Caecilius, what say you?" asked Pompey.

Caecilius hesitated. "This is not a court of law as I understand it. But I agree that the most heinous of crimes, which indeed this is, would surely be thought to merit the gravest of punishments."

Pompey turned back to Crassus, whose face was now white with sweat.

"Good. Well since we're all agreed, I for one have always been in favor of swift justice."

There was a rasp of metal as Pompey extracted from his belt the bloodstained short sword previously wielded by Lucrio. Caecilius started forward in alarm and Caepio moved to shield Hortensia's view. But neither Hortensius nor Cato made any move to check Pompey as he advanced on Crassus, who had stumbled backwards on to his sleeping couch.

"Don't!"

The tip of the short sword buried itself harmlessly in the crimson coverlet as Pompey's aim went awry. Crassus rolled off the couch and cowered on the floor. His co-consul paused before attempting to strike again, the tip of his blade hovering above Crassus's belly. He glanced over at Hortensia, who had ducked out of Caepio's protective embrace and was now standing in the middle of the room, an imploring look on her face.

"Forgive me, madam. I had forgotten there was a lady in the room. Caepio, you should take your wife home. This is no place for her."

Hortensia held up both her hands placatingly as though soothing a head-shy horse.

"General Pompey, you must not."

"This is not for your eyes, my dear. Go home, you will be honored in the same breath as Cloelia for your bravery this day, but now you must leave this to us."

She turned to face her father and his companions. "Please, Papa, Cato – listen to me. Caecilius is right, this is not a law court."

The expression on Caecilius and Cato's faces made it obvious they strongly disagreed with this statement. Impatience creased Pompey's face.

"Hortensius, you take her out."

But Hortensius didn't move and Hortensia took advantage of her father's silence.

"I have a right to speak. You cannot kill him," she insisted. "If you do, you will cause the very chaos that your own murder was intended to create."

Pompey snorted. "Don't talk nonsense, my dear. Once people hear what this guttersnipe was planning and how narrow an escape the Republic has had, believe me, they will be celebrating and sacrificing in the name of Jupiter, not rioting in the streets."

"And then what?" she demanded. "What happens after he is dead? Will you accept another consul in his place?"

Pompey's hesitation was a fraction too long. "Of course." He glanced around the room and nodded magnanimously at Hortensius. "Why, your own father would be just the man for the job. He'll be consul anyway at the end of the year."

Hortensia looked at her father for a moment before turning back resolutely to Pompey. "And are you so sure that you and my father have the full support of the Senate?" she asked quietly. "That there will not be those who accuse the pair of *you* of corruption and conspiracy?"

She received no reply. Hortensius was eying his daughter intently, and Caepio too looked thoughtful. After staring at her and evidently undergoing a severe internal struggle, Pompey at last muttered:

"I may not be able to buy people's loyalty like Crassus here, but we've proof haven't we? There's your testimony, the Vestals, the forger. Your man here told us about the slave-boy in the Temple – and we have this will, by Jupiter!" He held up the document scrunched in his fist.

"Rumor doesn't respect proof though, does it?" answered Hortensia gently. "And neither my testimony nor the forger's nor the Vestals' will carry as much weight as a man's in a Roman court, not if enough of Crassus's supporters cry foul. Do you really want Rome to split itself down the middle again? Brothers siding against brothers, fathers fighting on opposite sides from their sons? You have a duty to prevent that. You have the power to stop it. You are the greatest general in Rome, sir. Isn't the only way to conquer to make peace?"

Her vibrant voice filled the chamber with its warm timbre, leaving silence in its wake. The tip of Pompey's sword wavered above Crassus's heart like a silverfish suspended in a current.

"What exactly is it that you want me to do then, madam?" he asked slowly, staring down at Crassus's petrified face. "Pretend that nothing has happened? Smile and act as though this . . . this traitor and I are the best of friends?"

"Yes," she said baldly. "For the sake of the Republic, you must. What has happened tonight must never leave this room."

Every eye in the room was fixed on the hovering tip of the sword. The only sound emanated from Crassus's throat as he sucked and wheezed. Slowly, very slowly, Pompey lowered his arm.

Crassus began to stagger to his feet. "I'm indebted to you, madam," he croaked. "I was beginning to think that common sense would never prevail in this discussion and I still protest that –"

The words whimpered and died as Crassus found himself grabbed by the neck of his robes and slammed against the wall.

"You listen to me you little shitbird," growled Pompey. "If you so much as fart in a way that I don't like the smell of, I'm going to cut out your scrotum and use what's left of your prick as a door knocker. Do you understand? This isn't over between you and me."

Releasing Crassus, who slid groggily down the wall, Pompey turned to Hortensius, Cato, Caepio and Caecilius, addressing them bullishly.

"Gentlemen. You came here to expose a conspiracy and now you are being asked to join one. Do you agree to it?"

Caecilius, Caepio and Hortensius all nodded. After a long delay, Cato grudgingly followed suit.

"Good. Then the pact is sealed. To sweeten the deal, old Crassus here promises to lend Hortensius and Caecilius his full support during their consulship – don't you, Crassus? – and he'll make an anonymous donation to the state treasury too. Five million sesterces should just about do it, what do you think?" He waved his sword in front of Crassus's nose and received a mumbled reply.

"What about Dolabella?" interjected Cato, clearly still disgruntled. "What are people going to think when they find his body on the Appian Way – and those of all your men?"

"They will think precisely what they were supposed to think. That the pirate menace has struck again. I see it will behoove me to exercise some authority in that regard," answered Pompey with a glint in his eye.

He turned next to Hortensia, favoring her with a twisted little smile and a brief salute. Then he strode toward the door, pausing on the threshold with the bloodstained short sword still in his hand. He held it out to Lucrio, subjecting the Lusitanian to long, searching scrutiny as he did so.

"You're a useful man in a fight. Someone obviously taught you well. I'd give something to have you serve alongside me one day."

Lucrio took the sword and returned the look unblinkingly. Pompey's piercing eyes wandered to his left forearm. Where the leather guard had been torn away, the skin there was lighter than the surrounding area and a faded circular mark was just visible. Pompey nodded purposefully.

"Those come off, you know. Lime and gypsum. Old soldier's trick. Some swear pigeon shit works too, not that I've never tried it. You might want to think about it though. A man needs to be able to forget his past sometimes."

He departed into the corridor. Beckoning the others to follow, Hortensius placed an arm around Hortensia's shoulders and swept the entire party out of the room. As they emerged into the open air and began to walk steadily up the Palatine Hill, Caecilius glanced at Hortensius, a look of pithy disapproval on his face.

"I've said it before and I'll say it again, Hortensius. You should never have taught your daughter how to speak."

XXXVI

Rome. January 1, 69BC

HORTENSIA SAT ALONE IN HER FATHER'S STUDY. IT WAS A COOL DAY, even for the first month of the year, and a fire had been kindled in a brazier in the middle of the room, well away from her father's precious papyri collection. She found it hard to tear her gaze from the twisting flames and wondered idly if this was how it felt to be a Vestal, the monotony of their daily duty by the hearth alleviated by the mesmeric comfort of gazing into the heart of the blaze. One of the lumps of wood settled slightly, sending a spark shooting out of the bronze basin, and she watched it glowing for several minutes on the tile floor before it slowly turned black and finally dissolved into grey ash.

Her eye fell once more to the document unrolled across her knee. The thin red string that had kept it in its coil lay on the floor. It was a small scroll, covered with an uneven, scrawling hand as though its author were only half literate, and contained just two columns of text. The first appeared to be a statement from a landowner in the Roman province of Asia, who testified that he had never faced any intimidation at the hands of its provincial governor; the second was a description of a farm in the province, detailing its precise location and the delineation of its boundaries, and avowing the landowner's willingness to see it pass into the hands of the governor, in the event of his own death.

Holding the document out over a low cedar table placed in front of her chair, Hortensia leaned forward and with the aid of a little make-up scoop from her mother's dressing-table, levered up some of the crumbled ashes from below the brazier and tipped them over the bottom edge, letting the surplus fall on to the cedar table. With one finger, she lightly rubbed the grey powder into the papyrus. A word appeared, like a vein coming to the surface of the skin, written in what appeared to be a light, sepia ink. She stared at it for a few moments then let it drop to the ground where it joined a pile of other documents, many – though not all – with the same faint, one-word imprimatur inscribed across the corner.

Hortensia sat back in her chair and stared deep into the flames. She did not hear the door opening behind her and started up quickly at the sound of it being closed. Caepio was standing there.

"There you are. Your mama said you had gone into the garden."

"I did, but it was too cold."

"Are you ready to go? Your mama has already set out with Quintus, we'd better hurry if you don't want to miss your papa's speech."

She hesitated, then nodded, touching the back of her hand to her cheek, which was red and flushed from the heat of the fire. "Yes. Just give me a moment. I'll be out soon."

Caepio opened the door. Then he closed it again. He came over to his wife, scanning her face, seeing the redness in her eyes and the puffiness in her cheeks that owed nothing to the brazier's warmth. Then he noticed the papyri scattered on the floor. Bending down to pick one up, he scanned the contents, and after a long, difficult pause, finally looked up at her again with sadness and regret in his face.

"Don't judge him too harshly, my dearest."

She shook her head, not looking at him. "No. I know . . ."

"Your father was – and is – one of the finest advocates Rome has ever seen. He has won many cases by the sheer force of his rhetoric. But he cannot stand to lose. Even when there was little risk of failure, he felt he had to make sure of victory, he convinced himself it was necessary . . ."

She nodded again, blinked away a few more tears and took a few aimless steps about the room, staring up at the rolls of papyri.

"I don't know if this will help," Caepio continued, after another difficult pause, "but I think I know now why he was in such a strange mood at the time of Verres's trial. He was worried Dolabella was going to expose his visits to the forger, that much we already know. The fear of humiliation weighed heavily with him. But I think he was ashamed too. In a way, it made him more determined to face Cicero, to prove that he could win without tricks, with just the power of his voice alone. The burden lifted from him just before your wedding, when he told Dolabella he wouldn't give in to his blackmail."

"He only did that because he knew he could prove Petro's letters for fakes," said Hortensia quietly. Caepio did not answer immediately.

"Perhaps. But you know, I still think it brought him back to himself. He was looking forward to the chance to prove his skill against that of a worthy opponent, even if only to himself. However of course Cicero proved himself a little too worthy, and your father didn't get the chance. He realized from the first day of the trial that his days as king of the law court were over. And in a strange way, he accepted it."

He looked over at her, but she didn't turn around. Slowly he gathered up the papers scattered on the floor, examining their corners, sorting them into two piles and retying them.

"Where did you find these?"

"With his other case files," she said listlessly, nodding in the direction of the alcoves behind Hortensius's writing-couch. Caepio took one pile and replaced them in the alcoves one by one. Then he took the other and dropped the scrolls in the brazier. "He won't know," he said in answer to Hortensia's questioning look. "Once a case is over, he doesn't tend to revisit it. He prides himself too much on his memory."

He extended a hand to her. She walked across the room and accepted his embrace. From within it came a muffled question:

"You thought he might have been involved, didn't you? When I told you about what Lucrio heard at Tiberius Dolabella's house."

"It did occur to me," he admitted. "The encounters with Dolabella, your father's strange mood, the fact that there seemed to be a great deal of money involved in whatever was going on, which has always been Hortensius's greatest weakness. I wanted to protect you. But on reflection I realized my own foolishness. Your papa is a flawed human being,

Hortensia. Like you, like me. But in the end, he would never have betrayed the Republic. He loves it too much. More than that – he loves you. He sees himself through your eyes."

He felt her sigh and they both watched as the papyri softened and turned black in the glowing bronze bowl.

THE STREETS LEADING to and from the forum were thronged with people. Flowers squashed underfoot stained the paving stones with splashes of crimson and yellow, while giggling children darted between the adults' legs, hands linked so as not to lose touch with their friends. Sausage and oyster sellers did a busy trade along the Sacred Way, so too the sign sellers flogging wooden placards daubed with the names of both the incoming and outgoing consuls.

At the heart of the forum itself, on the steps of the Curia, Hortensius and Caecilius acknowledged the cheers of the public, flanked on either side by their consular predecessors Crassus and Pompey, and supported by a full cast of their fellow senators. Their pristine white togas, edged with purple, made them visible even to those toward the back of the vast crowd, and there were bursts of cheering every time one of the great men spied a pocket of supporters carrying their name aloft on a placard and raised an arm in hearty salute. Just off to the side of the Curia, the candidates' families had been given their own place to stand, and they too nodded and smiled as they received the salutations of nearby well-wishers. For Caecilius, there was Claudia, splendidly arrayed in a new gown of saffron-yellow and almost bursting out of it with uxorial pride. Hortensius was represented by Lutatia, Quintus – wearing a stony expression and irritably refusing his mother's quiet prompts to look a little happier for the sake of his father – and Hortensia, who was accompanied by Caepio.

Looking out over the sea of animated, cheering faces, Hortensia spied six distant figures, also dressed in white, observing the scene from the steps of the Temple of Vesta. She whispered something in Caepio's ear and he nodded; then she slowly made her way round the edge of the vast crowd until she reached the temple. Ascending the first step, she placed her hand in Cornelia's outstretched one as she came down to greet her.

"I am glad to see you. This is a happy day for your family," said the Chief Vestal graciously.

Hortensia nodded. "Yes it is. And for Rome."

"And for Rome." Cornelia smiled. "After all, we – and only we – know what might have been." She turned and beckoned to Fabia, who came down the steps to join them and bestowed the warmest of smiles upon Hortensia. They all contemplated the scene on the Curia steps for a few moments, then a small, freckled boy of nine or ten, wearing a white tunic that was too big for him, came tripping down from the temple.

"Do you need a parasol, *domina*? For your guest?" he asked timidly. Cornelia shook her head in dismissal.

"I know it's odd, but I feel sorry for what happened to Felix," Fabia confessed to Hortensia, as the little slave clambered back up the steps to the Temple. "He was just a boy. He must have felt important for the first time in his life . . ."

"You have no reason to feel sorry for him," chided Cornelia in a low undertone. "He is more fortunate than he deserved. If we had told the Pontifex the real reason we wanted him sent away, instead of saying we had caught him peeping again . . . A silver mine in Africa is a better fate than a sack in the Tiber."

Hortensia and Fabia exchanged glances but neither of them said anything. Another cheer went up from the crowd. "I had better go back," said Hortensia. "I will come back and see you all soon. I promise."

Fabia accompanied her to the bottom step. "I wish you could have met Helena," she said in parting. "She was brave, like you."

"Then I'm not surprised you and she were such good friends," said Hortensia.

Fabia smiled wistfully. "Yes, we were. I hope now that you and I can call ourselves friends."

"Of course we can," said Hortensia warmly.

"I am glad. I told my sister all about you, how clever you are, how much spirit you have. She said she could see it in you too."

"Do I know your sister then?" asked Hortensia, much surprised. Fabia looked equally taken aback.

"But surely I told you?"

"No. Who is she?"

"Well, I hope you won't mind. I know your families are not the best of friends," stammered Fabia. "She is Terentia. The wife of Marcus Tullius Cicero."

She examined Hortensia's face anxiously for a reaction.

"So that's why . . . I knew your face reminded me of someone," said Hortensia wonderingly.

"Are you angry I spoke to her about you?"

"No," said Hortensia after a moment's pause. "I'm just . . . surprised."

She smiled reassuringly and squeezed Fabia's hand. "Goodbye. Come and visit me on the Palatine whenever you like."

"I wish it could be as often as that. But I will come one day."

They said their farewells again, and Hortensia slowly made her way back around the edge of the crowd toward the Curia. She could see that Caecilius was now addressing the crowd, his patrician, slightly reedy tones not quite commanding enough to reach beyond the first few rows of his supporters. As she threaded her way through the thickening crowd of spectators, her attention was caught by a dark-haired little girl sitting by herself on the steps of the Temple of Castor and Pollux, scratching away at the surface of a wax tablet with a stilus that was too big for her small hand. Hortensia went over to her and was greeted with a gap-toothed smile of delight.

"Hello Laelia, where's your mama?"

"Shopping for our supper. She told me to wait here for her."

She peered behind Hortensia, as though expecting to see someone else with her.

"Where's Lucrio?"

"Lucrio has gone away for a little while."

"Where did he go?"

"He went to Lusitania, a long way away. He used to live there when he was a little boy you see."

"Is he coming back?" demanded Laelia.

Hortensia reflected that she had asked herself the same question many times. It had been four months now with no word. Not that she had expected Lucrio to be much of a correspondent.

"I hope so. He went to back to look for someone." She bent down to inspect Laelia's tablet more closely. "That's a beautiful picture. Are you drawing the forum?"

Laelia nodded and patted the step next to her for Hortensia to sit down. She pointed at the obscure etchings on her tablet.

"This is the sun, and this is a temple, and this is the street, and these are the shops."

"And who's this?" Hortensia traced one finger over a row of lopsided smiling faces in the corner of the tablet. "Are these the people doing their shopping?"

"No, that's me, and that's Mama and that's Papa."

Hortensia glanced at Laelia, who had bent her head over her tablet once more and was adding extra details to her portraits, her dark tresses hiding her own face from view. After a moment, without looking up, Laelia spoke once more.

"Mama says you and Lucrio found the men who took Papa away."

Hortensia hesitated, and nodded. Laelia carried on digging the tip of her stilus into the red wax for a while, then she turned her solemn brown eyes on Hortensia.

"Did you punish them?"

Again, Hortensia nodded gravely. Laelia turned back to her tablet.

"Mama says when I finish this, she'll give it to Papa for me. Then he'll always have a picture of us to look at. I think he misses us."

Hortensia closed her eyes briefly over the tears that had formed there. Laelia brushed some wax shavings off her drawing and held it up to admire. A huge smile suddenly dimpled her cheeks.

"Look! There's Lucrio!"

Hortensia squinted at the tablet, thinking Laelia must have added Lucrio to the picture. But then she saw that the little girl was pointing to someone coming toward them out of the crowd and the smile that lit up her face was even more joyful than Laelia's.

She stood up as he came toward them. He was very brown and he looked tired but she was relieved to see that he appeared otherwise to be in good health.

"So you have come back," she said warmly.

"Yes, *domina*, I have come back," said Lucrio with a slight smile, holding out his hand to Laelia, who thumped her fist into it and demanded without preamble:

"Did you find the person you were looking for?"

Hortensia's eyes met Lucrio's, an anxious question there. He smiled and closed a hand briefly around Laelia's little fist.

"I did. They were where I expected them to be." He took the tablet being waved at him and admired it. "What a beautiful picture."

"My father will be pleased to see you," said Hortensia. "Your timing couldn't be better, as you can see."

"Yes, that is why I came to find you, *domina*. Your mother asked me to come and escort you back. Your father will be making his address to the crowd soon."

"The great showman. His audience awaits," she acknowledged with a smile. She rose from the step, placed her hand on Laelia's silken head and then after a moment's hesitation, bent down and kissed her cheek.

"Your papa does miss you, Laelia," she whispered. "But he will always love you and be with you."

They said goodbye to the little girl, who was reluctant to let them go, and Hortensia let Lucrio take the lead in guiding them back toward the Curia. She looked up at him appraisingly, searching for answers in his unreadable face.

"I'm glad to see you. Did you indeed find . . . the answer you were looking for?"

"Yes, I found it, *domina*."

"And?" she pressed.

He paused to steer her past a gaggle of chattering families blocking their path. When they were side-by-side again, he glanced down at her and smiled a little at the anticipation in her expression.

"Three grave-markers, on the edge of the olive grove. All lined up in a row. The people who farm the land now say they have been there these fourteen years, ever since they took it over. They left them there out of respect."

Hortensia's face twisted in anguished sympathy.

"But what about your other family?" she asked after a pause. "Your uncle and aunt . . . the ones you said farmed nearby? Did they have anything to tell you?"

"My aunt Luciana died some years ago. My uncle Caucenus told me that when they found my father and mother and Taio, they were all dead. He buried them himself. So you see, there can be no doubt, *domina*." Lucrio was silent for a moment before the wry smile returned. "As you can imagine, my uncle and my cousins were very surprised to see me."

Hortensia shook her head in sorrow.

"I'm so sorry Lucrio. He was an evil man. It was just like him to say something to torment you even from beyond the grave."

"Yes, *domina*. Still, at least I have no doubts anymore, and I am glad to have had the chance to go back. The farm was just as I remembered it. Even my father's vegetable patch was still there."

They were now near the spot where Lutatia and the others were dutifully applauding Caecilius, but were forced to wait while a line of goats, their horns trailing colored ribbons, were led toward the steps of the senate house as part of the preparations for the great sacrifice of thanks which would take place there.

"Did you ever find out which of them knew?" he asked suddenly.

Hortensia's brow wrinkled in puzzled enquiry. Lucrio gestured toward the men lined up behind her father and Caecilius.

"The senators. The ones who signed the will. Were they all part of the conspiracy, apart from your father and Albinus?"

Hortensia glanced up and scanned the row of faces looking out from the Curia. Crassus. Metellus Pius. Marcus Cotta. Julius Caesar. All of them smiling and waving to the crowd.

"I don't know," she admitted. "Maybe Pompey has his suspicions.

But I suppose we'll never know for certain. What good would it do? It's all over now."

She glanced up at him warily. "So what now? Did you just come back to say goodbye? Are you . . . are you going to go home again?"

"No, *domina*. I lost my home a long time ago."

"You'll always have a home here, with us. Won't you stay?"

"I'm not sure it's in my power to leave."

"Well of course it is, if you truly wish. My father gave you your freedom. No one has the right to stop you."

As usual, she couldn't read the look he gave her. But there was something in it that made her feel strange, as though he was simultaneously keeping her at bay and yet willing her to see something else. Suddenly she felt a warm hand on her arm.

"So you found her, good. Come on Hortensia," boomed Hortensius jovially. "Your old Papa is about to put on a show."

He drew his daughter's hand through his arm, saluting some of his supporters in the crowd with a theatrical wave, and turned to lead her back to join the other members of their family. But first he paused and peered more closely at Lucrio.

"Back from your travels, are you? Good. I didn't make you a free man just so that you could swan about on holiday. What are you going to do with yourself now? Found an occupation yet?"

"Not yet, *domine*."

"Well while you make up your mind, you can have your old job back at Laurentum if you want it. I suppose I'll have to pay you this time."

"You are too good, *domine*," replied Lucrio drily.

"Yes I am, aren't I?" Hortensius peered more closely at him. "And I see you've got rid of that thing while you've been away," he commented sardonically, nodding at Lucrio's right arm where a small patch of white skin showed up against the brown. Lucrio glanced down before meeting the challenge in Hortensius's eyes.

"Maybe your politicians have something to teach us after all, *domine*," he said.

The faintest curl of a smile tugged at Hortensius's mouth. The crowd was now shouting his name and he tucked Hortensia's hand under his arm again. Leading her up the steps of the Curia, he glanced down at her and pinched her cheek before raising an arm in salute. Gradually the crowd quieted and Hortensius began to speak.

"My fellow Romans," he boomed, his rich, magnificent voice echoing effortlessly round the forum as Caecilius's had not. "This is a wonderful day for myself and for my family." He beamed down at Hortensia and made a desultory gesture toward Lutatia and Quintus, still standing on the slope next to the Curia before hushing the crowd with a grand sweep of his arm. "But more than that, it is a wonderful day for our city. It is a wonderful day for our empire."

As the crowd roared its delighted response, Hortensia glanced behind her along the row of senators to where Crassus and Pompey were standing side by side. As usual, Crassus was wearing a smile as wide as his handsome face, as though he were in full agreement with the mood in the forum. He was nudging Pompey and pointing into the crowd as though he had just spied a mutual friend of theirs. By contrast, Pompey's habitual air of good-humored jollity seemed muted. He acknowledged his supporters in the crowd with much waving and grinning, but there was a hint of boredom about his manner and though he nodded at Crassus's asides, he made no attempt to show any other sign of amity with his fellow outgoing consul.

Gazing farther along the row to the other side of the Curia, where more senatorial wives and children were corralled in a group, Hortensia spied Terentia, who was engaged in conversation with her sister-in-law Servilia. As she stared curiously at Cicero's wife, the older woman caught Hortensia looking at her. She nodded her head slightly as though in knowing greeting, but Hortensia didn't know how to respond and so she looked away as though she hadn't seen her.

Hortensius raised his arms again and the crowd eagerly obeyed his command.

"I know you will want to join with me in expressing the gratitude of the entire Republic to the two men in whose footsteps my colleague

Caecilius and I have the impossible task of following." Hortensia was the only one close enough to see the sparkle of mischief which had kindled in her father's blue eyes. "I know too that you, as much as I, would like nothing more than to see these two remarkable sons of Rome making one last show of unity. Pompey, Crassus – step forward and shake hands so that the city of Rome may offer you its grateful thanks!"

With the crowd in full voice, Pompey and Crassus had no choice but to turn to each other. Crassus put out his hand first, and the two men clasped hands, the veins straining against their knuckles, and smiled out at their audience. As they released their grip, it was Pompey rather than Crassus who shot Hortensius a look of pure malice.

But Hortensius didn't seem to notice. Instead, he turned to his daughter, squeezed her shoulders and bent his head to murmur in her ear. She could only just hear him over the ecstatic cheering of the crowd.

"What do I always tell you, Hortensia? Give them a show."

His face was full of mischievous delight and pride. She smiled up at him, put a hand to his temples and dutifully smoothed a strand of his slick black hair back into place. "As you say, Papa," she replied.

AUTHOR'S NOTES

MY INSPIRATION FOR THIS BOOK – AND THE SERIES THAT WILL FOLLOW – was the historical character of Hortensia, who I first met when I was researching my previous book *The First Ladies of Rome*. All that is known of her survives in short literary references which preserve her identity as the daughter of Cicero's great law court rival Quintus Hortensius Hortalus, and her reputation as one of the very few women in Roman history known for her speech-making abilities. These were praised by (amongst others) first-century historian and advocate Appian, who wrote of her: ". . . by bringing back her father's eloquence . . . Quintus Hortensius lived again in the female line and breathed through his daughter's words."

Although Hortensia herself almost certainly never spoke in the Roman law court, other women are known to have done so before a law was passed in the late Republic to put an end to what was seen as a scandalous practice. Hortensia lived through one of the most politically tumultuous periods in Roman history and through her family connections was well acquainted with many of the key players of the day. Most of the characters in my book are real-life figures, including Hortensia's husband Caepio and the Vestal Virgin Fabia, not to mention titans of Roman history such as Crassus, Pompey, Cato, Brutus, Cicero and Julius Caesar. Others such as the young Lusitanian gladiator Lucrio and the villainous Tiberius Dolabella are fictional creations of my own – though the Dolabella family did contribute several major players to the Roman political scene, including Publius Cornelius Dolabella, who also appears in the book.

In setting off down the path worn by so many writers of historical fiction before, I have been guided by the principle that where known footprints of history exist, I have done my best to tread carefully around them. Otherwise, I have felt free to go my own way. Hortensius and Cicero's famous showdown at the trial of Gaius Verres is well documented and has been recounted in fiction before. It is not my particular concern to offer an alternative viewpoint on that trial. This story is Hortensia's and part of the fascination for me is in imagining how a young woman with her intelligence, courage and determination might fight to make her voice heard in a society deeply resistant to women playing any part in public life, let alone the law court of which her father is king. To speak was a man's job in ancient Rome and the great pleasure in weaving a life for Hortensia was to bring into being a woman who could confound that expectation.

ABOUT THE AUTHOR

ANNELISE FREISENBRUCH WAS BORN IN BERMUDA IN 1977, AND studied Classics at Newnham College, Cambridge, receiving her PhD in 2004. In 2010, her first book *The First Ladies of Rome* was published by Jonathan Cape in the UK and by Free Press in the United States (where it appeared as *Caesars' Wives: Sex, Power and Politics in the Roman Empire*). It has since been translated into several languages and Annelise has appeared on television and radio to talk about her research. She has taught Latin for ten years and is currently the Head of Classics at Port Regis School in Dorset. This is her first novel.

To discover more please visit Annelise's website: www.annelisefreisenbruch.co.uk

Or follow Annelise on Twitter: @afreisenbruch